You Should Have Told Me

Leah Konen is a graduate of the University of North Carolina at Chapel Hill, where she studied journalism and English literature. She lives in Brooklyn and Saugerties, New York, with her husband, their daughter, Eleanor, and their dog, Farley.

Find her online at leahkonen.com or on Twitter and Instagram @LeahKonen.

Praise for *You Should Have Told Me*

'This gut-wrenching and breathlessly tense thriller perfectly captures the vulnerability, desperation and helplessness of a new mother trapped in a nightmare scenario. Raw, unflinchingly honest and emotionally compelling, with themes of family and trust'
Allie Reynolds, author of *Shiver*

'Readers are going to love *You Should Have Told Me*. There's so much to unpack in this taut, compelling thriller. New motherhood, a missing husband, a ton of secrets, all brilliantly written and plotted'
Samantha Downing, bestselling author of *My Lovely Wife*

'Unique, cleverly plotted and emotionally resonant, *You Should Have Told Me* is the rare thriller that manages to be both a dazzling page-turner and a moving meditation on what it means to be a mother today'
Andrea Bartz, bestselling author of *We Were Never Here*

'*You Should Have Told Me* is an urgent, read-in-one-sitting story . . . a tightly constructed thriller'
Katie Gutierrez

'Raw, brave and gripping . . . the flawless writing is both emotionally resonant and tantalizingly suspenseful'
Samantha Bailey

'With breathless suspense and cliffhangers in nearly every chapter, Leah Konen has written a pitch-perfect thriller with a plot so propulsive the pages practically turn themselves'
Megan Collins

Praise for *The Perfect Escape*

'Clever, complex and expertly planned.'
Rachel Abbott, bestselling author of *Right Behind You*

'Full of secrets and twists, *The Perfect Escape* is a fast-paced,
edge-of-your-seat thriller about a group of friends who may not
know one another as well as they think. With its eerie setting,
unsettling plot, and shocking reveals, this book had me completely
captivated from the first page to the very last.'
Megan Miranda, author of *Such a Quiet Place*

'Nobody writes twists like Leah Konen – this woman puts
Hitchcock to shame . . . A gripping, whip-smart, and unforgettable
pulse-pounder that left my head spinning. With its intricate
plotting and truly shocking reveals, this thriller is both an
addictive page-turner and a brilliant examination of female
friendship, shame, and betrayals.'
Andrea Bartz, author of *We Were Never Here*

'When three women embark on a trip to forget their broken lives,
they become embroiled in the centre of a murder investigation. *The
Perfect Escape* is a clever, locked-room mystery that is compulsively readable and impossible to put down!'
Wendy Walker, author of *Don't Look for Me*

'The type of captivating, masterfully-constructed thriller
you'll consume in a breathless rush – and then flip right
back to the beginning to figure out how the author pulled
it all off. Konen keeps the shocking twists coming
while wringing nail-biting tension out of even the smallest
moments. I couldn't put it down!'
Layne Fargo

Praise for *One White Lie*

'Intense, unpredictable and completely addictive – *One White Lie*
is everything a great psychological thriller should be'
T. M. Logan, author of *The Holiday*

'Remarkably insidious. Extremely readable.'
Caroline Kepnes, author of *You*

'*One White Lie* reads like the best Hitchcock film never
made . . . An assured and astonishing debut from an author
destined to become a big name in thriller fiction.'
Sarah Pinborough, author of *Behind Her Eyes*

'It's rare that a novel keeps me guessing until the very
last page – but *One White Lie* delivers in a big way.
It's absolutely terrific.'
Sarah Pekkanen, coauthor of *The Wife Between Us*

'Hooked me from the start . . . This book has everything – engaging
characters, a unique story, and an ending that will blow you away.'
Samantha Downing, author of *My Lovely Wife*

'I love Konen's writing style – super pacy and whizzes you
along – I couldn't put it down until I knew how it ended.'
Sandie Jones, author of *The Other Woman*

'Compulsively readable, a gripping page-turner. The tension
builds with every page. Each shocking twist is followed by an
even more shocking twist. This is one of those books you'll want to
read again the moment you finish. A masterful psychological
thriller that will leave you breathless.'
Lisa Regan, bestselling author of *The Drowning Girls*

'Skillfully captures the unnerving tensions that come with building
your chosen family while never knowing quite who to trust.'
Marie Claire

You Should Have Told Me

LEAH KONEN

PENGUIN BOOKS

PENGUIN BOOKS

UK | USA | Canada | Ireland | Australia
India | New Zealand | South Africa

Penguin Books is part of the Penguin Random House group of companies
whose addresses can be found at global.penguinrandomhouse.com

 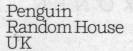

First published in the United States of America by G. P. Putnam's Sons,
an imprint of Penguin Random House LLC 2023
First published in Great Britain by Penguin Books 2023
001

Book design by Ashley Tucker
Printed and bound in Great Britain by Clays Ltd, Elcograf S.p.A.

The authorized representative in the EEA is Penguin Random House Ireland,
Morrison Chambers, 32 Nassau Street, Dublin D02 YH68

A CIP catalogue record for this book is available from the British Library

ISBN: 978–1–405–94751–0

www.greenpenguin.co.uk

For my mother
and all mothers

Prologue

HE KNOWS.

He knows, and he's planning the worst.

I burst through the wooden door, shaking with adrenaline from what I've just done.

Foolish. Far-fetched. Sending him away like that. But I had no choice. I've been over it and over it. I had no choice.

I beeline through drunk girls and the guys trying to lure them home, past the bartender I've never liked and the pool table whose felt is rough, patched in spots.

So many corners of this godforsaken bar. So many places to hide in plain sight.

And then, the booth—what I've come to think of as our booth. The one farthest from the door. Out of sightline of anything but the men's bathroom.

No one in it—too tucked away. Table empty but for a tealight candle whose wax has swallowed its wick.

My hands run frantically along each oak seat. Nothing.

How could I have made such a stupid, thoughtless mistake?

Knees down, crouching forward: Beer-sticky floor. Peanut shells. Business cards. Dingy napkins. A widowed earring. Nothing of mine.

I push up, and my head bangs against the table. Pain aches through my temples.

And then, through the ache, the realization: outside. Has to be outside.

I rush to the door to the alley, always cracked open with the same single brick.

A squeak of hinges, and I'm out in the cool night air.

Most people don't come back here. The other patrons go where you're supposed to, out front.

But I can't risk him seeing me. Peering through the window to clock yet another one of my failures.

I scan the alleyway. Dim streetlight. Crumbling brick walls. A dumpster in the corner. And there, right in the middle of it all, against one of the bricks that had come loose, the two butts of my Parliaments, still half-glowing.

I rush forward, running my fingers along the ground, but nothing. Nothing.

Then I hear it behind me, the squeak of hinges. The opening of the door.

I turn in horror, watch the light fill the open doorway, morphing him into nothing more than a shadowy silhouette.

One that's coming straight for me.

I try to push myself up, but I stumble, my hand connecting with another errant brick, my palm mashing into my hot cigarette butts. Temples throbbing harder. Breath seemingly gone. The reality of what's happening suffocating me.

The shadow looms closer, the door shutting behind him, cutting us off from anyone who could see.

I know it then as true as I've ever known anything.

He's caught me.

He's won.

FRIDAY, MARCH 15

FRIDAY, MARCH 16

10:43 a.m.

A COLD-BLOODED SCREAM, PIERCING THROUGH THE CLOY-ing music.

I looked down to see Freya writhing, unlatched from my breast, my nipple shriveled up from the shock of exposure, the air chilly despite the beating sun.

Heads instantly turned my way, the families of Kingston gawking at the new parents who never should have brought such a young baby to a concert aimed at older kids. Freya followed her scream with a monkey cry, an *eeee-eeee-eeee* I'd never heard before becoming a mother, one that was so common now.

Max reached into the backpack and pulled out the llama pacifier—Freya's favorite—but I shook my head and pressed her, maybe a little too firmly, back onto my boob. She stopped, thank god, just as the two guys in front went into their next verse.

"Now what do we do two times a day, every day?" the one with the extremely bushy beard asked, tapping at the face of his guitar.

"Sometimes even three times!" the other guy answered, resting his pick briefly between his teeth and stretching a pair of heavily tattooed arms.

Then, in tandem, as if the answer were the most exciting thing in the world: "We brush our teeth!"

The crowd, a smattering of families scattered across the grass of Forsyth Park, cheered along, and the song continued. *When we wake up in the morning and get ready for the day, we brush our teeth, wa-hoo-a-doodley-doo, we brush our teeth, one time and definitely two . . .*

One woman was still looking our way, even though Freya was quiet now—a beautiful woman, one you might even call striking, with piercing eyes, creamy skin framed by chunky bangs, and long glossy hair. I looked down, avoiding her gaze. Stared for a moment at the heavy wool blanket Max laid out a half hour ago. Shifted against the grass, the earth still hard and thawing beneath us, an Ides of March cold emanating from beneath. I hated to be watched as a mother. I always felt as if I weren't measuring up.

By the time I looked up, the woman had turned around, back to the music, back to her family. Max squeezed my hand, grounding me. "You okay?"

I nodded, forcing a smile. Max's dark-brown eyes shone, and his wavy hair, due for a cut, flopped in front of his eyes, his beard covered lightly in this wax product I'd got him one Christmas, his crow's-feet crinkling as a smile stretched across his face. He looked terribly handsome still, despite the lack of sleep, despite the circles beneath his eyes. What's more, he looked hopeful, brimming with new-parent bliss, a burp cloth tossed over his shoulder for the moment Freya needed it. He was so good, his presence the balm that softened the rough edges of my emotions, the highs and lows and super-lows of our post-Freya world. When he was beside me—helping, supporting, looking at her with such awe and love—I almost felt it would all be okay.

I supposed it was destined to be this way, I thought, as I adjusted Freya on my breast. Max had been all encouragement, all assurances, from the moment he found out I was pregnant. He was thirty-seven when I met him, with a sense you could almost feel, seeping from his pores, that it was time to slow down. His band, the Velvet Hope, a synth-y alt-rock act that I genuinely loved, had brought him a bit of indie and festival-circuit fame but little in the way of money. Shortly before we'd met, he'd thrown most of his energy into a business offering music lessons to kids in Manhattan and Brooklyn. By the time he moved in with me six months later, he had a nice little operation going. Two instructors working under him. A reputation among the Upper East Side and Park Slope elite, buoyed by the fact that rich parents could hire *the* lead singer and co-founder of the Velvet Hope to teach their kids guitar chords.

"This is a blessing," he'd said, when I'd showed him those two lines on the test, my face pale, my palms cold, caught between uncontrollable tears and panicked breaths. "This is a *good* thing."

Now, Max leaned down and kissed the bottom of Freya's six-week-old foot, covered in a knit bootie his hippie aunt Tammy had crocheted just for her. Freya's crying, her fussing and needing, never seemed to bother Max the same way it did me. He took a sip of coffee, the foam of his latte leaving a light print of white against his reddish-brown mustache. "You know we saw these guys in Brooklyn, right?"

"Really?" I asked. Brooklyn felt like a foreign, faraway land now, even though it was only two hours south.

"Totally," Max went on, stretching his legs out, wiggling his toes beneath the black suede Vans he always wore. "The band was called Roadkill. It was that show at the Bell House, the one with the strobe lights that didn't have the warning, where the girl passed out because of all the flashing."

"*That* show?" It had been one of those early Janie-and-Max moments, not so early that we were still playing it casual, but early enough that the world felt like its own kind of magic as we ambled through it, hand in hand. We'd gone out to a French restaurant on the Brooklyn waterfront, blowing Max's newly arrived, meager-yet-momentous royalty check on Chablis and steak frites. We'd found our way to the show after, rolling into one of our favorite venues much drunker on each other than the two glasses of wine we'd each had, Liana holding space for us near the stage. The three of us shook and shimmied and sang along like you can only do when you have absolutely nowhere important to be the next day. All fun and games until a girl dancing next to us passed out, Max instantly jumping into action, clearing the crowd, calling an ambulance, the three of us waiting outside with her friends until she was taken to Brooklyn Methodist. Such a hero he seemed, then and now. The type to swoop in and take care of things when someone was in need. The type who never thought: Someone else will do it. The type whose convictions turned so seamlessly into actions.

Max raised an eyebrow. "The very one. I hope that girl was okay."

That's Max for you, I thought, my heart swelling at how

lucky I was to have found him. Still worried about a girl he didn't even know from however many years earlier.

"Anyway," he went on. "The relevant info is, these guys never really made it in the indie scene, but I googled them when I saw this in the *Daily Freeman*, and they have something like ten successful kids' albums. They're making real money. It's crazy."

I took in the duo properly: Ratty T-shirts. Gauged earlobes. Hats that looked plucked from the dusty shelves of one thrift store or another.

I turned to Max. "Is that something that you'd want to do one day?"

"Never say never, right?" he replied. "Freya would love it, I'm sure."

It wouldn't be the same. It would be just another thing that's been taken over by the baby.

Max, ever the optimist, was happy he'd left the Velvet Hope. It was me who seemed to miss it more, the life we'd had before Freya had turned everything to oversized maxi pads, cracked nipples, and burp cloths.

The woman up front turned again, and for a moment, I forgot about bright stage lights and loud music and the magic of *before*. "See that woman," I said, quiet as I could. "She keeps looking at us. At me and Freya."

Max looked her way, and she immediately turned around. "Who?" he asked.

"The one with the long hair," I said. "And the mermaid tattoo. I know Freya was screaming, but I can't do anything about it now."

Max hesitated, in that way he had of hesitating these days,

when he thought I was about to get upset. He slipped his hand over mine, squeezed slightly. "It's a kids' concert. Wailing children are par for the course."

I nodded, then slipped my hand from Max's and took out my phone, checking the time. His parents and Liana, who'd been staying in their own rentals in town all week, were due to meet us in just over an hour. Carl would be his usual cheerful self, would see the lack of sleep in my eyes and look at me with compassion. Brenda was another story. I'm pretty sure she lost any bit of warmth she may have had in one of the many rooms of their elaborate Westchester house. At least I'd have Liana, Max's oldest friend, and my friend, too, after all our years together. Besides, even though family brought its own kind of stress, it was nice to be surrounded by people. To feel less alone.

My phone rang loudly—I'd forgotten to turn off the ringer—and my heart raced at the name on the screen: *Bryan CLIENT*.

Quickly, I turned the volume all the way down with my right hand, holding Freya tighter with the elbow of my left arm so the sound wouldn't disturb her sucking—then flipped it over, slipping it beneath my thigh.

It continued to vibrate, and as it did, it was like I was back there, at the agency last May, the day after everything changed. Eli's assistant, the one whose name I couldn't remember because he changed assistants so often, walking toward me purposefully, her lancelike heels leaving pockmarks in the corporate carpet, her prominent eyebrows cinched in a knot.

Sitting at the desk I'd called my own for years and never thought I'd have to leave, stomach churning, sweat already prickling the back of my neck, I'd imagined the assistant spitting in my face—or slapping me across it. I'd pictured her crossing her spindly arms and saying the words that taunted me, aloud, for all to hear. *We all know what you did.* But she hadn't, of course. She'd only pursed her lips. "Eli wants to speak to you."

"Now?" I'd asked. "I don't have anything on my calendar—"

Molly, art director turned best friend, had looked at me, raising an eyebrow.

"Now," the assistant said firmly, and she'd flipped around, not waiting for a response.

By the time I stood, the sweat had moved across my body—in my armpits, on my shoulders, at my temples—cold and shimmering, where everyone could see. *We all know.* I knew if I didn't hold it together, I might be sick, right there on the nasty low-pile carpet, a shade of taupe that was already a little too close to bile, and the one element of the big-windowed loft space that hadn't been updated when Eli had taken over this floor to start his own agency.

I'd never forget how their eyes seemed to follow me. Jay, the junior designer I'd pushed to hire only a few weeks before. Ani, the account director I'd once beat out for a promotion but who'd remained a close friend. Eric, the video editor I'd made out with at an agency Christmas party, long before I met Max. *We all know what you did.*

The carpet had morphed to gleaming polished concrete as we approached Eli's office, and the woman's heels took on a metronomic click, like a doomsday clock. Eli's door was open, and the elongated space was flooded with the glimmering light of the sun reflecting off the Hudson River, illuminating shelves of golden awards and photos with celebrities, dignitaries, and a cast of hangers-on. The assistant turned away, leaving me on my own, and my stomach churned again. I took two cautious steps inside, and across the room, Eli looked up from a spread of glossy photos. "Janie," he said. "Come in." My pulse rang in my ears, whooshing, as Eli cleared his throat. "Please shut the door behind you."

"Agency stuff?" Max asked now, nodding down to my phone, which had finally stopped vibrating. All my clients were logged into my phone that way, or at least they had been.

"Don't they know you have a baby?" Max went on. "And that you don't even work there anymore?"

"I'm sure someone didn't get the memo," I said, almost smoothly. "Clients, you know. They'll figure it out."

Max shrugged and leaned down to kiss the other one of Freya's bootied feet.

Up front, the woman looked back again, and for a brief moment, she stared, her eyes widening, her mermaid tattoo peeking from behind the cuff of a denim jacket, as if it wanted to come out and swim.

She turned back, and the man next to her, whose face I couldn't see—no more than a black jacket and a gray hat—leaned closer to her, slinking an arm around her. A child danced happily in front of them, his curly brown locks bouncing along with the music, his movements a bit spastic in that awkward child way.

Great. Now, not only was I the mom who couldn't keep her baby quiet, I was the one who didn't turn her phone off, either. How quickly you become those people, the people you never expected to be.

As if on cue, Freya pulled off my boob, began to scream. I struggled to get her back on, but it was no use. She was done:

with my milk, with this excursion, which had been so important to Max. With beautiful women who looked at us, judging.

Max offered the pacifier again, and this time I took it, popping it into Freya's mouth and holding it just so. It was green and rubbery, with a fuzzy pink llama attached to the bottom. Molly had picked it out for us, and even though our pediatrician said another brand was better for newborns, it had been the only one Freya would take. Literally. We'd tried others, and Max had even bought a couple more with the loveys attached, but Freya somehow knew the difference, was horrified if we came at her with anything other than the "llama in place of your mama," as Max called it now.

Freya's wails stopped instantly, but the pacifier would only buy us a few minutes. Max gathered our things, jumping into action like he always did, then took Freya from me, and I stood, waiting to see if the woman would turn back again.

She did. And for a second, I thought I could see pity in her eyes.

Like she could see me, mother to mother . . .

In a way that dear, sweet, naive Max would never truly understand.

2

8:27 p.m.

MY FATHER-IN-LAW'S BALD SPOT WAS SHINY WITH SWEAT AND ringed in straight white hairs that clung to his scalp. Hunched over the table in the kitchen of the Victorian two-bedroom Max and Freya and I had been staying in for a little over three weeks, lifting a bite of beef stew to his mouth, Carl looked like an oversized Keebler elf, his face pink and doughy, and he acted like one, too. Warm and jovial, he had a belly laugh that shook his uniform of Lacoste polo shirts and shapeless khakis, and a complexion that was ruddy from his lifelong affinity for fine wine and whiskey, neat. Next to him, Max's mom, Brenda, made quite the contrast. Thin and elegant, with a fine nose, dark eyes, salt-and-pepper hair cut neatly beneath her chin and a Bergdorf wardrobe in shades of gray and black. Carl and Brenda both came from money, whereas we Walkers were always scraping by—but Carl somehow remained the guy you'd love to sit down and share a beer with, whereas Brenda always acted like she had a stick shoved up her bony little spin-class-sculpted ass.

Max's parents weren't really my in-laws—not legally, at

least—but they'd felt like family since the moment I met them, on a visit to Westchester a couple of months after Max and I started dating. Carl had poured Max and me a few fingers of good whiskey, led us to the formal living room to delight us with the latest Otis Redding album he'd procured on vinyl, and had asked about my parents, my work, and my favorite Jane Austen novel before Brenda even brought out hors d'oeuvres. He'd made sure I'd taken down his cell phone number in that very first meeting—"in case you need anything, *ever*"—and in spite of Brenda's pursed lips and the sheer number of fine-silver forks laid out for dinner (one for salad, one for the main course, and one for dessert), I'd felt instantly welcome, protected, and safe. Like I had someone to look out for me in all the ways my own parents couldn't. Three years in, and Brenda was still cold and reserved, but I loved Carl more and more each time I saw him. And now, our bond was stronger than ever. Freya had tied us together, a tiny little branch that made us all part of the same tree.

I found my seat next to Liana, and she smiled, her eyes glowing. She looked radiant, healthy and well rested, her golden-brown hair properly brushed. "I told them to wait."

"It's okay," I said, trying to ignore the sour smell emanating from the bottom of my top. "Baby time isn't very reliable. You learn quickly never to wait."

Liana and Max had always been a package deal. They'd met when they were nine years old, neighbors on their idyllic street in Scarsdale, New York. They'd gone to school together at NYU, and the Velvet Hope had formed from the halls of the Steinhardt Department of Music in Greenwich Village. They'd even been roommates in their twenties in Bushwick, along with their three other bandmates and a rotating cast of characters who took key roles in the stories they inevitably told after either of them had a few drinks. Molly had once asked if I found Liana threatening, but though she was gorgeous, I never had. Max and Liana were like brother and sister, and Liana always seemed to have some artsy man-about-Brooklyn waiting in the wings of her life. Their careers had diverged since Max left the band, but their friendship remained strong. She was an honorary member of the Bosch clan and one of my dearest friends.

"She asleep?" Max asked, catching my eyes across the table.

I nodded, setting my phone faceup next to my plate so I could keep an eye on the camera pointed straight into Freya's bassinet. "Finally."

Max smiled sheepishly, and I looked down at my stew, my stomach rumbling. I hadn't had anything to eat since lunch, which we'd had with Carl and Brenda and Liana in town. Afterward, we packed into our rental cars and drove to the woodsy rail trails to meander past a small waterfall. We'd had a perfect upstate day, even if Freya didn't seem to enjoy it quite as much as her grandparents had.

I took a bite. The stew was warm at best and had an almost gelatinous skin on top, but it was sustaining anyway. I quickly took another.

"Freya's such a good eater," Carl said warmly, a bit of gravy clinging to his neatly trimmed mustache. He refilled his wineglass and took a gulp. "Max was the same way, you know."

"Never stops, really," Brenda added, her voice clipped. "It's such a lot of work, breastfeeding." The question remained unsaid but implied all the same: *Don't you want to switch to formula? I fed Max on it, and he turned out fine.*

"It is," I said. I didn't have any issue with formula, itself—Max and I used it when I needed a break—but I was sick of Brenda's constant feedback.

"I think what Janie's doing is great," Liana piped in, backing me up, and I shot her a smile. I was glad to have her here, softening Max's mother's edges. "Don't they say that mother's milk is this perfect balance of nutrients and antibodies—everything a baby needs?"

"However a baby gets fed is the right way," Max said, echoing what he'd read on one of the mommy blogs and making me love him even more. "Nursing. Formula. Whichever."

Brenda nodded, as if Max had just taken her side, and Liana caught my eye, raising her eyebrows.

"I can't believe it's already our last night," Liana said. She'd gone out of her way not to book any gigs so she could come upstate for a week with Max's parents. She'd wanted to spend as much time with Freya as she possibly could. And it was nice to have her here, her feminine energy a salve, her offbeat stories a reminder that the world continued to turn, that Brooklyn would always be Brooklyn. What's more, she was another human, another person—along with Max—who stood between me and isolation.

The first week of new motherhood had been filled with celebratory visits from friends and Max's parents, every one of them a welcome distraction from leaking boobs and leaking eyes, and then my own mom and dad had come up, stayed for a week in a hotel I'd paid for. Then there was the preparation for the move up to our rental in Kingston mid-February, the time it took to settle in. And now this visit, which was over as soon as it had begun.

There was nothing else scheduled, only endless hours and days to fill. The thought was terrifying.

I took another bite. The stew was quickly on its way to cold, but I was ravenous nonetheless. Feeding Freya, every calorie seemed to burn off instantly, dissipating in my rare bouts of sleep. The baby weight was already nearly gone, the only little bit left collecting in a pocket of fat above my C-section scar.

My phone buzzed, an alert flashing across the screen, and my shoulders knotted up instinctively, fearing another call from Bryan, but it was a text from one of the college girls, Bree, on a chain with my three favorite hall mates from North Carolina.

Paging Janie. How's the day treating you? Six weeks is finally here, it really does get better every day!

My friends from college, who'd stayed local after we graduated, had all had children earlier than me, in that way so many do when married and not living in New York City. Their kids were starting kindergarten now, mastering reading, and I loved each one of the College Littles, as we'd taken to calling them, fiercely. The girls had been so happy when they'd found out I was pregnant, and despite my panic-fueled moments and hour-by-hour hesitations, I'd included them in the process, sending ultrasound photos, head-circumference measurements, and details of my not-limited-to-morning sickness in the early days. Yet now that Freya was here, I didn't quite know what to say to them, how to put all the feelings swirling within me into words. So I opened my camera roll and added the two most recent photos of Freya. That would tide them over. It was all anyone wanted in the end. Not to know how you were but to see photos of that beautiful smiling baby you were supposed to adore so much.

I sank my teeth into a chunk of beef, feeling it go stringy in my mouth, shoving another forkful in just as quickly, then guzzled from my oversized water bottle, turned pink with the berry-flavored fenugreek supplement I'd started taking to boost my milk supply.

I tried not to be too jealous of the good Cabs Carl had bought at the local wine shop this afternoon—a pair of eighty-dollar bottles of wine, purchased to celebrate his and Brenda's first grandchild. Both of Max's parents had urged me to have some; Brenda had made a point when they'd opened the first bottle over an hour earlier to tell me that she'd enjoyed a glass of wine here and there when Max was first born, to take the edge off. (Yet another benefit of formula.) But in spite of my desire, I'd said no. I didn't want to have to count the hours, worry about having to dump my precious milk if I got too sauced.

Brenda lifted her glass and cleared her throat loudly. "Carl," she said. "Put your phone down."

His eyebrows scrunched up, and in his expression I saw a hint of the anger that occasionally came out—always directed Brenda's way and typically after he'd had at least two drinks. "Sorry," he said with a terse sigh, before taking another sip. "Work stuff." I didn't blame him for his annoyance—Brenda drove me nuts, too—but this week especially, he'd been a bit on edge. Drinking more than usual and snapping more, too. Max had been fretting about it since his parents arrived. He thought Carl's consulting projects were to blame for the stress, for the drinking that wasn't a problem yet but maybe could be one day? Max thought it was time for his dad to stop working for good and focus on his health, on retirement—on Freya.

Brenda waited until the phone was back in Carl's pocket to speak. "To you both," she said, rather formally, as if a statement had been prepared ahead of time. Brenda had worked in PR for years, back when PR in Manhattan meant wearing designer clothes and accumulating contacts in a meticulously organized Rolodex. "You know every generation, the rules change, the suggestions, the precautions—all that. I mean, we put Max to sleep on his tummy, and *he* lived." She forced a laugh at the joke, then raised her glass even higher. "But truly, when you ask yourself what makes a good parent, I always think it's best to look at the baby. Dear Freya"—Brenda glanced to the stairs that led to our room, as if Freya might flutter her eyes open and hear us even now—"it's clear just looking at her how healthy she is, how happy she is, how secure she seems in her surroundings—anyone can see that you two are good parents. A good father," she said, eyeing her son. "As I always knew you would be."

Then she looked at me, hesitated just long enough for the words to cut. "And a good mother. Freya is lucky to have you."

"Hear, hear," Carl said. "We always knew that one day our baby would have a baby. Because you're still our baby, Max. You'll always be."

"I wasn't so sure," Liana piped in. "But I'm so glad you did. Freya is the luckiest girl in the world."

"No, no, no," Max said, a smile spreading across his lips. "*We're* the lucky ones. We have her."

———————

WHEN THE STEW was soon gone from my bowl, when there was nothing left to consume, no more seconds to spoon around or crusty bread to chow down on, Liana got up, taking her dish and mine, and Max followed.

Brenda went deep into planning mode, announcing aloud what they needed to do tomorrow to check out from their rental, and Carl poured himself another glass, eyeing Brenda as if daring her to comment.

Over the clinking of dishes going into the ceramic sink, the rush of the tap, I tipped back my water, emptying it in one gulp, my mouth suddenly dry, then rose from the table to fill it.

In the kitchen, I found Max and Liana, facing each other, in quiet but tense whispered conversation.

I cleared my throat.

They both jumped, then looked at me—guilt on both of their faces.

I knew it then. I knew it so truly: they'd been talking about me.

"I'm just getting water," I said, squeezing around them and their impromptu tête-à-tête. I opened the fridge and pulled out the pitcher, pouring it as quickly as I could, heat in my face, tenderness in my boobs, droplets of water spilling onto the counter.

"Great, we're just finishing up the dishes," Liana said, far too cheerfully.

"You need anything else, Janie?" Max asked as I shut the fridge. "We're here for you, you know."

And there it was, the practiced careful kindness in Max's

voice, like I was something brittle, something that could crumble under barely any pressure at all.

I made my way back to the dining table, gulping down the water as fast as I could, my face suddenly hot, blushing with shame.

Max was such a joyful father, his support so kind, his love for me and Freya so true . . .

I knew if I wasn't careful, I was going to shatter it all.

3

10:11 p.m.

THE CREAKING WAS AWFUL AND ANIMALISTIC, AND IT WAS followed by a loud thump.

I opened my eyes and pushed myself up. Max was in the foyer, kicking off his shoes.

"I fell asleep?" I asked groggily, the info fitting together like puzzle pieces. Max had gone out to walk his parents and Liana to their respective rentals, right downtown. They were heading back tomorrow morning—Carl and Brenda to Westchester, Liana to Brooklyn.

"Believe me, you needed it," Max said, leaning over the sofa for a kiss, his beard scratchy against my chin. When he pulled away, his hair fell across his eyes. "I opened the video monitor app on your phone so you could hear her in case she needed you."

"I barely remember laying down." I reached for my phone, checked that Freya was, indeed, still breathing, then tapped out of the monitor app.

There was a text from Molly, who'd been checking in almost religiously to see how I was doing. Molly, my coworker who was so much more than a coworker, was single, proudly childfree, and fiercely confident. Not to mention the closest friend I'd made since moving to the city.

"What took so long?" I asked, glancing at the time. "You left an hour ago."

Max took a seat next to me. "My dad wanted to get a 'celebratory drink.'" He made air quotes. Max was always making air quotes. It had endeared him to me from the start.

"Really?" I asked. "After all that wine?"

"Yup," Max said. "There's a wine bar close to their place. He and my mom were still there when I begged off, my dad savoring the last few sips of some overpriced port. Thankfully, the place closes any minute now, so they'll have no choice but to go home."

"Damn, maybe you're right," I said. "Maybe he really is drinking too much."

"I know," Max said. "I need to talk to him. We talk about everything, but . . . this seems so hard. I mean, he's my dad. How can I tell him how to live his life? How can I act like I'm better than him?"

"I don't know," I said. It was a lifelong battle of mine, and I still hadn't figured it out. My parents' finances had always been a mess, their decisions never quite thought out. They were still together—and seemingly happy—in a suburb of Raleigh, North Carolina, but they'd only just started to emerge from the hell of declaring bankruptcy years earlier. Judging them, criticizing them—hell, even helping them financially, as I'd done on and off over the years—it threw the balance off. Parents cared for children, not the other way around.

At least good parents did.

"Anyway," Max said, "I don't want to burden you with

this. You must be exhausted after a week of activities with all of us. We can be kind of a lot, I know."

A lot is better than *alone*, I thought. Busy is better than all these endless hours, just me and her . . .

Max leaned back, sinking deeper into the cushions. "But I *am* glad you're still up." He drummed his fingers against his jeans, like he always did when he had something to say. He was going to do it, wasn't he? He was going to finally say what we'd both been thinking: That I was falling apart. That I wasn't up to this. That I needed serious help. That I wasn't half the mother Freya deserved.

And just like that, tears blossomed in my eyes.

"Janie," he said, instantly going into protective mode. His fingers linked through mine, and he gave them a squeeze, making me feel safe, in spite of everything. He squeezed harder, and I couldn't help it: more tears came. From his jeans pocket, he retrieved one of the handkerchiefs he always kept on him, one that was trimmed with teal, his name emblazoned in the corner. I'd given him the set for his birthday the year before. Carefully, Max dabbed it beneath my eyes, soaking up the wet. "Janie," he said, biting his lip. "What is it? You can tell me anything." He took a deep breath. "You can say it, whatever it is."

I stared at the circles beneath his eyes, a chapped bit of skin at the bottom of his lip, wondering if I really could tell him anything. I was supposed to, I knew that. That was the basis of a healthy relationship, wasn't it? And yet, I wasn't sure. Max was exhausted, too, only he always found a way to pull it together. Better than me.

"It's just . . . it scares me. Everyone leaving. It being . . . only us."

Max sighed, and it almost sounded like a sigh of relief. "Scares you?"

I pressed on. "When we're all alone, I feel like, I don't know, like this hurricane is taking me over, like something is building, this . . . this *dread*."

"Dread about what?"

I hesitated. How could I even explain it to him? He'd already written Freya three different songs, pen and ink in a hot-pink notebook he'd bought just for her. She inspired him, and he seemed to inspire her. When Freya cried, his voice was soothing; he'd make up songs on the spot, ditties that flowed easily from his lips. I, on the other hand, found myself staring, slack-jawed, wondering what I'd gotten myself into, knowing only that the longer I was near her, free of other people, other things to distract me, the more I felt this . . . despair . . . deepening as night approached. It was hard to pinpoint what exactly I feared: that something would happen to her; that I'd be up all night; that she'd cry and cry and cry and nothing would stop her; that I'd fall asleep feeding her, crush her beneath my weight; that I'd finally lose my damn mind. Snap!

"You're so good with her," I said. "I wish . . . I wish I were more like you—"

"What are you talking about?" Max asked, his thumb making circles in my palm. He must know, I thought. He must. He saw the way the tears seemed to leak from my eyes at the slightest provocation, the way I never quite knew what to do with the baby I was supposed to love so much.

"You're incredible," he said. "I knew you would be. And it's getting better—right? She's sleeping in longer stretches. She's going more time between feedings. It's hard, sure, but we're doing it." Max leaned in then, wine and Altoids strong on his breath. He kissed me softly, and I wanted to savor it—the taste of him—and I found myself wishing, not for the first time, that it was just Max and me.

Wishing we could go back. Before the birth. Before the pregnancy.

Before work had imploded, too.

Max's lips lingered on mine a moment, and I thought about it, I did.

My OB had cleared me for sex and exercise one week before, but I still felt too raw—physically and emotionally. I was a live wire, all my emotions balancing on a knife's edge. All I knew about myself, about my life, teeter-tottering. Precarious.

Max sensed my hesitation and pulled back. "You look beautiful, you know that," he said. "You have that mother's glow."

"You mean grease from not showering in two days?"

Max pushed my hair from my face and tugged at the end of a lock like he always did. "I'm serious. You're stunning."

"Thanks," I managed. "I don't feel it."

"It's okay," he said. "You'll get there."

I swallowed, the shame filling me up inside. "This is harder than I thought it would be. Than . . . than anyone told me."

"I know," he said. "For me, too."

I tugged at the fringe of one of the pillows. "For you, it comes easily. I can tell."

Max's eyes widened like he wanted to tell me something.

"What is it?" I asked.

A pause, stretching between us. "It's not always easy for me, either, Janie," he said finally.

"I know," I said. "I don't mean *easy*, not like that. But you're such a natural. The way you are with her . . ."

"I'm far from perfect."

"I'm not saying you're perfect," I said. "I'm saying you're better at this than me."

He shifted closer to me. "I've been stressed, too. I've been—" He hesitated. "I've been . . . completely overwhelmed, like I'm treading water just to get by, just to . . . just to do all the right things." Max looked away, then back at me. "I mean, there's been so much on my mind, too. I've been trying not to show it, because you have so much on your plate, with feeding her and being her mother, with the birth and the C-section and the recovery, but that doesn't mean it hasn't been harder than I thought. Sometimes I feel like I'm barely making it through."

My lips parted, and it was such a relief to acknowledge it, how hard, how awful this was. Not to lie to ourselves anymore, pretending like it was all okay.

It was such a relief, it's like the words tumbled out:

"Do you ever wish we'd made a different choice?"

Max's hand, still in mine, went slack.

"What? You mean that we . . . that we didn't have Freya?"

I pulled my hand away. "I didn't mean . . . only it was so nice. I was happy, just the two of us."

"Am I not doing this right?" he asked, his shoulders cinching up. "Am I not supporting you like I should?"

"No," I said quickly. "No, it's not that. It's just such a lot of work, minute in and minute out. It's all-consuming, and before . . ."

Max's eyes narrowed. "All the work, all the sleepless nights. None of it matters. Because we have *her*."

I nodded unconvincingly, feeling like a child being scolded. "Of course. I know—"

Max stood suddenly, shaking his head. "You really don't sound like yourself, Janie."

My chest constricted. "I'm tired. Sorry." I wasn't sure what I was apologizing for, but the word felt right all the same.

"Maybe you should sleep in the guest bedroom tonight, so you can catch up on some sleep," Max said. "I'll do the first feeding."

"You don't have to—"

"I want to," he said. "You deserve—you *need*—a break. We can talk more about this . . . about *everything*, tomorrow."

"Okay," I said. "But . . . are you sure you won't fall asleep down here?" I asked. It had been happening more and more, Max passing out on the couch, leaving me upstairs, with her, alone. He always came up when I called for him, but even those moments, in the dead of night, not having him there, they terrified me, kicking that dread, that despair, into high gear.

"Don't worry," Max said. "I'll handle it when she wakes up."

Then he smiled, the warmth back in his eyes, for a moment, at least.

I pressed my lips together, trying to make up for the terrible thing I'd just said. "I wasn't being serious. I only meant that I can't do this without you. That I need you, more than I've ever needed anyone."

"I know," Max said. "Of course you can't. And you don't have to." He leaned in for one more kiss. "You can count on me, Janie. I *promise*."

SATURDAY, MARCH 16

4

3:16 a.m.

THE WAILING WAS LIKE A TIDE, LIKE A GRAVITATIONAL PULL, RIS-
ing and falling, like the contractions that had washed over me
during my thirty-six hours of labor.

I made my way through the rental's expansive backyard,
toward the corner in the very back.

Max had shown me the nest just last week. He'd been
pulling weeds, making room for a bed of perennials that had
already begun to poke through—verdant green spikes that
hinted at spring's coming. At first, it looked like nothing more
than a puff of gray-and-white fuzz, but then I'd spotted the
eye, glassy and black, a whole world inside it. A baby bunny.
Nuzzled in among its brothers and sisters.

Now, the wailing seemed to intensify as I rushed through
the backyard. The bed was covered with green leaves, and I
dropped to my knees, pushing the brush aside.

There, I saw it. A single baby bunny. Jaw unhinged, ears
pinned back, a face that could only look horrific.

Screaming.

My eyes burst open. It was pitch black, and the smell was
all wrong. No hint of Max's earthy scent or Freya's baby

sweetness. The duvet was scratchy, and I pushed it away from my chin.

I was in the guest bedroom, of course. Max had done the first night feeding. Was it already time for the second?

I fumbled for my phone on the nightstand in the dark, knocked my water bottle to the ground, thanked my lucky stars the cap was screwed on tight, and finally found it.

There were no notifications, which was strange, since I thought I'd woken a few hours ago to the buzzing sound of a text, too sleep-deprived to give it a real look. I must have dreamed it.

I checked the time. Just after three—exactly when Freya had been waking for her first feeding of the night. I sat up in bed, ready to go check on her. Had Max fallen asleep downstairs again? After he promised?

My feet hit the floor, the wood cool beneath my toes, but then, suddenly, the screaming stopped.

I paused a minute, frozen in place, waiting. It didn't pick up.

I breathed a sigh of relief. It had probably taken Max longer than normal to change her or get her bottle ready. I forgot sometimes, how much more complicated it was for him to feed her.

I sank back into bed and stared at the ceiling another minute, but there was no sound, only silence. I turned on my side, pressed the extra pillow over my head, shut my eyes, and almost instantly found sleep.

MY EYES OPENED again. The cries were louder this time, as if shooting through my brain. I looked at my phone. It felt like it had only been minutes, but in reality it had been half an hour. What the hell?

Freya cried louder, and I jumped out of bed, rushed down the hall, and burst into the bedroom.

She was squirming and writhing, like a turtle stuck on its back, trying to turn over.

I tugged at the chain, turning on the small lamp on the nightstand. Our bed was empty.

So Max *had* passed out downstairs. A spark of anger boiled in my belly. He *promised*.

I leaned over the bassinet, and as Freya's eyes caught mine, she wailed even harder, as if asking me why I'd done this to her, brought her onto this earth.

"I'm here, baby. I'm right here."

She only screamed louder, like she alone could see me for who I really was. It was almost like she *knew*.

I slid my hands beneath her, lifting her to me, and as I did, I felt a squish beneath my right hand. Careful not to trip, I carried Freya to the changing table, tried to set her down as gently as I could.

A new bout of screams poured from her mouth the second she hit the mat. Hands fumbling, already wet from where the shit had soaked through her diaper, I tugged at the Velcro of her swaddle. She cried louder at the harsh ripping sound, and I pulled at the snaps of her PJs like an EMT tearing off someone's shirt to tend to a gunshot wound.

The mess, yellow and seedy, was everywhere, spilling from the top of her cheap, bought-in-bulk Pampers, leaching across the dinosaur print of her PJs, coloring her white swaddle a sickly hue. I pulled the fabric away from her body, her chubby legs and flailing arms fighting me every step of the way.

Finally, she was changed and latched on my breast, her jaw wide open, like the baby bunny's had been in my dream.

On my phone, I started the feed timer and selected my left breast. It was insane, how much we tracked, and I found myself wondering if we had to, but something about it also made me feel in control, a tiny bit of power in a new normal where I had almost none.

After a moment, her sucks became rhythmic. Near silence invaded the room. And with the silence, dread. The realization, cutting through my sleep-deprived haze, of what I'd blurted out to Max.

You told him you didn't want your own baby. Is there anything worse?

I tried to ignore the thought, but it was no use.

You confirmed to him what he already knew; he wanted this, not you.

I'd spent every moment since I'd graduated college working toward what I wanted. A good job, an apartment I could call my own, the monetary security I'd never had growing up. By the time I held the Clearblue Easy in my hand, I was four years into a thirty-year mortgage on a modest co-op in Bed-Stuy, two years into my relationship with Max, and still holding on to a faint hope that I might hit VP at the ad agency before I turned thirty-five. Pregnancy was never one of the ducks I'd been working so hard to get in a row. It scared me so much that in my panic, I'd gone to Molly first, not Max, terrified of this being real. And when I did tell Max, just a few hours later, he'd been so happy, so overjoyed, so sure that this was a serendipitous chance. He'd reminded me that we weren't exactly getting any younger, and he even talked over the decision with his dad, something that made me uncomfortable but I didn't feel I could forbid him from doing. Carl, of course, had been thrilled at the prospect of a grandchild, and it made Max even happier, even more hopeful.

So I'd convinced myself I could do it, that this was our chance, our baby, and that was that—after all, how could I deprive the people I loved of so much joy? Through my pregnancy, through nauseous days and late nights, through my departure from the agency in December and the shocked look on Molly's face when she heard I was leaving, I'd prayed they would come, all those maternal feelings the world had promised me. And now, I *still* found myself praying for those fluttery butterfly feelings, the ones I felt when I'd first met Max, only even more powerful. That was what everyone always said, wasn't it? Love like you'd never known it before.

Freya popped off my left boob, and I did the dance of arranging her on my right, then started the timer again. How could anyone love doing *this*?

Good mothers can. Just not you.

Ten minutes more and she was done. My pulse raced, blood pounding in my ears, as I set her back in the bassinet, watching her squirm—my whole body tense, hoping she'd stay asleep—but then, miraculously, and it always felt like a miracle, every time she fully shut her eyes, she stopped stirring. She was out.

Part of me wanted to go downstairs, yell at Max for leaving me alone with her, show him how hard this was for me, how much I was falling apart. Another wanted to curl up in his presence—his warmth and support and empathy—and ask for assurances that this would be okay.

But sleep tugged mercilessly at my eyelids, and I slipped into our bed instead. There would be time for all that tomorrow.

For now, I needed rest.

5

6:08 a.m.

WHEN MY EYES OPENED AGAIN, THE FAINTEST LIGHT WAS PEEK-
ing around the edges of the bedroom's drapes.

Since the moment Freya had been born, I don't think I'd
ever woken to anything less than her cries, but now, the room
was quiet. Max's side of the bed remained empty.

I crept out of bed, looking in on Freya. Her lips were
pressed lightly together, her eyes shut, eyelashes fanned out,
her head ringed with dark downy hair that seemed to be either falling out or regrowing each day. In these moments,
when she was snuggled up in her swaddle like a little bug in
a rug, it was impossible not to feel *something*. She was an angel, in that way that Bree and the college girls had promised
she would be. A picture that made people all over the world
embark on the crazy, impractical, and often unnecessary path
of parenthood.

Too bad you don't feel like this when she's awake.

Careful not to disturb her, I headed into the hallway and
down the stairs, the walls cast with an eerie dawn glow, just

enough light to lend a gray pallor across every surface, softening edges and elongating shadows.

At the foyer, I paused. The diaper bag and Freya's bucket
seat were sitting in the corner, and next to it, my shoes, black
Chelsea boots that had been the only pair to still fit during my
pregnancy, were tossed by the mat, as they always were. I
stared at the space next to them, trying to comprehend.

It had never made a difference to us. We were never that
fussy, and my Bed-Stuy apartment was never that nice. And
yet, there had been a whole paragraph in the rental's welcome
binder about the quality, the fragile constitution of the place's
"uncorrupted original heart pine floors." It had become a joke
between Max and me, one of the few things that was easy to
laugh at these days. If Freya's spit-up ever hit the floor (and so
often, it did), one or the other of us would call out: "Oh no!
I have corrupted the original heart pine floor!" Still, we did
our best to follow the owner's rule number one: *NO SHOES
INSIDE*. After a few days, it had become habit.

Max's shoes, the black suede Vans he always wore, the
ones I'd seen him taking off last night—they weren't there.

Where is he?

I turned toward the living room and its stone fireplace,
built-in bookcases, and oversized leather sofa, its back to me,
obscuring my view.

There was no noise, no wheeze or intake of breath, only
the sound of my own. I took another step forward and took in
the vignette.

Nothing, no one, on the sofa. No Max.

I found my phone in the pocket of my robe and dialed
Max. It rang five times, each one making my pulse pick up,
then hit his voicemail:

"Hey, you've reached Max. I'm not here right now—well, I am, because this is a cell phone, but for whatever reason, I can't answer. You know what to do."

"Max," I said. "It's six in the morning. I woke up to Freya screaming. I'm wrecked, and I need a break. Where *are* you?"

He probably just stepped out, I thought. For diapers. For wipes. For . . . for *something*. He's probably about to walk in any minute now.

I dialed him again—same rings, same voicemail—then tapped into the app for the video monitor, which kept twenty-four hours of footage of Freya's crib, recording every time there was movement, but there was nothing more than an occasional squirm. Max hadn't been in our room at all.

I returned to the foyer, trying to puzzle this out. The small wooden table, where we normally tossed our keys, had my set but not his. On the coatrack, Max's Carhartt jacket hung, waiting, but his lighter North Face layer, the one he grabbed when he was stepping out for only a minute—to take out the trash, to get some air, a moment's break from Freya's screaming—did not. I checked the chest pocket of the Carhartt, the two diagonal ones on the side, the three on the interior. No phone, no wallet, no keys, not even so much as a receipt—Max tossed them all in the trash the moment he got them. There was a handkerchief, but he had those in just about every pocket.

I turned away from the coatrack, walked into the kitchen, not that I expected him to be there, then turned back, stopped at the bottom of the stairs: What if Max had slipped into the guest room after I'd left it? Maybe he'd done even more drinking, maybe he'd pulled on his coat and shoes to get some air. Maybe he'd gone back inside and crashed on the couch.

Maybe he'd woken up sometime between when I last fed Freya and now, knowing he'd broken his promise, worried that in the chaos of his dad's drinking, he'd forgotten to examine his own. Maybe he went to the guest room so as not to bother me.

At the top of the stairs, I headed toward the second door on the right.

The bed was empty, sheets rumpled just as I'd left them at three a.m.

I dialed Max again, waited for the five rings. The voice-mail I'd once thought was so cute, the first time I'd gotten the message, on the way to our second date together, at one of the mom-and-pop Williamsburg restaurants that had become a Sweetgreen or Chipotle when the neighborhood had been invaded by developers. How long ago that seemed now.

"Max," I said. "Seriously, where *are* you? You're freaking me out. Wherever you are, come home." I took a quick breath. "I need you."

As if on cue, Freya began to scream.

6

7:03 a.m.

THERE WAS STILL NO SIGN OF MAX BY THE TIME I GOT FREYA TO sleep again, nearly an hour later.

My body wanted to crash into the mattress, pull the covers over my head, sleep until her screams woke me. *Sleep when the baby sleeps*, that's what everyone said. But everyone didn't count on your partner up and disappearing in the middle of the night.

I ducked into the bathroom, the white tile cold, edging on anemic, and stared at my reflection. I was a mess. My hair looked like a rat's nest, tangled and weblike at the ends. My eyes were somehow even more ringed than they had been the day before. A pimple on my chin seemed to have bloomed in the last hour.

I leaned forward, splashed water on my face, and began to brush my teeth. The bathroom door creaked open—I hadn't shut it all the way—and a rush of cool air crept in from the hallway. The house, situated right downtown, was old, what real estate agents would call charming, and complete with the sorts of Instagram-worthy details you never saw in newer homes. Exposed beams on the ceilings. Wide planked floors. Arched doorways and iron vents that allowed the heat from the woodstove to rise into the second story. Two bedrooms, one bath.

And yet now, with Max nowhere to be found, every creak of a floorboard, every shadow and gust of wind, every bit of age, down to the discolored grout between the subway tiles, made it feel more decrepit than charming. A dead zone, where Freya and I were trapped.

Maybe I should have listened to Molly and Bree, who'd thought we were crazy for removing ourselves from the city in a time that was so isolating already. No matter how much I explained that there were tons of people from Brooklyn up in Kingston now, which had gotten exceedingly hip in recent years, Molly insisted it wasn't the same. Maybe she was right, maybe we should have stayed. Or gone to Westchester, near Carl and Brenda, who'd been strangely against the idea of us coming here. But I'd always loved this town, since I first came up with Max, loved the little haven for Brooklynites tucked between the Hudson River and the Catskill Mountains. I'd always wanted to live here but had never wanted to give up the city. Parental leave felt like our chance, and so we'd booked it way back in September. I'd been worried about work then, sure, had been since that awful night in May, but I was doing my best to adapt. I hadn't known that my job would be over by the beginning of December, only a couple of months before Freya would be born. That between COBRA and this rental, we'd put a significant dent in our savings, savings that weren't so robust these days, since we'd emptied Max's generous trust from his parents and poured it into equity on the co-op, eager to get our monthly payments down.

Coming up here was a bit reckless, but did I really regret it? I doubted Brooklyn would have been better—only more claustrophobic—and our daily family excursions in the stroller were wonderful, if difficult. Putting Freya in a cute onesie, bundling her up in a muslin blanket, layering on makeup to pretend like I still cared, and performing our parenthood for the residents of Kingston lent an air of hope to the day-to-day, like putting on a filter, the real picture instantly appearing better. And in those moments, sipping a decaf latte that wouldn't mess with my milk, eating peppery arugula and house-made sausage, Freya's cheeks pinking from the country air, I almost believed the dread and panic would stop.

I finished brushing and spat into the sink, my eyes catching Max's comb, clean and free from hair. Just last week, I'd plucked every last follicle from it. I told Max I couldn't stand the mess when he asked me why. Thankfully, he hadn't asked more than that.

Back downstairs, I walked to the living room, jumping at the sound of a squeal, hairs standing up on the back of my neck, ready to rush to Freya. But I heard it again, and it was clearly an animal of some sort. A coyote? Did coyotes howl at seven a.m.?

I sat on the sofa, pressed my palms to my thighs. Forced myself to take a few deep breaths. To think.

I dialed Max again.

Five rings. Click. The message. Beep. Already, the routine had become familiar.

"Max, I don't know what's going on. I don't know when you left or why. I don't know where you are. Please, call me. Let me know you're okay." My voice cracked at the end, and

I hung up as tears spilled from my eyes. "I can't take care of her alone."

Of course you can't. You'll fail her even more than you already have.

I tapped back to my contacts, hesitating a moment, then found Carl's number. It rang three times and then—

"Janie." His voice was warm but scratchy, and he cleared his throat. He sounded tired.

"Sorry if I woke you," I said.

"Don't apologize," he said. "You didn't. How's my favorite baby girl?"

"She's fine," I said. "Sleeping."

"We had such a great time with her, you know," Carl said. "But it went by way too fast. When you three are back in the city, you have to come out to Scarsdale. Not just for a day but—"

"Carl," I snapped.

The line hung blank. I'd never spoken to him or Brenda that way before. "I'm sorry, but I . . . I didn't call to talk about Freya. Is Max there?"

"Here?" Carl said, his voice raising a pitch. "Why would Max be here?"

"He's not here," I said. "I haven't seen him since last night."

"Last night?"

"Yes," I said. "When Freya woke up in the middle of the night, he wasn't in our room. I went to feed her, but—"

"Is the car there?" Carl asked.

"I don't know," I said, glancing out the front windows and seeing a navy sedan and a hunter-green minivan. "Max dropped us off after the walk yesterday. He parks in a different place each time—you know we don't have our own spot."

"What about the car key?" Carl asked.

"It's not here. It's on Max's key chain. He's the one who always drives."

"Well, there you go," Carl said. "He probably went out. Er, he was talking about needing diapers just last night. There's a Target nearby, yes?"

"When did he say that?" I asked. "At the bar?"

"The *bar*?" Carl said, his pitch rising at the word.

"The *wine* bar," I clarified. "He said you all stopped for a drink."

"Oh," Carl said. "Right. Yes, well, you know. To end the trip. To celebrate. I wouldn't really call it a *bar*, not in the traditional sense."

"Does it matter?" I asked. I did not have the time to make Carl feel better about his drinking by pretending he hadn't gone to an actual bar. "Did Max say anything else? Did he check in to make sure you got home okay? I know he was a little worried about you."

"Worried?" Carl asked, his voice clipped.

"Well, he just said you'd . . . you'd all had a good bit to drink."

A pause on the line, hanging there, and I felt awful, the same slick, oily feeling I got in my stomach when I had to talk to my own father about finances, as if children weren't supposed to ever know better than their parents—or parents-in-law.

"No, we didn't talk after that, Janie," Carl said, his voice resigned. "He left, and the wine bar closed, and that was that."

"Okay," I said. "But I'm . . . I'm a bit freaked out. This isn't like Max."

Another pause, an agonizing beat too long. "I'm sure he's out getting supplies, like I said. You've tried calling him, I assume."

"A bunch of times," I said quickly. "He's not answering."

I could hear Brenda in the background, saying something too muffled to make out. "Look, Janie, is there any sign of foul play? Any real reason to be so concerned?"

"I don't know," I said. "I don't think so, but—"

"There you go," Carl said. "I'm sure he forgot his phone or something. I bet he'll be walking in any minute." He paused for a beat. "We're about to get on the road. Brenda has a doctor's appointment at eleven that she really can't miss."

"Okay," I said. "If you really don't think I should worry—"

"I really don't think you should worry," Carl said. "Keep calling him, and I'll call him, too. And if you don't hear from him in a couple hours, call me back, okay?"

"Okay."

"You're not on your own here, Janie. You have us. Remember that."

"Thank you," I said. "Thank you for saying that."

"Now give my baby girl a kiss for me. I'll check in later."

Call ended, I stared at the phone in my hands. Was I making something out of nothing? Was Max really about to turn up any moment, his hands full of diapers and wipes and all the things Freya needed? Was this yet another way I was coming apart, my mind and body so raw, so fragile I couldn't handle even the slightest change in routine?

I forced myself to count to ten. Then, calmly as I could, I looked through the house again—for Max's phone, for

anything that would give me so much as a clue as to where
he'd gone. I ransacked the couch cushions, the hamper,
searched soaked-through burp cloths and the pockets of
jeans. Nothing.

Back up in the bathroom, I found the antidepressants Max
took every morning. The suitcase we'd brought up with us
and the dopp kit full of toiletries. Lotion we chose together in
Ireland—made with the herbs and flowers that grew in the
dry, arid Burren.

I opened the cabinet under the sink, my pulse picking up
as I did, but there was nothing but cleaning products and a
cardboard box shoved way in the back—Max didn't go there.
He never cleaned the bathroom. Never, ever, ever.

I was zipping up his dopp kit when the tile caught my eye,
a couple of droplets from Max's last shower still clinging to
the ceramic. Max had been complaining, these past few days,
about the state of the hot water in the old house. It was hard
to get a shower to last longer than ten minutes—fifteen, tops.
And Max had always been a long showerer. He liked the feeling of having hot water rush over him; it calmed his anxiety
and depression. Liana and his bandmates had teased him mercilessly about it when they used to go on the road—*Who the
hell wants to take a long shower at a Motel 6?* My stomach
seemed to fold in on itself, pretzeling, as the scenario played
out in my head. Max had been talking about wanting to look
at the hot-water heater, down in the basement. I imagined the
rickety floating steps, the ones without so much as a handrail,
that descended below. I pictured the rock-hard bluestone
foundation that the house had been built on, pools of water
seeping into the foundation's cracks. The binder that came
with the rental suggested we familiarize ourselves with the

basement, in case of an emergency, and we had, if only briefly. It was impossibly dark and damp. You could stand upright in only half of it; the other half sloped up into nothingness, the rocks forming obscure angles. And it was cold. So cold. With cobwebs in the corners, mice droppings sprinkled about like fresh-grated pepper.

Max, I thought, my heart clenching in my chest. Max.

What if he'd gone down there to check on the heater—what if he'd slipped?

I rushed through the hall and down the stairs. Quickly, I pulled on my boots, zipping them up without socks.

I cinched my robe tighter and headed past the kitchen, past the side door and the back door, to the one that led down to the basement.

I whipped it open—it was incredibly dark—and fumbled for the pull chain of the light, thoughts racing in my head.

What if he's down here?

What if he hit his head?

What if blood is pooling, leaching out across bluestone?

What if you're all alone now? No one but you and her.

Finally, I found it.

Click.

The room flooded with sickly yellow light.

A wash of relief, so sweet I could almost taste it.

The room was empty. No Max to be found.

But then the other side of that relief, the equally ugly side of the coin.

No Max to be found.

The father of my child was still gone.

7

8:43 a.m.

"HI, BABY," I SAID WHEN FREYA WOKE AGAIN. "MAMA'S HERE."

Freya squirmed at the noise, a frown appearing, but it turned upside down when her eyes opened.

"Did you have a nice sleep?"

She yawned as if to answer my question, her mouth gaping wide.

I lifted her from the bassinet, rested her gently on the changing table, and pulled at the Velcro of her swaddle.

"Crazy night," I said, as her blue-gray eyes blinked at mine. I'd read somewhere that it was good to talk to babies as much as you could, help them learn language. When Max—or anyone else—was around, I tried my best to say all the things you should say. *Oh aren't you just the sweetest little baby in the whole wide world? Do you have the chubbiest little cheeks and the most perfect little face?*

Now, I hardly saw the point.

"We don't know where Daddy is," I said, unsnapping her onesie and checking her diaper. It needed a change. "We haven't seen him since last night. He didn't tell Mommy where he was going. He didn't tell Grandma or Grandpa, either. Mommy is confused."

I finished changing her, grabbed a fresh onesie from the drawer, lowered my voice to almost a whisper.

"Mommy is terrified."

Freya burped, as if to answer me, then cried out again. She was hungry, I knew.

She was always hungry.

And we were all alone. Until Max came back, at least. Because he *was* coming back, from wherever he was. He had to.

I sank into the rocking chair, grabbed my nursing pillow, and arranged Freya on my left side. She cried harder, but after a few tries, she latched.

"We don't know where he is," I said, rocking back and forth, Freya sucking away. "We have no earthly idea when he's coming back. We're worried he's hurt. We're worried something happened to him."

On my phone, I tapped into the feeding-tracking app and started the timer. It felt almost absurd to time her now, obscenely meaningless. *Hello, Officer, I'd like to report my missing partner, and also my daughter nursed for sixteen minutes on the left side this morning.* But at the same time, it felt strange not to. As if that would be confirmation, acceptance, that something was deeply wrong.

After a minute, Freya paused to swallow, and I pushed my breast farther into her mouth, worried she'd lose the latch if I didn't. She sucked again, hungry, happy.

I dialed Max again. Five rings and then the message.

Dialed again. The same. And again. And again.

Was the ringing a good thing? Proof that his phone was out there, buzzing away somewhere, and not buried in the sludge of the Hudson River or the rocky banks of Esopus Creek? Not smashed against a brick wall or already reset by someone who'd mugged my partner so they could get their hands on the newest iPhone? Did people even do that any-more, steal phones? They were so ubiquitous, it seemed silly, no matter their cost.

I rocked the chair a bit faster as the other side of the thought occurred to me.

His phone was still working, so that meant . . .

What if Max was safe somewhere, staring down, phone in his hand? What if he was *choosing* not to answer us?

Why would he answer you? After you told him you didn't even want your own baby?

Would he? Could he? Would he really dare abandon us . . . on purpose?

Freya pulled off, breaking her latch, as if she could sense the change in my demeanor, could taste the anger in my milk.

No. It wasn't possible. He wouldn't.

She cried again, and I lifted her to my shoulder, rapped at her back, beating her like a drum, the only way to get a good burp. After a minute, it came, and so did the feeling, hot and wet on my shoulder. The sour-sweet smell of her spit-up. I mopped it up with the rag, then switched her to the other side. She fussed a minute before she got on, and I dutifully started the timer again.

The minutes passed painfully slowly, with no end to this hell in sight. Usually, after the morning feed, I handed her over to Max. He'd play with her a bit, settle her in her bouncer or her lounging pillow, let her suck on the llama pacifier, give me a minute to brush my teeth, shove down a bit of yogurt before she was hungry again. But there was no Max now. No break. The not knowing when he would return, when he'd relieve me of my duties, was terrifying. So many minutes, so many hours, without Max's sweet stories and cooing sounds. Just the two of us, and she'd see right through me. She'd see how much I doubted myself, doubted everything. How difficult this was for me. How bad I was at this.

She'd know it if she didn't already: That I didn't love her half as much as I should. That sometimes I wondered if I loved this strange, needy alien even a little bit at all.

I could hold her now and hate her, for bringing us all of this, for changing our lives in this way, and at the same time, I knew it, deep inside me, I couldn't hate *her*. She hadn't asked for this. We had. She'd done nothing. She deserved all my love, all my affection.

She deserved a good mother.

A good father.

I'd assumed she'd have that at least.

No, I thought, pushing it all away. She *did* have that. I was being ridiculous. It had only been a matter of hours.

When Freya was fed and dressed, we made our way downstairs, and I set her up in the bouncer—which would entertain her for approximately eight minutes, if I was lucky, at which point we'd switch either to the swing or the play mat or the lounging pillow we kept on the sofa—and headed to the kitchen to get myself more water.

As I was pouring it from the tap, I saw it:

The side door, the one that led to the garden that we never, ever used. The deadbolt was in the vertical position . . . unlocked.

I racked my brain, struggling to remember if it had been like that when I'd gone down to the basement just an hour ago. Had Max gone out last night and used that door instead? But why? Or had he come back in, slipped away while I was up feeding Freya just now?

Or, worse, had someone else come in? I rushed forward, turning the lock to horizontal, twisting the handle and pulling to check it had engaged. Then I surveyed all the doors, all the windows, all the corners of the house where someone could be, not satisfied until I'd looked into each and every closet, behind every curtain.

When I was back downstairs, my heart pounding, my breaths short, Freya already starting to lose interest in the toys hooked to her bouncer, I called Carl again. It rang only once, then went to voicemail. I tapped into my call log, saw the word *Mom* from a week earlier, but knew it was useless. They were on a European cruise. Far from cell reception and unplugged, for the most part, from everything else. Spending money they didn't have. Enjoying a life that wasn't really theirs to live, one that I had at least half funded for them. Out of service. Out of touch.

Instead, I started a different call.

"Hello?" she said. The surprise was there in her voice, impossible to miss. She hadn't expected to hear from me—not like this. Our friendship lived on texts, on Instagram DMs and Facebook posts.

"Hey," I said. "It's Janie."

She laughed. "I know."

"I don't know who else to call. I need your help."

8

9:54 a.m.

FREYA HAD MOVED FROM THE BOUNCER TO THE SWING TO MY boobs and back to the bouncer by the time Liana arrived.

I opened the door for her, and she quickly walked inside, her golden-brown hair pulled into a messy topknot. She wore threadbare jeans and a faded Talking Heads T-shirt. Her face was bare, free of makeup, but she looked impossibly chic.

"I'm sorry," I said. "Carl and Brenda weren't answering, and I didn't know what to do."

"Don't apologize," Liana said, then wrapped me in a quick, firm hug. "I don't know what's going on, but we'll figure it out. I promise." She walked into the kitchen and began to pull mugs from the cabinet. "Do you mind? I rushed over, and I'm wrecked without caffeine."

There was something different about her, and it took me a minute to place it. *Alcohol.* Vodka, maybe. Or even gin. Stale, mixed with sweat. Leaking from your pores the next morning.

How many times had I been to a show with Liana and Max, had we all ordered rounds of tequila shots, cheap

Tecates? Too many to count. Liana, co-founder and keyboards for the Velvet Hope. Liana, beloved on the Brooklyn indie-music scene, always dragging us to see a show featuring one friend or another. Liana was a social butterfly in a way Max never was. I'd loved it, that feeling of being in the know, of being part of a world I'd never been privy to before, as if Liana had handed me a key to a whole other city, one of neon lights and dusty floors.

Between Liana and Molly, Ani and my other friends at the agency, there had always been something to do.

There had always been freedom, fun, on the horizon. Nights to look forward to. Days to trade stories.

It was a world that felt so entirely far away now, so closed to me: *Mothers, Keep Out*.

I pushed away the thought, focusing instead on the one thing I could do. I pulled out my phone, searched for the Find My app.

"What are you doing?" Liana asked, dumping ground coffee into the filter and water into the pot.

"Max's phone," I said. "I have his password. I can log in to iCloud to find his location."

"Oh," Liana said. "Of course. Good idea."

I nodded. "I thought of it just before you got here. I should have checked it sooner, but I was so . . . so . . ."

Liana didn't wait for me to fill in the blank. "Of course you were." She flicked the switch to brew, and a red light came on. She leaned against the counter. "Go ahead, then," she said. "Hopefully it will clear this whole thing up."

I tapped open the app, my fingers shaking with anticipation.

We used it frequently these days, because I was *always*

misplacing my phone. I was so focused on Freya, on all her many needs, it was like my limbs no longer worked correctly. The connection of hands to brain had been somehow severed, like the umbilical cord from my placenta to her, and I would leave things . . . everywhere. A clean bottle on the shelf of a bookcase. A burp cloth by the bread box in the kitchen. My phone deep in the sofa's cushions, left beneath my pillow upstairs in the bed, sitting on the bathroom counter. Max would use my Apple ID to log in to iCloud on his phone, make sure my device was still in the house, and show me the location, a little dot on the map—then play the sound—*ting-ting-ting*—the phone announcing its presence from wherever it was.

I was already logged in, and my phone, my computer, the iPad we used to check on Freya's baby cam, all showed up, three dots on the map. All inside the house.

I keyed in his email—musicmanmax@gmail.com—then carefully typed his password, one that hadn't changed in years: Daisy, his first cat. First letter capitalized, second letter replaced with the *at* sign to get a special character in. Plus his birthday: October 8. D@isy108. Passwords were so annoying, he always said. Once you got one that worked, you kept it.

I tapped the button to log in, got an immediate error, then shook my head, trying again. I'd probably made a typo.

I did it again, carefully this time.

Again, a rejection.

The letters were so tiny, and my thumb still so bloated, and the characters turned to dots the second I punched them in. I must have made a mistake.

I tried it again.

A message.

We noticed you entered an old password. Your password was changed fifteen days ago. This is your third attempt.

I stared at the message, at its tiny clerical font.

Your password was changed fifteen days ago.

It must be a coincidence, I thought. Maybe a password had gotten compromised, and Max had to change it.

"What is it?" Liana asked. "Janie, you look like a ghost."

"It's nothing," I said. "I guess . . . I guess Max had to update his password. Apple, you know, they're always making you change it."

"Oh," Liana said. She blinked twice, breaking my gaze, then forced a reassuring smile. "I'm sure it doesn't mean anything."

But I could see it, there in her eyes, as much as she was trying to hide it. Liana didn't look the least bit surprised.

Before I could press her further, she turned away from the pot and walked to the living room, straight to Freya's bouncer. "Coochie coochie coo, my little Frey Frey," she said, kneeling down to pinch Freya's toes, which were wrapped up in footed PJs. "Did you go easy on your mommy last night, or did you keep her up every hour?"

Liana turned to me, and it took me a minute to realize she was talking to me by way of the baby. This stuff came so naturally for other people, but never in a million years would I have thought to talk to another adult that way. "Oh," I said quickly. "She wasn't up any more than normal, but, Liana— you don't think he was *trying* to keep me out of his phone, do you?"

Liana returned to the kitchen and the gurgling coffeepot. It wasn't even close to done, but she pulled it out anyway, filling her cup halfway, the machine dripping onto the hot plate. It sizzled as she put the carafe back.

"Sorry," she said. "I told you I'm a mess without caffeine. And more than a little hungover." She opened the fridge and splashed some milk in her cup, then shut the door and turned to me. "Like I said—like *you* said—I'm sure there's some reasonable explanation. And when Max comes back, you'll get it."

I bit my lip, not entirely sure I believed her. "You went to the bar with them last night, then?"

"The wine bar with Carl? God, no. I am not about to spend fourteen dollars on three ounces of port. Besides, it looked like Brenda was going to smack him across the face. No, uhh, I had a prior engagement."

I raised an eyebrow.

Liana burst out laughing. "Sorry, it's not some big secret or anything. This guy I used to hook up with who left the city to find himself in the Catskills. He lives right downtown. I went to his place. It's that guy, Joe, the one who was always wearing that snapback with the puffy paint on it."

"Puffy Paint Guy?" I asked. "He lives *here*? And you didn't say anything until now?"

Liana blushed. "Sometimes I swear *everyone* from our old Brooklyn days lives here now. Besides, I'm not sure reuniting with Puffy Paint Guy is worthy of the evening news."

Liana was right. There were a lot of Brooklynites up here. Just a few days earlier, I'd seen a guy I'd dated for about three weeks in my twenties in line for coffee, and there I was, a baby in tow. I'm pretty sure we both pretended not to recognize each other to avoid the awkwardness. And that's not to mention the acquaintances I knew were here from Facebook or Instagram and simply had yet to run into, people who'd fled when the city got too tough.

Suddenly, I felt a twang of unspeakable jealousy—Liana was still so very connected to that old life—and if I weren't spending every moment tending to Freya, I could be, too. Reuniting with an old friend over coffee. Meeting up for a beer after a casual hike on the rail trails.

None of that for me, thank you. I was saddled with responsibility. With Freya.

"So," I said, trying to find lightness, however I could. "Does Joe still have the hat?"

"He does not," Liana said. "Now, it's a Herschel beanie and lumberjack shirt. He's fully embraced the Catskills aesthetic."

In spite of myself, in spite of everything, I burst out laughing.

Liana walked from the kitchen and took a seat on the couch, right beside Freya's bouncer. "Enough about my exploits," she said. "Tell me everything. Tell me exactly what happened."

I brought her up to speed as much as possible, skipping only one detail—the secret I'd shared with Max before I went to bed, one too shameful to voice again.

Freya screamed just as I was finishing, as if announcing the end of my story with a wail. I waited a beat, then two, to see if her cry was a one-off, but she carried on.

"One second," I said, standing up. "Let me get her pacifier."

Freya's cries intensified, following me down the hall.

The diaper bag was in the corner of the foyer, a black backpack I'd insisted on using instead of something bright and boldly patterned or—lord help us—quilted. I dug through the contents. Tiny diapers. A packet of wipes that had come open and started to dry out. Premade formula bottles. A teether that Freya had absolutely no interest in.

The llama pacifier wasn't there, the only one she'd deign to use. I flipped over the bag, shaking out its contents, the mess of an infant splaying over the hardwood floors. Nothing. The last place I remembered seeing it was on the car ride back from the excursion the day before. I checked Freya's bucket seat, sitting in the corner, but it wasn't there, either. It had probably fallen on the floor of the car. Shit.

Suddenly, the crying stopped, and I leapt to my feet, rushed back into the room.

There was Liana, Freya between her legs, Liana's heels bouncing up and down, soothing her. She cocked her to the side, looking only at Freya. "Now what do you have to be upset about, baby girl?" She was so good with kids, a fact I'd seen in full display all week, one she attributed to a brief stint nannying on the Upper West Side, but I knew better: she was a natural.

A natural in all the ways you're not.

"I think we should look for the car," I said. "It's not out front, but Max parks in a different spot each time, and now that you're here, now that you can help me get her outside, that's what we should do."

Liana's heels took on a new pattern, swishing like windshield wipers. Freya loved it. Liana took a sip of coffee, careful not to get any on Freya. "Then let's do that," she said. "And at least we'll know . . ." She paused, her eyes locked on Freya, as if she were intentionally avoiding my gaze. "At least we'll know if Max has it or not."

"Do you really think he would just . . . drive off?"

"Of course not," Liana said quickly. "But let's look for the car first. Like you said."

I nodded along, but there was no denying it.

Something was very wrong here.

Liana knew it as well as I did.

9

11:05 a.m.

IT TOOK NEARLY A HALF HOUR TO GET OUT THE DOOR. I HAD to feed Freya, change her, repack the diaper bag, get out the stroller, position everything just right. Then Liana and I had to get the whole mess onto the porch, down the steps, through the wooden gate and onto the sidewalk.

Liana had asked if we should drive around in her car, a lipstick-red Toyota whose license plate proudly read VLVTHP, but that wasn't an option. There was no way to safely secure Freya. The base that her bucket seat clicked into was in our rental car, wherever that was.

Outside, the three of us paused next to an oak tree, branches still bare from the winter. I engaged the stroller's brake and opened the diaper bag, pulling out a long spiral stuffed animal with a smiling fox head and a bushy, squeaky tail, one of the many gifts I'd gotten from the baby shower Brenda and Liana had thrown me in Westchester. Freya blinked twice, then offered the fox a coy smile. It wasn't her llama, and it wouldn't stop her from crying, should she start, but it might entertain her for a few minutes, enough for the rolling of the stroller to lull her to sleep.

"All right," Liana said, her eyes on her phone's map. "Where does Max normally park?"

"Anywhere on these blocks, really," I said. "Sometimes it's harder to find a spot than others, especially on the weekends."

"Let's do five blocks each way, okay?" she said. "I doubt he would have gone farther than that . . . just to park."

The words, the second half of her sentence, hung in the air as Freya stared at the toy and an older woman walked past, pulling her knit cardigan tight across her bony chest.

Just to park.

It was the way Liana said it, as if there were so many other things Max could have done with the car.

He wouldn't have gone farther than that . . .

. . . unless what you said to him changed everything.

. . . unless he wanted a fresh start.

. . . unless he was leaving you.

"Janie," Liana said, and I realized she was staring at me, waiting for a response. That often happened since Freya. My mind would go somewhere else, like when you rushed to the top of a staircase and forgot what you'd been after the minute your foot hit the last step. I was lost in the intricacies of my new life with Freya. Mommy brain.

"Sorry," I said. "What was that?"

"Five blocks each way. That good?"

"Yes," I said. "But I don't think he would *leave* us, Liana. And it wouldn't explain the door, anyway. Something could have happened. Someone could have—I don't know, come in and . . . and—Max wouldn't ever leave us. Not on purpose."

Liana paused. There was no denying it—she did. Then she reached out a hand and grasped my shoulder. "I'm sure he wouldn't."

There was something rhythmic, almost meditative about it, rolling the stroller as Freya drifted off, every bump in the bluestone path like a note in the lullaby, rocking her fast to sleep.

The people who did pass us, they smiled, completely oblivious to the chaos that had descended upon Freya and me, imagining, perhaps, that Liana and I were a couple, or that she was a good friend, up for the weekend to help me care for the new baby.

And *everyone* loved a new baby. Loved to coo. Loved to peek into the stroller and see that poreless skin and those shut eyes, so peaceful, like they were contemplating whatever heaven they'd come from. Max called it the Baby Pass. People made way for you in line. They offered you the best tables at the café. They said hello and wished you well, so consumed with the joy of seeing a creature so pure.

I squeezed at the handle of the stroller, then stopped, my phone lighting up from where I'd perched it in the caddy.

A text from Molly.

Freya looks so happy and angelic! Know you're busy but would really love to catch up by phone or FaceTime soon. It's been awhile! Hope things are OK

I swiped away at the notification, then tapped into the college group text, marveled at the way their conversations had continued on without me, all the girls responding to the photos I'd sent last night, all of them telling me how cute Freya was, asking me how I was doing, trading their own photos and videos of their quickly growing kids. Everyone wholly unaware that since sending those pictures, my world had imploded.

"Wow . . . Janie Walker?"

I looked up to see Ani, a friend from the agency I'd barely kept up with since leaving. Her hair was cut blunt at the shoulders, and she was dressed in a black-leather trench and platform heels, as if she'd been plucked right out of SoHo. Classic Ani.

"Ani," I said. "I didn't know you were here."

"I live here now!" she said earnestly. "As of last week! Traded city life for this and not mad about it at all. I've been meaning to text you, but life's been chaos with the move."

"Wow!" I said. "You never said anything about wanting to leave the city."

Ani and I had once been so close it would have been unfathomable for her to move without telling me everything about it.

She laughed. "I know, right? But here's a good transition. My real estate agent calls Kingston 'Brooklyn North.'"

"And you're still at the agency, right? Molly didn't say anything about you leaving."

Ani nodded. "I'm going to be working remotely a few days a week and taking the train down when I have an important meeting. Just got made VP, actually."

"Oh," I said. "Congrats. I know you've been working for it a long time."

"Well, not quite as long as you, but close!" she said, and I smiled awkwardly.

Liana tucked a bit of hair behind her ears, and I cleared

my throat. "Sorry," I said. "This is my friend Liana. Liana, Ani. Ani, Liana."

"Max's bandmate, right?" Ani stretched out her hand, and Liana shook it briefly. "I can't believe we haven't met before." Then she leaned over the stroller. "And this must be Freya? Molly's passed pictures around. She's an absolute doll."

I felt a pang at the thought of Freya's photo circulating the office, of the world continuing on without me, a world I had enjoyed so much.

"How's full-time-mom life?" Ani prodded. "Like I said, I really have been meaning to text you to check in."

"It's great," I lied. And then, to add a cherry on top of what everyone seemed to want to hear: "Hard, of course, but . . . fulfilling, you know."

"I'm sure! You know children aren't for me, but I love loving on other people's kids. Let me know if you ever need a babysitter. Get you and Max a date night."

My pulse ratcheted up, but I forced a smile. "That's so generous of you."

"I mean it," Ani said. "And how is Max anyway? He's left the band completely now, right?"

He's left the band. He's maybe even left us.

"He's good," I said. "You know, adapting to being a dad."

I stole a look at Liana, but her eyes were locked on the ground.

"Well, I should be going," Ani said. "I'm due to meet a friend for brunch. Another Brooklynite, of course. So good to run into you, though, serendipity! And please give me a call when you want a sitter. Or when you want to leave Freya with Max and catch up over drinks with me." She smiled mischievously.

"Of course," I said. "I will."

I pushed the stroller forward and waited until Ani was around the block, completely out of sight and out of earshot, before turning to Liana. "You must think I'm such a phony."

She reached for my hand. "I don't think that at all. Please understand that whatever's happened, it's not your fault. You don't deserve any of this."

I squeezed back, but Liana didn't know the truth:

In some ways, I did deserve it.

I really did.

WHEN THERE WAS nowhere left to check, when it was painfully clear that the car wasn't going to be found, Liana begged for more coffee and something to eat. We stopped in at the French bakery up the block from our rental, one Max and I had been to once or twice for baguettes, Freya still fast asleep.

The bell rang behind us, and the Provençal-yellow walls seemed to glow with cheerfulness. The scent of semolina rushed into my nostrils, and a French woman with all-gray hair said, "Isn't she a sweet one?"

I'm not sure if it was the fact that I'd just seen Ani, the way she brought my agency days so physically back into my present, but when I looked at the man at the front of the line, caught the salt-and-pepper hair, the thick black glasses, the ones I'd found so intellectual and at least a little bit attractive, the neatly trimmed beard and well-fitted blazer, I was sure it was Bryan, the client who'd unexplainably called me yesterday.

I took a step back, my stomach jumping into my lungs, shame filling me up inside. In a flash I was back there again, crowded into that private karaoke room in Koreatown, the one with fake leather banquettes and a digital songbook on an old iPad. High on the rush of the client meeting, belly full of ramen from the Asian-fusion shop on Eleventh Avenue, brain ruminating on what Eli had said: "I can tell we're close to signing them again. Let's seal this."

I'd spent the night doing my best to do just that: Ordering Hendrick's martinis and twenty-six-dollar pot stickers at dinner. Suggesting karaoke afterward because I knew it was the sort of thing Bryan would love—a guy who was swimming in money but fancied himself a man of the people. The whole Mark Zuckerberg sweatshirt thing.

Everything had seemed so simple that night. Work hard. Play hard. Make money. Rack up a tab. Bryan had kicked us off with his rendition of Rick Astley—"you've been Rick-rolled!"—Eli had chimed in with Joy Division, and Molly and I had done TLC's "Waterfalls," both of us knowing every last word to Left Eye's rap, competing with each other to see who could spit it out faster. It had been so fun, that night. I'd looked around: at Molly, at Ani, at Eli, at Bryan and the money his account promised us, at the city and all its strange ways, and I'd been happy. Maybe it was the last time I really was. Because in less than twenty-four hours, I had sabotaged it all—one horrible mistake, and my career had begun imploding.

The man in front of me now stared, his eyebrows narrowing, and Liana put a hand on my arm. "Janie," she said. "Janie, what's happened? What's wrong?"

I came to, from the murk of my own past, from this apparition I'd somehow created from the chaos of sleepless nights and stirred-up shame, and I could hear in an instant that this man's voice was all wrong, could see that his smile was, too.

It wasn't Bryan, not even close, just another thirtysome-thing, well-dressed, well-groomed man. More proof I was los-ing it. Seeing things—people—that weren't even there.

"I'm fine," I said, shaking my head. "I don't think I want a coffee. I . . . I need some air. And she needs to get home for another feeding."

I felt their collective gaze as I backed out the door, the bell clanking behind me, Freya waking at the sound.

Pulse pounding, feet heavy against the pavement, Freya fussing in the stroller, I strode down the block, Liana strug-gling to keep up.

"What happened back there?" Liana asked.

"Nothing," I said. "I thought I saw someone I recognized, but it wasn't him. It doesn't matter."

"But it does," Liana said. "You can tell me, whatever it is."

We were interrupted by the sound of sirens in the distance.

"Oh god," I said, my heart kicking up a notch. "Oh god."

Liana shook her head. "It could be anything, Janie. Any-thing."

But as we made our way back, as Freya began to wail, echoing the sirens herself, I found myself praying, just about as hard as I ever had before.

Please be okay, Max. Please, god, just be okay.

I can forgive anything if you'll only come back.

10

1:43 p.m.

BACK IN FRONT OF OUR RENTAL, I MARVELED AT THE SHEER number of steps required to get a baby inside and situated. Remove bucket seat from stroller. Fold stroller. Carry up porch steps. Swing back and forth to temper crying. Fumble for keys. Set car seat down. Fight with straps and buckles to get baby out. Check diaper. Carry to sofa. Lift shirt. Paw at the hook of the nursing bra. Latch on. Liana's help was only proof positive that it was a dance made for two.

What would I do if Max didn't come back? What if she cried and cried and cried and all I could feel was that raw animal hatred that would sometimes sneak up since she was born? What if it happened like the newspapers always said it did? What if I just . . . snapped?

"What do we do now?" I asked.

"Now?" Liana said. "Now we eat something."

"I can't . . ." I protested. "I'm not hungry."

"Don't you need to eat extra calories to feed her?"

Five hundred a day, that was what the doctor said, and I'd

dutifully done it, even when I wasn't hungry, because I had to try, for her.

"Anyway," Liana continued, "I'm still hungover, and I can't think straight without some toast at least. What have you got?"

"There's sliced bread on the counter," I said. "Some eggs in the fridge." They were eggs from the farmer's market, the one that set up shop in downtown Kingston on Saturdays. Max and I had gone a week ago, just before everyone got in. In a different world, Max and I would be going there today. These eggs were the special kind, the multicolored ones, pale green and yellow and baby blue and pink, like little gemstones, arranged in a row for us to marvel at. Last week, I'd taken a photo of them, along with Freya asleep in the stroller, posted it all to Instagram, used it to show everyone that I was adjusting fine . . .

A crack of eggs, shaking me from my thoughts. Then the sizzle of the pan, the pop of the toaster. Freya unlatching and latching back on.

Five minutes later, Liana set a plate in front of me. Freya was asleep on my chest, a blessing, but it meant I couldn't move.

"Okay," Liana said. "Let's start with what we know. The car obviously isn't here."

And the llama pacifier, I thought, something I needed badly, especially now that we were here on our own. I dug my fork into the eggs as the salty smell invaded my nostrils, forced a bite into my mouth.

"No," I said, swallowing it down and taking another. "I suppose it isn't." It seemed to lessen the possibility of Max having been abducted through the side door, but it raised other possibilities. Winding roads, ditches filled with crunched-up steel and not-yet-melted snow.

And Max, was he out there, waiting for us to find him? Was he suffering? Or was it all over already? Was he already . . . gone?

"Have you talked to anyone else?" Liana went on. "Other friends?"

"No, but you know Max." I shoved another forkful into my mouth. "It was the band and me. He didn't need a lot of people."

"Right," Liana said. "I'll call our bandmates. Just to check. And you should call Carl again, too."

I nodded robotically.

"What about your parents?" Liana asked.

"They won't be any help," I said. "They're on this cruise. In Europe. Two weeks."

"So they *did* do that," Liana said. "Wow."

"They're just a couple of days in," I said. "I'm not even sure how I would contact them. I told them things were fine with Freya and not to check email, to make the most of it."

Liana raised her eyebrows. She knew how much I'd helped my parents over the years, both before I met Max and after. Five hundred for a car repair here, a couple grand for a security deposit there. They were my parents, and in spite of everything, I loved them. I, an only child just like Max, was all they had.

"I don't need to hear it, Liana," I said. "Not now."

When I'd learned that they'd been saving up for this cruise to celebrate their thirtieth wedding anniversary, I'd been surprised, sure. Molly, Liana, even Max, who'd always gone out of his way not to judge them, had been shocked to learn that they weren't saving up to reimburse me for all the help I'd given them over the years.

But what did I expect? For them to put their extra money into a college savings plan for Freya? To rent a place in Brooklyn for a month and come up and help us out when we were back in the city? To save for the wedding I'd never had and that I'd always known I'd be paying for if I did? (To the horror of Carl and Brenda, I'm sure, who still believed in that age-old, sexist, classist, and heteronormative mantra *The bride's parents pay for the wedding. They just do.*) To simply pay me back?

Besides, the money I'd given them had never been presented as a loan. It was a gift, a recognition that I had more than they did, and family helped each other out. I didn't resent them for wanting to enjoy their lives now that the bankruptcy had finally fallen off their records, now that the creditors were no longer knocking down their doors . . .

Or maybe, actually, I did. Maybe with each new phase of my life I wanted, so desperately, for them to be different. For them to be quote-unquote *normal* parents, the ones who show up. Who help, not hinder. For them to be the parents I still sometimes naively dreamed that they'd one day wake up and be.

"What am I supposed to do, ruin their trip?" I asked. "Even if you think they shouldn't have taken the cruise, they're still on the damn thing. They're at sea. I don't even know when they get to the next port."

"Okay," Liana said. "Okay, I get it. Do you have information for the car?"

"You mean the plate number?"

"The police will want it, if it comes to that."

I flashed to a dark ravine, the front and back of the rental car smashed to smithereens, Max trapped inside. "I can find it," I said. "But, Jesus, Liana. Even if Max had gone to Target or something for baby supplies, the trip's a straight shot, right down 9W. If something had happened, we'd . . ." I hesitated, thinking of the sound of those sirens. "We'd know by now."

Liana shook her head. "It's too early to start thinking that way, Janie."

"Is it? If something didn't happen to him, then where on earth could he have gone?"

Liana paused a moment. "I *really* don't know." It was the way she said it, where she put the emphasis. *Really*. As if she *should* know.

As if Max would tell her anything and everything, even if he wouldn't tell me.

"Listen," she said. "Let's talk to his parents once more before we involve the police, okay? Maybe he's been in contact with them."

"But why would he call them and not me?"

She didn't answer. She simply lifted the phone to her ear, already making the call. As if they all knew Max better than I did.

For the first time ever, I wondered if maybe they did.

11

3:01 p.m.

IT TOOK AN HOUR FOR CARL TO FINALLY CALL US BACK, ONE I spent feeding Freya, off and on, my ass merging with the cushions of the sofa, trapped in my very own baby jail.

"Carl," I said, adjusting Freya. "We've been calling and calling."

"I'm sorry," he said. "Brenda had an appointment, like I told you. No word, still? Max hasn't come back?"

"No, Carl," I said, his casual verbiage sending me into a state of half alarm. Why wasn't he as scared as I was? "No *word*. And there was a side door unlocked, and Liana and I can't find the car, and—"

"Liana?" Carl asked. "I saw that she called me. She's with you?"

"Yes," I said, my voice clipped. "You and Brenda left. Who else was I supposed to call?"

"Of course, Janie," Carl said. "I didn't mean it that way. I'm just trying to understand. I didn't—we didn't realize you were quite so worried. And he could still turn up, Janie, he could—"

"Turn up in a ditch," I snapped.

As soon as I said it, I wanted to take it back, erase my words like I wanted to erase the words I'd said to Max the last time I'd seen him. Because it took it out of the murky darkness of my mind, into the harsh light of reality.

The line was silent.

"*Carl*."

He cleared his throat. "I'm so sorry," he said finally. "But believe me, I know Max, and he can be a little flighty sometimes, fail to realize how his actions impact other people, and I really don't think you should let your mind go there. It's only going to upset you, and it hasn't even been twenty-four hours."

Upset me?

"This isn't me being an emotional new mom, Carl. This is serious. Max isn't here, and he's *not* flighty. Not with me, at least. He's never done anything like this before. Never in all the time I've known him."

"I'm not saying you're being emotional—"

"Then what *are* you saying?"

"I'm saying in a few hours, this is going to be a completely different situation. He'll turn up."

"What do you think, he's some lost sock? Aren't you *worried*?" I asked desperately. "He's your *son*. It's time to—" I eyed Liana, who was typing away on her phone. "It's time to call the police."

"The police," Carl said, the pitch of his voice rising with alarm. "What on earth are the police going to do?"

Freya unlatched, let out a tiny Freya sound. I got her back on quickly. "File a missing person's report, for one."

"Well for that, I'm pretty sure we need to wait twenty-four hours."

"Carl," I said. "This isn't fucking *CSI*." It was strange—I don't think I'd ever sworn in front of him or Brenda before, and yet it felt natural now, justified, like the proper reaction, the worried reaction, the reaction of someone who actually gave a shit about Max. "You can file a report at any time."

"Come on, Janie," Carl said, and I heard it then, the anger of his that sometimes brewed beneath the surface, that I'd only ever seen come up toward Brenda before. "You know what that will do? Use up valuable resources when, for all we know, Max is clearing his head."

Clearing his head? What kind of Westchester WASPy denial fuckery was this? "Is there something I need to know?" I asked, point-blank. "Did Max tell you something? Something that's causing you to react this way?"

Max talked through all his life decisions with his dad. Always had, and the unplanned pregnancy had been no exception. Yes, sometimes it felt strange that Carl knew I had considered not having Freya, but Max's closeness with Carl was something I'd grown used to, something that had never felt threatening until now. Had Max gone straight to his dad last night, too? I imagined him picking up the phone, reeling from our conversation. *She doesn't even want Freya, Dad. She told me she wishes we hadn't had her. I don't know how I can be around someone like this.*

"Did Max say something . . ." I clarified, "about me?"

"Oh god, Janie, of course not," Carl said quickly, and his old voice was back now, the anger gone, evaporated before me, as if it had never been there. "What could he possibly say about you? Max adores you. You're his family. You're *our* family."

A hint of relief, however tiny. "Then why aren't you more worried?"

"Because Max, he's an anxious person. You know this. I

do, too. And a baby is very stressful. Let's let a few more hours pass. He's probably going to come marching through that door any minute, feeling like a fool. Apologizing like hell."

I pulled the phone away. "Carl wants to wait," I said. "To call the police."

Liana shrugged. "Maybe we should."

"I still don't understand," I said, the phone back on my ear. "Where do you think he is? Hanging out in a motel somewhere? He wouldn't do that, not without telling me."

"I can't say exactly, Janie," Carl said. "And I can see why you'd be scared. But if the car isn't there, and the car key isn't, either, then the most likely scenario is that he *did* go to get some space and that he's going to turn up any minute now. Okay? And if he doesn't, you call me right back, and we'll call the police, the whole works. I *promise*."

I took a breath, halfway between arguing and relenting— then froze.

A sound outside, followed by flashing lights, illuminating the sheer drapes that hung in the front windows for privacy, strobing, morphing them into some sort of terrible disco ball.

I stood, holding Freya to me, and rushed to the window, and there it was, my fears materialized.

The vision that was about to change my world forever.

"I have to go, Carl," I said, my voice stilted and robotic. "The police are here."

12

3:07 p.m.

THE LIGHTS STOPPED. THE DOORS SLAMMED. ONE. TWO.

A man and a woman emerged.

Through the wooden gate, up the stone steps. Onto the front porch.

I made for the door, fear pumping through every vein and capillary, probably invading my milk, too. My left arm still holding Freya tight to my body, feeling the squishiness, the heat of her skin, I didn't even wait for the knock. I turned the handle and pulled the door open, winced at the creaking sound. Liana stood next to me.

The man was young, with a pudgy baby face, pasty-pink skin, a strong nose, and bushy dark-brown eyebrows, which raised at the sight of me, a baby attached to my breast, flesh white and veined and there for him to see, the other breast covered only by the flimsy cotton of my nursing bra, a wet circle darkening the gray fabric where my milk hadn't gotten the memo to stop flowing. He looked away, finding his shoes, but the officer next to him, a Black woman who looked to be in her forties, with tightly curled hair pulled into a low bun, trained her eyes on me. The baby, our display, didn't scare her, and I wondered if she had kids of her own at home. Probably, I thought.

And she's probably a much better mother than you.

"I'm Officer Duncan," she said, revealing a smile of ultra-straight teeth. "This is Officer Cary. We're here because there was an incident last night—"

"Oh my god," I said, my voice wavering. "Oh my god, you've found him."

It played out before me then, every conversation I would have to have with Freya, how her father had loved her beyond words, how he'd been so good with her, and it was a terrible tragedy right after she was born. Things like this happened sometimes. You never thought they'd happen to you, but everyone couldn't beat the odds, now, could they?

Freya wouldn't remember a thing. About the only parent who ever truly loved her.

He probably went out for a drive after you said what you said. He was probably so disturbed and distracted that he crashed the car into a ditch, and now it's all your fault.

Then, like a slap, another realization, cold in my bones: one of never-ending aloneness. Every second and hour. Three hundred and sixty-five days times eighteen years. Even then, it wouldn't be over. I was a mother now. That meant forever. I was a mother, and I would have to do it all alone, something *he* had wanted, not me, something I wasn't remotely ready for.

Then the third realization, the one that should have come earlier. Max, my Max.

The man I loved so dearly. My partner in all the ways that mattered.

Officer Duncan shook her head. "I'm sorry, I didn't mean

to scare you. We're here to speak to Max Bosch. We have no reason to think he's in danger."

"You don't understand," I said, pulling Freya closer to me. "He's not here. I haven't seen him since last night. I was about to call you. I was about to—"

"Janie," Liana said, and she took my hand, squeezing it, but I quickly shook her off.

"I was about to file a missing person's report, and now you're here—" I said, my words, my thoughts, jumbling together, tears filling my eyes. "You're here, and you're talking about an incident, and . . . and . . ."

Duncan raised an eyebrow, and the two officers exchanged a look, an invisible conversation passing between them. It was almost like I could see their ears pricking up, this new information definitely something to them. Something potentially very big. But . . . *what*?

"Ma'am," the man, Cary, said, finally turning back to me, "we can absolutely get started on a missing person's report. And we can hopefully get some info that straightens this out." He nodded to Freya. "Would you like to get more comfortable, perhaps?"

"No," I said, tears spilling from my lids now. "Tell me why you're here. You're scaring me to death. How can you possibly know Max wasn't hurt?" I said, my voice aching. "How in the world could you know that?"

Duncan held up a hand. "Slow down, ma'am. Please. We just want to hear exactly what happened, when you last saw your husband."

"Boyfriend," I said, correcting her. "Partner. Whatever. Her dad," I said, nodding down to Freya, snot dripping from my nose now. I wiped it away, like a child. I wiped it away as

Freya still sucked at my tit, all sense of propriety—of decency—gone.

"Okay," she said. "And you live here with him?"

"It's a rental. We live in Brooklyn. We wanted to—to start her life up here, with woods, with space, in the country."

With roads Max could skid across. With dark ravines where he could tumble to his death.

"Please," I said, staring at Duncan, willing her to give me an answer, to offer something that would make this make sense. "Please tell me why you're here." Words poured forth then, as if boiling over the top of a pot. "He isn't answering his phone, and we can't find the car, and—and—a side door was unlocked—" I paused for breath. "And now you're here, and I don't know what happened, and you're telling me he's not in danger, but how do you know that?"

Freya began to cry, a wail that pulled apart any remaining strength I had left.

Tears streaked down my cheeks, and I wiped away more snot.

Cary shifted his weight. "We are very sorry for scaring you, ma'am. We can tell you're upset."

"There was an incident at the Three Crows Tavern," Duncan said. "Only a few blocks away from here."

I shook my head and sniffled, trying to understand. "The wine bar?"

Duncan narrowed her eyes but continued. "We're going around the neighborhood, trying to get a fuller picture," she said. "That means we need to speak to everyone who was there last night. Including Mr. Bosch."

"But I saw him afterward," I said. "I spoke to him. He was back here, safe. He woke me up. He—"

"Janie," Liana said, so firm, so loud, I couldn't do anything but stop. "The wine bar is not the Three Crows. I've been to the Three Crows. I went there—er—the other night. It's not the same place Max went with Carl and Brenda."

"Carl and Brenda?" Duncan pressed.

"Max's parents," Liana and I said in unison.

"All right, let's take a beat," Duncan said. "You're telling us that your partner was at two different bars last night?"

"All I know about is the first one," Liana said. "His dad wanted to stop for a glass of dessert wine. The place was something with *Grape* in the name."

Cary tapped at his phone. "Upstate Grape," he offered.

"Yes," Liana said. "Yes, exactly."

"Okay, then," Duncan went on, pulling out a notepad. "Glad we cleared that up. So Mr. Bosch was at Upstate Grape last night. With his father and mother—"

I nodded. "Carl and Brenda Bosch."

"And he went to Three Crows after that."

"No," I said. "No, he was home before eleven. He sent me upstairs to get some sleep. He was going to do Freya's first feeding. He wouldn't go back out. There was no reason—"

"Ma'am," Cary said, cutting me short. "We have a credit card receipt that places Mr. Bosch at the Three Crows Tavern just after midnight."

I shook my head, my mind reeling at the thought. Max, going back out? To a bar I'd never even heard of? Last night, when he was supposed to be helping me? Resting up so he could feed Freya?

An image filled my mind then, a puzzle piece fitting into place. Had Max gone out the side door so I wouldn't hear the squeaky hinges of the front? Was *that* the explanation?

I turned to Liana, but her lips were pressed together. Her face was pale.

Why would Max have gone out? And to a bar that had had an *incident*, no less. A skipped-out-on tab, a bar fight, a stolen purse—those weren't *incidents*. An incident was . . .

"What happened?" I asked again, standing up straighter, as if to brace myself, not even caring that my chest was showing. "What in the world was this *incident*?"

Cary jumped in then, his eyes trained directly on me.

"An apparent homicide," he said. "In the alleyway behind the bar."

My pulse beat, loud as a drum in my head, just like it did all those times I carefully set Freya down after a feeding, praying she'd stay asleep. As if life and death were on the line, as if I'd consider selling my own soul if it meant she wouldn't stir, open her mouth wide, and scream for more, if it meant I'd get a couple of hours of oh-so-precious sleep.

But no matter how bad it felt, that *wasn't* life and death. This was.

"What?" I asked, struggling to process. "What did you say?"

"Ma'am, should you— Are you sure you don't want to—" Cary nodded to Freya, who continued to suck, and I couldn't believe he gave two shits about accidentally seeing my nipple, alert and exposed, even for the tiniest of moments. I bet he watched porn late at night on his phone. I bet he had no problem with seeing a nipple or two then.

My spine stiffened, and I set my lips firm. "Someone was murdered, and *this* is what you're worried about?" I glared at him. "She's hungry. She needs to eat."

"Of course she does," Duncan said. "But perhaps you'd like to sit down for this conversation."

"I don't need to sit. I need to know how you know Max wasn't hurt. Wasn't . . . killed."

"The victim is a woman, ma'am," Cary said finally. "That's all we can say."

At first, relief.

It wasn't Max. It was some other person. Some woman. With other people who loved her. Other people who depended on her. Call it callous, call it cruel, but this was someone else's tragedy, not ours.

Then my eyes caught Liana's, and I saw what I'd been searching for all day—from her, from Carl: fear. Hot, raw fear.

Max had been at the bar. At midnight. He had been at the bar where a woman had been killed.

And he hadn't come home.

A murderer was out there, and my partner was gone.

"You understand why we want to speak with him," Duncan said.

"Yes," I said. "Yes, I do."

"And are you sure you don't know how we can get in touch with him?" she prompted. "Because if you're protecting him—"

"Protecting him?" I snapped. "A murderer is out there, and he's *missing*. I'm not protecting him. *You* should be."

Duncan stood up straighter. "Let's get started on that missing person's report, then."

The scream came so suddenly, so frighteningly, that for a moment, I didn't even recognize it as hers.

For a moment, it was disembodied, some primal scream. That of a dying woman. Of a man in danger. Of grief. Of need. Of death, even.

But it wasn't any of those things, was it?

I looked down to see Freya, popped off my boob, sucking in breath, in the way babies do, revving up, and I knew it was coming, the sound I abhorred so much, the sound that was like crunching glass or nails on a chalkboard. The sound the US government used to use to torture people. Freya wound up, her face going red as the air filled her belly, her diaphragm, her throat, blowing her up like a balloon. And there was that excruciating pause, where I wondered for a second if she was going to stop breathing. I felt like her life and mine hung completely in the balance.

Then it came. Another scream.

I pulled her to my chest, took a couple of steps backward. Looked at Duncan only.

"You better come in."

13

8:17 p.m.

MY HANDS SHOOK AS I PULLED THE BEDROOM DOOR SHUT that evening, Freya asleep behind it.

The hours had passed in a blur of events so unexpected, so disconnected from the life I'd ever thought I'd live, that it was hard to even count them as real, as anything more than a fever dream of fears.

There had been papers to fill out. License plate numbers to rattle off. Rental agreements to forward to Duncan's email. The cops wanted the address to our place in Brooklyn, Max's email and cell phone number. His age, height, approximate weight, and what he was wearing, from that North Face layer to his worn-out Vans. A recent photo (or two). Ideas of anywhere he may or may not be.

There were questions to answer, too.

When did you last see Max? *Last night.*

Did he seem okay to you? *Yes, he seemed fine.*

And still, more details. The circumstances of Carl and Brenda's visit, of Liana's presence, and all their contact info, too. Questions about Max's friends, his other acquaintances.

About women he may or may not have known, the implication blind and naked on both Duncan's and Cary's faces. New fathers didn't go out to bars at midnight on Friday nights to stock up on formula, that was for sure. They didn't go for very good reasons at all.

It felt like ages before Duncan and Cary were gone, before they'd left with promises to "do what we can" and demands we call them the second Max resurfaced.

By then, it was Freya's witching hour. The time of day when new babies decide that screaming is better than anything else. With no Max, no "llama in place of your mama," it had all been up to me. Liana could only do so much to help.

But now, Freya was asleep. Even a little early for her, as if the chaos of the day had tired her as well. Now, there was nothing to do *but* process.

At the top of the stairs, I hesitated, listening to the clink of dishes downstairs. Liana must be in the kitchen, tidying and cleaning, maybe even pulling something together for dinner.

I needed some time to myself—to think.

I turned away from the stairs, walked down the hallway, past the guest room, already filled with Liana's things, into the nook at the end of the hall, the sound of dishes replaced by the pitter-patter of rain on the old roof.

Max and I had turned this alcove into a home office of sorts, moving a chair from downstairs in front of the small hallway table. Our computers—twin MacBook Airs, mine rose gold, his silver—were there. I pulled his toward me slowly, my hands shaking as I thought about what Carl had said. *A baby is very stressful. He's probably going to come marching through that door any minute, feeling like a fool.*

For the first time since I'd woken to Max being gone, my brain crawled toward the seedier possibilities. After all, what did men do when they needed to de-stress? It was a tale as old as time, wasn't it?

That wasn't Max. It never had been.

Max loved with such loyalty, such . . . trust.

Trust was hard to come by. I knew that well.

I opened his laptop, was greeted by Max's avatar in a circle in the middle. I clicked on it, and then I was in—there had never been a password to access his computer.

I checked his email first, scanning it carefully.

Nothing unexpected: REI promotions. *New York Times* newsletters. Updates from the baby milestone app we'd both downloaded. A few back-and-forths with music clients of his. Invites to shows from Liana and other bandmates.

Squeaky clean.

Because that's how Max lived or because he'd been busy deleting?

I opened his browser instead, queued up the full history, desperate to find something, anything, that would give me a clue as to why he'd gone to that bar, what had happened there.

That was fruitless as well. Nothing more than news articles and searches about how to get a baby to sleep or tips on preventing SIDS. Nothing to hint that anything untoward was going on, that soon he would be gone.

I flicked through his desktop, his downloads folder— nothing.

My phone buzzed, and I scrambled to answer it, hoping for an update from Duncan or Cary. Or a call from Max that could put this nightmare behind us.

"Carl," I said.

"Janie, I'm glad I got you. Freya asleep?"

"Yes," I said. "On the earlier side, thankfully. Liana called you, right?" I asked. Freya's needs had been so all-consuming, I'd tasked Liana with updating Max's parents on everything that had transpired with the police.

"Yes," Carl said, and was I mistaken, or did his voice already have a bit of a slur to it? "Yes, she did." He cleared his throat, as if to erase his last couple of drinks. "I'm so sorry you're going through this, Janie. I really am, and, look—I know you've already made the report, but I still think we should try to stay calm, tread carefully on this one."

"'Tread carefully'?" I asked, gobsmacked. "A woman is dead, Carl. Murdered. And Max was—"

"Max had nothing to do with that," Carl said firmly. "It's entirely coincidental."

"What if Max saw something?" I asked. "What if he tried to intervene and the killer went after him? What if he's in danger?"

"I don't think that's likely, Janie," Carl said. "We need to keep our heads on straight. We need to not act rash here."

"I'm not being *rash*," I said. "I'm not being anything but normal. It's you who doesn't seem in touch with what's actually going on. That your *son* is missing. That your son could have seen a murder. That he could be in horrible danger, if he's not already—"

Dead. If he's not already dead.

"And what if he didn't?" Carl asked, the slur back in his voice now. "Do you really want him wrapped up in this? Do you want him to lose all his clients? To never be able to work again? People don't exactly want their children taught by people caught up in murders, Janie. You need to think about what you're doing here. For Max and for you and for Freya."

"I am thinking about Max," I said. "Lately, it feels like I'm the *only* one who is."

I hung up, blood rushing, pulse pounding. I hung up on my father-in-law, the one I'd loved almost as long as I'd loved Max, who'd taken me into his family, who'd been the rock my own parents could never find a way to be.

I was done with them all: With Carl, pussyfooting around the truth that was right there in front of him so he could make time for another glass of wine. With the cops, who thought some clandestine affair could explain Max's absence better than anything else.

Even Liana had been hesitant to see what was going on, taking Carl's side, urging me to wait to report Max missing. Normalizing behavior that wasn't the slightest bit normal at all.

What was wrong with them? All of them?

I pushed back, the chair legs scraping against the hardwood, and keyed "Three Crows Tavern" into my phone's map.

If anyone was going to find out what the hell happened to Max—where he was now—damn it, it was going to be me.

14

9:28 p.m.

I STARED AT THE PLAIN BRICK FACADE, THE THICK GLASS WIN-
dows, a wooden sign above the door.

BAR

I checked the map to confirm. This was definitely it. Even
though Kingston was small, I'd never been on this street, a
couple of blocks off the main drag. Buildings sandwiched it
in, no way to see the alleyway from here. It seemed so
insignificant—so unassuming.

Inside, it was dimly lit, with dusty, sticky floors, and the
Smiths blaring from an actual jukebox, not one of those digital
things that had become ubiquitous in recent years. Spacious,
with plenty of nooks and crannies to tuck yourself away in,
but still—a dive.

The crowd was young and Saturday-night drunk, even
this early in the evening. Girls in their early twenties—or
maybe even younger than that, but with fake IDs—were scattered in groups, gathering in the way that young women do.
Guys were speckled among them, holding cold PBRs and Bud
Lights and looking for a way in. A chalkboard advertised beer

specials and two-for-one well drinks, which would explain the raucous attitudes, the hangovers that would inevitably come tomorrow. The whole scene made everything somehow worse. *This* was where Max had come the night before to get away from me? Not a whiskey tasting room or that Upstate Grape place, but here? A place that catered to college kids and twentysomethings?

Why, Max? I thought. Why did you come here? What happened to you when you did?

Because he wanted to get away from you. You and all the terrible things you told him. You and all the terrible things he was about to find out.

The bar was in the corner, lacquered wood that stretched across one entire side, but my eyes homed in on a back door, one that must lead to the alley. I pushed through the crowd, made my way to the shut door. I reached for the handle, a silver industrial thing—

"Hey."

I turned to see a freckled boy, dirty rag in his hand—too young to serve alcohol but just old enough to work here. "It's locked. If you want to smoke, you have to do it out front from now on, that's what Dave says."

The boy turned around before I had a chance to ask why. I headed toward a bartender who looked at least a little bit older, with shaggy hair and a Ramones T-shirt. I took the only empty seat at the bar, the one on the corner, and pressed my palms against the wood, trying to relax, to get my wits about me.

"Well drinks are two-for-one," the guy said. "Domestics are four bucks a pop. What can I get you?"

My first real drink out in who knew how long, and I

wanted it to be good, at least. Well liquor would not do. "Hendrick's and soda?" I asked.

"Huh?"

"Tanqueray, then. Soda and extra lime."

"It's not on special," the bartender said.

"That's okay."

He poured from the green glass bottle generously, topped it off from a button on his fountain, added two limes, and pushed the drink in front of me. "That'll be eight."

I nodded, reaching for my wallet. There was no easy way in. No caution tape. No crime scene. Nothing more than a locked door to explain all that had happened the night before. Still, I had to try. "I'm surprised you're open," I said cautiously. I pulled my credit card from its slot, avoided the bartender's gaze. "After what happened last night."

When I looked back up, the bartender was wiping down the counter.

"It's just so shocking," I said, pressing on. I pushed my card forward, my fingers shaking slightly. "To think that something like that could happen right here in town."

The guy still didn't meet my eyes.

"The woman?" I prompted. "The one who was killed?"

"Listen, lady," he said, glancing surreptitiously right, then left. "I don't know how you know about that, but the owner told us not to discuss it, okay? It's not good for business."

I licked my lips. "I don't want to get you in trouble. It's just my . . ." I hesitated. "My *friend* was here last night, and we haven't heard from him since. I was wondering if you saw him."

"I'm serious," he said as he took my credit card. "I wasn't here, I didn't talk to any police, and the little I do know is not supposed to be public knowledge. Now, should I leave your tab open?" he asked, the conversation obviously over.

"Sure."

He turned around, and I took a sip of my drink—a gulp, really—trying to quash the churning of my stomach. Had I really thought it would be so easy? That I could cruise up to the bar and ply someone for information like a character on a bad TV show?

This was a complete dead end, that much was obvious. Should have been obvious from the moment the boy stopped me from even trying to open the back door.

Part of me wanted to leave, turn around right there, but what did I have to go back to? Liana going on about how we had to listen to Carl? Freya waking up to accost me with every one of her needs? Max still absent from our bed, our home?

I took another sip, letting the gin slip across my tongue. The drink was so good, the liquor floral, almost sweet.

Another sip. It was hitting me fast now, after so long without drinking anything more than a mouthful or two of wine. It was hitting me very fast indeed, softening all the weeks—months—of pain.

The jukebox changed, and that song came on, the old one my roommate and I used to listen to when I first moved to New York. By one of those late-aughts bands that had the word *Bells* in their name.

Around me, the crowd seemed to thrum and pulse—young people wondering where a Saturday night was going to take them.

This used to be me, I thought, for the second time that day. Maybe in a slightly classier joint, but the effect was the same, wasn't it? Before my pregnancy, going out, slurping up the city's offerings like a bowl of Momofuku noodles, it had been my thing. So common for me, so frequent then. *Out* had so many meanings, but it was always that—out. Living. My pores, opening up, like the world was a sauna, and I was there to sweat out the bad stuff, soak up the good. It didn't really matter where *out* was, just as long as it was, and I was part of it.

Now, that world was so far away. Liana hadn't even wanted me to come here. She thought the whole errand was foolish, and I suppose it was. But for a moment, I didn't care. I was out, wasn't I? I was a woman again, not just a mother. And with the gin already going to my head, a song I'd loved so much in a different life building to its final chorus, I could almost imagine it, that this really was my life, that I had the luxury of freedom and self-determination. That every single minute of every single day didn't revolve around somebody else.

And in that moment, I wanted it so badly, so deeply. I wanted seedy bars and spur-of-the-moment spin classes. I wanted Brooklyn Steel shows and bike rides down to the Promenade. I wanted packed ad agency meetings and the adrenaline of a tight deadline. I wanted to drink my drink and order another and another and another after that. I wanted to infuse my breast milk with poison, and I wanted it to not even matter, because I never wanted to feed her again. I wanted out. I wanted my old life back.

I wanted to run, to disappear, as maybe Max had.

Only a mother couldn't run, could she? It was biological. The mother filled out the birth certificate. The mother wore the hospital band that matched the baby's. The mother was the constant.

Men could leave. Things could get hard, and they could go

out and clear their heads, go to a bar, forget it all. And if it was really bad, they might never come back. And sure, it made them assholes, sure, it made them losers, but society would always accept them in the end, society would redeem them, one way or another. Another girlfriend could be had. Another family, maybe, one day, when they were ready this time.

Mothers didn't leave, did they? It was too horrible, too antisocial, to even comprehend. Mothers didn't disappear. Mothers didn't get caught up in things like this, things that took them away.

I remember watching that movie, the one with Meryl Streep and Dustin Hoffman, several years before, long before there was any talk of a child of my own, before I'd met Max, even. *Kramer vs. Kramer*. Meryl Streep gets fed up with motherhood and just . . . goes. It was so easy to hate her in that movie, so easy to paint her as a monster. What she'd done was so evil, wasn't it? So wrong?

I remember in high school, reading *A Doll's House*, internally cheering for Ibsen's brand of feminism, however imperfect, and then being horrified when Nora simply leaves her children behind.

A mother exits. A door shuts. *Fin*.

Never could I have imagined then, as a teenager who traded futures like they were baseball cards—maybe one day I'll have three kids, or maybe I won't have any and I'll make loads of money and go on nice vacations—that I would find myself in a situation where my own partner had gone, where I was wishing, desperately, that I could go, too.

My phone rang, vibrating against the bar, shaking me out of my fantasy. Molly's name lit up the screen.

My finger hovered over the button. I needed her in a way I hadn't only twenty-four hours earlier. I took another sip and tapped to answer. "Hello?"

"Janie," Molly said, as if momentarily dumbfounded. "You answered!"

"Yes," I managed.

I stirred my drink, took another sip, the bar raucous and loud around me.

"I hope I didn't interrupt anything. I have no idea what a new-mother schedule is these days."

"Don't worry," I said. "There isn't one."

Molly laughed. "Where are you?"

"A bar," I said. "A few blocks from where we're staying."

"Date night!" Molly said, practically squealing with delight. "Wait, is Ani babysitting? She told me she ran into you. God, don't let me keep you."

My voice cracked, but I managed to get the words out. "No," I said. "Just me."

"Oh," Molly said. "Well, Mama's night out, just as important, right? Max home with Freya. Love that."

Heat rose to my face. "Not exactly."

"What do you mean?" Molly asked. "Who's with her?"

"It's fine," I said, but already my voice was cracking. "It's nothing."

"Janie," Molly said. "It doesn't sound like nothing. And you don't sound okay."

My eyes began to well, but I held the tears back.

"My mother, you know, she had really intense postpartum with my little sister," Molly said. "I was eight. I remember. You can tell me, whatever it is. We can get you help."

"It's not that," I said, but even as I said it, how could I be sure? I *was* falling apart. Long before Max left. But it wasn't *only* that.

"Then what is it?" Molly asked earnestly. "Janie, it's *me*."

My pulse pounded with fear, with shame, and I wanted to make something up, protect my secrets, but I found I couldn't lie about this. Not to my best friend.

"Max isn't here," I said, barely able to get the words out. "Max is gone."

"What do you mean, he's *gone*?"

Already, in a matter of hours, the story had become familiar. Something I delivered on repeat now, something I might be repeating for a very long time. A story I would have to tell Freya one day. "He wasn't here this morning. I'm worried something happened to him. I'm—"

"Oh my god, Janie," Molly interrupted me. "Did you call the police?"

"Yes."

"Did they start a missing person's report?"

"They're doing what they can," I said.

"Who's with Freya?"

"Liana," I said. "She's—"

"Jesus, Janie. And he didn't leave a note or anything? He didn't give you any clue as to where he went?"

Shame once again reared its ugly head. "I don't know that he *went* anywhere, Molly. I'm worried something's happened to him."

A pause. "Okay," Molly finally said. "Of course you are. I just . . . I know parenthood can be hard on people. I know Max has some mental health issues . . ."

So everyone thought he'd left me, then. His own parents.

The police. Liana. Now Molly, too. And her pity was too much. Liana and Carl and Brenda, they belonged to Max. Molly was mine.

"I'm coming up there," Molly went on. "You can't go through this on your own—"

I wished, suddenly, that I could take it back. She was already so horrified, and I hadn't even told her about the murder. It wasn't like Molly could actually do anything to help me—she could only be a witness to my undoing. "No," I said. "No, don't come. I'm okay. I mean, I'm doing what I can, I—"

"Janie."

"No," I said again, my voice pleading, because the thought of her seeing me like this—alone, lost in the world, a partner gone, a baby needing—was too much. The thought of her telling me Max had left me on purpose, face-to-face—I couldn't handle it.

"No," I said, firmly now. "I have to go, Molly."

"Janie, just—"

"Please don't come."

I hung up the phone before she could say anything else.

THE GIRLS—YES, girls; they couldn't have been more than twenty-three—were decked out in that way that only early-twenties girls in a bar can be. Not just in dark eyeliner and skimpy tops that didn't suit the weather at all, but their faces were practically slathered with naïve excitement—with hope. Bree and I used to take a whole afternoon post–World Civ, flicking through each of our "going-out tops" for a Friday night.

"Six weeks old?" the girl in the middle of the trio, the tall one with an asymmetrical haircut and a heart-shaped face, said. "No shit. That's . . . *young* young. It's amazing you can get out at all."

"I know," I said. "But, believe me, I need it."

"So where's your husband?" the girl next to her asked.

"Boyfriend," I said.

"Baby daddy!" the third girl squealed, setting off peals of laughter.

"Yup. Baby daddy," I said, endearing myself to them. "He's at home, watching her." It was amazing how easy it was to lie. But everything was easy with the booze in my system. Easy to text Max: *If you really are ok, I'll never forgive you for this. A woman is dead, you asshole. We're terrified.* Easy to grab my second drink and walk up to a group of girls more than a decade my junior who were hovered around the bar's back door and say hi, weasel my way into their conversation.

"Is it as hard as it sounds?" the middle one asked. "One of my high school friends has three kids, and her life looks fucking miserable."

I sucked down more of my drink. "It actually *is* kind of miserable!"

The girls laughed uncontrollably.

"But you love her more than anything, right? It's worth it?" one of the others asked.

"Oh, it's totally worth it." Another lie—just as easy now.

I sipped more of my drink and nodded to the back door. This was my chance. "Do you know why it's locked tonight?" I asked. "They usually don't make a big deal if people smoke out there, right?"

The girls exchanged glances, their faces lighting up with secrets. I'd been right to approach them, right to count on twentysomethings to delight in gossip, to have information I couldn't get otherwise. The girl in the middle raised an eye-brow. "So they're *saying* that there are some loose bricks in the alleyway, and it's not safe or something."

"But that's not the whole story?" I asked.

She leaned forward. "So honestly, and I only know this because my sister is dating a town cop, but someone was supposedly *murdered* out back. I guess she was found this morning. I can't even believe they're open."

"What?" I asked, gasping perhaps a bit too dramatically, but the girls didn't seem to notice. "Right here?"

The third girl nodded. "Crazy, right? Kingston is so, you know, *sleepy*."

"But no one knows?" I asked.

The middle girl nodded. "I mean, it's only a matter of time, right? The only people who really go into the alley are the people who work at the businesses that back up to it, and I definitely saw cops at the intersections this afternoon, but you can't see anything from the street. I think they're keeping it quiet, or trying to, at least." She shrugged. "Maybe to aid the investigation. To catch the guy, whatever."

My pulse quickened, and the drink in my hand began to shake.

"You okay?" one of the other girls asked.

"Yes," I said, forcing my hand to be still. "Just haven't had this much alcohol in a while, between pregnancy and breast-feeding."

The girls laughed.

I took a final sip. "Aren't you scared, then? A murderer on the loose and everything?"

The middle girl shrugged. "So again, this is not common knowledge, but the woman who died, I talked to her once, and I don't have proof or anything, but I would bet my life it was her husband. Every time she came here, she was always going on about how good it was to get away. And, I mean, it kind of always is, isn't it? With women?"

Relief washed over me. The husband, of course. It was always the husband, like the girl said. This had nothing at all to do with Max.

"So do you know much about her, then?" I asked. "The woman who died?"

"Not much," she said. "But she was kind of a regular. She always came on the early side on Wednesdays, which is usually when I come, too. One of my friends and I have a weekly meetup, you know? Anyway, I only talked to her once, but she was super gorgeous. Even for someone in her late thirties or whatever. Her name was Grace."

I took a deep breath, because now that I was here, I had to check. "Do you know if she knew someone named Max?"

The girl shook her head. "No clue. We only talked that once. But I know she'd usually come with another woman. Not a guy or anything."

I nodded, and then the girl bit her lip.

"The only other thing I know is that she lived in that old brick house across the street."

SUNDAY, MARCH 17

15

10:03 a.m.

THUMP-THUMP-THUMP.

Thump-thump-thump.

Thump-thump—

My eyes burst open. Freya was crying, but beneath it, the sound echoed.

I stood, slipping into my robe, my head pounding, undid her swaddle, and pulled Freya from the bassinet. She writhed in my arms like a snake.

The thumping continued. There was someone at the door. The police?

Downstairs, I peered through the window to see Liana. I hadn't even realized she'd gone out. Holding Freya to me, her body still squirming, I opened the door.

"I'm sorry," Liana said, her shoulders slumped. "God, I must have woken you up. I tried calling and texting but . . ."

I spotted my phone in front of the door, lit up with notifications, where I must have tossed it as soon as I'd gotten home from the bar. After talking to the girls, I'd left, unable to look away from the house across the street, all brick and surrounded by an actual picket fence, one I'd stared at, telling myself desperately that all of this had nothing to do with Max. Once I was back in our rental, I'd gone straight to the pump to relieve some of the pressure of the milk, poured the mess down the sink, and ambled up the stairs to get whatever sleep I could before Freya woke again. And she did wake. What felt like every couple of hours, but it was impossible to know because I didn't have my phone on me, and I'd been too exhausted, too busy warming frozen milk and making bottles, to remember to bring it upstairs.

Now, I looked at Liana, more than a little confused. "Where were you?" I asked. "And why didn't you use the key?"

"I was getting a latte," Liana said. She looked down to her obviously empty hands. "I'm sorry I didn't get you one . . . they didn't have any decaf espresso. I locked the door behind me because I didn't want to leave you and Freya in an unlocked house, but then somehow I lost the key you gave me. Do you have a spare?"

"That *was* the spare," I said, remembering all the times Liana had misplaced things before. It was part of her charm, something I didn't find all that charming right at this moment.

"I really am sorry." She reached for Freya. "Can I help you?"

"No," I said. "And it's okay. I'm just tired. And I need to feed her."

"Okay," she said. "Let me make you some breakfast, then."

A few minutes later, Freya was latched on. Toast was on a plate. A cup of decaf coffee was in my hand.

"Were you . . . okay . . . last night?" Liana asked, her eyes wide, caring and kind. "I tried to stay up, but I was too exhausted."

I took a bite of toast, made just how I liked it—slathered

with butter and jam. "I went to that bar, and I met some girls there—young ones—they said they thought it was the husband who did it, who killed that woman."

"That makes the most sense, doesn't it?" Liana said, taking a bite of toast. "Isn't that usually the case?"

"Right," I said. "Just—do you know if Max ever knew anyone named Grace?"

"That's the name of the woman who died?"

I nodded. "That's what the girls said."

Liana puzzled over it a moment, then shook her head. "I don't think so. It doesn't ring any bells."

"You're sure?" I asked. "Any people he dated before me? People associated with the band? Anything?"

Liana finished off her toast, then shook her head. "You meet a lot of people when you're in a band, but I swear to you, I don't know a Grace."

"Okay." I took another bite. Liana was telling the truth, I was sure of it. "But we still don't know where he is. And if this husband did kill this woman, what if Max saw it? He was at the bar that night, at least the cops are saying so. What if he's in trouble? What if . . ."

I couldn't bear to say the rest.

"Listen, Janie, I know why you would think that way, but I'm hoping—I'm praying—that Max's leaving is a coincidence, that none of this is connected."

"But then how would that explain where he is? I've been over it and over it, and nothing makes sense."

Liana took a deep breath. Then she pushed her plate aside and stood, making her way to the kitchen.

I followed, Freya clutched in my arms.

Liana began opening and shutting cabinets.

"What are you doing?" I asked.

Her back stayed to me. "Making a drink."

"It's not even noon."

"I know," she said, reaching for the whiskey Max kept in the cabinet above the microwave. When she'd poured a couple of fingers over ice, she walked past me, into the living room. Like a robot, I followed her, Freya still latched on.

I sat back down, and Freya pulled off. I reached for the burp cloth hanging over the back of the armchair, but it was damp and sour, overdue for a wash. There was a bin by the sofa, where we kept a fresh stack, but it was empty. The laundry was Max's chore, not mine, one he apparently hadn't kept up with the past couple of days.

I sopped up the milk as best as I could with the old rag, then delivered Freya into the electric swing, desperate to get her out of my arms. I turned on the vibrations and the music, the cloying digital sounds of "Mary Had a Little Lamb," and she settled immediately, her eyes beginning to close, lids heavy, as the swing went to and fro.

Liana tipped her glass back, and the smell of liquor turned my stomach after my two drinks last night. Her eyes fixed on some obscure point in the distance, like Freya's did sometimes. Then she cleared her throat and took another sip of whiskey.

"Max . . ." she started. "He's a good dad. He . . . he loves Freya. He loves . . ." Her eyes met mine. "You. But he isn't perfect."

I felt ill. "Why are you saying it like that? What do you know?"

Liana scooted slightly away from me on the sofa, and the

message was beyond clear: *I know things that you don't. Things that might break you in two.*

"What is it?" I asked. "Christ, just tell me."

She squirmed, messing with the pillow behind her back. "I'm sure you noticed that Carl has been very calm through all this. And, to a point, I have, too."

"Yes," I said, narrowing my eyes. "None of you seem very worried at all."

"There's a reason for that," Liana said, licking her lips, taking another sip. "You see, Max has disappeared before."

10:27 a.m.

"WHAT DO YOU MEAN, HE DISAPPEARED?"

Liana pressed her palms to her thighs, spreading out her fingers. She had such long and beautiful fingers, ones that danced over the black-and-white keys of her keyboard, that flicked on the synthesizer and filled the venue with delicious, soul-invading bass.

"The first time was in college," Liana said. "It was our sophomore year. We'd just started the band. Max was always a good student, always as book smart as he was musical, and he screwed up. He missed a test—completely forgot about it. It was twenty percent of his grade or something." Liana huffed. "We didn't know that, at first. This happened on a Thursday, and we didn't see him on Friday, and none of his friends or his roommate or his classmates did, either. He and I almost always went to this dive bar on Friday nights, and he wasn't there. We figured he was holed up with whoever he was dating at the moment—sorry, but you know how he was before he met you—that week it was a girl named Sarah. I didn't really get worried until Saturday. We had this gig—some rich Tribeca kid's birthday—and Max didn't show. He wasn't answering calls or texts. We thought maybe he went home to Scarsdale. When we still didn't hear from him on Sunday, we called Carl and Brenda. I was sure he was going to be there, but Brenda said he wasn't, and she hadn't heard from him, either, and he usually called his grandmother on Sunday mornings, and he hadn't done that. Carl and Brenda ended up coming into the city, and we found Sarah, and she also said she hadn't seen him."

My stomach lurched. "Did you report it?"

Liana shook her head. "Brenda wanted to, but Carl said Max was just being Max, blowing off steam somewhere, and to give him a day. So we waited. And then, Monday morning, bright and early, Max was in our eight a.m. music composition class. Showered, shaved, a smile on his face. I managed to hold it together until class was over, then I cursed him out on the edge of the park. He apologized. He explained about the test and getting worried, and he said he had everything under control, and—god—it's like he almost blamed me for getting his parents involved. He said there was nothing to worry about and he was fine; he just needed some time away." Liana scoffed. "He apologized to his parents, and he talked to his professor and used his Max charms to get the guy to agree to let him make up the test. I didn't talk to him for a week, but after a while, we fell back into our easy friendship."

"And you don't know where he went for those few days?"

"No," Liana said. "He never told me. He said he was fine and not to worry."

"Did you worry?"

Liana laughed a bitter, awful laugh. "Not until it happened again."

."Again?" I asked. It was hard to believe, even in spite of everything that had happened in the past thirty-six hours. Max, sweet, reliable Max. Max, disappearing. *Poof.* More than once. A whole history, a whole part of his narrative he'd never shared with me, not even in those tender moments when I'd told him about lying to my parents about the details of my first car wreck, that I still felt guilty for how much it cost their insurance when we were already so financially unstable. I'd confessed my secrets, my misplaced shame, and he hadn't done the same.

All that time, Liana and Carl and Brenda had known. In actuality, it was a secret they kept together, a pact of sorts. One that was on their minds when we sat down to dinner, when we opened a bottle of wine. When we cooed over Freya. When we made plans for our future.

They all knew something I didn't.

"Yes," Liana said, looking me straight in the eyes. "Twice more, actually. Hold on," she said, standing now. "I need to get some water and another piece of toast, or else this whiskey is going to hit me way too hard."

Liana went to the kitchen, and I glanced to Freya, wondering how long she'd sleep. Everything was like this now, an hourglass turned over, sand dripping down the slope, plopping in a mound beneath. The worst of it was, you never, ever knew how much time you had. Your muscles would tense, your shoulders stiffen at the tiniest sound, because one cry, and you were on again, your body wasn't yours, your baby owned you for however many hours until she slept.

As if listening to me, to my internal thoughts, as if they were somehow siphoning off to her like nutrients through the umbilical cord, Freya stirred. Her eyes opened, and they fluttered, and I looked away from her, knowing if she saw me, it would all be over.

I stared at my feet, and I counted to ten, my counting in sync with the *swoosh-swoosh-swoosh* of the electric rocker. I heard the click of the toaster and water filling a glass, making the ice inside go *pop-pop-pop*. I looked back to Freya, and thankfully her eyes were shut. She looked so beautiful, I almost wanted to cry. She looked so beautiful, I almost felt like I could love her, in my way. I could find a way to, at least.

I almost felt like if I could get Max back, it would all be okay.

Liana returned, taking a seat right next to me, digging into her toast.

"The next time was when Max and I were living together—all the band in this loft space in Bushwick. He and Ethan and Jeremy—our first drummer—"

"I know who Jeremy is," I said. How quickly had Liana forgotten that I used to do all these things, too?

"Sorry," she said, brushing some crumbs from her mouth. "Anyway, the boys went to the Jersey Shore for a long weekend. One of Jeremy's cousins had a house there. They went to Atlantic City one night, and Max lost a stupid amount of money at one of the blackjack tables. Like, nearly a month of rent. So he told the boys he wanted to go home and was going to catch the Greyhound back."

"But he didn't?"

"No, but I didn't know. I thought he was with Jeremy and Ethan, as planned. It wasn't until Tuesday, when they got back—Jeremy walked in and saw me in the living room and asked me if Max had been sulking all weekend. I still remember the way the ice ran through my veins. I asked him what he was talking about. I told him I'd thought Max was in Jersey. We called all our mutual friends and eventually decided to call his parents again—at least to check if he was in Westchester. Brenda got the story out of us pretty quickly. She and Carl were worried, but slightly less so this time around. They didn't come to the city, but they told us to call them if Max didn't turn up the next day."

"Did he?"

"He did. He didn't have an explanation. He just said, again, that he was fine, and that there wasn't any reason to get his parents involved. And this time I was furious. It's what made me move out. I couldn't live with someone who was going to act like that. There were some girls I knew from my college a cappella group. They had a place in Astoria. I jumped on it. Max and Jeremy and Ethan stayed roommates, and who knows? Maybe Max did it again, but neither of them were the type to keep tabs on anyone. I didn't hear about it, if he ever did disappear."

"And that was it?"

Liana took a quick sip of water. "No, but that was the last time I was involved, thankfully. I told Max—and I promised myself—that I would never intervene with his parents again, and I kept my word. But it did happen again. It was his girlfriend, this time."

"Angie?"

Liana nodded. "They got in an argument, and Max screwed off to who knows where. She gave it a night, but she called me in the morning. I told her I hadn't seen him and forced myself to leave it at that. But eventually, she called Carl and Brenda, and they did the whole song and dance again."

"How long was it this time?"

"I'm not sure," she said. "Two, three days? I wasn't the best support to Angie, I'll fully admit it. I told her I didn't know anything and took myself out of the situation. He did turn up, like he always did, and I have no idea what he told Angie, if he accounted for his whereabouts at all, but I think that was the beginning of the end with them."

My stomach felt suddenly heavy, and I remembered Max telling me about Angie, the girl he'd been with for a year and a half and lived with for six months. "We weren't a good match, living together," he'd said. "Our lifestyles didn't align at all."

Had that been a lie, too, a cover-up for a history of disappearing?

I replayed yesterday's visit in my mind, trying to make it gel with this new information. "But how does this fit with a woman dying?"

"Look," Liana said, "I was as scared as you were when they basically told us a murderer is on the loose, but once I really thought about it . . . about Max's . . . *history* . . . it does seem like an awful coincidence. You were there last night. It was a busy bar, wasn't it?"

I nodded.

"It must have been packed on Friday. And so this terrible thing happens to some woman, and obviously they have to check with everyone who was there, but that doesn't mean anything more than that."

"But why was he there in the first place?"

Liana hesitated, her eyes catching mine briefly, then sighed, looking away. "I have to think he was stressed out. From . . . from all kinds of things. Freya. Our visit. Carl's drinking. If you'd seen the way Carl was stumbling around even before we got to the wine bar, you'd have been worried, too. It . . . it must have all gotten to him, and so he goes out, he does what he does to . . . to decompress, and then he freaks out even more, and he gets in his head, and . . . and he leaves because that's what he does. Max leaves when things get hard. He only ever does it for a couple of days."

I pressed my lips together. "So that's it, then? He left because Freya and I were too much for him. That kind of thing?"

Or because he found out about you, what a mess you are, what a fraud.

I stared at Liana, wanting her to say no—no, Max would never, ever do this to you—no, he loves you too much for any of that.

When she looked at me, there was only pity in her eyes.

"I don't know, Janie. I don't know what else to think."

17

10:53 a.m.

"WHY DIDN'T YOU SAY ANYTHING, CARL?" I ASKED, AS SOON AS I answered his call. I was tucked into the small alcove, my would-be headquarters for investigating what the hell had happened to my partner. Freya was downstairs, Liana left with instructions to give her a bottle if she got tired of her swing.

"I'm sorry, Janie. I'm so, so sorry. We all thought he was done with that chapter of his life."

All. The word was such an exclusion, so casually cruel.

"I've never understood why he did this," Carl went on. "Why he felt he needed to escape this way." He sighed, and when he spoke, there was genuine sadness in his voice. "I don't understand it now. I'm his father. If he's not okay, he should come to me."

"Or me," I said. "You know, the mother of his newborn child?"

"I know," Carl said. "Janie, I know." His words were clear now, not wine-tinged, as they had been the night before.

"We talked so many times yesterday," I said. "You didn't think even one of those times I deserved to know?"

Carl cleared his throat. "Brenda and I discussed it, but we were hoping Max would return and we could put it all behind us. And even now," Carl went on, "this is still what he could be doing. He doesn't know there's this—" He paused. "This— *murder* investigation." Carl pronounced it like it was a dirty word. "It hasn't even hit the news yet."

"He would know if he answered his phone," I snapped. "If he read his texts."

Carl didn't say anything back.

"Listen," I said. "You've got to tell me now: Did Max say anything . . . anything to you when you were here, to make you think he would leave me?"

"No," Carl said. "Nothing at all. He mentioned—you know—that you were having a bit of a hard time of it, but that's all. And that happens for so many mothers, Janie. It's totally normal."

My chest tightened, and rage flared in my belly. "I don't need you to explain motherhood to me, Carl."

"No," he said quickly. "I know you don't. I'm only sorry I don't have more to give you. But I want you to know that even though we think this is going to resolve itself any moment, we've got a lawyer now, just in case."

"A lawyer?" I asked, dumbfounded. "You don't really think Max had something to do with this?"

"We don't think that at *all*, Janie. I know he didn't have anything to do with it. I know it as true as I know my own heart. But you have to admit, someone disappearing right around when someone else gets killed—it doesn't look good. So it's a precaution," Carl said. "For you, for me. For Max. It's a precaution that Brenda and I can afford, so we're taking it."

FINGERS PRACTICALLY BURSTING with energy, I tapped away at Max's computer, desperate for an answer, for some new piece of info to cling to.

First, I searched his emails for anything from a "Grace," "Gracie," or even "Gracee," but came up with nothing, confirming what Liana had said, that there wasn't any relevant history with someone of that name. I turned to Google next, entering in any combination I could think of in an attempt to get more intel: "Grace dead woman, Kingston, NY," "murder Grace Three Crows Tavern," "apparent homicide downtown Kingston."

I didn't get so much as a promising hit.

I opened a new browser window, loaded Facebook, and searched Max's friends for anyone named Grace, but again, no one. Then I opened a new tab—I could check Instagram to see if any of his followers were named Grace, instead—but as soon as I started to type, a list of frequented websites populated beneath.

There it was, second from the bottom: iCloud, the hub for Max's Apple devices.

I froze, hardly able to believe it. I should have realized it before: if Max used this computer to log on with his Apple ID and his new password, if it was saved, I could use it to check his current location.

My heart raced with promise, with hope.

Max's Gmail, all of that, it filled automatically. And why not? I would never have thought to look through his computer. I never had the time or mental space to do anything but feed and take care of Freya, try to take care of myself.

I loaded iCloud.

The log-in screen appeared, and I clicked into it. There, directly beneath, Max's email filled in, as well as a password, obscured by large black dots but there all the same. I hit return, and it felt too easy, like there was no way it could possibly work, but then, so simple and straightforward it seemed almost miraculous: a greeting.

Welcome, Max.

My heart leapt, and I hovered over the button. It was hard to believe I could possibly be this close to knowing where Max was.

A spinning wheel, and then I was in. A map of our streets, adorned with two dots. A list of Max's devices.

Max's iPhone. It was grayed out, marked "offline."

Damn it.

But beneath it, a second device.

Max 2.

Max 2?

What the hell was that?

I racked my brain, wondering if there was something else, an old iPad of his, an outdated iPod touch?

I couldn't think of a thing.

I returned to the map, hovered over the dot.

Max 2 was in this house. I clicked the dot. Then the button to play a sound.

For a moment, sheer silence, and it was like I couldn't even breathe, and then, there it was.

I jumped to my feet, followed the pinging sound down the hallway, found myself in front of the guest bedroom door.

I turned the knob, entering the room. Liana had only been here twenty-four hours, and yet her things were everywhere.

Denim jackets. Neon tops. A makeup bag turned on its side, half its contents spilling out. I stepped over strewn-about clothing, following the pinging sound. At first I thought it was coming from the nightstand, but the drawers were empty. Next I checked beneath the bed. Closer, but still no cigar.

I lifted pillows, pulled back the rumpled sheets, trying to find the source.

Then I knelt on the left side of the bed—Max's side—and slid my arm between the mattress and the box spring.

At first, there was nothing, but I pushed farther, the bedding eating up my arm, all the way to my shoulder.

I swiped back and forth, back and forth.

Then, there it was: a cool, smooth feeling.

My breaths came fast as I grasped it with two fingers, retrieved it with a surgeon's precision.

I held it there, pinging awfully in my hands. I tapped at the alert to silence it, then stared at the phone.

A picture of us on the lock screen, me and Max—a selfie on the Brooklyn Bridge—one from so many years before, from one of our early dates.

A phone Max had long ago upgraded, that I could have sworn he'd traded in, but that in fact had been with him, waiting to be put to use, the whole time.

Max's phone.

No, not Max. Not *my* Max, at least.

Max 2.

18

11:06 a.m.

WE THINK OF OUR LIVES AS ONE THING, AN EVER-RUNNING program, a channel that's always on, one that stars yours truly, like *The Truman Show*.

But really, our lives are made up of chapters, ones that are clear and distinct from one another. And there are events and moments—page breaks, if you will—that usher us from one chapter to the next.

Moments that aren't moments, really, that aren't equal to their length of time, that have so much more weight than those other moments, those other minutes. Moments that seem to hold a lifetime within.

Stepping on that plane, alone, that would take me to New York.

Meeting Max after his show.

The birth of Freya.

Moments that act as a cleaving, dividing our lives into before and after.

But here, in my hands, this was one, too. One I'd never expected, so soon after the recent new chapter of Freya's arrival.

This was more, somehow, than waking to Max gone, or to the police showing up on my doorstep, or even to Liana informing me of Max's habit of disappearing when things got tough.

This was the page break, the new chapter.

The proof, sturdy and solid, that Max wasn't who I thought he was.

I stared at that photo of us on the Brooklyn Bridge. We'd gone to a show the night before, and it was the first time I'd slept over. I'd been holding back with Max, made it a full six or seven dates before sleeping with him. I was worried about the band thing, even though I didn't get those vibes from him at all. I didn't want to be one of *those girls*. And so we'd waited until it had become near impossible to wait anymore. The next morning, high on the physicality of each other, pheromones leaching from our pores, we'd gotten bagels and decided to walk across the Brooklyn Bridge.

It was an hour walk from Max's apartment to the bridge itself, plus the trek over and back, but the time had simply flown. We'd had so much to talk about—his childhood in Westchester, mine in North Carolina, our favorite neighborhood Italian spots and the age-old pizza question: to fold or not to fold. I told him I'd recently become a little bit obsessed with the Norse goddess Freya, reading all the mythology I could find, how she was the "party girl" among the goddesses, with a fondness for good times and fine things. I told him I found her predilections so very feminist, how she couldn't be bothered to care what others thought of her. At the time, I'd had no idea, not a single earthly clue, that Freya would come to have new meaning—for me, and for him, too—that I'd cling to that name through my pregnancy, hoping that by calling her something I'd always loved, I'd find a way to love her, too.

I breathed in and out, trying to calm my heartbeats. Max and I looked so damn *happy* in this photo. My smile was wide, revealing my gums. His was more muted—Max never smiled fully for pictures—but you could see it in his eyes: that spark, that excitement of fresh, new love. He and I knew it even then, in our way. We knew this was something very real, something that would see us through not only more dates but a whole season of our lives. We knew we were each other's; it was so dazzlingly clear.

I felt a lump forming in my throat. Even then, Max had known things about himself, things he must have already decided he was never going to share with me. Had he simply been waiting for things to get hard to disappear?

Why didn't you tell me?

Why did you just go?

Liana and Carl had never said anything about an alternate life, about separate phones, about new passwords and secrets kept from the person he was supposed to be closest to.

Oh, come on, like you don't have secrets, too.

I swiped to open the phone, revealing a prompt for a passcode—six numbers. I tried Freya's birthday, then our anniversary, then Max's birthday, then mine, and, finally, Carl's birthday, since he and his dad were so close. The last one worked.

There were only a few standard-issue apps on the home screen, and I tapped into the internet browser, checked the search history.

Two searches only, both from nearly three weeks ago.

Three Crows Tavern address
Three Crows Tavern hours

I opened the text messages, the calls, but there was nothing, which made sense. The phone had no cell service. It was no longer part of our plan. There was only Wi-Fi.

How else could he use this phone to talk to someone? Facebook Messenger? Instagram? None of those apps were there. I even opened the calculator app—I'd read somewhere that people used it to hide bad things on their phones—nothing. I swiped left to see if there was anything stored on another page, and there it was, sitting pretty. WhatsApp, the messaging service that was completely encrypted. The one that kept no record, that couldn't even be subpoenaed. I'd read about it last year, a case that wound its way through our byzantine court system. The app wouldn't give investigators the info.

It was an app for doing secret things.

Or not so secret, of course. It was the same one I used to send texts to the college girls. The one I used for the mommy group I'd joined when I found out I was pregnant.

It could be nothing, absolutely nothing.

Once I was inside, it was beyond clear that it *wasn't* nothing. There were several messages from Friday, starting at 10:58 and ending at 11:19. All from a ten-digit phone number that hadn't been saved under anyone's name.

Can you meet me? Usual place?

I really need to see you tonight.

This is important. Please.

*Text me back or I'm going to call your real phone. She's going
to find out.*

I need to see you. I need to see you now.

My heart raced mercilessly. I couldn't believe it. I really
couldn't believe it.

I scrolled up. Through a string of texts.

On Wednesday:

Still on for tonight, right?

And an answer from Max:

Yes.

Another on the Wednesday before:

Tonight still good?

From Max:

Yup, see you at 11.

I kept scrolling. It was the same pattern the week before.

The first message had come just a couple of days after we'd
arrived in Kingston.

*The place is called the Three Crows. He thinks I'm at book
club. Come as soon as you can.*

And a confirmation from Max:

Okay. Should make it out by 11.

I scrolled through everything again. By the looks of it, there were three meetings total, not counting whatever had come out of the messages on Friday.

I imagined Max coming up here dutifully every Wednesday to check the phone, shoot off a confirmation while I was stuck downstairs, Freya glued to my boob. While she was covering me in spit-up, while I was changing a nasty yellow seedy diaper, while she was screaming and I was trying to get her to calm down in her electric swing. While I was napping, while Freya was napping, while I was falling apart, tears on my cheeks in the shower, so very many times.

I prayed hard that these texts had nothing to do with this Grace woman, my anxiety ratcheted up so high that for a moment, I felt like I could have even accepted the heartbreak of an affair so long as it was only some random woman, some woman he'd met . . . somehow . . . someone who had nothing to do with this . . . *murder.*

Taking a sharp breath, I grabbed my own phone instead, then keyed in the phone number from the messages and started a call, hoping the woman on the other end would answer, her voice proof that this woman, whoever she was to Max, was alive, at least.

I lifted it to my ear, my hands shaking.

It went straight to voicemail.

"Hi, you've reached—"

For a millisecond, every other possibility flashed before me, any other name—Jessica, Amber, Mia—

"—*Grace*—"

No, Max, no, no, no.

"—*I can't talk right now, but you know what to do!*"

19

11:10 a.m.

THE DOORBELL RANG. IT RANG WHILE I WAS STARING, DUMB-founded, at my phone in one hand, Max's hidden device in the other. Secrets and betrayals resting in both of my palms.

The police, I thought. Again, the police.

On instinct, I slipped Max's phone back beneath the mattress and deleted the call I'd just made from my own. The bell rang again.

Liana was at the door by the time I was downstairs, one hand reaching toward the knob, Freya propped in her other arm.

I grabbed my baby from her and stood straighter, bracing myself for Duncan and Cary as Liana opened the door.

"Molly?"

My best friend stood there, as if materialized from nothing. She'd gotten a new haircut—a bob that very much suited her, and I pictured her and Ani discovering some hip salon together—and new glasses, too, frameless ones that felt oh so nineties. She glanced at Liana, then trained her eyes on me. "In the flesh!"

"Molly," I repeated. "I told you not to come."

Freya began to cry, and I bounced her in an attempt to calm some of the fussing as Liana stood frozen, one hand still on the door.

"I'm here to help, Janie," Molly said, ignoring the fact that Liana was here doing just that. "You *need* help."

I shook my head, moisture forming in my eyes. "I can't—"

But Molly was already stepping across the threshold, into my secrets, into this new world.

Liana held the door open another moment, looking to me for guidance, but what could I do? Throw my best friend out?

I shrugged in acceptance, and Liana shut the door.

"She's gorgeous," Molly said, smiling at Freya, as if all of this was normal. As if she wasn't swooping in to save me but simply here to pay Mama and Baby a visit.

"I should really feed her," I managed.

"I could still give her a bottle," Liana offered.

"No," I said, resigned. "If I'm in reach, she won't want a bottle."

"Then by all means, feed her," Molly said. "Don't let me stop you."

On autopilot, I took a seat on the sofa, situated Freya, pulled my top up and my nursing bra down. Freya latched on happily, and Molly sat next to me.

Liana looked from me to Molly and back again, shifting her weight from foot to foot. "I'll make some coffee," she said finally, before turning and heading straight to the kitchen.

"What a beauty," Molly went on, shaking her head, her straight black hair slinking about like flapper's fringe. "I mean, I know I saw her when she was first born, but god, she's changed so much already."

"Thank you," I said, my brain still trying to compute. "But, Molly, I told you I was okay. You didn't need to come."

"Well, you didn't sound okay," Molly said. "And if I'm overreacting, fine. I'm staying with Ani. She's desperate to show off her new place, and she's been on me to plan a visit, anyway, so I texted her this morning and took her up on it."

"Ani?" I asked, my heart racing. "Did you tell her about Max?"

"No," Molly said. "God, you're always so worried about what other people think. I didn't tell her anything, okay? Just that it would be nice to see you and I was desperate to get out of the city. Besides, Ani doesn't matter right now. Is Max back?" Molly asked. "Has he called you, at least?"

"No," I said, my voice catching in my throat. "No, but—"

"Then I was right. You're *not* okay."

Freya popped off then, smiling sweetly, suddenly more interested in Molly than the buffet on my chest.

Molly's hands shot out toward Freya, her nails a perfect plum shade, one I was strangely jealous of. "At least let me hold that gorgeous girl of yours?"

I rehooked my top and relinquished my baby, who nuzzled into Molly's rather ample chest and began to root around, as if looking for more food. Molly only laughed and adjusted Freya, so her face was closer to hers. "None from me, little girl. The good stuff only comes from your mama."

It was so normal, what was happening. My best friend cooing with my sweet little baby. It was so normal, and it made it so painfully obvious—a stark relief—that things were not normal.

Hi, you've reached Grace!

Molly adjusted Freya so she was wedged perfectly between her raw-denim-clad legs, bouncing her just so.

"How did you even know where I was staying?" I asked.

"The address was on the birth announcement."

"Oh."

"Look," Molly said, turning toward me. "I'm not going to be on top of you or anything. I'll be at Ani's like I said, working remotely. We're both on a big project anyway. But I'll be right here in town. Because you need me. I *know* you need me."

It was so horrifying, the fact that Molly could soon know all, that Ani could be wrapped up in this, too. *Hold your head high*, that was what my mother always said. *Don't let the neighbors find out.* There were so many years when things were not okay at home, when my parents' credit card bills piled up, when one misstep in the dance of what got paid when meant the power would get shut off, the internet would suddenly be gone, or the car my dad had bought to replace our old clunker would be temporarily repossessed. Through all those years, I'd done what my mom and dad told me to. I didn't tell any of my friends at my public but very moneyed high school about the creditors on the phone or the spottiness of our utilities. No lights? No internet? No problem, so long as no one knew. Keep it in the family. Don't air your dirty laundry.

It's no one's business but ours.

For a moment, I felt it so sincerely, that pull of privacy, of protection, of shielding my family's business from those who might judge. From Molly and her freedom and her self-awareness and her caring kindness—from Molly, "I just want you to be okay, I'm on your team always, you know that." It wasn't the same pull I'd felt when the police were at my door. That was sheer terror, fear, and survival. This was subtler, more nuanced. A higher level on Maslow's goddamned hierarchy of needs. The need for acceptance. For Molly not to know how much I'd messed up my life. How little I could trust my partner and, in turn, how little I could trust myself.

"Janie," Molly said, her voice so earnest, so terrible, so kind. "Janie, what is it? There's something else you're not telling me. I can see it."

Liana came back then, steaming cups of coffee in her hands, and the air in the room instantly changed, the closeness that Molly and I so easily fell into dissipating with Liana's presence. "Everything okay?" she asked.

No, it wasn't, and neither Liana nor Molly knew the whole of it.

Could I tell them, really? Could I lay it all bare before them? The secret phone? The secret life?

"Janie," Molly said. "Tell me what else is going on. *Please*."

The funny part was, I didn't have to answer.

An answer was there in that moment, right outside my door.

An answer in the form of flashing lights.

"Oh my god," Liana said, quickly setting down the coffees. "They're back."

Molly and Liana followed behind me—we were a pack of frantic women picking up the pieces of an absent man.

I opened the door to see Duncan on her own.

"Hello," she said, her eyes landing on each one of us, however briefly. "Hello, Liana."

Liana nodded, and Duncan's eyes turned to me. I cleared my throat, tried to say what a normal partner would say, not a partner who'd just discovered a string of text messages to a murdered woman. To Grace. "Max is still missing."

"Is he?" Duncan asked. She cleared her throat; her whole tenor had changed from yesterday. Then, it was all about gathering info, submitting a report. Now things had quite obviously changed. "And you haven't heard from him?"

"No," I said, my heart beating quickly. In my periphery, I saw Molly stiffen, and I wished, so badly, she wasn't here. "No, but I . . . I found out something . . . something I didn't know yesterday."

"Did you?" Duncan asked. "And what's that?"

My pulse pounded in my ears, as the woman's voice message rang there, too. I could tell Duncan everything, secure my place on the right side of a murder investigation, but I wasn't ready. I didn't know what was going on, but I still couldn't believe Max could actually *kill* somebody. And besides, Molly was here. I couldn't lay it all out like this. It was horrifying . . . humiliating.

Instead, I could lay out part of it—I supposed I had to.

"Liana," I said. "Do you want to tell Officer Duncan what you told me?"

Liana's eyebrows shot up, but quickly, she composed herself. "Right," she said. "Right. I've known Max a long time, and he has a habit of running off. So I think he's probably just taking some time to himself. Getting some space from the baby."

Molly slipped a hand in mine, a hand for comfort, a hand to root me to this earth, but I pulled mine away, used it to support Freya instead.

"Like I said," Liana went on. "He has a habit of acting this way. He kind of freaks out and leaves."

Liana laid it all out meticulously: the first time, the second time, the third time. She put Max's secrets on display, Molly there to hear every one of them, and I felt it intently, that deep, deep shame, like I had when my high school BFF Jessica asked why my parents' car was in the shop so long. Or when my first boyfriend argued that electricity was very reliable in our part of town, and there hadn't been any storms, when I'd been forced to tell him I didn't have power that day. Duke Energy may have kept (or not kept) the lights on in our home, but my lies certainly brightened the facade of our fake-middle-class suburban life.

Molly was obviously shocked, but Duncan seemed anything but. She almost looked . . . *bored.*

"Listen," Duncan said, when Liana was finished, "we may have had reason to believe all that yesterday—even this morning—but not now." She trained her eyes on me. "A witness has come forward, alleging that Mr. Bosch met with the victim specifically on Friday night. And now he's gone."

Victim, I thought. The victim, Grace. Grace, in a brick house. Grace, who texted my partner too many times.

"And how would this *witness* know?" Liana asked. "Was this person with them or just making things up? Covering their own tracks?"

Duncan pressed her lips together, ignoring Liana's question, and all my training, all my years of entertaining clients, made it so painfully clear. There was something else here, too. More news. More than just a new witness. Facts that would make this so much worse.

"The thing is," Duncan said calmly but firmly, "and this is why I'm back here, trying to glean any information I can from you. The thing is, it's not just about a woman anymore."

"What do you mean?" I asked.

"There's a child involved, too. The victim's son. A minor, only six years old. This isn't just a murder investigation." Her eyes flashed, and I saw genuine anger in them. Genuine rage. A mother's rage.

"This is a kidnapping investigation as well."

20

11:21 a.m.

"JESUS CHRIST."

It took me a moment to realize the outburst had come from Molly.

Freya began to fuss, and I hugged her to my chest, easily falling into the patterns that had been firmly established since she was born—patting her butt rhythmically, rocking back and forth as I bounced on my toes, anything to get her to stop crying. "I should feed her again," I said to Duncan. I'd only given her a little bit before Molly had taken her from me. It wasn't enough. It was never enough.

"Well, we need to talk," Duncan said. "And we need you to cooperate. I can't impress upon you how crucial it is that you help us now, instead of hindering us."

I swallowed, Freya's cries building. "Okay," I said, raising my voice to be heard over Freya's wail, too broken to even think about resisting. "I guess you should come inside."

We set up in the living room, me in the wingback armchair, Duncan in the oversized one opposite, Liana and Molly on either side of the couch, bookends. I lifted the flap of my top, the one specifically put there to make this easier. When I'd bought the shirt, forty-five dollars at that baby boutique in Brooklyn, I'd imagined using it in a coffee shop, at a brewery, or in the park. Never had I imagined that it would be used now, when I was sitting here, being grilled about my partner's role in a murder. And not just a murder, a kidnapping. My god.

Quick as I could, I unhooked my nursing bra, then grabbed my nipple between two fingers, held Freya's head in the other hand, popped her on—smash!—and she latched on immediately.

Finally, quiet. Peace. A collective sigh of relief around the room, as if we were in yoga class, breathing in sync. I looked up to Duncan, then to Liana and Molly, and the image didn't feel so far off. It was as if we were in some other setting, some other ritual. Women coming together to care for a baby communally, to depend on one another, to hold one another up. A nursing support group, a Mommy and Me class, a postpartum Pilates session.

But no, that wasn't it. *This* collection of female energy was here to address a missing man, one mother abandoned, another one murdered, a stolen child.

"Thank you for cooperating," Duncan said. "An autopsy has come back, confirming homicide, but we cannot move forward until we can speak to your partner."

Autopsy, Christ. The word was such a clear cleaving, putting Duncan on the good side, all of us—the bad.

Freya's sucks increased in speed, and I felt, somewhere deep inside of me, somewhere buried so far down and difficult to access, those motherly feelings I knew I was supposed to have. And that part of me couldn't imagine anything more horrible on earth than someone killing a mother, kidnapping a child.

I counted to five, steeling any reserves of energy I still had. God knew between Freya and Max, I was almost wholly depleted. "Max would never take someone's child," I said. "He wouldn't hurt anyone at all." I nodded down to Freya. "He *has* a child. And why didn't you mention it when you came yesterday? Why has this suddenly changed course?"

Duncan made a quick, succinct note on her pad with a ballpoint pen. "There was some confusion. The child was supposed to be sleeping over at a friend's house on Friday night. In the chaos of the investigation, the child's father didn't go over to pick him up until Saturday evening, when he discovered the boy had never been at a sleepover at all."

"And that's not suspicious?" Liana demanded, her voice pulled tight. "That this man didn't even know where his own kid was?"

Duncan's eyes ping-ponged between the three of us. "With all due respect, we're not here to talk about anyone but Mr. Bosch."

"But——" Liana said.

"Isn't he the most likely suspect, in any case?" I asked. "The husband? I went to that bar, the Three Crows, last night, and some girls there even said that this woman was always trying to get away from him."

"Please," Duncan said. "We do not need you to be moonlighting as an investigator, Ms. Walker. Right now, all we need from you is to help us find your partner. And like I said, this witness we have now reliably puts the victim and your partner together on Friday night. We need you to help us here."

My heart beat mercilessly.

"You have all his info from the missing person's report."

"We need more," Duncan pressed. "Friends, family he could be staying with. That sort of thing. Anything that could aid us in any way."

And so we gave it. Carl and Brenda's address. Contact info for the remaining members of the Velvet Hope. The name of Max's music business. His former agent and manager. Anyone he might have reached out to.

"How about anything else we should know?" Duncan asked when we were done. "Anything that could help us find him, no matter how small?"

My throat tightened. Carefully, I pulled Freya off my left side and did the whole song and dance on the right. The whole time, I thought of the phone, tucked beneath that mattress. The phone that so clearly connected Max to Grace.

Could I really give it to them, prove that the two had been together several times before, spread out Max's secrets for Duncan and Liana and Molly to see? The conversations were in WhatsApp. There was a chance, if I didn't share them, that no one would see those messages but me.

Besides, I couldn't believe Max could really kill a woman and take her child. If I did, I *would* tell Duncan everything. I would have to.

Or was I just telling myself that? Was this yet another way my would-be motherly instincts had failed?

No, I thought. Max wouldn't. Max *couldn't*.

Max is loyal. Unlike you.

"There's nothing," I said, my voice strong and steady as I caught Duncan's eyes.

"You sure about that?" Duncan asked, clicking her pen twice.

"Believe me, I wish I had answers." The words that followed were not a lie at all. "I wish I knew where my partner was, but I don't."

Duncan stood. "I'll leave you to it, then."

"Wait," I said. "Aren't you going to tell us . . . what happened? To the woman, I mean."

To this mother. This *dead* mother. Grace.

Duncan only stared.

"The autopsy," I clarified. "How she died."

"We haven't shared it with the press yet; we're holding back while we look into a few things." Duncan blinked twice, then narrowed her eyes. "But I might as well tell you, so long as you stay quiet. You deserve to know just how serious this is. It was blunt force trauma, to the back of the head."

"Couldn't that mean it was an accident?" I asked. "That she . . . that she fell?"

"Yes, it is possible that she fell," Duncan said, her voice clipped. "But that doesn't mean it was an accident."

She paused briefly, before delivering the rest of it.

"You don't fall that hard without being pushed."

21

12:24 p.m.

"YOU DIDN'T HAVE TO KEEP EVERYTHING A SECRET," MOLLY SAID, lifting a bite of eggs to her mouth. "This is way more serious than Max being gone."

We were sitting in Outdated, Kingston's coffee shop–cum–eatery–cum–antique goods clearinghouse. You could supposedly buy anything in the place, from the chairs beneath your butt to the hangings on the walls. Beyond the gimmick, the food was delicious, the coffee fair trade—a little slice of Brooklyn up in Kingston, New York. A spot that had become a favorite over the past few weeks.

In lieu of a response, I dug into my food: a scramble of free-range eggs, organic kale, and local goat cheese. I was ravenous, as always, and though a tiny part of me wondered if the cheese was pasteurized, if the same rules applied in nursing and pregnancy, I was too overwhelmed to care.

As soon as Duncan was gone and Freya was down for a nap, Molly had jumped at the chance to take me to lunch—I knew she wanted to talk to me without Liana around—and I'd been too shaken, too thrown, to do anything but go along.

And now, decaf coffee in cup, potentially dangerous cheese on my fork, hangover slowly wearing off, I had to admit it was a welcome change. A woman, going out to lunch. Catching up with a friend, like friends do.

"Have you told your parents?" Molly prodded.

I shook my head.

"What about Bree? Any of the college girls?"

"No," I said. "They're busy with their own kids. Their own families."

"So you've been dealing with all of this on your own?"

I shoved more eggs into my mouth, then took a gulp of coffee, washing them down.

"It's not even been two days. I haven't been thinking straight. I called Max's parents, because they'd just been with us, and they didn't seem worried, and afterward I called Liana, and she came over, and we just—we tried to do what we could. I told *you*, at least."

"Only because I happened to call you, because I practically forced it out of you. *And* you were drunk."

I set down my fork. "What do you want me to say, Molly?"

"Nothing," she said. "I get it. You keep your cards close. But listen, and I know you're not going to want to hear this, but you can't let them take charge of this whole thing."

"What do you mean, take charge?" I asked. "Liana and Max's parents, they're like family to me."

"Family who's going to keep up appearances, however they can."

"What does that mean?"

"It means they're going to protect Max, they're going to protect their own reputation, they're going to keep their perfect little Westchester world intact. That's who they are."

I scoffed. "Is this about the baby shower again?" Molly had wanted to plan something small and intimate and completely me, but Liana and Brenda had beaten her to the punch, hosting it in Scarsdale, the two of them concocting the sorts of Pinterest cupcake towers and color-coordinated napkins that were anything but my style but thoughtful all the same. Was it a little unkosher that my mother-in-law and my partner's best friend planned it and not my people? Sure, but my mom hadn't come through on planning one in North Carolina, and Molly had been late to the game.

"Janie," Molly said, reaching a hand across the table and grabbing mine. "Believe me when I say this: I don't care about the baby shower, no matter how WASPy Westchester it was. I'm *worried* about you, and I'm worried that Max is gone, and you've only got people around you who are his, first and foremost."

"But they're *not* just Max's people—they're Freya's family. They're all I have, they're—"

"What about *your* family? Your actual family? The family you haven't even called?"

"I haven't called them because I've never been able to rely on them in the way I can rely on Max's parents, okay? They're on a European cruise. I told you that—"

"Fuck their cruise," Molly said. Heads began to turn our way.

"Keep your voice down," I said. "Everyone's going to hear you."

"Jesus Christ, Janie, this isn't the moment to care about what other people think. This isn't the time to take it all on yourself so people don't see you suffering. This is serious. I saw the look on that cop's face. She either thinks you're covering for Max or is close to thinking it. Whatever happened, whatever he's involved in, do you want to be part of it, too?"

I paused, tears welling in my eyes.

"I'm sorry," Molly said. "I'm sorry for being so harsh. It's just—god—I feel like I don't even know you anymore. You're my best friend, but you haven't been yourself in . . . in *months*. Leaving the agency, barely answering your calls . . ."

Leaving, I thought bitterly, as if it were that simple. Instead, I had built myself a coffin and climbed right in.

I forced the words out, the words I'd trotted out to Max as well, all through the pregnancy I should have enjoyed far more than I did. "It was hard on me, the pregnancy."

Molly shook her head. "You're doing it again. You're telling me a story. You're putting your perfect little narrative out to the world. How am I supposed to help you if you won't ever be honest with me?"

"You're not supposed to help me," I said. "I didn't ask for your help. I didn't ask for any of this."

Molly took my hand in hers again and squeezed. "Something happened," Molly said. "Before you even got pregnant. I know it. You were so upset. You were so . . . so unlike yourself. Did Max do something? Did he hurt you? Did you keep it quiet so people wouldn't judge you? Because it's okay, Janie. There's nothing to be ashamed of. There's—"

I whipped my hand away, as if hers were on fire. "No, of course not."

"You can tell me, you know. I'm on your side."

Tears spilled over my lids, streaming down my cheeks, salty on my lips. I wiped them away with the back of my hand.

"Did he hurt you?" Molly asked again. "Please, Janie. Just tell me."

I shook my head viciously, then locked my eyes on Molly. "You've got it all wrong, okay? *He's* not the one who hurt me."

Molly's head cocked to the side—like a sweet dog, trying to understand what its owner had just said.

I lowered my voice but kept my eyes on hers, because it had been so long now, so much shame, so much weight, so much pulling me down into an underworld of my own making, and I couldn't bear it another moment more, no matter what Molly might think of me.

"I'm the one who hurt him."

22

12:33 p.m.

A YELLOW TAXICAB. A HOTEL'S THOUSAND-THREAD-COUNT sheets. The sound of the shower running on the other side of the door.

I pushed the images away, as I had been pushing them away for nearly a year now, then stared at my hands. "I slept with Bryan."

Silence, and then I couldn't help it—I stole a look up. It took a moment for Molly to put it together, but then, in her eyes: realization.

"Bryan, our client? Your *work husband*?"

I nodded, my cheeks hot now. Molly had jokingly used the term about Bryan and me, because we got on so well. But it never meant anything—she'd even said it in front of Max. Now, the words filled me with shame.

"Oh my god," Molly said, and when she spoke next, her voice was a whisper: "You *cheated* on Max?"

More tears spilled over as I remembered that morning, the sick feeling in the pit of my stomach, the stench of bodies permeating the room's stale air. The hairline crack in the plaster overhead. The one I'd stared at, wondering. How had I done this? How had I let it go this far?

"I'm sorry," Molly said. "I didn't mean to say it like that. I'm surprised is all. What *happened*? I didn't even know you two were . . ."

"We weren't," I said. "We aren't. I mean, yes, I always found him a little attractive—I think most of the straight women and at least half the gay guys at the agency did—and I know that we were close, and we always had nice banter, but it stayed on the professional side. At least I thought it did."

"It did," Molly said. "I wouldn't have called him your work husband if I actually thought there was something there."

I closed my eyes, reeling from the memory. "I promise you, there wasn't. It's just, that night at karaoke, the week we re-signed the account. Bryan was . . . it was late, and we were singing duets together, and he was saying how it was time for me to become a VP, and we were both so drunk, and . . ." I let my voice trail off, unable to finish the rest. "I guess it just happened. The next morning at work, I was sure everyone knew. You and Ani and everyone in the office. I was sure that's why Eli wanted to talk to me. I was going to be let go for jeopardizing such an important relationship by sleeping with a client. But Eli only wanted to tell me they'd signed on for another two years."

I could still see Eli in that office, offering me a rare smile: *I just got off the phone with Bryan, and he says I'm crazy if I don't make you VP. I'll have to keep that in mind.*

Molly gazed at me a moment, before her eyes widened. "Oh my god. Is that why you left? I've been over and over it, because you never, ever seemed like the sort to become a mom and hop off the career ladder—did it have something to do with this?" Molly shook her head. "But that was way back in the summer. You didn't leave until December."

I took a sip of coffee. "I thought I could make it work, and for a little bit, I did. I had one of the junior account managers handle most of Bryan's business while I focused on my other accounts, and when I had to step in, I mainly interfaced with one of Bryan's colleagues."

"Okay," Molly said.

"But in the fall, Bryan's colleague left, and the account manager got moved to a different business, and it was just me and Bryan. It was unbearable, and I thought about leaving every day. And then Eli pulled me aside in November, said he could see me making VP next year, after returning from maternity leave, but that I would be fully on Bryan's account for the next two years. I freaked out. I told him that I'd actually been planning on giving my notice so I could focus on motherhood."

"But you could have asked for a different account," Molly said.

I shook my head. "My relationship—my *business* relationship—with Bryan was one hundred percent the reason why I was on the VP track. The fact that we got on so well was my biggest asset at work. There wasn't another option."

Molly shook her head, unable to comprehend. "But that's not fair, that's not—"

"A line was crossed, Molly. I couldn't go on like that, not for years on end."

"But Bryan crossed a line, too, and *he* got to keep on doing his thing."

I shrugged. "Maybe it's not fair, but it is what it is."

"That's bullshit," Molly said.

"So what if it is?" I asked, resigned now, and relieved, that someone finally knew. "But it's what happened."

"Did you tell Max?" she asked.

When I spoke, my voice was quiet. "I wanted to, but I just . . . I couldn't."

I waited for Molly to ask the other question, the one that plagued me, too, but she didn't. She left it. She took what I'd told her at face value.

"Janie," she said, leaning forward. "I get it, I do. You feel guilty. Of course you do. So you fucked up—it happens. But this—what's happening now—this is not your fault. And you can't go on defending Max because you feel guilty about this *freak* thing. What's happening now, what's happening with this investigation, with that police officer, it's serious. God, it's life and death. You need to call your parents. You need to open up. You need to stop worrying about what everyone thinks about you and let people actually be here for you."

"Even if I could get in touch with my parents, it would take them days."

"So come stay with me and Ani. Go back, get Freya, and come over. Her house has like four bedrooms, and she's not even dating anyone at the moment. We can all hang out for a few days if you want to be close to the investigation, or we can go back to Brooklyn, whatever you want. Just come with me. We'll figure this out."

"I don't want to drag even more people into this," I said. "Not Ani, too."

"Janie," Molly said, her voice softening. "I know you've always held yourself to this impossible standard, but things happen. People cheat. It's so common it's almost normal. But you know what is *not* normal? Disappearing on your daughter's mother. Getting caught up in a murder investigation. In a kidnapping."

"Max wouldn't—"

"Max isn't here to defend himself."

I stared at Molly, at my best friend. And my heart felt so heavy, so frail, because it was what I'd been thinking, too.

"Please," Molly went on. "Let me be here for you. You shut me out with this Bryan thing, when I could have helped you." She blinked, and I saw tears in my best friend's eyes. "Please don't shut me out again."

23

12:55 p.m.

IN THE DAYLIGHT, GRACE'S HOUSE WAS GORGEOUS. EIGHT identical windows set off the first and second stories, and shutters flanked each one, so close to the windows they almost looked like they were kissing.

My fingers shook as I pulled open the creaky gate.

This was foolish, maybe even dangerous.

Those girls at the bar had told me Grace was eager to get away from her husband. And now I knew beyond a shadow of a doubt, proof contained in all those messages between them, that Max and Grace had been meeting. If I'd found them, maybe her husband had, too. Maybe he'd been angry, maybe he'd killed her, maybe he'd even hurt Max.

Still, this man was the only person in the world who might have answers.

I didn't pull the gate shut behind me, leaving an exit should I need one, and walked up the stone steps, my pulse pounding strong in my temples.

On the porch, I stared at the antique knocker, in the shape

of a lion's face—it was vicious, that knocker, as if it could leap from the door and eat me alive.

I lifted my hand to it, rapped against the door three times.

For a moment, nothing. I thought of Ani's address here in Kingston, sitting safely in my text messages, the way Molly had practically begged me to come before we'd parted outside the restaurant, how she'd promised to call me in a couple of hours and show up at my door if I didn't answer. I could leave this place, grab Freya, get my things, and go to them now.

I could put Max's alternate phone, Max's alternate life, behind me.

But then, a shuffle of footsteps. A door opened just a crack. A decision made.

The man had shaggy hair, fair skin, and a beard that was an Irish sort of red. "If you're a reporter," he said, "I swear to god, I'm calling the police."

"No," I said. "I'm not a reporter—"

"I don't want any offers for funeral services, either."

"God, no. I'm not—"

"Who are you, then?" His eyes were deep-set, deep brown, and though I expected to see only hatred coming my way, what seemed to live there, more than anything else, was sadness.

"The woman, Grace, someone told me she lived here."

He winced at the name, as if I'd placed a shard of glass to his chest, twisted it, and buried it beneath the skin.

"You loved her," I said, the words out before I could stop them.

"Yes, I loved her. She's my—" He stopped, and his eyes crinkled up, moistening. "She was my wife."

"I'm sorry," I managed. "I'm sorry to show up like this."

"What the fuck do you *want*?"

I flinched at his words, and the knowledge that I could be standing in front of a killer came back full force. "My partner, I think he met her that night, and he's gone now, too, and I'm trying to figure out what happened. I'm trying to get some answers, the only way I know how."

The door opened another crack, and now I could see a well-worn T-shirt, the slightest paunch of a belly, black sweatpants.

"Who's your partner?" the man asked.

I swallowed. "Max Bosch."

The man stared at me a minute and in his eyes, I saw a million things pass—anger and hurt, grief and betrayal. It looked so genuine, so real. He looked so unassuming. That didn't mean anything, did it? He could have killed her. He probably did. Still, I had to make him think I was on his side if I was going to get anything from him at all.

"I know I'm probably the last person you want to see right now," I said. "I'm sorry—I don't even know your name."

"Daniel," he said, the door opening another crack.

"Daniel," I repeated. "I'm—" For a half second, I imagined giving him a fake name, but decided to keep it simple instead. "—Janie, and until the police showed up at my door yesterday, I had no idea that any of this was happening at all. I was completely in the dark. Whatever was going on between your wife and my partner, I had no clue. And I don't think he hurt her—I *know* he didn't hurt her—but he's not here, and all I want is to find him, to figure out what happened, to get some information. To tell my baby daughter where her daddy is. I swear."

The man stared at me, assessing, then sighed. "We're together in that, at least. I need to find him, too. And I'll do anything I can to make that happen."

He opened the door wider.

"I guess you better come inside."

24

1:03 p.m.

THE LIVING ROOM WAS A TESTAMENT TO THOSE WHO WERE gone. An oversized sofa had a stain from what looked like a juice spill, crayon portraits—one labeled, in a child's scrawl, "MOM," the other "DAD"—hung on either side of a TV stand littered with errant race cars and LEGO bricks of all sizes.

In the foyer, hooks held a black purse and a red one, as well as a denim jacket with a mermaid patch on the back—all things that must have belonged to Grace. It was as if either one of them were about to walk in any moment, a mother's voice, warm and loving, a child, bursting through the door with energy, with life.

I felt a sudden pang of empathy. No matter what had happened between this woman and Max, she didn't deserve to die. Her son didn't deserve to be left without a mother, without the one love that was supposed to be so constant in his life.

Her son didn't deserve to be taken, wherever he was.

I was suddenly struck with the terrifying thought of returning to our rental, of Freya being gone as well. It was so strange, these two forces. One moment, I resented my baby and all the ways she made me feel like a screwup, made me feel unworthy. But at the same time, beneath all that, I wanted to protect her so badly, in a way that absolutely consumed me. I wanted her to be happy, and I wanted her to be fed and clean and well rested and well nourished. I wanted her to grow into this beautiful and smart and kind and wonderful girl. I just doubted, so very deeply, that I was the one who should usher her through life. That I had it in me to do so. And that was what made me hate her, in my darkest moments. The knowledge that I was going to fuck her up completely.

I heard water running in the kitchen—Daniel had said he would make us tea—and my eyes found the door, the deadbolt that was turned upright, open and unlocked. The grieving-husband bit could be nothing more than an act. I could be putting myself at risk, and what would Freya do if both her parents were gone?

I took out my phone, suddenly desperate to see her. I opened the video monitor app, tapped *LIVE*, and there she was, still sleeping. I watched the subtle rise and fall of her swaddled chest, and the desire to care for her was so deep, so consuming, that in that moment, I prayed I would find a way to be enough.

My phone rang then—Carl—but I ignored it. There was a clink of china in the kitchen, and Daniel reappeared, the fixings for tea in his hands.

He set the tray on top of a coffee table in the style of a trunk, rough-hewn wood, something that would grace the pages of a Pottery Barn catalogue. I briefly imagined a six-year-old leaning over this table, coloring portraits of his two favorite people. My stomach twisted, entrails knotting.

"It helps me," he said. "The rituals. Grace loved her tea in the afternoon. It feels weird to have a day without it." Daniel passed me a mug, a mint-green thing with a handle in the shape of a mermaid tail, something that looked like it was straight out of an expensive shop in Brooklyn. He took his own mug, one that said *DIA Beacon* on it, and added a scoop of sugar before slipping a silver receptacle from his back pocket. It took me a moment to realize it was a flask, it felt so out of place in the surrounding display of stylish middle-class familial comfort. "I know I probably shouldn't be talking to you," he said. "But the cops aren't doing shit for Grace."

He poured some liquor into his tea, then lifted the flask, an offering. "You want some?"

"Me? Oh," I said. "I'm okay."

He shrugged, pulling it back, then took a sip. From the scrunch of his lips, it must have burned.

I set down my own tea, adjusted myself on the chair. "So you came home on Friday, and she and your son, they were gone?"

Daniel nodded. "I was out late on Friday. I had a meeting in the city. Grace said she was going to meet up with one of her girlfriends—Erica—they usually met on Wednesdays for some book discussion thing, but she said Erica was going through something and needed to talk. She told me Sutton was at a sleepover and that she might be out late. She doesn't get too many nights like that to herself, so of course I urged her to go."

I nodded, my spine tingling, as I thought of that message on Max's phone.

He thinks I'm at book club.

"I work in real estate," Daniel went on. "I was out late, doing a walk-through, dinner, drinks after—the whole works— and when I got back, well after midnight, I should have—I didn't know that he'd—I thought she was enjoying herself while Sutton was at a friend's." Daniel's eyes began to well. "I didn't think—" He hesitated, and his voice cracked with emotion. "I *loved* her. She was my *everything*."

Daniel stared at me then, like a lost puppy, or one of those animals you see on nature documentaries, after their mother, the matriarchal leader of their little pack, has been snatched away. The grief emanating off him was unbearable. It filled the room, heavy and solid; you could cut it with a knife. His head fell into his hands, and his body shook uncontrollably.

I hesitated. Even before Freya, I'd never had maternal instincts, wasn't the sort to wrap my arms around a friend when they were falling apart. I was much more likely to offer some sort of solution, however pat, to make them feel like their situation wasn't as bad as they thought it was, to reason a way out, to fix it. I wouldn't show up on someone's doorstep like Molly would, sure they needed to unload their emotional pain. Quite the opposite—I'd give them space, let them come to me if and when they wanted.

Only now, I felt it, within me: the need to help this man who was falling apart, who seemed grief-stricken and broken and truly, genuinely hurt. Who didn't seem guilty at all.

So what does that make Max?

I stood and inched around the coffee table, and I found my-self, almost on instinct, sitting down next to this man I didn't know from Adam. Without thinking, I reached my arm out, looped it around him, pulled him close to me.

His body shook harder, and he didn't resist me, he only leaned in, and I could smell on him a staleness, as if he hadn't showered since he'd gotten the news. I noted a hint of ciga-rettes baked into his clothes, and I wondered if he was truly a smoker or had picked up a long-kicked habit because of every-thing that had happened.

I let my hand fall from his shoulder to his upper arm, and it was surprisingly muscled compared to the rest of him. I squeezed then, letting him know I was there—me, another human, caught up in this chaos—me there, suffering along-side him.

He looked up, and his face was so close, and I had a sud-den, awful fear that he was going to do something wild like lean in and kiss me. It was so unusual, so rare, for me to be so close to another man. He didn't, thank god. Still, he looked at me, staring, as if reading me, all my fears and failures, every-thing I'd done wrong with Freya.

His eyes were stern when he spoke.

"It was him, you know," he said. "He killed her, and he took my son."

I reared back, instantly pulling away, returning to my chair.

"He didn't," I said. "He wouldn't."

"Who did, then?"

My eyes caught his, and I didn't say it outright, but I didn't have to.

"I wasn't even home," Daniel said. "And I was never at that bar. Max was. And what about Sutton?" He went on. "You think I did something to him? He's my *child*."

"I don't know," I said. "I don't—"

"The police said Max was seen with Grace on Friday. That means she lied to me about meeting her friend. That means she'd probably lied to me before. All I can think is that something . . . developed between them, and that she tried to break it off. And Max got angry, and he—he—" Daniel's shoulders shook. "Maybe he even wanted a fresh start. Him, Grace, and Sutton. And when she said no, when she resisted . . ." Sobs racked his body, but Daniel kept going. "He probably thought he could sweep her away, finally make it work, make up for everything he did before. Be one happy family."

"One happy family?" I asked. "What are you talking about?"

Daniel looked at me then, his face pained, his shoulders slumped. "You said you wanted answers, didn't you?"

No, I thought. Not answers like these. Maybe Max had had an affair—fine—maybe things had been going on with this woman. But to want to start a new life with a random woman and someone else's kid? It wasn't Max at all. Maybe I didn't know what Max really felt about me, maybe he did sneak away from me to be with some other woman. Maybe we were just two people who lied to each other about the things we did with other people. But one thing was clear above all else: Max adored Freya. He would never, ever leave her behind. She was his daughter. She was his daughter, and he loved her more than anything.

"He would never leave us, not like that."

Daniel's eyes pierced mine. "And yet he's not here, is he?"

I sat up straighter, feeling like I'd indulged this man too much. He was grieving, he was out of his mind, obviously creating theories, things to fill the gaping hole in his heart. I set down my mug and stood. "I should be going."

"So you don't believe me?"

My words were strong for the first time. "I can believe a lot of things, but not that Max would leave Freya. He's her *father*. Why would he want to go and start a new family when he already has one of his own?"

Daniel's eyes flashed with anger, but then just as quickly, they softened. And there in them, not grief anymore. Not kindness. Pity.

"I see," he said. "So you didn't know the backstory at all."

My heart began to race faster, but I forced some calm into my voice. "I told you," I said, grabbing my bag and pulling it close. "I never heard about your wife until yesterday."

"Right," he said. "Well, I'm sorry to be the one to have to tell you."

I turned, and I could see the door, there in my periphery. I could leave, I could run off, and I could avoid whatever it was that he was about to say.

I couldn't help myself. I had to know. "Tell me what?"

Daniel took a sip of booze-soaked tea, then stared, his eyes piercing, splitting me apart.

"Max is Sutton's biological father."

25

1:15 p.m.

HEAT.

In my face. The back of my neck. The pits of my arms.

I needed water.

I ambled forward—around the coffee table, around Daniel—toward the door that led to the kitchen.

To glossy subway tiles. To a Sub-Zero fridge littered with drawings obviously done by a child.

Max's child?

I jolted toward the farmhouse sink and reached for the faucet—

Too late.

My stomach twisted, and I bent over, the counter hitting my belly, just above my scar, lighting it on fire, and bile, hot, sour, bitter, lurched up my throat and into the sink. Onto a child's cup with fire trucks printed around the edge, now spattered with bits of the eggs I'd eaten at lunch.

I flicked on the water. As it came out, I absurdly felt the letdown of my milk, saw the first bits of moisture appearing in two ugly spots on the front of my shirt. I cupped my hands and sucked in water, rinsing my mouth and spitting it out, then repeated the process.

"You really didn't know any of it?"

I spat out the rest of the water and turned to see Daniel. The pity was in his eyes again.

"It can't be true," I said, my hands behind me, still on the sink, as if propping me up.

Daniel grabbed a few paper towels and handed them to me. "They met about seven years ago. At one of Max's shows."

I pressed the towel to my lips, soaked up water and bile.

"Grace was fed up with dating. No guys would commit. That kind of a thing. She'd had this really bad date where the guy stuck her with the bill when she said she wouldn't go home with him that night. She was sitting at the bar alone, and when Max finished his show, he found her there." Daniel sighed. "I guessed they shared a couple of beers, commiserated or something."

I could almost see it playing out. At the bar of the Bell House. Or Coco 66. I could see Max smile, say, *"Fuck those guys."* Something like that.

"Then they were matched on one of the dating apps a month later. He asked her out properly, said everything she wanted to hear." Daniel's lips pressed into a thin, firm line. "They fell into a relationship. They were joined at the hip. They were getting serious. You can guess what happened next."

I didn't want to hear it. Not from him. Not like this.

"She got pregnant. She told him, and after that, he was done with her. Didn't answer her calls, her texts. When she went to his place, his roommates told her he wasn't home. He cut off all contact. I think some people call it 'ghosting.' The rest of us call it what it is: being a prick."

"Max would never do that. How do you even—"

"She told me," Daniel said. "I met her a few months later. She was four months pregnant and barely showing. I was down in the city for work, and we both loved Modigliani. There was an exhibit at the Met. We started talking. I asked her to dinner. She said—" He hesitated. "She said she wasn't dating because she was pregnant. I just wanted to be around her, to talk to her. We did go to dinner, but we were just friends at first. But we kept in contact. You have to understand, she had no one. Her parents were dead. She had friends, but transient city friends, not the type you can rely on to raise a baby." He looked at the fridge, at Sutton's drawings, then back at me. "It wasn't any big sacrifice or anything. I loved her. It made sense for me to invite her up to Kingston. We were meant to be together." His voice cracked. "All these years, all these years I was always glad Max was such a prick, because if he hadn't been, I never would have found her." Daniel shook his head bitterly. "And now look what's happened. He killed her. He killed her, and he's taken Sutton from the only father he's ever known."

"No," I said. "Max wouldn't."

Daniel's eyes locked on mine. "Wouldn't he? Until about five minutes ago, you didn't even know he had another child."

I wiped my hand across the back of my mouth and pushed past Daniel. Back to the living room, back to my things, scattered on the chair. I gathered them together, but Daniel kept going.

"He wanted to make up for lost time," he said, following me to the door. "He wanted to build a life with Grace. And when she said no, that wasn't okay with him. He always got what he wanted. He always put himself first."

I turned around.

"I'm sorry about your wife," I said. "I'm sorry about your son. But Max didn't hurt them."

I grabbed for the door and made my way as quickly as I could down the stone pathway, my hands clasping desperately at the gate, beelining toward home.

Daniel's words looped around my head as I walked through Kingston's vibrant blocks, passing expensive strollers and gurgling, happy babies, babies and mothers who weren't caught up in the mess Freya and I were in. Babies and mothers and fathers—fathers who were present, who were there, who were not fathering other babies in secret, who were not surrounded by murder and abduction and all sorts of things a father should never be part of.

He killed her.

He killed her, and he's taken Sutton from the only father he's ever known.

I couldn't *really* believe it—could I?

Max wasn't a killer. And, god, he would never hurt a child.

Max loved Freya. And in a natural, innate, *fatherly* way—so much more than I did. Unlike me, he was able to feel all the feelings he was supposed to. To do the dance, day in and day out. Freya was his first child. She had to be.

Not to mention, Daniel's story wasn't without its share of holes. If he had any proof—Max's name on a birth certificate, a paternity test—he surely would have shown it to me.

All of it was just words, words about a woman who wasn't here to tell the story herself. And all of it painted Daniel in an extremely positive light: Saving a pregnant woman, being the dad Sutton never had. Loving Grace despite all the baggage she brought with her.

Daniel could have killed her. All of this could be a story to make himself look better. And yet . . .

I'd seen grief, loss, there in Daniel's eyes. I'd seen hurt and betrayal. I'd seen the things I felt myself.

What if it all *was* true? What if Max really was Sutton's dad? What if his meetings with Grace were part of a full-on affair, one that had gone on for who knew how long? What if he'd pined for the years he'd missed in his child's life? What if he'd justified the whole thing because he knew about Bryan, because he knew everything?

Could I really trust anything Max had told me when he couldn't even trust me?

I turned at the corner of John and Wall, walked through the rainbow crosswalk I'd found so enchanting when we'd been up here before. I'd suggested Kingston—that idea had always been mine—but had Max only been so eager to do it, even after I'd left my job and we both knew it was financially unsound, because it would bring him closer to Grace?

I continued down Wall Street, approaching the Old Dutch Church. Under the shade of one of the huge elm trees that lined the graveyard, I took out my phone, dialed Max for—what?—the millionth time? It went straight to voicemail, as it had done so many times now, only this time, I didn't hear him—this time, it was only a cold, falsely cheerful robotic woman.

"The mailbox of the person you're trying to reach is full."

I ended the call, then dialed again. The same voice. The same damn message.

"The mailbox of the person you're trying to reach is full."

A tightness in my throat, as if even out here, surrounded by air fresher than I'd ever had in the city, I wouldn't be able to get enough oxygen.

Max hadn't answered once since he disappeared, but still, his inbox was there, a lifeline if I needed it. Now that was gone, too.

I wanted, so badly now, to call him, scream at him—"Did you really have a child you didn't tell me about? Did you hurt Grace? Did you kill her? Is Sutton with you now?"

But I couldn't. Not anymore.

Then, like an answer, like some sort of cosmic reply—

My phone rang, my screen displaying an 800 number. My fingers prickled, and somewhere, deep down, I knew this was more than a spam call pushing a car warranty. I tapped to answer. Lifted the phone to my ear.

"Hello."

A sigh, and then a shuffling sound, like someone was adjusting the phone, pulling it closer to their ear.

"Hello," I said, my heartbeats fierce, a million miles a minute. "If you don't say anything, I'm hanging up."

There was a pause, a breath, and I knew it for sure then, I knew it before he spoke.

"Janie," he said. "Please don't hang up."

His voice was so deep, as warm and rich as a fresh pot of coffee, and yet a little gruff, too. A voice that had made many a woman swoon, me notwithstanding. A voice I had craved, had prayed for, had been desperate to hear since I'd woken up Saturday morning, Freya's cries piercing my ears.

A voice that belonged to a man who might have done awful, brutal, unspeakable things.

A man who'd left me, and left Freya. A man I hated so fiercely but couldn't help but love.

"Please," Max said again. "Don't go. Just give me a chance. I can explain."

26

1:33 p.m.

"IS FREYA OKAY?"

Max asked this as if it were the most natural thing in the world, as if he were only calling, like a father did, to check in. *Did she nap well? Is she fussy? Maybe give her some gas drops—or are we doing gripe water now? How are you hanging in?*

The line hung there, taut and tense between us. I wanted to yell, scream, ask him how he could leave me on my own when he knew I couldn't handle it.

"She's . . . she's fine," I managed, my voice wavering, cracking at the end. "She's sleeping now. Liana is watching her. Where *are* you?"

"Listen, Janie. You can't tell anyone I called. Not my parents, not Liana. Not any of your friends. No lawyers. No one, okay? It's too risky. I didn't even know if I *should* call because I don't want to get you in trouble, but I saw it all hit the news, and I had to let you know I was okay. I had to hear your voice."

"News?" I asked.

"It's in the *Daily Freeman*."

I shook my head, pushing back tears. "I found your phone. I . . . I know about Grace. Did you . . ." I steeled myself. "Did you kill her?"

"No, Janie. God, no. I would never. She asked me to help her. She was in an impossible spot. I didn't have a choice."

"You always have a choice," I practically spat. "You always, *always* have a choice."

There was a rushing sound in the background, the honk of a horn. Traffic? A highway?

"Where are you?" I asked again.

"I can't talk long. I'll be back as soon as I can, as soon as I figure this out. I'm in too deep now. I have to finish what I started. Stay close, please. Don't leave me yet."

"Wait," I said. "Just wait."

"Janie, I have to—"

"Is it true?" I asked. "Is he your son?"

A pause, one that sent my insides roiling. A pause that killed me, tore me apart inside. "Janie, I have to go. I'll call again as soon as I can."

"Max, don't—"

"I love you. You and Freya. More than anything. Please believe me."

"Is he with you? Sutton?"

"I have to go," he said again. "Stay where you are for now. Goodbye."

Before he could end the call, there it was, impossible to miss, a voice in the background: "How much longer?"

The call ended, and I stared at the phone in my hands, my pulse pounding, my world coming apart.

The voice I'd just heard . . .

It was the voice of a child.

27

1:37 p.m.

I STUMBLED BACK, TURNING, LOOKING FOR A BENCH, BUT there wasn't one, so I eased down clumsily onto the sidewalk and leaned against a stone pillar, knowing if I didn't, I might fall over, right there in the middle of town.

I took in the view across from me, shaken.

A local bank. A historical society. Safe, simple things.

The voice had been unmistakable. Sweet, higher-pitched, a hint of a whine. Freya would speak like that one day. Her lungs, lungs that had formed in my womb, that had started working, breathing in and out amniotic fluid when I was as round as a watermelon, would keep growing and growing, and one day they wouldn't only emit monkey sounds and baby wails. One day, there would be full words. *Mama. Dada. How much longer?*

Would she even know and love that second word, *Dada*? What would it mean to her? A man on the other side of a plexiglass window? Someone she spoke to through one of those phones they always showed on TV?

How could we possibly come back from this when he had Sutton, a six-year-old who drew pictures and drank from a fire truck cup?

How much more? I thought desperately, staring at the cracks of the stone sidewalk, touching my fingers into the dirt between them. How much deeper did the deceptions go? How much worse could it get?

"Are you okay?"

I looked up to see an older man—silver hair, thin-rimmed glasses—hunched over, leaning toward me. "Miss, do you want me to get you some help?"

Even this stranger can see it. Max's guilt is tinging you, too. Everyone will know soon.

"I'm fine," I said, widening my eyes, entreating the man to believe me. "I got a little winded, is all. Needed to sit for a moment."

"Do you want me to call a doctor?"

I forced a smile. This man probably loved the Good Samaritan story in Sunday school, probably always stopped for messy women in the midst of falling apart. Loved to be a hero, whenever—wherever—he could.

She was in an impossible spot. I didn't have a choice.

"I'm fine. *Really*," I said, my voice firm now.

"You shouldn't be alone anyway, young woman like you. There's a murderer out there, you know."

My phone rang then, and I jumped. "I need to get this. Like I said, I'm fine."

"Okay, okay, lady, I was only trying to help."

He shook his head and walked off, and I grabbed at the phone desperately, hoping for another call from Max. "Carl," I said with a sigh. "Hi."

"Janie," he said. "I'm glad I caught you. We think you should come to Scarsdale. If Max makes contact—*when* Max makes contact—we'll tell him to come here, too. We can figure everything out. Brenda and I can hire a nanny—a night nurse—whatever you need. You're family, Janie. I hope you know that. We can help you, until Max comes to his senses. We want to help you."

If Max makes contact. What would Carl say if he knew he already had? If he knew that Max had told me—begged me—to stay close?

"Carl," I said, buying time. "This is so fast."

"I know," he said. "But listen. The police told us about the child. This is bigger now. And the news has got ahold of it now, too. We don't know where Max is, what he's gotten caught up in. We need to stick together here."

"I know," I said, but already I could feel myself betraying him and Brenda.

"So come, then. Today."

"No, Carl, it's too soon—"

"Please," he said.

"I'll call you later. Promise. I have to go."

I hung up before he could say anything else. I'd never lied outright to Carl before. He was family to me, just as he'd said, but he'd kept secrets from me—and now I had mine. I pushed myself up, leaned against the fence instead, and navigated to Google, typed, "Grace murder the Daily Freeman."

There it was, finally—the hit I'd been looking for. I tapped on it, and the article loaded, but a paywall popped up, obscuring it—*Subscribe to support local journalism!* Fingers clumsy, I found my credit card, practically ripping it from its space in my wallet, keyed each digit in.

The first thing I saw was a photo of the bar I'd been to the night before. Beneath it, in bold letters, the story I'd been waiting for.

KINGSTON WOMAN, 38, FOUND DEAD IN APPARENT HOMICIDE, CHIEF SAYS

KINGSTON, N.Y.—A 38-year-old woman was discovered fatally injured Saturday morning in the alley behind Three Crows Tavern on North Front Street, city police said. Details have only just been released by the police.

Kingston police identified the victim Sunday morning as Grace P. Akins.

Officers reported responding to a report of a woman found dead around 9:30 a.m. The 911 call was placed by Dave Welch, the owner of Three Crows Tavern, who discovered Akins when he arrived Saturday morning.

The victim was taken to HealthAlliance Hospital's Broadway Campus, where she was pronounced dead. Autopsy results have yet to be released to the press.

According to her Facebook page, Akins was a stay-at-home mother and was married to Daniel Akins, a real estate developer. Her six-year-old child, Sutton Akins, has not been seen since Friday morning.

The Kingston police chief, Arnold Agnew, said that the department is following tips, interviewing witnesses and those connected to the deceased, and seeking cell phone evidence. No suspects have yet been identified.

"We're following every lead we have, both about the victim and her son, and we'll see where those leads go," Agnew said.

Agnew asks anyone with information about the homicide or the whereabouts of the child to contact the Kingston Police.

I scrolled down, impatient, but there wasn't anything more than that. Only ads for local restaurants and bespoke vitamins.

I scrolled back up, making sure I hadn't missed anything, but there was no photo of Grace. I needed to see her. This woman, this mother, this person I couldn't even hate, no matter what she'd done with Max, because she'd never, ever deserved to die.

Then a line caught my eye: *According to her Facebook page.*

I opened the app and typed in her name, making sure the spelling matched that of the article: *Grace Akins.*

Two others came up first. One in California. One in Iowa.

And then, directly beneath. A Grace Akins from Kingston, New York. Details next to a tiny thumbnail photo.

I tapped it, landed on her profile, the image of her bigger now, spread across my screen.

Oh. My. God.

There she was. Wide eyes, not looking back surreptitiously but gazing at me directly. Creamy porcelain skin. Chunky cool-girl bangs and long glossy brown hair. Lips painted a bright red, not pursed or pressed together but smiling for whoever was behind the camera. She was gorgeous, truly striking.

The kind of beautiful you didn't forget.

There, along the edge of the photo, a glimpse of her arm, of her mermaid tattoo. It hit me then, the details from Daniel's living room practically flashing before my eyes.

You should have known. You should have put it together by now.

The mermaid patch on the back of the denim jacket.

The swoop of the scaly tail on the handle of the mug.

It must be her thing. Her very own motif.

She was the woman from town, the woman from Friday, the woman who'd been looking at me—a glance here, a head turn there—while Max and Freya and I had been spread out on a blanket, listening to kiddie music, trying to enjoy ourselves.

A concert I hadn't even wanted to go to, but Max had insisted.

I thought it had been our last normal day, but it hadn't.

She'd been there, watching me.

Grace had been there all along.

28

1:53 p.m.

IT WAS RIGHT IN FRONT OF ME THAT DAY. THE MAN SITTING next to Grace, whose face I'd never seen, was Daniel. The boy playing in front of her, the one with the curly hair—Max's hair?—dancing to the music: Sutton.

How much longer?

Grace, a beautiful woman, with a beautiful family. A woman who looked happy. A woman who had no idea that Friday would be her last.

All of it was too painful, too awful, too raw. Even after all I'd been through these last few days, here I was, alive. Here I was, with Freya.

I scrolled down. I wanted more. Every detail about her. Anything I could possibly get my hands on.

Lives in Kingston, N.Y.

Works at Living That Stay-at-Home-Mom Life

Married to Daniel Akins

Nothing more. I wasn't a friend of hers, and she hadn't shared any more publicly. I was about to return to Google when my eyes caught another line. Words I'd seen so many times, in so many other situations, words that had never felt dangerous until now.

Liana Price is a mutual friend

Liana? What the fuck?

Molly's words rang through my head:

They're going to protect Max, they're going to protect their own reputation, they're going to keep their perfect little Westchester world intact. That's who they are.

Images flashed to mind: Liana and Max whispering in the kitchen, the way she hadn't looked surprised by Max's changed password, her trip this morning to get coffee, her nearly belligerent insistence that Max was innocent, her answer when I'd asked if Max knew anyone named Grace: *It doesn't ring any bells*. Did Liana know more than she'd let on? Was she protecting herself, too? Had she somehow been wrapped up in this the entire time?

I stumbled forward and turned onto Main Street, reeling in shock, anger, disbelief. My phone buzzed with a new text from Molly, but I ignored it, tucking my phone into my pocket. I had to get home. I had to make sense of what I could.

Finally, I was in front of the rental. I rushed up the steps, dashed across the slatted porch, and turned the handle of the door.

Locked. I fumbled with the keys, got the right one, felt the twist, shoved the door open, the creak like a screech now, a wail.

I rushed down the hallway, my ears pricked for the sound of Freya—crying or cooing, burping or farting, squirming around and testing out her so recently formed lungs—but there was only silence, and in a moment, I saw why.

There in the living room was Liana, propped up in the wingback chair, Freya nestled happily into the crook of her arm, sucking on a bottle, one of the types we'd paid extra for because they were supposed to mimic the feeling of a real breast. It was beautiful, really. Like a Renaissance painting, mother and child.

Was it all a big lie?

Liana smiled, as if nothing in the world was wrong. "She seemed hungry when she woke up. I was going to call you, but I figured you deserved the break."

"You knew Grace," I said, the words spat out, an accusation. "You knew her, and you told me you didn't."

"What?" Liana asked, dumbfounded. "What do you mean? I *don't* know a Grace. I promise."

"Don't play dumb," I said. I reached for Freya, craving her warmth, the solid, tangible presence of my baby. Suddenly wanting her out of Liana's hands. She fussed as I took her, but I popped the bottle in, and she was quiet again. "Grace is your friend. I saw on Facebook."

"Wait," Liana said. "Wait, *what*?"

"Grace Akins," I said. "She's the one who's dead. And you knew her. You didn't think it was important to tell me? Even after I asked you—point-blank?"

"No," Liana said. "I swear to god I have no idea what you're talking about."

I felt the squish of Freya's diaper. She would need to be changed soon. Just as soon as she was done with this bottle.

"Daniel says Grace was Max's ex-girlfriend. He says her child . . . her child is Max's."

Sutton, who was with Max now. Whose voice I'd just heard.

"What are you talking about?" Liana asked, her eyes widening in the sort of shock that didn't look remotely practiced, put on, or rehearsed. "Who's Daniel?"

"Grace's husband," I said, patting Freya's butt offhandedly. "I went to see him—"

"Hold on," Liana said, with a shake of her head. "Hold on, I thought you were at lunch with Molly."

"I was," I said. "But afterward, I decided I needed answers, and his house is downtown, right across from that bar, and—"

"And so you visit a potential murderer?" Liana looked genuinely worried, as if everything was so precariously balanced, and I was about to tip the tower of blocks right over. "If Max didn't kill this woman, and we *know* Max didn't kill her, then her husband did. Isn't that obvious? And you're going over there, you're—"

"And what if Max *did* kill her?" I snapped.

Liana looked at me, horrified. "Jesus, Janie, what's wrong with you?"

"With me?" I asked, anger surging to my cheeks now, Freya somehow heavier in my arms. "You think there's something wrong with me because I don't trust Max anymore, because I don't trust any of you?"

Liana reached a hand to me, but I shook her off. "Please," she said urgently. "Believe me. There was never an ex-girlfriend. There was never a child. There was never any woman named Grace."

"You sure about that?" I shot back. "Because her husband says that Max and Grace had a whole illicit affair and that their son, Sutton, is Max's biological child."

Liana reared back. "And you *believe* him?"

"What am I supposed to believe?" I asked, adjusting the bottle so Freya could get more milk. "Max isn't here to explain. Max fucked off to who knows where, and there's an old iPhone, up in the guest room. There's a phone, tucked under the mattress you're sleeping on, full of WhatsApp messages between him and *her*. Full of details about all the times they were going to meet."

And he called me, I thought, as I watched the formula drip down the sides of the bottle, liquid and powdery at the same time. He told me he was trying to help her. And I heard Sutton's innocent voice.

I couldn't tell Liana that. That was a secret too deep. That made me complicit, too.

"For Christ sake, *you're* friends with her," I went on.

"Janie," Liana said. "I'm friends with maybe two thousand people on Facebook. It must be some random thing—"

"It's not," I said. I pulled Freya closer, balanced the bottom of the bottle beneath my chin, and retrieved my phone with my free hand, tapped into Facebook, flipped it around for Liana's eyes. "See?"

Liana took my phone, and she held it in front of her face, and for a minute, there was nothing—no recognition—but then her eyes widened. "Oh."

"So you *did* know her?" I said, my voice pleading. "You did."

Freya whined, and I tipped the bottle all the way up, letting her have the last few drops, watched as she sucked hungrily.

"How did you know her?" I asked, my eyes locked on Liana's. "*Please.* If you care about me at all, if you care about our supposed friendship, you have to tell me everything. *Now.*"

For a moment, Liana looked like she wanted to argue back, but then her face softened. She seemed to make a decision.

"I swear to you I had no idea this was her."

She sighed, as if setting down a boulder she'd been carrying all along.

"When I knew her, she called herself Rae."

29

2:13 p.m.

"SHE WAS NEVER A GIRLFRIEND," LIANA SAID. "I PROMISE YOU."

The bottle was empty now, and Freya began to whine. I tugged down my top and latched her on. She nursed slowly, easy and lackadaisical. She wanted comfort, nothing more. How could I blame her?

"Rae," I said, testing the word on my lips as I held Freya close. Not Grace, but Rae. Rae with the mermaid tattoo. Rae with the beautiful hair. Rae who was dead now, who'd been murdered, who would never get the chance to hug Sutton again.

"Give me your phone," I said.

"What?" Liana asked. "Why?"

"I want to see Grace's whole profile," I said, my voice earnest. "I want to know everything I can about her."

"Okay," Liana said. "Okay." She slipped her phone from the pocket of her tattered jeans, unlocked it, opened Facebook, and passed it to me.

In the search, I keyed in "Grace Akins," tapped on her profile. Freya squirmed, seeming to sense I was focused on something other than her. She let out a cry and unlatched, the suction tugging at my nipple, making it feel tender and dry. Carefully, I latched her back on.

I flicked down Grace's timeline, past messages that had only just been posted—*Please tell me this isn't about you? Oh god, Grace, I can't believe it*—to a photo of her and Sutton.

I paused, staring at it. Sutton's eyes were wide, his nose straight and strong, his hair curly, dark brown, his eyebrows thick.

"Oh my god," I said. "He looks like Max."

"Let me see," Liana said, and I flipped the phone around.

Her eyebrows shot up, but she tried to downplay it. "He looks like a kid, Janie. Lots of kids have those features. It doesn't mean anything. And you have to understand," Liana said. "He and Rae were never serious. She was just a girl Max met after a show."

"But that's *exactly* how her husband said they met."

"What I mean is it wasn't anything more than a hookup thing, I promise you. I think it was shortly after he and Angie split, obviously well before he met you. I only met her a handful of times. It was *never* a relationship."

My thumb continued to flick through Grace's Facebook photos—images at the Ashokan Reservoir, a shot of one of Sutton's drawings, a family photo—her, Sutton, and Daniel—looking for something that would give me answers. Anything that would explain why she and Max had reconnected as they had. It all looked so . . . normal.

Her life looked peaceful. Happy. Sweet.

"It was nothing," Liana went on. "I swear to you."

"And that's why you stayed friends with her on Facebook all these years?"

"God, Janie," Liana said. "I friended everyone back then. Put them in our marketing group, blasted out event invites to shows. You know that. I'm not friends with this woman, if that's what you think. I didn't even know her real name was Grace. Back when I knew her it was Rae, R-A-E, even on Facebook, and her last name, god, I can't even remember, something with a C, but not Akins."

"What was she like?" I asked.

Liana's eyes turned down. "She was nice, Janie. She was really nice."

A weight in my gut, a knowledge so true: she didn't deserve to die. She didn't deserve any of this.

"But just because she was a nice person," Liana repeated, "that doesn't mean what this man said was true. She and Max weren't serious, and they didn't have any sort of relationship . . ." She hesitated. "I would have known."

"How can you be sure?" I asked.

"Because I'm his best friend," Liana said firmly, a hint of protectiveness—ownership?—in her voice. "He told me when he liked someone. He told me when it was more than . . . you know." Liana wrinkled her nose. "Max said something to me, the day he met you. He said, 'This is different.'"

"Liana," I said.

"I'm not saying that to make you feel any sort of way, I promise. I'm saying it because you can't just *believe* this man."

"Max had secrets from you, too," I said. "He never told you where he went or what he was doing all those times he disappeared."

"That was different," Liana said.

"How?"

"It just *was*."

Freya popped off, and I rehooked my nursing bra, got her situated in the swing, and turned the vibrations up high.

"What about everything else?" I asked. "You and Max talking quietly on Friday. The way you didn't even look surprised when I told you he changed his password."

Liana hesitated, her eyes connecting with mine, then sighed. "I don't know, I guess I just . . . I thought something was up with him this week. I thought he was acting different. And so I asked him on Friday, and he said there was nothing going on."

"What about this morning? Where were you, really? We have coffee here."

Liana looked down at her hands, then back up again. "I'm sorry," she said. "I shouldn't have lied. I went to tell the police about Max's history of disappearing. I thought it was important that they know, so they wouldn't, you know, think it had to do with the murder."

"So *that's* why Duncan didn't look surprised when I made you tell her. She'd already heard. Why didn't you say something?" I asked.

Liana shrugged. "I didn't want you to think I was betraying Max, but I actually thought it would make him look more innocent, I promise. That's why you wanted to tell Duncan about Max disappearing, too, right? Your reasoning was the same."

"Yes," I said. "But that was before I knew all this." I gestured wildly, Liana's phone still in my hand. I looked to Freya in the swing, whose eyelids were heavy again. I could go right now, if I really wanted. Freya was fed and sleepy. I could get her into the stroller, pack up the important things. Leave this house, and all Max's deceptions, behind. Freya and I could be at Ani's within the hour. Molly and Ani could help me. I could call my parents, and maybe they'd actually show up for me for once, and somehow, we'd all figure it out. Or I could go to Carl and Brenda, let them hire me that night nurse.

Stay close, please. Don't leave me yet.

That was what Max had asked of me, but I didn't know if I could do it. Not when everything between us had been poisoned with so many lies.

There was a sudden off-putting smell wafting up from the baby swing. I'd forgotten about the dirty diaper. Something so mundane, so ubiquitous in the life of a new parent.

"It's too much," I said, looking up at Liana. "It's been so hard, all of it, even before this. The feedings, the diapers, the constant battle of trying to get by. And I don't have any of the right feelings. I was never meant to be a mother, I've been coming apart the whole time, and that was *before* all this. That was when I had Max to help. I don't know what to do—where to go from here."

"I'm here," Liana said. "I'm here as long as you need me. I swear."

I pressed my lips together, tried to ignore the smell of shit, Freya's eyes shutting now, oblivious to the mess her body had just created. "Molly wants me to come stay with her. She thinks Max is caught up in—"

"Is that what you want?" Liana asked, cutting me off.

"What I want?" I repeated.

"Yes," Liana said.

What I wanted—*all* I wanted—was to rewind. To find a way to somehow go back, to before I ever heard about another child of Max's, or a Grace or Rae or anyone.

I wanted to go back to before I'd ever found that damn

phone with its history of texts. To before I'd discovered that Max had changed his password, to before he'd disappeared.

Before I'd told him the worst thought, the thought that made me feel so very sick inside: that sometimes I looked at my baby, the baby I was supposed to love more than life itself, and I wished we hadn't had her.

But in truth, I wished we could rewind before that even. Before those early difficult days. Before those endless sleepless nights. Before the chaos of birth. Before the unplanned C-section. Before the trials of pregnancy, of knowing my body was no longer my own.

Before that awful night with Bryan, my drunken stupidity turning what I'd always thought was a harmless flirtation into something so much more, sacrificing everything I'd ever held dear.

I wished I could go back to me and Max. Simple and easy and in love.

I shook my head, bringing myself back to the present. "I don't know what I want," I said. "Maybe it would be better to get out of this place—" I gestured around the house. "To put this all behind me. To move on."

Liana shrugged. "Look, I would be mad, too. Furious. And Max isn't perfect. Believe me, I know that. And maybe they were meeting—hell, maybe there even was an affair." Her eyes found her hands. "But as awful . . . as *terrible* as that is—" she said, before catching my eyes again. "I *know* he wouldn't kill anyone, and I think you know that, too. I know he wouldn't hurt a child. I know that at the end of this, all he's going to want is to be in Freya's life. And so even if you hate him, even if you can never forgive him, if any part of you believes that Max is innocent of these terrible things, if you want him to continue to be Freya's loving father, you know he needs us. And I fear that if we leave it will look like we believe he's guilty, too."

I stared at her, so badly wanting to trust her words.

But how could I, really? Liana didn't know that Sutton was with Max now.

How could there possibly be an explanation for that?

I jolted, my musings cut short.

Once again, there was a loud, urgent knocking at the door.

30

2:29 p.m.

MOLLY STOOD ON THE PORCH, ONE HAND ON HER HIP. "I TOLD you I was coming over if you didn't answer."

I looked away only briefly. "Yes, you did."

She walked in without waiting to be asked and made her way to the living room, then waved a hand dramatically in front of her face. "Oof, it smells awful in here."

"Freya's diaper," I said.

"Should you change her, then?" Molly asked, gesturing in the direction of the swing.

"Not while she's sleeping," Liana said, sitting up straighter on the sofa, a hint of protectiveness in her voice. "You never wake a sleeping baby."

Molly ignored Liana and turned to me, her voice quiet but firm. "Do you want me to help you pack? While the baby is down?"

"Molly," I said, "I never said I was coming. I haven't even had time to think about it."

Molly's eyes caught Liana's, and Liana averted her gaze, staring at her feet.

"We don't have to tell Ani why, you know. We can make something up. It's fine."

"It's not that," I said. "It's not just that, at least."

"So what's your plan, then?" Molly asked. "You're just going to stay here and wait for Max to show up? For the police to come after you next?"

Stay close, please. Don't leave me yet.

I walked from the room, not wanting to risk waking Freya.

When we were in the kitchen, Molly stepped close, lowering her voice, taking advantage of this tiny bit of privacy. "Did Liana talk you out of it, is that it?"

"No," I said. "I mean, yes, she thinks it's best we stay where we are, but it's not only that."

"What is it, then?" Molly prodded. "What is here that's so important? You need to focus on you, Janie, not him."

Max, I thought. Max is out there, calling me from somewhere. Max asked me to stay.

And then there was the other thing, too.

Sutton's voice on the line. Was I complicit if I didn't go straight to Duncan, tell her what happened? If I ran back to Brooklyn—if I holed up in Westchester with Carl and Brenda—would it look like I was running, too? And if I *did* tell Duncan about Max's phone call, what would that mean for him?

Maybe it was something I could have more easily done were I not a mother. Maybe if it were just me and Max, I could cut and run, let the cards fall where they may. But he wasn't just Max anymore. He was the father of my daughter.

If I gave him up, where did that leave me? Leave Freya? I needed time to think.

"Molly, it's not that simple," I said. "There are things

about Max that I didn't know, that I'm learning. And I'm trying to make sense of those things, and Liana *knows* him. She gets him, gets what's going on in a way you never will. She's not ready to just abandon him—"

"Of course she's not," Molly said, throwing her hands up. "She's on his side."

"He's my daughter's father. I can't just throw him to the wolves. Liana gets that. I wish you did."

Molly huffed, and I knew it wasn't fair, but it was true. "So I guess I'm the enemy now?"

"You're not the enemy," I said. "You're my best friend. But—" I hesitated. "I don't know how you can help me now. Not when it's all so black and white to you."

Molly's eyes were wide and sad, unbearably hurt. "How can you think she can help you when I can't? After everything we've been through?"

I bit my lip. "Because I know what you want, but I—I can't—he's Freya's father—"

"Oh my god," Molly said, lowering her voice conspiratorially. "Janie, what do you know?"

"Nothing," I said, my heart racing.

"Something happened between lunch and now. Something—"

Everything happened between lunch and now, Molly. Everything.

"—something that's changed you. Did he . . . did he call you? Do you know where he is?"

"No," I said instinctively. "No, of course not."

Molly reached for my hand, and tears sprang to my eyes. How was she so good at reading me? How did she know me inside and out? "Janie," she said. "You have to be careful, or you're going to risk your own life, too. You know that, right?"

"I don't know what you're talking about," I said, shaking her off. "You're making things up."

"I'm not," Molly said. "Because you never could say no to what Max wanted of you. Not with this pregnancy. And now, not with this."

My stomach ached suddenly. Her words were low, below the proverbial belt, and I hated her for them. I hated her because they were probably true.

When I'd gone to Molly when I found out I was pregnant, she'd told me I could do whatever I wanted, that Max wouldn't even have to know if I didn't want to tell him. Molly might not have known everything, but she knew what mattered: that I was terrified—absolutely terrified—of having this baby. Of choosing this path.

"Are you glad it's turned out this way?" I asked, my voice acrid and bitter now. "Proof you were right? That I wasn't up to this and Max wasn't, either?"

"Don't say that, Janie."

"Why?" I asked. "It's true, isn't it?"

"Listen, I know I didn't immediately get on board when you told me you were pregnant. I know I doubted whether Max was really the type to take on the whole Brooklyn dad thing. Whether it's what you wanted. But you can't really think that—god—that I'm happy all of this has happened. I love you, Janie. All I want in the whole world is what's best for you—you and Freya. I don't want you to get caught up in his mess. I want to protect you, and I'm not sure that's where Liana's head is at."

"Maybe Liana wants to protect us all—me and Max and Freya. Did you ever think of that?"

Molly lowered her voice. "Does Liana know that the only reason you're sticking around is because you feel guilty about some stupid drunken mistake? You don't owe him this, Janie. Nothing you did deserves this."

"That's not the reason," I said. "I swear it's not." But I didn't really know that, did I? It was impossible to separate one thread from another—pull too hard, and everything could unravel.

Molly frowned, changing tack. "So this is your plan, then? To stay here, waiting around for someone who left you? Hanging on to some hope that a horse isn't really a horse? Come on, the cops are literally on your doorstep. A woman is dead. A child is missing."

And not just a woman, I thought. A nice woman, someone who used to call herself Rae. Someone who had obviously loved Sutton dearly, even a quick glance through her timeline proved as much.

How much longer?

"For all either of us know," Molly said, "Max could have killed her."

I shook my head desperately. "Don't say that."

"Why?" She shrugged. "It's the truth. You know it as well as I do."

Anger surged in my belly. It was one thing for me to say it, for me to wonder, but it was another for her to put it into words. "I think you should leave," I said. "You telling me you think the father of my baby is a murderer, it's not actually helping."

"Really?" Molly asked. "Seriously?"

"Yes," I said, surer than I'd ever been. "Please just go."

Molly threw up her hands, then backed out of the kitchen, making for the door.

One hand on the knob, she turned back.

"By the way," she said, "I emailed your mom."

"You *what*?"

"She needed to know," Molly said. "Good luck, Janie. Call me when you come to your senses. I'm right down the road."

31

7:35 p.m.

"WE WERE HOPING YOU WOULD RECONSIDER COMING down to Scarsdale." Carl and Brenda gazed into the screen of our FaceTime, a call that had come in exactly at seven thirty, when they normally tried to say goodnight to Freya before bed. As soon as I'd told them Freya was already upstairs having a bottle with Liana, the true reason for their call became clear. "We have resources," Carl went on. "A lawyer. Everything you need."

I hesitated, knowing Carl was at least partially right. Since I'd sent Molly away, every second that wasn't dedicated to the minute-by-minute grind of watching Freya had been devoted to my new grind: googling. Looking for another news hit. Checking social to see if anything had appeared there. Using Liana's phone to parse through everything I could find on Grace's Facebook page, discovering little more than vacation photos and a confirmation, deep in the caverns of her timeline, that at one point she *had* been called Rae. I was a sitting duck, waiting for the story to hit national news, waiting for my parents to call with questions of their own, but not willing to leave this place until I had something more to hang on to. Not only for Max, for me, too.

"I'm not ready yet," I said finally. "But listen, I need you to be honest with me . . . did Max have a child before Freya?"

Blank stares, coming my way.

"What did you say?" Brenda asked.

"A child," I said. "A biological child. Grace, that's the name of the woman who was killed, or maybe you might know her as Rae. She knew Max. Apparently they dated before, and her child, Sutton, is Max's."

How much longer?

"According to whom?" Brenda huffed. "Are people just making up wild stories now? The police didn't say anything like that."

"No," I said. "The woman's husband."

"You *spoke* to him?" Brenda asked. "Is that really a good idea—"

"It doesn't matter," I said. "Just tell me. Did Max ever say anything? Could he have known Sutton was his? Could he have . . . abandoned him?"

"That's absurd," Brenda said.

"So you never knew anything about Rae or Sutton?"

Carl scoffed. "In terms of girlfriends, there was only Angie and then you. Period."

"Janie," Brenda said. "I say this from the bottom of my heart. I truly believe if Max had learned he was a father, he would have come to us the moment he knew."

"You're sure about that?" I asked.

"Yes, I'm sure," she said. "I'm his mother."

A pause stretched across the line as I looked from Carl to Brenda. There was nothing more to say.

"Listen," Carl said, breaking the silence. "Our lawyer needs to meet with you. If it's not going to be down here, then he'll have to come up there."

The thought sent shock waves through my body. What could I tell him? Max had said to tell no one, lawyers included. "No," I said. "I'm not ready for that."

Carl continued on as if I hadn't said a word. "His name's Rick Courtland. He's the best out there. He'll get in touch with you tomorrow." He and Brenda exchanged yet another look. "Listen to him, Janie. Please."

"But I don't—"

"Just answer his call, if nothing else," Brenda said, her voice earnest. "Do us that favor, at least."

WHEN I LAID Freya down an hour later, I watched as she squirmed, wriggled, and then, peacefully, went still.

My beautiful, perfect baby. Too perfect, almost. Some parents had real anxieties to contend with from the start, babies who needed ultrasounds and CAT scans. Babies who had to spend months in the NICU. I'd been one of the lucky ones, hadn't I? One of those mothers who'd been given the gift we all say we so desperately want: a healthy baby. That was it, wasn't it? That was all it was supposed to be, if you loved like a mother should, if you loved in the right way, selflessly, from the bottom of your heart.

You don't love that way. You can't. Grace probably did.

Maybe it should have been you instead of her.

I stared at Freya's bud of a mouth and her cheeks, as puffy as a chipmunk's. There were so many things she didn't know. That her mother walked the fine line between love and hate toward her on a daily—hourly—basis. That her father was gone, caught up in something her mother couldn't even begin to understand, something that required lawyers now, strategies. Something that involved a boy, Sutton, who was only a little more than a handful of years older than her. Something that had resulted in the death of Grace, of Rae, of a woman who loved mermaids and loved her son, a woman who was torn from her family—torn from this life. Freya didn't know that the wave was building, and it would inevitably crash onto the shore, that this clusterfuck would only get bigger and bigger, and her father had somehow gotten himself into the center of it, the eye of the hurricane.

I backed away, out of the room, pulled the door shut behind me, then carefully, quietly, I returned to the guest room. I went straight to the edge of the mattress where I'd slipped Max's second phone into its hiding spot.

It was still hanging on to a little charge, and I tapped it to life. There were no more messages in WhatsApp, but why would there be? Grace was dead.

I checked every app again, the search history, the camera roll, but there was nothing that I hadn't found the day before, so I tucked it back under the mattress, exactly where I'd told Liana I'd found it. If she wanted to look at it herself, I wouldn't stop her. I no longer saw the point.

I went through the rest of the room, careful not to miss a thing, desperate to find something to fill in the gaps from

Max's phone call, one so short, so incomplete, it was hard to believe it had happened at all.

I checked each nightstand, opened the drawers of the dresser, searched through the small trash can. I opened the trunk of extra blankets, lifted out each patterned, woolen layer, to see if Max had shoved something beneath.

Secret lives left remnants, didn't they? They couldn't only live in apps on a second phone. I knelt down, shoved my arm between the mattress and the box spring. My fingers slid around the coolness of the phone, and I pulled it out, flicked through everything one more time. Nothing.

I stood, tossing it onto the bed, and, hands on my hips, stared at the rumpled sheets, the pillow, still imprinted from where Liana's head had been, a dress of hers and a pair of underwear tossed on the edge of the bed. If Max had hidden one thing, he must have hidden others. I imagined Liana sitting downstairs, watching trash TV, oblivious to what I was about to do.

They say a mother can lift a car if her child is trapped beneath it, adrenaline and fear pumping through her, and that was what I thought of as I pushed up the mattress with two hands, Liana's things flailing off, sheets falling to the other side.

Only I wasn't saving Freya, of course. I was chasing some answers to help with my own sanity, and the intensity, the urgency, did make the mattress come up easily, did allow me to push the whole thing off the other edge so it hung there, like the top of a trapdoor, waiting to shut. Snap!

Adrenaline coursing, sweat on the back of my neck, I didn't expect to find anything. I swear to god, I didn't.

I gasped when I saw it.

It was familiar—and not familiar—at once. For a moment, it really was hard to compute.

An empty, folded cardboard box, with words printed boldly across the front.

Your DNA Home Paternity Test

32

8:45 p.m.

I STOOD, PRACTICALLY FROZEN TO THE SPOT, HOLDING THE evidence I'd been after in my hand. The box was completely empty—there was no report, nothing to read at all. It was trash, nothing more. Trash that Max hadn't wanted me to find, that he was probably too scared to toss out here at the rental. Shoved under the mattress until he got a chance to throw it away somewhere outside. Still, it was evidence, wasn't it? Proof that there had been questions. Proof that there had been fears.

It had to be to determine his relation to Sutton, I thought.

It can't be for Freya. It just can't.

I stumbled to the bathroom, tossed the empty box on the floor, then knelt against the tile, grimy and due for a clean. I whipped open the vanity's cabinet doors, pushed aside toilet bowl cleaner and Windex, paper towel rolls and a box of tampons, a pack of fresh sponges and a spray bottle of Lime-A-Way, eager to see what I knew must be there, to hold it in my hands.

Max never cleaned the bathroom. Never in all the time

we'd been together. He did other things—he pulled his weight, I swear—but he never did that. This place had felt safe. A lockbox made of ammonia and chlorine instead of fireproof steel.

My fingers hit my target, and I retrieved the box. Discreetly packaged in brown corrugated cardboard, but addressed to me nonetheless. I opened it up, found the box contained within, and took in the differences.

The box I'd found under the mattress was green, whereas this one was yellow.

The box I'd found under the mattress had a bearded man on it; the man on mine was clean-shaven.

The box I'd found under the mattress showed a girl, not a boy.

The box I'd found under the mattress said *Your DNA Home Paternity Test*, and this one said *Family Solutions Testing*.

And yet, they were essentially the same.

Between me and Max, we had the remnants of two different paternity tests—one I never thought he'd find, one he never thought I'd find. The irony was almost poetic.

Carefully, I opened mine, flipped past the paperwork I'd filled out on the floor of this bathroom, fingered the sterile collection containers, one holding Max's hairs, fished from his brush that always sat on the bathroom counter, one holding Freya's, plucked from her tiny, fragile head.

I hadn't had the guts to send the test back yet. I hadn't had the courage to open Pandora's box.

I closed it up carefully, handling it like I was on a bomb squad, like the secrets within could be triggered any moment, obliterating everything I had left, then replaced all the cleaning products and shut the cabinet doors.

Molly hadn't put the timing together, but why would she? She'd only just learned about what happened with Bryan, and besides, you didn't keep up with other people's calendars like you did your own. And no one was aware of calendars like a pregnant woman.

Only I knew all the possibilities.

I knew I should have told Max. I should have told him that first morning after waking up in Bryan's hotel room, regret and shame and a hangover swimming through my stomach, liquor likely still coursing through my veins. But Max was out of town, traveling with the band. I didn't want to break the news of what had happened, tell him over the phone I'd gotten drunk and gone to Bryan's hotel room. When Max got home a few days later, I was so happy—so relieved—to see him, and our bodies found each other's almost immediately, and then I lay there, knowing that if I was going to tell him, I should have done it before we slept together. I should have done it the moment he walked in the door.

In those in-between days, the guilt built, of course it did, but in ways it felt like it all had been nothing more than a temporary moment of insanity, like it could go away if I didn't think of it—ever. I knew, deep down, that I had no real feelings for Bryan. That we were friendly, yes, that he was good-looking, sure, but it wasn't ever something I'd really wanted: it was nothing more than a horrible, drunken mistake. I had to protect the most precious thing to me in the world—me and Max.

And then, the missed period. Then, the pregnancy test. The horror as I watched those two lines appear in that window. I called Molly, told her I was terrified, but she thought it was only around the pregnancy, not the details of conception.

I did consider terminating and not even telling him, but in all likelihood, it was Max's. He and I had slept together only the day before that night with Bryan, a few days after when Max returned from his trip, and again the day after that. According to my calculations, my frantic googling, it was most likely I'd gotten pregnant the week before what happened with Bryan anyway. Besides, Max and I never used condoms—I was on the pill, a pill that had failed in one way or another, apparently—and surely Bryan would have wrapped it up for a drunken hookup.

So I told Max about the pregnancy, I even told him about my reservations about having a child, but he was so thrilled, so over the moon, I couldn't tell him the whole of it. How could I? In all likelihood, it was nothing. Nothing at all.

And when Freya was born, god, she looked so much like Max, she really did. The point of her chin. The arch of her eyebrows. The adorable little lines of her nostrils.

In the hospital, I felt like I could handle it. The nurses were there, checking in on us every hour, and the nursery was a refuge, allowing Max and me to get a bit of sleep.

But then, those first days at home were so hard, and Freya wanted so much, nursing hour in and hour out, never taking a break. It felt like hell, a hell of my own making, a hell I never would have chosen if I could have gone back.

That feeling built and built, and in my dark hours, feeding her deep into the night, I would look at her features, and I would wonder. I knew the timing wasn't quite right for her to be Bryan's—I knew in my heart she was Max's—but at the same time, I didn't know anything, did I? My world was coming apart at the seams, breast milk leaking through the cracks.

So I ordered the test just after we arrived in Kingston,

hoping to put any lingering doubt behind me—if I ever got the guts to send the thing in, at least.

Now, I stared at the box that had held the other test—Max's test—the most terrible idea plaguing my mind.

Had Max figured it out? Had he discovered my secret somehow? Suspected what had happened, doubted his own connection to Freya?

Had he ordered this test, plucked his own hairs, and Freya's, too? Only he had had the guts to send it all in when I didn't, and now it was out there, processing in some lab? What if this had nothing to do with Grace, with Sutton, at all?

Or what if . . . what if this was the discovery that had sent him running to Grace in the first place? What if this was the missing piece that made everything make sense?

The chance was slim, I knew it, and yet I had to know, and only one person could possibly give me an answer.

I grabbed my phone, my fingers working quickly. I didn't have his number, but in a few minutes on Facebook, I found him anyway.

I sent him two messages, hoping and praying he checked this account.

Can you meet me? I need to talk to you right now.

And then, to be safe.

Somewhere public this time.

33

9:45 p.m.

"WHAT D'YA NEED?"

The bartender was a man of middling age whose hair was clipped neatly, and he wore a standard-issue black button-down shirt. Behind him, liquors of every type lined the walls on leveled, mirrored shelves—the place was a far cry from the Three Crows, even though it was only four or five blocks away.

I straightened up as I scanned a paper menu secured onto a faux-leather folio. What my body needed was a nice cup of coffee—or, hell, a good night of sleep—but the rest of me needed escape.

"Dirty martini," I said. "Hendrick's, if you have it. Extra olives."

"We do," he said. A slight hesitation, and then he rested his palms on the bar, looking at me earnestly. "Listen. I hate to even say this because it's none of my business, but are you on your own tonight?"

"No," I said, my shoulders tensing. "I'm meeting some-one."

"Okay. Good." The man smiled bashfully. "I feel I have to tell any women out tonight to be careful, especially if you're drinking. Not sure if you saw the news, but a woman about your age was murdered only a few blocks from here. Nothing like this has ever happened right in the middle of town. We're all a little shaken."

My face flushed, deep shame filling me up. Here he was worrying about me, and yet my own partner was at least somehow caught in the midst of tragedy. "Thanks," I said. "I'll keep that in mind."

The bartender nodded, then set off to make my drink, grabbing a stainless-steel shaker, filling a martini glass with ice, retrieving Hendrick's from the highest shelf, and grabbing a small bottle of vermouth. I glanced around. The place, his suggestion, was the sort of cozy and nice that wasn't trying too hard—or too shabby, either—a place I would have picked myself. A burnished wooden bar of some dark sort of wood stretched across one side of the room. The interior was finished in shades of deep green and smoky blue, and there was a casual glamour about it. The only other patrons were a couple—on a first date, perhaps—in the corner, and a pair of men my dad's age who looked practically glued to the barstools on the short end of the bar—the place's very own Cliff and Norm. There were no women on their own—or even together—and I wondered how much that had to do with the news that had just been released.

A text popped up from Liana.

Hope you're getting some space to decompress. Not to be a total mom about it, but I'll wait up for you. I don't like you out on your own with this murder still unsolved.

The bartender splashed in liquids and began to vigorously shake, and I looked at the time, then turned back to the bar's door. He should be here by now, and I wondered if he'd lost his nerve, if he wasn't coming, if I was the enemy now, and I'd have to sit with the uncertainty on my own, ask myself, *What if what if what if*?

What if Max knows what a fuckup you really are? What if Max found out the truth? That you don't even know for sure that he's Freya's father?

I checked my email, wondering if Molly's missive had gotten to my parents or if they were making good on their vow to "disconnect" for this trip. Perhaps I'd get something in the early hours of the morning, during Freya's first waking, while I was feeding her a bottle of formula or warmed milk to account for the Hendrick's that would inevitably still be in my body.

The bartender presented the concoction, centered perfectly on a black cocktail napkin, four olives speared onto a toothpick, the upward slope of the glass sweating with condensation.

"Thank you," I said. I lifted it to my lips, taking the smallest of sips. It was everything I wanted: salty and cool, strong and a tiny bit sweet from the vermouth, from the floral undertones of the gin. "It's perfect."

As if on cue, a scrape of chair legs behind me.

Daniel.

His hair had been brushed, and he'd put on fresh clothing since I'd seen him. Perhaps he'd showered, perhaps he'd done something to clean himself up. And still, there in his eyes, the unmistakable signs of grief. A puffiness to his lids. Bags beneath them. A blank stare of loss.

Was it real, or was it all an act?

I wanted to believe in Max's innocence—I loved him so very much, he was mine, and I thought he always would be—but sometimes it felt like the cards were stacking up so high on the other side, tipping a scale I had no control of. Even Liana couldn't dismiss the possibility of an affair with Grace. And Liana was determined to defend Max, any way she could.

Daniel raised his eyebrows, acknowledging my presence, but didn't say anything more, just ordered a scotch and soda and leaned against the bar, as if impatient for the numbing effect of the alcohol on its way.

Though it was a simple order, the bartender prepared it with the same attention to detail, the same easy swagger, as he'd used for my martini, and we stood there, the two of us silent, questions and secrets and betraying (betrayed?) partners like ghosts between us.

"Should we go to a table?" I asked, as soon as his drink was up. Daniel nodded.

I led the way, and for a moment, liquor already going to my head, it felt so familiar, this ritual, this dance. How many dates had followed this exact pattern? Belly up to the bar for drinks, then cozy into a corner to get to know each other a little better. There was a high to it, to all those dates before Max, like being tipsy on too much wine, even if the hangover came quicker than it ever did with alcohol, the promise wearing off quickly, leaving disappointment in its wake.

Then Max came along, and he changed all that. With him, the high hadn't worn off after one date or two or three or four hundred. It had lasted.

Lasted until the rug was ripped right out from under me.

Daniel and I nestled into the booth, his hand clinging to

his drink as if it were a security blanket. He took a sip and set it down, then took another sip immediately. Security blanket? More like a pacifier.

"Thank you for meeting me," I said. "And I'm sorry for running off so quickly this afternoon. I was in shock."

Daniel's eyes flashed to mine, and I expected to see anger, but there was pity instead. "Of course you were," he said. "He hurt you, too. He hurt all of us. And now he has my son. And if there's anything you can tell me that can help me find him, I'll take whatever chance I can get."

My heart beat mercilessly, and I twisted the glass along its circle of condensation, avoiding Daniel's gaze. What would this man do if he figured out that I was complicit now, too?

"I don't know where Max is," I said finally. Truthfully. "But I know he would never hurt a child."

You can't say take *anymore, can you? Because he would. And he did. And now you're covering for him. As if you haven't fucked things up enough already.*

Daniel took another sip of his drink. "It's always the same, isn't it?"

My eyebrows narrowed. "What is?"

"There are two kinds of men. Bad ones and good ones. Men like Max, and men like me."

"Max isn't—"

"Let me finish," he said. "*Please.* Men like Max, they show up, say the right things, and they give their whole song and dance. Hell, maybe *they* even think they're good, in some twisted way, but when they don't get what they want, that all changes."

Max's words rang in my head: *I had no choice.* As if he was some Good Samaritan, like that old man leaning over me, outside the church this afternoon, someone who just *had* to get involved. But Max could have chosen me. Chosen Freya.

Why would he choose you when you've lied to him from the start?

"And you know why they get away with it?" Daniel went on. "Because they prey on people who want to see the best in others. People like you. People like Grace. It was something I loved about her, how she was always so willing to forgive." His voice cracked at the end. "But it's what got her killed."

I swallowed back my own objections, because for now, they were nothing more than words. And in this moment, what I needed to know more than anything was whether Max had found out about Bryan, whether he'd suspected he might not be Freya's father. It somehow felt so core, so key, to understanding everything else.

"Do you know—" I finally looked up. "Do you know if Max and Grace ever got a paternity test? To prove that Max was Sutton's father?"

Daniel cocked his head to the side. He stared at me a moment, as if reassessing me, as if I were smarter than he'd given me credit for. Then he adjusted himself in the booth, reached into his back pocket, and came up with something square and white—papers, folded into quarters.

"Yes," he said, setting them on the table before me. "He did—*they* did. I would have shown you earlier, but I didn't find this myself until a couple of hours ago."

Hands shaking, I unfolded the pages. On the first one, a logo sat on top, the same design I'd seen on the empty box I'd found:

Your DNA Home Paternity Test

For a moment, I felt relief. The test had been used to determine Sutton's parentage, not Freya's. Max didn't know about Bryan. He didn't know my secret, my awful shame. He didn't know what a terrible person I truly was.

But on the other side of that relief was horror.

My eyes scanned the paper, devouring the info as quickly as I could.

Client: Maximillian Bosch
Mother: Grace Akins
Child: Sutton Akins
Alleged Father: Maximillian Bosch

There was all sorts of other information, case numbers and time stamps and sterile, clinical terms like *mouth swab*, ID numbers that had something to do with genetic markers and matches.

Among all of that, two things stood out.

The date, just this past week.

And the "conclusion," the damning parts in bold caps, impossible to miss.

*Based on our DNA analysis, Maximillian Bosch **IS THE BIOLOGICAL FATHER** of Sutton Akins.*

34

10:11 p.m.

DANIEL SIPPED HIS DRINK PATIENTLY WHILE I LOOKED OVER the report, all five pages of it: through the appendix, through the markers the company looks for, through the explanation of the process, through pie charts and illustrations, graphs used to back up the fact that was suddenly beyond a shadow of a doubt—or with 99 percent accuracy, as the report itself proclaimed.

I looked over it all, knowing that this was what I would be looking at if I ever sent my own test in. Knowing that, for now, it didn't even matter. For now, I had my answer, a foregone conclusion:

Max had another child. A child before he ever had Freya. That photo of Sutton, a mini facsimile of Max, the resemblance hadn't been in my head. It was real.

A week earlier, it would have been impossible to believe, and now, here it was—proof, in my hands—and proof ringing in my ears that Max didn't just have a child, he had Sutton. A motherless boy whose photos I'd pored over on Grace's profile. A boy caught up in unspeakable things.

How much longer?

I folded the papers back into a neat square, then pressed them beneath my palm, as if I could mash them into the wooden table, as if they could become a bit of the ephemera of this place, like an abandoned coaster or one of the napkins that the bartender had slipped beneath our drinks.

"I don't understand," I said. "If Max had known he was Sutton's father all along, like you said, then why would he have needed a test?"

Daniel sighed. "Grace . . . she put my name on Sutton's birth certificate. Max left her long before the birth, and it seemed simpler than having to go through the whole adoption process. To give Max any of his parental rights back, Grace and Max would have to petition the court to have that changed. To do that, you have to submit genetic proof."

I shook my head. "You're saying the man who supposedly abandoned Grace and Sutton wants them back so much that he's willing to jump through all these legal hoops? Is he an absent father or a present one?" I asked. "You can't have it both ways."

"I think he's a man who changed his mind. Who, for whatever reason, wanted to start fresh with Grace and Sutton. And as much as I hate the idea, I think Grace at least entertained it. I know it always bothered her that Sutton had no connection to his bio dad, that we didn't even really tell our friends or acquaintances the truth. She knew we were going to have to tell Sutton his history at some point, because once he got old enough, he could do one of those DNA tests and find out anyway. So maybe that's what led to their reconnection, but I think she had second thoughts about what she was doing with

Max. I think she changed her mind, and Max wasn't okay with that."

Daniel's theory was outlandish, but at the same time, I didn't have a better one to offer. I knew Max had Sutton, I just didn't know why.

"Have the police seen all this?" I asked, changing tack.

"I called them as soon as I found it, a couple hours ago. I made copies and scanned them straight to the station."

I released my grip, pushed the papers toward him. He adjusted in his seat and returned them to his back pocket. "After you left, I could barely sit still," he said. "I tore our bedroom apart, and I found this deep in the back of her closet. I knew I needed something to prove what I was saying, more than my story of the events." He sighed. "You know the police hardly trust me. I'm the husband. I'm the one who didn't call anyone when she didn't come home on Friday night, who went to sleep when my wife and kid weren't there. Who didn't even know Sutton was gone until later. I knew there had to be something, *anything*, to back up my story. And then, there it was."

I swallowed, trying to focus. "Was there anything else? Anything else you found?"

"No," Daniel said. "Only this." He took another sip of his drink, and his whole body seemed to crumple. "I wish she had come to me, the second Max got back in touch. I wish she'd shared everything with me, instead of . . . of doing *this* behind my back. I should have known something was off, questioned why she was always going off to that stupid bar across the street, the one she knew I hated and would never set foot in." He turned up his nose, as if he'd smelled something rancid. "She didn't have to go running back to Max's arms just because he showed up, wanting another chance. And even if she made some mistakes, I would have found a way to forgive her. No matter what happened, I never would have stopped fighting for our family." Daniel's shoulders hunched, and a sob escaped his throat. "If she'd only known how much I loved her, how much I loved Sutton, none of this would have happened. Max wouldn't have been able to take her from me."

I PAID MY bill and exited the bar, leaving Daniel there, still nursing his drink, feeling the pull—almost gravitational—to be away from this man, from his messy grief and his horrible theories, from those papers now tucked inside his back pocket.

Outside, I sucked in the fresh air, like if I breathed deep enough, I could change the facts of the situation. I stumbled forward, the martini already going straight to my head, even stronger than the gin and sodas I'd had the previous night.

In a few blocks, I reached Wall Street, the rainbow crosswalks slicked with a light drizzle. I hated them, suddenly. I hated any stupid Instagram photo I'd shared of them. I hated all the pictures I'd shared of Max, holding Freya, feeding her, cuddling close to me in bed, her tiny body between ours.

I hated it all, because it was a lie, wasn't it?

All of it was a lie.

Gin going to my head, drizzle soaking through my coat, for a moment, all I wanted was to cut and run, leave Max and his secrets behind. But who would I turn to if I did? I was a mother now, and mothers needed whole *villages* to raise children. And the first person in your village, it was supposed to be your partner.

I knew that women did it all the time—alone.

But they're better women than you. They can do it. You can't. You couldn't even do it when Max was right there with you, right there by your side.

After all, who were we, Max and me? Nothing more than a pair of liars, trading mistruths like other couples traded morning kisses.

But as I stumbled forward, I knew it deep down. I didn't hate him. I loved him as much as ever. And I prayed there was something—some explanation—to hold on to.

I gazed to the right, down the street. That way led back to the rental, to where I should be, guzzling water, telling Liana I'd cleared my head, checking the freezer for a perfect-sized pack of milk and trying to get a few precious hours of sleep before Freya woke again.

To the left was that other place. Daniel and Grace's home, and just across the street, Three Crows Tavern.

My heart gave a tiny leap, the sort you got when you were a teen, taking a sip of liquor, a drag of a cigarette for the first time. Doing something that probably would only hurt you but jumping in headfirst anyway.

I hesitated only a moment, and then I turned left.

Chasing answers.

Chasing Max.

35

10:36 p.m.

THREE CROWS WAS ALL BUT EMPTY.

And in its emptiness, it looked even trashier, even divier, than it had the previous night, as if the people packed in had covered over its flaws like cheap drugstore concealer.

The news had cast a pall over the whole place—only one or two guys were scattered around the tables, and it was even harder to picture Grace or Max inside. I supposed that was what made it the perfect cover. A place Daniel would never set foot in. The sort of place I wouldn't, either.

The bartender was a woman this time, younger and freer than me, with blond highlights, red lipstick, and a white midriff T-shirt that showed off a belly-button ring and a nut-brown tan, even though we were barely out of winter. She seemed more suited to Florida than upstate New York, and she smiled as I took my choice of unoccupied seats. "Bud Lights and PBRs are two dollars, well drinks two-for-one."

"I thought that was your Saturday-night special," I said.

She laughed. "It's our every-night special."

I nodded, then ordered a Bud Light, more to have something to hold than for any other reason, the martini still swirling around in my head.

She turned and squatted before a small fridge, revealing a lower back tattoo—a rising sun—and grabbed the bottle.

She twisted the cap off, then handed it to me, setting it atop a flimsy napkin. I pushed a few bills her way, and she smiled, tapped some buttons on the register, and tucked the tip into her pocket. I cleared my throat, knowing this was my best chance. Another bartender, another opportunity.

"Is it always this empty on Sundays?" I asked.

She raised an eyebrow, then shook her head. "Not usually."

My heart beat hard against my ribs. "I assume it's because of what happened."

She rolled her eyes. "You know, Dave doesn't want us talking about it, but, *hello*, it was in the *Daily Freeman*. People know what happened. People *deserve* to know what happened. And even yesterday, gossip was swirling. Three different friends texted me to ask what I knew."

I snaked my fingers around the bottle. "I guess it's good that it's finally hit the news, then. No need to pretend."

"Not good for tips, but yeah," she said. "Better for people to know."

"Er, I'm actually a friend of Grace's," I said, finding the lie like you'd find a pack of tissues in your purse. "I know she was here that night, that she was meeting someone."

"Right," she said. "The dad."

I reared back. Had this woman, this girl, known that Max had a son long before I had? The thought was dreadful. Disgusting.

"You *knew* him?" I asked.

"Only from the bar. Did you?"

"No," I said quickly. "Just in connection to Grace."

She shrugged and began cutting up a lime.

"Were you here on Friday?" I asked, desperate not to lose her.

The girl kept slicing but eventually shook her head. "Not me, thank god. I know the killer was probably someone Grace knew and all, either her husband or that guy she came here with, but still. A murderer out, stalking back alleys. Scares the shit out of you. That's why I thought it was crazy that Dave was trying so hard to keep it quiet."

I took a small sip for courage. The beer tasted like college and bad decisions. "I'm trying to find out more about Grace's . . . relationship to this guy she was meeting. It's all so unexpected, so hard to comprehend."

The girl stopped cutting and looked up at me, perhaps noting the genuine grief in my eyes. The emotion was real, even if the facts were slightly different. "You're not a reporter, are you?"

"No," I said.

"Because I don't want my name showing up in some article. This job pays my tuition. I'm getting my master's. It's not cheap, you know."

"I swear," I said. "I'm just a friend."

She glanced back and forth. There was barely anyone here, and that counted in my favor. "What do you want to know, exactly?"

"You must have seen them together before, right? Grace and . . . this man?"

She tugged at a loop of her jeans. "Sure."

"More than once?" I asked.

"Yeah," she said with a shrug. She nodded to the back corner. "Last few Wednesdays, she would come in with someone else—a girlfriend—but later on she'd wind up talking to this guy. They'd have a drink, usually no more than one or two, then leave—always separately."

I nodded. It tracked with all the WhatsApp messages I'd read. "I hate to pry, but did either of them talk to you? Tell you why they were meeting?"

"No," she said. "That's not really my business anyway."

There was no one else to serve, but the girl's eyes darted about, looking for an exit.

"How did you know he was the father, then?" I asked. "If you never heard them talking?"

"Oh," the girl said, her eyes widening. "When I was making his drink, he was always on his phone, flipping through photos. Checking some video monitor to see the baby sleeping. I asked him about the baby—I love kids; well, I love kids that aren't mine—and he said he was a new dad. Had a little one at home. Funny name, too. Fiona or something, but more uncommon. Frida, maybe? Something like that."

Freya, I half wanted to scream. *Freya*.

"He seemed absolutely crazy about her, the way he was always looking at her photos."

My heart ached. He *was* crazy about Freya. He *is*.

"I thought he was just a regular guy," the bartender said. "And now people are saying he skipped town? That the police are *looking* for him. Now, that's a surprise." She went back to cutting her limes. "I mean, freaking out and meeting some woman at a bar because you have spit-up on you day and night, that's one thing, but killing her? It's a little hard to buy. I didn't talk to him much, besides to make his drinks, but he

looked so nice, so . . . normal. He really didn't seem the type."
She paused then, pursed her lips. "But I guess that's what
they always say, after something like this happens. Neighbors, you know. That he didn't seem the type. I guess you
never really know someone, do you?"

"No," I said. "No, you really don't."

She grabbed a Tupperware container, tossed the slices in,
but I couldn't leave it at that. I had to know more. I had to
hear it from someone who had seen them together, at least.
Who'd watched their meetings unfold.

"I know this is kind of forward, but do you think he and
Grace were sleeping together?"

The girl raised an eyebrow, then pressed the top of the
container, sealing it tight. "Usually if two people come in
here, it's to—well, you know . . . It's a precursor."

"Sure," I said.

She crossed her arms. "But I mean, this past Wednesday,
it was pretty clear."

My heart raced, and I felt like my world was about to split
in two again.

"Why?" I asked. "What happened?"

"This woman came in, and lord was she mad. He got an
earful, that's for sure."

"I'm sorry," I said. "I don't understand. Grace was mad?"

"No," the girl said, and she delivered it with all the matter-
of-factness of a report on the weather.

"Not Grace. The guy's wife."

MONDAY, MARCH 18

36

3:02 a.m.

THERE WAS ANOTHER WOMAN, TOO.

The thought was there the moment I opened my eyes, Freya's cries waking me from what little sleep I'd managed to grab hold of.

"Hold on, baby," I said as she writhed in her swaddle. "Hold on, I have to make you a bottle."

In the kitchen, I grabbed frozen milk, filled a bowl of warm water, waited.

The bartender's words had been shocking, and my initial reaction—*What did you say?*—was met with little more than a casual shrug—*I mean, I guess I don't know that they were married. But by how mad she was, I assumed she was his baby's mother.* I'd entreated her for a physical description, anything, but it was clear in an instant I'd pushed her too far. *This is getting weird, okay? Now I see why Dave told us not to talk about this stuff. If you want another drink, let me know.*

Now, staring at a package of frozen milk, willing it to melt faster, I tried to make sense of the little she'd given me.

There was another woman. Not just Grace, but someone else. Some *angry* woman. Someone who thought she had claim to Max's affections, too.

I bobbed the milk up and down, wondering how harmful it would be to chuck the thing in the microwave. Freya wailed from upstairs, my boobs pulsing at her cries.

"I heard Freya crying."

I jolted at the sound, turned to find Liana.

"Is everything okay?" she asked.

No, I wanted to scream. *No, everything is not okay. Max is the biological father of a missing child.* For all I knew, Max could have been fucking all the eligible women in Kingston, New York.

"She's hungry," I managed. "And I had too much to drink, so I can't feed her."

"Oh," Liana said. "Is there anything I can do?"

"No," I said. "This is almost ready. Go back to sleep. Please. Sorry she woke you."

Liana stood rooted to the spot. "Did something *happen* tonight?" she asked. "When you were out? You seem upset."

Part of me wanted to tell her everything, but I knew it would do no good. Liana would find a way to defend Max. She'd take his side, just like Molly said. "Did something happen? I'm raising a child alone because my partner is gone and possibly wanted for murder and kidnapping, so yes, I'm upset."

Liana's eyes widened, but she quickly composed herself. "Right," she said. "Right. I'm sorry. That was a shit thing to say."

My eyes began to well, and Freya's cries somehow got even louder, cascading down the stairs, swirling around us.

"No," I said. "No, *I'm* sorry. I shouldn't snap at you. You've been so much help."

Liana rushed forward, wrapping me in a hug, but the pressure only hurt, making my boobs ache more.

"I have to feed her," I said, pulling away.

"Okay," Liana said, turning for the stairs. "I'll see you in the morning."

I snatched the packet of milk, emptied it into the bottle, twisted the cap, and tested a squeeze on my wrist—it would do.

Upstairs, I rushed to Freya, who was angrier than ever at having been left so long.

I'm sorry, I wanted to tell her. I'm sorry you got a shit mother and a father who abandoned you and I'm sorry you have to suffer like this. I'm sorry we can't be better for you.

I picked her up instead, forcing some calm into my voice. "It's okay, baby girl," I said robotically. "It's okay. I'm here."

Her cries stopped the second the bottle was in her mouth, and for a tiny moment, holding my baby in my arms, doing what I needed to do, I felt like a mother   a real one.

She went back to sleep easily, but though I was exhausted, I couldn't. My boobs ached, still desperate to be emptied, and so back downstairs, I hooked up my pump, watched as the plastic flanges, the ridiculous contraptions that should be attached to a cow, not a human, began to leach the milk from my ducts, milk that would be poured down the drain.

And then something wild happened.

My phone, turned over on one arm of the chair, began to ring.

Not a text. Not a notification.

A phone call.

I flipped it over, breaths coming faster now, and for a moment, I thought maybe it was Max again, and all I wanted was to hear his voice on the other line, so I could tell him just how much I hated him.

The number wasn't one I recognized, and it had a plus sign at the front. An international call.

"Hello?"

"Janie." Of course the voice wasn't his, it was hers, and it was warm and open and caring, seeped with every bowl of chicken soup she'd ever brought me, every hug, every kiss on the cheek, every time she'd told me, *It's all going to be okay.* For a moment, none of our complicated history mattered. She was my mother, and it was good to hear her voice.

"Janie," she said again, and fresh tears sprung to my eyes. "Janie, we just saw Molly's email. We couldn't figure out how to make a call on Skype like you told us, so we're calling from the office of the ship. Oh god, what happened?"

The flanges tugged at my breasts, and I watched as milk streamed out. "I woke to Freya crying on Friday, and he was . . . he was gone. And now a woman has been murdered, and her child is missing. And . . . I didn't know who he was at all. It was all a lie. Everything. It's all . . . it's all ruined."

"It's not ruined," my mother said. "You have sweet, beautiful Freya. That's all that matters now."

"It's *not* all that matters," I said, anger surging within me, bubbling up beneath all the betrayal and hurt. "I'm alone. And nothing is going to change that. And it's not like, it's not like—"

It's not like I can rely on you.

"I'm on my own. I don't even have a job anymore. I'm

completely alone, and I have no one. No one to turn to. Nowhere to go."

"It's okay," my mother said, her voice calm and still and oh so motherly. "It's all going to be okay. It always works out. I truly believe that, Janie. Things always work out in the end."

They work out because I help you. They work out because you wait for me to save you like I always do.

"Besides," my mother went on, "Molly is there, yes?"

"Yes, and she wants me to go with her. She wants me to put all this behind me. Go back to Brooklyn."

"And what about Max's parents?"

"They're saying I should come to Scarsdale and stay with them."

"What do you want, Janie?" she asked. "Because those are both good options."

Tears coursed down my cheeks. I wanted to be taken care of, for once. By Max, sure, but by my parents, too. I wanted them to be the parents I could always rely on, not the ones that relied on me. Maybe if I'd ever experienced that myself, I'd know how to be a mother to Freya. But I'd spent so many years giving to my parents, dealing with their own dramas, I didn't have anything left.

Shit had hit the fan. My life had imploded. But I couldn't run home to them. I couldn't run home to anyone. I was it.

I was all Freya had—and would ever have.

"I don't know. I don't know what to do. I wish . . . I just wish you were here."

A hesitation, and in it, a confirmation. That I couldn't count on them, in the end. I already knew it, but it hurt all the same.

"Of course," my mother said finally. "Of course that's what we'll do. We'll come . . . we'll come to New York."

"You don't have to," I said. "It's fine. *Really.*"

"No, you're our daughter, and you need us more than you've ever needed us before. I'm sorry . . . I'm only sorry I didn't suggest it myself."

The tears came even harder then, and I gasped to catch my breath.

"Janie," my mother said, her voice soft. "Janie, I know I've made a lot of mistakes. I know I've leaned on you more than a mother ever should. But I love you more than anything," she said. "Please don't ever doubt that."

On the other side of the phone, out on a sea thousands of miles away, I could hear her crying, too.

"Let me take care of you as best as I can. I'm still your mother, after all."

37

9:48 a.m.

MORNING AGAIN. FREYA AGAIN. A NIGHT OF BROKEN, AWFUL sleep—again. A night alone. Again.

I tugged at the Velcro of Freya's swaddle, and her arms popped up, free and exposed, and she stretched with her whole body, a butterfly emerging from a cocoon.

Wordless, I undid the top snap and pulled down the zipper, exposing her pale bare tummy, the diaper I'd put on somewhere between five and six a.m., when she'd woken again, poopy and upset. Carefully I pulled out each arm, each leg, pudgy but fragile.

From the dresser, I grabbed a cotton onesie, pale pink, then froze at the words embroidered on the front: *Daddy's Best Girl.*

It had been a gift from one of Brenda's friends, the shower bursting with stuff like that. Every shade of pink and each piece of clothing emblazoned with slogans that were either cloyingly sweet or trying way too hard. *Cheeks for Days. Shine like Mama. Welcome to My Crib.*

Now I dropped the onesie, grabbed a plain black one

instead, and carried her to the changing table, blinking to keep my eyes open.

Even though my parents were dropping everything to come here, that wouldn't be for a few days. They weren't set to even disembark at the next stop—Naples—until Wednesday. Then they had to get a flight back to New York, which meant a train or a flight to Rome, another plane to New York City, and if I stayed up here, a car rental to make the two-hour drive to Kingston. Even after hearing my mother's tender words, I still found it hard to believe they'd actually make it through all those steps. I rescued them, not the other way around. They weren't going to magically change overnight, no matter how bad things had gotten for me.

I pulled the onesie over Freya's head, wiggled her arms through, and snapped the bottom before slipping a pair of booties on her feet. I pulled her into the crook of my arm—she somehow felt heavier, more substantial than she had even the day before; she was growing so fast—and walked carefully down the stairs.

It was quiet—Liana must be still sleeping—and I put Freya in the swing, set the vibrations just like she liked them, and started on a pot of decaf. I was filling the carafe with water when my phone buzzed with a text from Molly: a link to the *Daily Freeman*.

This just published. They name Max. I'm still here. Right down the road. Come whenever you need me.

I tapped the link, my heart jolting. I gripped the phone tightly, the pads of my fingers turning white, waiting to see which shoe would drop now.

His face caught my eye first.

A photo from his Facebook, one I'd taken on a trip to Zion National Park. A close-up shot, one that obscured his surroundings, the glorious canyons we'd hiked through that morning, the CamelBak strapped on his shoulders, filled with beef jerky and granola bars and the extra layer I'd brought but had shed very quickly.

The way they'd cropped the photo made it look so strange, highlighting the sweat on his brow, the far-off look in his eyes, the forced smile (Max never liked smiling for pictures), and I wondered if even that was done to make him look guilty.

In the end, the photo didn't so much matter, did it?

It was the words that were important—those awful, excruciating words, written in bold beneath.

POLICE ISSUE MANHUNT IN CASE OF MURDERED KINGSTON MOM

KINGSTON, N.Y.—City police have identified a key suspect in the homicide of Grace Akins, according to Kingston police chief Arnold Agnew.

Maximillian Bosch, a 39-year-old music teacher, is wanted in connection with the murder of Mrs. Akins, whose body was found Saturday morning behind Kingston's Three Crows Tavern, and the kidnapping of her six-year-old son, Sutton Akins.

Mr. Bosch, who lives in Brooklyn but had been staying in Kingston, has not been seen since Friday evening, according to city police. He had been a person of interest in the investigation but, after the discovery of what Agnew referred to as "key evidence," has now been named a suspect. The department is working with the state troopers and federal police as well as border control to apprehend the suspect and find the child. An Amber

Alert is being issued, and police are asking all residents of the tri state area and beyond to look out for a black Toyota RAV-4, license plate 6NV-4129.

When asked why it took two full days to issue an Amber Alert, Agnew said that the details of the missing child were "previously unreported by the child's guardian."

Daniel Akins, the husband of the deceased, did not respond to requests for comment.

Agnew asks anyone with information about the homicide and kidnapping to contact the Kingston Police.

I stared in horror as Liana rushed down the stairs, her phone in her hand, too.

"Did you see this?" she asked. "I just got a Google Alert."

I nodded.

"I don't understand," Liana said, shaking her head, her hair still a mess, makeup smeared beneath her eyes. "What could they possibly have found? What is this key evidence? Max would never—"

And then, cutting her off, an awful *beep-beep-beep*ing on both of our phones.

I stared at the notification, contained in a gray box.

AMBER ALERT

Beneath it, the details of Max's rental car, the same ones I'd rattled off to Duncan myself.

Oh god oh god oh god.

I fumbled with my phone, tapped at the alert to stop the beeping. Liana did, too.

But there was no silence, only the solid *thump-thump* of knocking at the door.

The police. Coming to get you. If anything happens to Sutton, it's all on you.

My body jolted, preparing for another fight.

Unlike Liana, I *did* understand. I knew Max had Sutton. I'd known since yesterday. And I hadn't said a thing.

I'm sorry, Grace, I thought. I'm sorry if I failed your son. I'm sorry if my own motherly instincts weren't enough to save him. I'm sorry if I didn't choose the right path, selfishly kept the information to myself. No matter what you did, you didn't deserve this.

Liana looked on the verge of crumpling, a delicate flower about to lose its petals. I pushed past her and went to the door, realizing as I did that it could be press. The media circus was only just beginning.

I peered through the window to see Officer Duncan. Slowly, I opened the door.

"Can I come in?" she said, her voice firm and unyielding, making it clear that it was anything but a request. "We need to talk."

38

10:02 a.m.

I OFFERED DUNCAN COFFEE AND WAS SURPRISED WHEN SHE said yes.

I poured the cups a little too full and brought them to the living room, my hands shaking so the liquid singed me. Liana was up in an instant, rushing back to the kitchen, returning with paper towels, dabbing at the mess, taking care of me like she had been for two days now.

Duncan stood to help, too, taking a cup from my hand.

We found our places as if this were a different sort of visit, only our body language betraying us—Liana's foot tapping nervously, my hands shaking, Duncan's eyebrows knitted together in thought.

Duncan lifted the mug to her lips, took a small sip. "She's in a good mood today," she said, nodding to Freya, who rocked back and forth, oblivious. Happy for a few minutes, so long as "Mary Had a Little Lamb" was playing.

"For now," I said, and I felt a prickle of rage inside me, knowing that I could buy myself even more Happy Freya

Time if I had that damn llama pacifier, suddenly overcome by all the little ways Max had hurt us.

Duncan leaned forward, almost like a friend would. "How are you hanging in?"

"No," I said, shaking my head. "Please don't do this. Don't pretend like you care about me. Just tell me whatever it is you need to say."

"I'm a mother, too," Duncan said.

"And what does that matter?" Liana interjected. "What does that have to do with Max?"

Duncan didn't give Liana so much as a look. Her eyes stayed trained on me. "It must be hard. I can't even imagine."

"No," I said. "You can't."

Duncan set down her coffee and folded her hands together. "You may have seen the news. And I imagine you got the Amber Alert."

"We just did," I said. "When did this happen?"

"Last night we found something that . . . accelerated things," Duncan said. She leaned over, digging in her leather bag and pulling out a folder. From it, she retrieved a color photograph. "You recognize this?"

An evidence photo. I could tell by the L-shaped ruler that edged the side of the image. The background looked like concrete—or asphalt—the charcoal-gray foundation of a sidewalk—an alley.

There, in the middle, a piece of fabric. Rumpled and rectangular.

A bold teal border, impeccably stitched. With three letters embroidered onto the bottom left corner: *M-A-X*.

M-A-X spells Max, I sang in my head, as if I were Elmo on *Sesame Street*.

It was the very same handkerchief Max had pulled out and handed to me on Friday night, used to sop up the tears that spilled before I told him I didn't want to be a mother.

Only now, it had become a canvas for red, pools of it, as if it were a topographical map of the Great Lakes region, every body of water a different basin, a different rivulet, of blood.

My breath caught in my throat. Could he, really? He wouldn't. He couldn't. There was no way. I'd loved him, god, I'd loved him more than anything. I'd loved him more than I'd ever loved Freya, even though I knew that was wrong, knew I should love her so very much more.

Had I loved a murderer? Was this my answer?

"Do you recognize this?" Duncan asked.

Half of me, the deranged part that was still singing, *M-A-X spells Max!* wanted to laugh. The irony was simply astounding. I'd gotten this set in Park Slope, a bougie shop sandwiched between a dry cleaner and a Blue Bottle Coffee. The girl with dip-dyed pink hair and an angel tattoo across her chest had smiled as I selected the set: "We can personalize them, if you want?"

Max wasn't the type to put his initials on everything, and besides, he had little feeling for his last name—Freya had taken mine, in the end, which had done exactly nothing in helping me love her—so I'd asked her to do *M-A-X*.

M-A-X spells Max.

"Ms. Walker," Duncan prompted, still waiting for an answer.

"I'm sorry," I said. "Yes, I recognize it, but that doesn't mean . . ." My voice trailed off. I didn't know how to finish the thought.

Freya began to fuss, and I stood, walked to the swing, averting my eyes from Duncan's, hoping she couldn't see the heat rising to my face. I imagined Duncan going to that damn shop, asking the angel-tattoo girl about this very purchase. Subpoenaing phone records, proving that I'd heard Sutton's voice over the line. I turned the speed of the swing up a notch—and the vibrations, too.

"This was discovered near the crime scene," Duncan went on. "We don't have DNA results on it yet, but you know what we are expecting. Mrs. Akins's blood. Mr. Bosch's DNA. We should have that in forty-eight hours or so."

Freya made a face, fighting the new pace of the swing. Again, I wished for that pacifier. More, I wished Max were here to answer for himself instead of leaving me to do it. I unlatched the buckles and pulled Freya out, holding her close to me. I returned to my seat, lifted my legs onto the coffee table, and propped her there in the crevice between my thighs. Lifting my heels, I bounced her up and down, up and down, while I softly hummed the rest of the song. The smile on her face said she was happy. She would have me do this forever if she could. Lately, it felt like that was what I *would* be doing forever. Trying to appease Freya, trying to keep her from screaming, forever and ever, all on my own.

M-A-X spells murderer?

"Why are you showing this to me?" I asked finally. "I saw the paper. I got the alert. What do you need me for?"

"Nothing," Duncan said, blinking slowly. "Everything will move forward, whether you cooperate or not."

"Cooperate?" I asked, continuing to bounce Freya. "I *am* cooperating."

I wasn't. I knew that, and she must, too.

"The truth is," Duncan said, "I was hoping that, seeing this, you'd understand. Your partner isn't innocent here. This isn't some sort of mix-up. This is real."

I know, I thought. *I know*.

But I only kept on bouncing Freya, not saying a word.

39

10:13 a.m.

SHE KNOWS YOU'RE GUILTY, TOO.

I stared at Duncan, Freya still bouncing along.

Even if I wanted to cooperate, even if I emptied every last droplet of love I had left for Max, the tiniest of dregs at the bottom of the wine bottle, even then—what could I possibly say?

The police would want to know why I hadn't said anything about Max calling before. My very silence would be aiding and abetting a kidnapping. If they knew I'd heard Sutton on the line and still did nothing, why wouldn't they suspect I knew about Grace's murder, too? I couldn't risk Freya losing both parents.

I needed time. Time to think. Time to speak to the lawyer Carl and Brenda had mentioned. Or to run everything by Molly. Molly always knew what to do. Maybe I could call her, tell her all . . .

"Ms. Walker," Duncan prompted.

"Sorry," I said. "I don't know what else you want me to say."

Liana sighed with relief. She still, *somehow*, believed in Max's innocence, that much was clear.

Duncan leaned back in the chair. "Ms. Walker, I don't think you want to hurt anybody. I think you're still holding out hope that there's an explanation for all of this."

"What if there is?" I asked, my voice so quiet it was almost a whisper. "You don't really know, do you? You don't have an explanation. That's why you're here asking me."

Even as the words came out of my mouth, they sounded weak, unbelievable. But it was better for Duncan to think I was holding out hope than to think I was actively holding back information.

"You're wrong there, Ms. Walker. Because I *do* have an explanation. A good one. Max Bosch was the father of Grace Akins's child."

She paused, eyeing me, but I refused to react.

"So you found out, then. I'm guessing in the last day or so. I'm not stupid, Ms. Walker. I may not be some fancy city detective, but I'm smarter than the lot of them anyway. Trust me. My mother always told me I'd have to work twice as hard to be taken half as seriously, and I have."

It felt as if my stomach was bottoming out, but I didn't say a word.

"It was very important to Mr. Bosch that this stay hidden from you. He didn't want you to know that he was a deadbeat, did he? That he had a child he'd completely abandoned? So he and Mrs. Akins came to an agreement. I presume once she saw him playing happy family with you, she no longer liked all the terms of that agreement. Only your partner had a lot on the line. You. A new baby. Too much to lose."

I bounced Freya faster.

"So he met Mrs. Akins a few times. Tried to get her to see reason. See that there was no point in telling you the truth. Only it didn't work, did it? She resisted, she told him she didn't care anymore. He killed her to shut her up. Perhaps the child saw something. Perhaps Mr. Bosch realized he couldn't leave the scared kid alone. We'll figure that part out, too, just as soon as we find them."

"No," I said. "No, it doesn't make sense. Daniel showed me a paternity test. If Max knew he was Sutton's biological father all along, why would he have gotten that done? It was completed so recently."

Duncan sighed. "I would urge you not to put too much stock into any of Mr. Akins's theories. Mr. Bosch may have simply been stalling by asking to do that test before Mrs. Akins told you. We don't know exactly why it was ordered, but it does not work against our case."

Duncan's story was so much more terrible than the one Daniel had told, because it was so much more . . . logical. Daniel wanted me to believe that Max was planning on running off with Grace and starting a new family with Sutton. Max wanted me to believe that he was only trying to help her, this woman from his past. But Duncan's theory was perhaps the most straightforward, the inevitable conclusion if you layered Occam's razor over the whole thing. Max hadn't wanted me to know that he'd run out on a child of his, and so he was trying to keep Grace quiet. She resisted, and he—and he—

No. I still couldn't fathom it. Not Max. Not the man I loved so much. And besides, what about the other woman? The one the bartender had thought was his wife? How did it explain her?

Duncan leaned forward again in her chair. "I'm not

guessing, Ms. Walker. We do have proof. Not just the hand-kerchief, but financials, too. Our forensic team has discovered payments to Daniel and Grace Akins from your partner's trust. Hush money, we believe."

I shook my head. "His trust?" I asked. "He had one at one point, but we emptied it more than a year ago. We used it to pay down the mortgage to lower our monthly payment."

"Perhaps there was another account that you didn't know about. The payments began this past spring. In late May."

I froze up, playing it all back. That would have been right around when . . . when I told Max I was pregnant. Oh god.

Had Grace somehow found out, too? Had she and Max been in touch, even then? Had he told her? Had he thought that a little money would make it okay? Pay off one woman before you start a family with another? Of course, such an ar-rangement could only go so far. Eventually, Grace would want real restitution. She'd see me, sitting there on a blanket at that damn kiddie concert, holding a crying baby with Max by my side, and decide that money actually *wasn't* enough, that the truth had to come out . . .

Would Max—could Max—really kill her to keep her quiet?

"Are you sure this is right?" I asked. "Like I said, the trust was empty. And Daniel said he didn't even know Max and Grace were meeting, and yet you say that the money was going to both of them?"

"Like I said, you shouldn't put stock in Mr. Akins's theo-ries. He may very well be hoping to avoid any sort of black-mail or extortion charges. We're pretty sure that's why he's become suddenly so forthcoming about the fact that he is not

Sutton's biological father, even though he still retains all legal rights. He likely expected this to come out."

"Blackmail," Liana said, clinging to anything to protect Max. "Don't you think if this Daniel is guilty of blackmail, he might be worth looking into for murder?"

Duncan didn't even glance Liana's way, only stared at me. I pulled Freya tighter, as if she were a shield from Duncan's questioning eyes, but she popped off, began to cry.

Duncan pushed herself up and out of the chair, taking her cue. "You know where I am," she said. "You have my information. Give me a call when you feel ready to tell us all you know. We'll be waiting. And the sooner you help us, the sooner we can help the child."

She set her coffee mug on the side table.

"The pieces are all in place, Ms. Walker. We're going to finish this, with or without you."

40

2:11 p.m.

MY PHONE WAS BLOWING UP.

Freya was *finally* down for a nap, and Liana was upstairs, phone set to silent, catching up on sleep herself, but I found myself paralyzed, sitting on the sofa, staring at the article in *Rolling Stone*, the first national hit, the one that kicked off this deluge, the one I'd already read countless times.

FORMER VELVET HOPE FRONTMAN WANTED FOR ALLEGED MURDER AND KIDNAPPING

Maximillian Bosch, the indie-rock darling and onetime frontman of the Velvet Hope, has been named as a person of interest in a murder and kidnapping.

According to Kingston, N.Y., police, Bosch is wanted in connection with the murder of Grace Akins, a stay-at-home mother, and the kidnapping of her six-year-old son. He was last seen Friday evening, and there's been no sign of his black Toyota RAV-4 since. Family of the victim could not be reached for comment.

Bosch, who made a name writing optimistic ballads laced with irony and set to heavily synthesized beats, left the band at the end of last year, citing "the desire to spend more time with my growing family," according to his Instagram post. Bosch was a founding member of the band, which was born out of the dives of Greenwich Village and NYU's Steinhardt school. He was the lead guitarist and lyricist for the group.

Though never quite a household name, the Velvet Hope made a splash on the alt-rock scene, touring extensively through the US and Europe and becoming a cult favorite on Northeast college radio stations and at indie-music festivals. Before the split, rumors had swirled around a potential tour and collaboration with Thom Yorke.

The Velvet Hope lead singer, Liana Price, issued a statement on Instagram after Bosch's departure late last year: "We couldn't be happier for Max and this next step of his journey."

Price could not be reached for comment on the unfolding situation.

If you have any information about Maximillian Bosch or his whereabouts, please contact the Kingston Police.

The scoop hadn't been picked up by *The New York Times*, or by any other major newspaper—not yet, at least. But *Rolling Stone* was enough, wasn't it? More than enough. The guy who'd written the story, the guy who'd been so easy to find on Instagram, was a "foodie and freelance music journo" who was "kickin' it" in upstate New York.

And that was all it had taken. One guy, perusing the local paper while having coffee probably in the same damn café I'd gone to for brunch with Molly. Some guy, seeing a headline, recognizing the name Maximillian Bosch. Realizing yes, it was *that* Maximillian Bosch. A music teacher now, maybe, but so much more. Putting it together. Texting his editor—*dude,*

I've got a story for you—writing it up quickly, publishing it just as quickly—goddamn internet journalism. Always on, always ready to destroy you.

Max wasn't famous. No one would ever recognize him. In Brooklyn, he looked like just about every other white guy indie-rock musician. Unkempt beard, soulful eyes, guitar strapped over his back. A little paunch of a belly from the affinity for craft beer and a lack of affinity for the gym. In all our years together, he'd never once been recognized by a fan or stopped for an autograph. Nothing like that. I didn't worry that paparazzi would be trying to take photos of our baby or that anyone cared in the slightest who I was.

Still, Max was a thread woven into the tapestry of pop culture just as so many others were. His songs were played for people's first dances at weddings, were written up in *Pitchfork*, were set to people's year-in-review movies on YouTube before the copyright infractions got them taken down. Their first hit was even in a Kohl's commercial, of all things. Half the reason his music-lesson business had been so very successful was because Park Slope, Williamsburg, and Upper East Side parents wanted to know not only that their kid was learning guitar, but that their kid was learning guitar from the *founder and former lead guitarist of the Velvet Hope*.

He was somebody, somebody worth writing about when they did something bad.

And now, it wasn't just a nameless bad man who'd allegedly murdered Grace and kidnapped Sutton. Now, it was Maximillian Bosch, you know, that guy who was in the Velvet Hope and who left the band last year. That guy we definitely saw once or twice at Mercury Lounge. That guy our old roommate went home with that one time. That guy who played Bonnaroo three years in a row. That guy, you know, the one we read about in *Spin*—or was it *Paste*?—back when they were actual magazines you could hold in your hands.

Now, it was Max who'd somehow left a handkerchief with his name on it at the scene of the crime, one of a set of six, four of which were sitting in his top dresser drawer right now— I'd checked.

My phone jiggled, ringing. Bree. I tapped to ignore it, then returned to the college text chain, read the flurry of texts again.

Janie, I just read.

Are you OK? How's Freya?

Please give one of us a call. We're worried about you.
What can we do to help?

You don't have to be ashamed or embarrassed. We love you.
We love Freya. We are standing by.

Another call, this one from a 212 number—Manhattan. It could be a journalist—I'd received two of those calls already and hung up on them both—but it could also be Carl and Brenda's lawyer. I needed to talk to him, now more than ever.

"Hello?"

"Am I speaking with Janie Bosch?" The woman's voice was chipper—too chipper for the situation—and apparently my status as partner and co-parent, but not wife, had gotten lost in translation.

"Janie Walker," I said. "We're not married."

"Oh," the woman said. "Apologies. I'm calling from the law offices of Courtland and Diaz. I have Rick Courtland on the line."

I licked my lips. "Okay."

A click, and then a voice was booming through. "Hello, Janie? Carl and Brenda told you I'd be calling?"

"Yes," I said. "Yes, they told me."

"Right. Okay. When was the last time you spoke with the police?"

I swallowed. "This morning."

"Nothing since then? Any calls, anything?"

"No," I said.

"Good, good," he said quickly. "You need to talk to them, you call me first. Carl has retained my services for you as well. Now, of course, we'll need to meet in person."

"Okay."

"I'm wrapping up here, but how's tomorrow morning? Ten? I can come up to Kingston. Carl has provided your address. We'll parse this out together and make a plan."

"Oh . . . okay," I said. It felt fast, but it also felt necessary. "Yes, okay."

"Don't go speaking with the police until after we meet. Got that? And if you have to, for any reason, you call me first."

"Yes," I managed. "Okay."

"Great. I'll see you tomorrow, then."

The call ended. So short, so to the point, and yet it felt like so much had changed. I had a lawyer now. Max, too. We were the sort who needed lawyers. The sort to dominate the true-crime section of *Rolling Stone*.

I returned to the story, to the comments populating beneath. There had been seven a few minutes earlier. Now, there were eight.

VinylGirl4 *Why am I not surprised? Are there any dudes who aren't actual monsters?*

RHCPFan *These guys were always overrated by insufferable hipsters. Good riddance.*

BrooklynBound *This dude was a TOTAL DICK to my friend like five years ago.*

Bongo51 *Cue the Netflix special in 3, 2, 1 . . .*

WestCoastBro *This is why we still need the death penalty. Guys like these don't deserve to live!!!*

CuriousReader *Here we go, another MAN tried in the court of public opinion before we have all the facts.*

ColdplayAllDay *Umm, who?*

VelvetHopeless *That's it. I'm deleting all their albums.*

Back to the Google search. The article had already been picked up by most everyone who covered indie music. *Brooklyn-Vegan. Pitchfork. Billboard.* SoundCloud's news site.

It had begun to seep into our social networks, too. Into the personal. Into the things all my friends and family; my old coworkers; the girl I'd bunked with in camp; Jessica, my high school bestie; and Jennifer, my high school enemy, would all see, because we all had to be so connected now. We all had to be "friends."

I tapped into Facebook, loaded Max's timeline. Already, it was filling to the brim. Names I didn't recognize, people who couldn't have been that close to him popping up to claim their Six-Degrees-of-Kevin-Bacon to this particular news story.

This you?

Dude, what's going on?

Never thought I'd see your name in this story!

All of them linked to the *Rolling Stone* piece, and all of them were already full of reactions. Shock and awe and angry emojis that looked like Edvard Munch's *The Scream*. Classic thumbs-up likes because apparently a lot of people actually *enjoy* watching their pseudo-friend's undoing on social media. The comments beneath each post were piling up.

This can't be real. Murder? Jesus.

There must be some mistake.

I always knew you were fucked up, man.

I tapped back onto my profile, assessed the damage.

Is this your Max?

Janie, are you OK?

I really hope there's some mix-up and this isn't about you . . .

I tapped out of my profile and onto Max's business page instead, the one he used for updates on his music lessons: the Brooklyn Guitar Guy. There had been nothing a few minutes earlier, but surely, it wouldn't be long.

My heart leapt as I saw it, beating fiercely, as it had done for every comment, every single post thus far.

It was long, and it was brutal.

I feel I must share this to protect other parents from this man. We hired Max, the owner and lead teacher behind "The Brooklyn Guitar Guy," to teach our 12-year-old daughter guitar. At first, he seemed like a normal guy and a professional teacher, but a few months ago, things started to change. He showed up late for two lessons, not okay when you're paying $150/hour. He even snapped at my daughter, which is seriously inappropriate for a music lesson. At the time, we chalked it up to him maybe going through some things, but we elected to take our business else-where. Now, seeing this story, I'm both relieved that I trusted my mother's intuition and horrified that we ever let him anywhere near our child. I hope they find this guy and he rots. I'll be hug-ging my daughter a little bit tighter tonight.

Tears swam in my eyes, and mortification invaded my ev-ery pore, my mother's words, her constant refrain from my childhood, practically ringing in my ears: *It's nobody's business but ours.*

Maybe it was, and maybe it wasn't, but it didn't matter, did it? All the efforts I'd gone to, to build a life that was worth something, to show that life to the world, to let them know I had it put together even when I didn't; that was all so pointless now. Futile. Forever, I would be the woman who'd been with Max the Indie-Rock Murderer, the Kidnapper. That would be my legacy. In some ways, it would be Freya's, too.

Still, I was alone. I had no one to help me. I wasn't up to the task of caring for Freya even with another human around—much less on my own.

We were all so very fucked. Max's business was over. His career was shot. Our relationship had been a lie through and through. I didn't even have a job. Hell, I was meeting with a lawyer the next day, a lawyer who knew things were already so bad that he'd advised me not to speak to the police.

They all knew now, and there was no coming back from it.

I went back to my own timeline, deleted every comment, then shut down the account, not that it would really do anything.

Max's downfall—and mine—was complete.

41

4:39 p.m.

I PULLED THE COVERS UP TO MY CHIN, IGNORING THE SOUNDS of Freya's intermittent fussing. I'd done what I had to do. I'd gotten my baby up from her nap, changed her, fed her, played with her, done bicycle kicks to rid her belly of gas and "tummy time" to build her neck muscles. I'd fed her again.

After that, I'd left her with Liana, ambled up the stairs, shut the door, turned off the lights, and crawled into bed, ignoring the calls that continued to pour in, ones from Bree and the college girls, from random numbers that I assumed were journalists, none of them with the 800 beginning that had shown up the only time Max had reached out. The only call I'd answered had been my mother's. She'd updated me on their arrangements—they should be here by Thursday night. I hadn't had the heart to tell her about the new evidence, about bloody handkerchiefs or secret hush money, but still, she knew enough. "I saw the *Rolling Stone* article," she said, just before she got off the phone. "You have to protect yourself, Janie," she said. "And Freya."

"You must be so horrified," I found myself saying, my voice snappish, seething with long-buried anger and resentment. "You must be so horrified that everyone knows. No one's business but ours, right?"

My mother had taken a quick, sharp breath. "This is different, Janie. You know it is."

Now, I stared at the ceiling, tracing the cracks with my eyes. Freya's cries stopped—Liana must have given her a bottle.

I picked up my phone, swiped away the myriad notifications.

I had to do *something*. I couldn't hang around waiting like a sitting duck—that was what she'd said.

And she'd been right. She'd been right about everything.

Molly answered on the first ring.

"Janie," she said.

The line hung blank between us. Now that I had her here, I didn't know quite what to say.

"I saw the news," she said finally.

"That's not even everything," I said. "There's a handkerchief of Max's—bloody—found on the scene. And he was—well, Duncan says he was paying Grace from a trust fund I didn't know about. That's it, isn't it? That's proof?"

"That's what it looks like to me." Molly cleared her throat. "I'm sorry, Janie. I'm so sorry for all of it. Did your parents get in touch with you?"

"Yes," I said. "They should be here on Thursday. Thanks for emailing my mom for me."

"I'm sorry it upset you, but I'm glad I did." A pause. "What are you going to do?"

"I don't know," I said, my voice cracking. "Even with all

the evidence, Liana still thinks there's some explanation, and the lawyer wants to meet with me tomorrow, but I don't—I don't even know if I can wait that long."

"Lawyer?"

"Yeah," I said. "Carl and Brenda hired a lawyer. Some hotshot from the city."

"For Max," Molly said.

"For all of us."

"Right," Molly said. "I guess it's better than not having anyone at all, but I'd still say that any lawyer hired by Carl and Brenda is going to put Max first."

"Yes," I said. "I know."

There was silence, and for a moment, I thought the call had dropped, but then Molly finally spoke. "I can't imagine what you're going through. I can't begin to imagine how hard this is, and how hard it is now, when you've only just had Freya, but I know that protecting yourself and Freya is the right thing to do, whatever that means. And I'm not saying that because I hate Max. I'm saying that because I love you. So if there's something—something big you know—that you're holding back from the police . . . Janie, I think you have to tell them before . . . before this gets any worse."

"You're right," I said, resigned. "I need to go to Duncan. I know I need to. I'm just scared."

"Can I come with you?" Molly asked.

I hesitated only a moment. "Yes, let me just check to see how Freya's doing and as soon as I can get away, I'll text you, okay? And . . . and the lawyer . . . he said I could call him if I had to talk to the police. When we get to the station, when I actually talk to Duncan, I'll put him on speaker. It's the right thing to do. I know this."

"It is," Molly said. "And I'll be right there, holding your hand when you do."

"Thank you," I said.

"You're welcome." Molly's voice was calm and smooth. "And listen, I know you're scared. I know you feel like you're on your own here. I know you feel lost, but you have to remember, you still have a community. And I've been asking around, and everyone at the agency, they'd love to have you. Fuck Bryan. Fuck all that bullshit. You can come back."

My heart seized up, and for an instant, I was back in that goddamned karaoke bar. For an instant, everything was hazy except for me and Bryan, singing "Islands in the Stream," parts switched. He did Dolly Parton, and I did Kenny Rogers. Arms linked around each other, swaying back and forth for the choruses, cheap vodka sodas in our hands, both of us laughing like hell. We thought we were so funny. Delightfully so.

I'd been over it a million times since, whether my fate was already sealed by the time we sang that song, whether it was just us in the room by then, but I could have sworn there was someone with us still, even if their face was hard to make out.

"Molly," I said. "You remember that night we all went out to karaoke?"

"The night you and Bryan—"

"Yes," I said. "Do you remember Bryan and me singing 'Islands in the Stream,' the Dolly Parton song?"

"I don't think so, Janie. I think I'd gone home by that point. Why?"

Singing that song had been the last time I could remember feeling like my life was on track. The last time before it had all gone to shit. It still felt, strangely, that if I could go back to that night, turn left instead of right, it would almost be like none of the rest of this ever happened.

"It's not really important—"

"Wait," Molly said, as if a lightbulb had gone off. "Do you want me to ask Ani . . . she's right downstairs. I mean, I don't know if you feel comfortable telling her anything, but—"

"Ani?"

"When I left, it was the three of you, I think. You, Ani, and Bryan."

"Right," I said, struggling to find Ani's face in the murky soup of my memories. "I guess I got you two mixed up. And no. Don't ask her. It's not a big deal."

"What happened with Bryan," Molly said, her voice soothing. Careful. "I know you feel bad about it, but it has nothing to do with this. With what Max has done to you."

"I know," I said. "I don't even know why my mind is going there. Let me go. I'll text you as soon as I'm ready to go to the station."

I hung up the phone, stared at it in my hands. I knew I had to do it. I had to rip off the Band-Aid, choose one path in the yellow wood . . .

But my phone rang, and I jolted, felt the vibrations against my palm.

An 800 number, just like . . .

I tapped to answer the call. Lifted the phone to my ear.

"Hello?" I said. "Max?"

"Janie." His voice was tired and hollow, and in spite of everything, I was glad to hear it. "Janie, I need your help."

42

4:47 p.m.

"MY HELP?" I ASKED, DUMBFOUNDED. "WHAT MAKES YOU THINK you deserve my *help*? When you . . . when you could have *killed* her."

"Janie," Max said. "I know I fucked up. I know I made a million mistakes, but I swear to you, I swear on Freya's life. I didn't kill Rae. I didn't hurt anyone, and I *know* there's got to be a way to prove that, to set things right. You're the only one I can trust. This is why I begged you to stay close, and you did, you did because you haven't given up on me—"

"But I have, Max. I have. I can't trust you, I can't—"

"I know, Janie, I know. And you don't owe me anything, but you're all I have. You're my only chance here, my only chance that Freya doesn't know her father through the bars of a prison cell. It's the only chance I have to keep Sutton from getting hurt."

"Max, I—"

"I'm at 16 Mill House Road in Prattsville, New York. It's an hour northwest."

"What?"

"Sixteen Mill House Road. Prattsville. Write it down," he said. "But don't tell anyone. Come as soon as you can. Come tonight."

"Max, you can't just—"

"Sixteen Mill House Road. I love you, Janie. You and Freya. You two are my whole entire world. You always will be, no matter what happens."

He hung up.

I stared at the phone, my hands shaking.

Sixteen Mill House Road. Max had said it three times.

I tossed the phone across the bed, then tugged open the drawer of the nightstand, scrambled to find a pen and a scrap of paper. On an old tag from one of my nursing bras, I scribbled with the pen, dragging it back and forth until the ink started to bleed.

I wrote the address, then held it in my hands, stared at it.

I wouldn't go; of course I wouldn't. It was too risky. Max hadn't attempted to explain a single one of his betrayals, much less the lot of them. I owed him nothing. Absolutely nothing.

Besides, there were certain things he *couldn't* explain. What about that blood on his handkerchief? Why would Duncan have made up a series of payments? Why would the bartender have invented another woman? He was talking about preventing Sutton from getting hurt, but *he* was the one who had Sutton. Sutton, his *child*.

I needed to go to Duncan, as I'd already decided. I needed to do the right thing.

I love you, Janie. You and Freya.

I shook my head, as if I could sift Max's words from my brain.

A quick knock on my door, and then, it opened.

I scrambled to hide the note, crumpling it up, closing my fist.

"Is Freya fussy again?" I asked, even though I knew she wasn't. I hadn't heard a single cry.

"No," Liana said. Her eyes were dead serious. She looked . . . scared. "Duncan's back. She said she wants to talk to you."

"Okay," I said, squeezing my fist tighter. "Okay. Tell her I'll be right there. I need a minute to get dressed."

Liana turned, looked at me.

"Shut the door," I said, my voice half a whisper.

Her eyes held mine a moment, as if there were so many things she wanted to ask, but then she left, pulling the door closed tight behind her.

I waited until I heard her feet on the stairs to unfold my hand.

Unfurling the scrap of paper, I stared at it, committing it to memory, employing a mnemonic device, as I'd become so good at doing when I needed to remember the names and faces of a boardroom full of potential clients.

When I was sixteen, I worked at the mill, I told myself. *I had a cat named Pratt.*

When I was sixteen, I worked at the mill. I had a cat named Pratt.

Sixteen at the mill. Cat named Pratt.

I grabbed the pen and scratched out the address, then tore up the paper in tiny little bits. I went to the bathroom, the tile cold on my bare feet, lifted the porcelain lid, and it clanked against the tank behind it. I dropped the pieces of paper into the water, watching as they turned translucent. I waited an appropriate amount of time, in case anyone was listening.

Then I pushed the plunger, watched as the pieces swirled around the bowl and disappeared.

Gone.

43

5:01 p.m.

DUNCAN WAS IN THE FRONT HALLWAY WHEN I GOT DOWN-
stairs, her hands resting on her belt, her hair pulled into a
tight bun. Liana was there, too, shifting her weight from foot
to foot.

"Ms. Walker. Glad you could come down. Hope I didn't
disturb some much-needed new-mother sleep."

"It's okay," I said, forcing the words out. "What's happened? Why are you here?"

She pulled out her notebook, clicked her pen to life, then
held it over her notepad a moment, waiting. "Has Max attempted to contact you at all?"

I replayed his voice on the other end of the line, pictured
those bits of paper swirling in the bowl. I thought of Freya,
and how much she needed two parents, and wondered if there
was any way in the world she could have them.

"Look," I said, trying to force some strength into my
words, "I spoke to a lawyer. He's meeting me tomorrow. He
doesn't want . . . he doesn't want me to do any more inter-
views with you until I do."

Duncan raised an eyebrow. "So that's how you want to play it now, Ms. Walker?"

"I'm not . . . I'm not playing anything," I stammered, but I knew that wasn't true. I *could* call Rick Courtland right now, put him on speaker, just as I'd planned. But Max had practically begged me for help—so he could know Freya, be in her life. So he could protect Sutton.

Could I really give him up like this when there was some chance, however small . . . that he was telling the truth?

You're my only chance.

Duncan cleared her throat, then looked at me. "Do you want us to find your partner, Ms. Walker?"

I hesitated. I didn't know how to answer that. I didn't know myself.

"Let me clarify: Do you want your daughter to see her father again? Healthy. *Alive.*"

I felt tears pricking in the corners of my eyes.

"Because there's a manhunt now," Duncan went on. "You know this. If he resists, if he keeps on running, if he doesn't think straight, we don't know how things are going to end here."

My heart raced, pounding against my ribs, and I blinked back new tears.

"Did something happen?" Liana pressed, stepping forward. "Because lawyers or not, we've already answered all these questions, and the answers haven't changed. We haven't heard anything from Max. Why are you so sure he'd suddenly make contact after days of radio silence?"

Duncan looked from me to Liana and back to me again, then sighed. "The child has turned up."

The child.

"The child?" I said, momentarily dumbfounded. For a crazy second, I thought she was talking about Freya.

"The deceased's son, Sutton. He's with a great-aunt in Maine. Unharmed. She found him on her doorstep this afternoon. With a bag packed. Like he was going on a trip. Mr. Akins will be on the first flight out to see him tomorrow."

"He . . . he's okay." It wasn't a question. It was a statement. He was okay, of course he was, because Max would never hurt Sutton. Never, ever, ever.

And if he hadn't done that, maybe he hadn't done the other things, either.

Maybe he had nothing to do with Grace's death at all.

What if Duncan really had made up the payments? Wouldn't I have known about another trust if there was one? Was she really above saying whatever she had to in order to get me to turn on Max? Could that bartender have been confused? Could one of Grace's friends have stormed in, angry that Grace was meeting another man? Could his handkerchief somehow have slipped from his pocket? Could someone else have used it, covered it in blood?

Was there a chance, however small, that Max was in the right?

"The boy is okay," Duncan continued. "Physically speaking."

"See?" Liana said. "Like we told you, Max wouldn't do that—"

"Did Sutton say what happened?" I asked, forgetting, momentarily, about my promise to the lawyer.

"He's not said a word," Duncan said. "Not one single word. We're doing our best, but he's obviously been through trauma. He's scared. We're sending a child psychologist to talk with

him, but we don't expect to have answers anytime soon."
Duncan's gaze bounced between Liana and me. "The investigation remains. None of this changes that. Now, is there anything, anything at all, you think we should know?" Duncan
asked.

I could still do it. I could get Rick on the line, get all of this
off my chest.

Sixteen at the mill. Cat named Pratt.

But that would be it, then. Max would be arrested. The
next time I saw him would be in a cold and sterile visitation
room, if I chose to see him at all. I wasn't sure I could actually
go to Max—that felt too foolish, too risky—but I could at
least wait to divulge his location until I met with the lawyer
the next day.

"No," I said. "No, there's not."

Duncan turned, and I walked her to the door. "Oh," she
said, reaching into her pocket. "I found this on your porch."

She pulled out something fuzzy and white, and for a moment, I thought of those baby bunnies Max had found nesting
in the garden, the ones I'd dreamed about the night I'd woken
to find him gone.

Only it wasn't a bunny. It was a llama. A fuzzy little llama
with a green silicone pacifier attached to the end.

The one I'd been looking for. The one I'd left in the car.
The only one that soothed Freya.

My heart practically stopped. My breath caught in my
throat.

Max. He'd been here. He'd been here to bring this back
to us.

It was so small, the pacifier, too small, really, to tip the
scales one way or the other, when there were so many lies and

betrayals on the other side. But it was so thoughtful, in that way Max had always had of being thoughtful, and it called to mind all the other thoughtful things. Post-it notes on the bathroom mirror so I wouldn't forget my work iPad for an important meeting. The way Max always had a burp cloth or two tossed across his shoulder, ready when Freya needed it. How he never failed to drop me off right in front of our apartment, even before Freya, and then go circle the block himself to find a spot. Tiny little ways to show he cared, so baked into the fabric of our lives that sometimes I didn't even notice, didn't even appreciate them as I should have. And now, this gesture tugged at my heart like very few things had since Freya was born, a pinhole of light among all the dark, reminding me that she and I—we were loved. Greatly.

"My daughter used the same sort of one," Duncan said, handing it to me. "Must have dropped from the stroller. You can toss them right in the wash. Just don't put them in the dryer. Learned that the hard way." She shrugged. "Or you can always wipe down the top of it—the germs are good for them anyway, right?" Duncan smiled, and for a moment, she wasn't a cop, only a mother.

I took the pacifier from her hands. "Thank you," I said. "Thank you for the advice."

"Call me anytime," Duncan said. "Lawyer or no, anytime you want to talk. *Please*."

I managed to hold back my tears until the door was shut behind her, but then they came gushing.

"What is it?" Liana asked. "What's happened?"

"It's the pacifier I was looking for," I said. "The one . . . the one Freya loves."

"Oh," Liana said. "It must have fallen then, like Duncan said."

"No," I said, shaking my head fiercely. "No, he brought it for us."

Liana gasped.

"He knew the risk and he did it anyway. He knew how much we needed it."

Max had helped me, in a way so small, but so meaningful all the same. And yes, it was bittersweet; yes, the damn thing had only been gone because Max had left in the first place. If none of this had happened, the gesture wouldn't have been needed.

Still, *still*. He was trying to make it right. He was thinking of Freya, of me.

Besides, it wasn't only Max who was in trouble. Max's phone call flashed to mind yet again.

It's the only chance I have to keep Sutton from getting hurt.

What did it mean? Why would he say that if Sutton was already safe with some aunt in Maine?

I had to know, because I believed in his goodness.

I had to at least *try* to help him.

Tears still coming down, I handed the pacifier to Liana, asked her to wash it, then went to Freya, pulled her from the swing, and set myself up on the couch with my nursing pillow, pulled my bra down, and latched her on.

I had to feed her now, because I might not be able to later. I nuzzled Freya closer, felt the downy hair of the nape of her neck, longest in that one spot—a baby rattail.

"Is there else anything I can do?" Liana asked, returning from the kitchen, the disinfected pacifier in her hands.

My eyes caught hers. "Do you have your car?"

"What?" Liana said.

"Your car."

"Did something happen?" she asked, her voice frantic now. "Besides the pacifier? Oh god—did you hear from him? Do you know where he is? You did, didn't you? Duncan was right. He called you."

"Listen, Liana," I said. "We can't talk like this. Not now. Not with everything—" I shook my head. "It's too risky."

Liana nodded, her lip quivering.

Sixteen at the mill. Cat named Pratt.

"If you really want to help, you'll lend me your car, and you'll watch Freya."

I stared at her.

"And you won't ask me anything else."

44

6:35 p.m.

"GOODNIGHT," I SAID, LEANING OVER TO KISS FREYA. "BE GOOD for Aunt Liana. Mommy will be back in a few hours."

Freya smiled, then burped loudly, and Liana and I both laughed, the tension broken, if only for a moment. "There's fresh milk on the counter," I said. "Four ounces."

I leaned over, kissing Freya once again. I'd spent all these past weeks resenting her very presence, wishing I could somehow go back, feeling like I was teetering so dangerously between love and hate for my very own baby, and yet, now, seeing her in another woman's arms, knowing I would not be putting her to bed at night for the first time ever, my heart tugged with protectiveness. *I'm going to see your daddy, baby girl,* I wanted to say. I'm going to try to fix this however I can. Try to save him for you even if he's already lost to me.

You think you can take care of this? *You can't even take care of yourself. You can't even take care of* her.

"All right," I said. "Call me if there's anything. Call me if you need me. Promise."

"I will," Liana said. "And, Janie——"

"Yeah?"

"I know I said I wouldn't ask any questions, but you aren't going to see that man, are you? Rae's husband? Because he must have done it, and the police aren't zeroed in on him at all, and it scares me to——"

"No," I said. "No, I'm not. I promise."

"Okay," she said, breathing a sigh of relief. "Then go. Go do what you need to do."

I turned, slipping out the back door, pulling it shut behind me.

I reached into my purse, checking. Wallet. Phone. House keys. Keys to Liana's Toyota. All there. I'd memorized the directions to the place, and I'd debated not even taking my phone, worried they could trace me, but I'd been too scared to be without it, knowing Freya was with Liana. What if something happened? What if she needed me? In the end, the risk had been worth it. Calculated.

The backyard was lit up with string lights, arcing across the yard, casting everything in a hazy, romantic glow. I glanced around to see if anyone was watching, then tugged on the cord, unplugging them, and instantly, I was bathed in black. A tiny relief. No one would see back here now.

I'd wanted to go sooner, as soon as Duncan was gone, but after Liana had agreed to lend me her car, I'd stepped out front, under the guise of checking the mail, and sure enough, there, at the very end of the block, was an unmarked black Lincoln Town Car I'd swear belonged to a cop.

I ambled across the patio and onto the grass, my eyes adjusting to the dark. I walked past the picnic table I'd planned on sitting out at with Max once the weather was a little warmer, past the firepit that was surrounded in paving stones, the edges catching the glare of the moonlight, past the stretches of yard Max had enjoyed so very much, even though it was cold when we arrived—"This yard would be a whole park in Brooklyn!"—past the flower boxes in the back that Max had taken to clearing out, the ones where he'd discovered the nest of baby bunnies, fur as white as the fuzz of the llama pacifier.

At the back, I found the gate, lifted the dinky metal latch, and pulled it only far enough so I could get out. It opened onto a tiny alleyway that ran behind all the houses back here. It stretched up and down, but I needed to go north, to where Liana had pointed out her parking spot, and I didn't want to risk the cop seeing me popping out of the alley, so I cut through the yard straight in front of me, a lawn lit softly by the glow coming from the back windows, praying whoever was in there wouldn't see me in the dark.

I crept across the grass, past the side of their house, a wraparound deck, flower beds that would likely be filled with blooming perennials sooner rather than later, a mailbox that was tilted, as if it might fall over any moment, and onto the street.

My hands began to shake as I glanced in each direction, looking for that black Lincoln Town Car. Nothing. Never in my life had I done anything like this. Sure, I could kick back a few martinis with Molly, but I was still a rule follower, through and through. I'd never had a run-in with the law, not even so much as a speeding ticket. In college, I didn't even have a fake ID, even if I partook in the beers my roommates purchased with theirs.

I turned right, like Liana had told me to do, walked

quickly up the sidewalk, illuminated by streetlights. A few paces up, I spotted it: Liana's lipstick-red Corolla, VLVTHP on the plate. Not exactly the most inconspicuous vehicle, but it was all I had. If someone caught me in town, I'd say I was going to the grocery store, or to Target, to get baby supplies. Once I was out of town, heading west—it was deep woods, deep country. I was hoping no one would be looking, no cops cruising, or at least no one to put it together who exactly I was. The search was out for Max's car, not Liana's.

I fumbled in my purse for Liana's keys and finally found them, hooked to a flip-flop key chain that said *Costa Rica*, one packed with plastic cards and tabs, from CVS to the Brooklyn Public Library.

Behind me, I heard the grumble of an engine. I jolted, the keys dropping from my hand, clanking against the pavement.

I leaned down to pick them up, and the car came closer. I heard it as it slowed, as someone stepped on the brake, and I froze, crouched down, and I knew it was all over now, that I'd missed my chance, that this was a stupid plan anyway, that my cover was blown.

The car picked up the pace, driving off. I looked up to see a blue Nissan with rideshare decals. Nothing more than a driver, looking for the right pickup spot.

I released a breath, used the fob to open the car, slipped inside, pulled the door shut behind me, took another deep breath, let it out.

I retrieved my phone, shot off a quick text to Molly, who'd called twice now.

Freya's super fussy, so I'm going to go to the station once the lawyer is here tomorrow. I'll call you.

Maybe I would and maybe I wouldn't. It all depended on what Max said.

I looked over the directions one more time, memorizing them, then turned my phone on Airplane Mode, so all the tracking was off. I shoved the key in the ignition, pulled my seat belt across my body, across the pooch of skin that still hung on around my tummy, clicking it in. I hadn't been in the driver's seat in years.

Hands gripping the wheel, knuckles already turning white, I began to drive.

In less than five minutes, I was out of Kingston, and I thanked the gods that the town was small, that there was no cop in my rearview—no anyone, for that matter. Nights like tonight were dead. Weekenders having gone home. Locals settling into the routines of their families, their lovers, their friends.

I made my way, easing onto Route 28, through empty road and dense woods, curving around the reservoir, the signs for parking to access the rail trail, the nature walk we'd done only Friday, Liana and Carl and Brenda in tow. Friday, and yet a lifetime ago.

I continued on past all the tiny towns that peppered this stretch of road like big black dots, waiting to be connected in a child's coloring book, one leading into the next—blink and you missed it—West Hurley. Shokan. Boiceville. Mount Tremper. Phoenicia.

It was dark, nearly pitch-black, and the only thing I could really see was the glare of my brights on the yellow paint line down the center, the monsterlike shadows of tree limbs reaching out over the road, temporarily illuminated by my headlights.

I drove not a mile over the speed limit, slowed before each turn, too afraid to miss it.

And then, there it was, waiting for me, the road marker flashing on and off in the light of my turn signal.

Mill House Road.

I turned, not hesitating. The decision had already been made. I had to get to him now, before I lost my nerve.

The road itself curved, back and forth, back and forth, switchbacking through woods, through mountainous terrain, the houses growing farther apart with every mile.

Sixty-eight Mill House. Then 34. Then 22. And then, finally, another marker.

Sixteen.

I turned onto a dirt road, the gravel like popcorn against the underside of Liana's car, and my heart began to ache as I approached a tiny house—one you could hardly call more than a cabin, with a little porch, a pair of windows, and weatherworn siding that had fallen off in places, a roof that looked like it must leak if it rained too hard.

My partner. The father of my child. He was here. In this decrepit, tucked-away place.

I flicked off the headlights and stopped the engine. I tucked the keys into my purse, then got out.

The air was cool, cooler than it had been back in Kingston, and slightly damp. I looked up. The sky was covered with clouds, and the full—or nearly full—moon behind them cast a silvery glow across the whole of it.

Wind rustled, shushing through the trees, and around me, somewhere, I heard the crack of a branch—an animal moving. In the distance, a *trickle-trickle* sound of a stream.

As I walked closer, stepping onto the porch, those sounds

disappeared, drowned out by the blood rushing in my ears, the *beat-beat-beat* of my heart.

I reached for the door, but it opened before I could knock.

"Janie," he said, his eyes filling with relief, with moisture, with pain. "I'm so, so sorry." His voice splintered with emotion, and tears spilled from his eyes.

"I fucked everything up."

45

8:01 p.m.

FOR A MOMENT, I HELD MAX IN MY ARMS, AND HE COLLAPSED into me, his head falling to my shoulder, which was turning damp from his tears, his body convulsing; an entirely broken man. It was such a natural reaction. Your partner breaks down, you wrap your arms around them. Simple as that.

I forced myself to pull away, push past him into the space. It was small and run-down, a door to what must be a bathroom in the corner, exposed pipes along that wall, a woodstove opposite. The walls were lined with mismatched planks, as if someone had made them out of whatever wood they could get their hands on, and the floorboards were creaky, gapping in places. A round table was smushed against one wall, a threadbare sofa was pulled out into a bed, and in the last corner sat an acoustic guitar and a trio of fishing poles. Altogether, it was no more than the size of a Manhattan studio apartment. Only not nestled in the urban jungle of Chelsea— tucked away here—where no one could find you.

Where a guilty person would go.

I turned around, locked my eyes on Max's.

"Tell me you didn't kill her," I said, my voice wavering. "Please, god, tell me now, face-to-face, that you didn't kill her."

"I didn't," Max said immediately, stepping forward to take my hand in his. "I promise you. I swear. And I never cheated on you, either. It was never like that at all."

I looked at my partner. It had only been a few days, but it was as if he'd aged ten years. His hair was matted down, his beard unkempt, his hands dry and cracked in a way that he, under normal circumstances, would never let them get. Save for the calluses that took permanent residence on the pads of his fingers, his hands were always soft, surprisingly so. But it was his eyes that were the worst. They were ringed in circles, bags heavy beneath his lids. Pure exhaustion, not dissimilar to the way I'd felt the first few days after Freya was born; the way I still felt now.

Only it was worse than that. Red and bloodshot, these were the eyes of a man who was tired and scared and yet cranking with adrenaline.

A man who'd spent the past three days running.

"Then what happened?" I asked, pulling my hand away. "Why are you here? What is going on?"

"I never hurt her," Max said. "And I never hurt Sutton. I was only trying to help them both. Her husband, Daniel, he's a monster. He was always difficult, I guess, always controlling—he always ran their finances, always made sure he knew where she was—he even made her stop going by 'Rae' just because he didn't like it. But I think she was okay with it because Daniel took care of her, her and Sutton. And then this last year, he went off the rails. She had only a meager allowance, and he tracked every single purchase she made. He got rid of their second car so she couldn't go anywhere without him. She had to keep her phone, her computer, unlocked, no passwords, at all times. And he got stricter and stricter with Sutton, punishing him. I guess a few months ago Sutton fell down the stairs, broke an arm, and she was sure Daniel had something to do with it. She needed a way out. She wanted me to help."

The story was horrible, and I felt compassion, empathy, for this woman, I really did, but at the same time, why did Max have to swoop in? Why did he have to get involved like he had?

"Even if all that's true, why you?" I asked, shaking my head, taking a few steps forward and sinking down onto the bed. "You had your own family to take care of. You had me. Freya. And I wasn't okay. I needed you."

"I know," Max said. "I know, Janie, I know." He came closer, sat next to me. "The timing was awful. But it had to be me, see, because I was Sutton's real father, but that's not what she'd put on Sutton's birth certificate. She put that Daniel was. And so the only way she was going to escape Daniel was to petition for sole custody."

I scooted back, creating more space between us. "And you were just like, sure? I'm down to no longer be a deadbeat dad. Let's do a test?"

"No," he said. "Not at all. And I wasn't a deadbeat," he said earnestly. "At least, I never knew I was. I didn't know she had a child," Max said, dropping his head, his elbows on his knees, a man lost. "I definitely didn't know *I* had a child. Before all this, Rae was just a girl I'd dated briefly. That's all." He looked back up, his eyes widening, as if begging me to believe him. "I was with Rae years ago, way before I met you. We hooked up for a couple of months, and then, I guess, I lost interest. I ghosted her. I know it's a shitty thing to do, but that was all. And that's the last I heard of her until December, when she contacted me. It was right after I shared on Instagram that we'd be coming up to Kingston after the baby was born."

I bristled, remembering the post. I had found it so sweet, he'd said something about us spending the first couple of months of our baby's life "surrounded by mountains." It had sounded so wonderful, and even though I'd quit the agency by then, belly fat, the person I would come to know as Freya kicking at my ribs, my uterus pressing against my bladder and making me have to pee once every five to ten minutes, I'd almost convinced myself to believe that it would all work out. Look what had happened instead.

"What did she say?" I asked.

"She said she lived in Kingston now and was hoping we could meet up and chat once I was here."

I shook my head, cursing myself for choosing Kingston, a place where so many Brooklynites had wound up, for helping to bring this all upon us. "Why didn't you tell me?"

Max winced. "I don't know how to say this, but a lot of exes . . . I mean, she's not the first to reach out like that. I figured she was drunk or something. I didn't think anything of it. I did what I always did. I ignored it. But then when we actually got up here, she reached out again. She said that she had a child, and that the kid was mine, and she—she sent a photo of him—and god help me, he did look like me, right down to his eyes—and it scared the shit out of me. I kept thinking—god—what if Freya had some bio-dad, sperm-donor guy and all her mother wanted was to talk to him and—I just, I loved Freya so much. I felt like being a dad, it was my superpower. And then at the same time, there was a possibility that I was this absent father to another human? I felt like such a *hypocrite*. So I agreed. I agreed at least to meet up once, to see what she had to say."

"You still could have said something," I said. "You could have come to me."

"I know," Max said. "I'm so sorry. But by then, you were having such a hard time."

I stood, walking from the bed, then turned back. "Did it make you feel good?" I asked. "Helping her when you didn't know how to help me?"

"No," he said instinctively. "It didn't." Then he shrugged, shamed and spent. "I don't know, maybe in a way it did. I could see you suffering, and like you said, I didn't know what to do. I could make Freya a bottle and burp her and put her down for naps and stuff, do the dishes and the laundry, but I didn't know how to make you feel better. I was sleep-deprived, going crazy myself, but at the same time, I had this joy, this joy of being in Freya's presence, and I could see you didn't. So yeah, maybe I felt even more pressure to do the right thing. I just didn't see how I could shut Rae down without even giving her a meeting."

I sank into a chair that creaked beneath my weight. "I don't understand why, when your partner is having the worst time of her life, you have to rush out to solve someone else's problems. This isn't like some girl passing out at a show, Max. This isn't like being the good guy who calls for help. This is huge. Life-changing."

"I know, but I thought meeting with her once was the right thing to do. And I thought I could handle it, just one small meeting. I thought I could keep it private. I'd brought up this old iPhone in case we needed a dedicated device for checking the baby monitor—I forgot you were bringing that iPad from work—and I downloaded WhatsApp because I knew those messages were super private. We arranged our first meeting. I wanted to keep all of it separate from you until I could get a handle on the situation."

"And that's why you changed your Apple password, too?" I asked. "To keep everything from me?"

"Yes," he said. "I got nervous you'd look up my location and see me at the bar. I'm sorry." He shook his head. "I know I shouldn't have done any of that. I know, now, what it looks like. But I swear to you. I love you. I love *Freya*."

"Don't," I said. "Just tell me what happened. Tell me how it got to this."

His chin dropped toward his chest. "I met up with Rae. She suggested the Three Crows. And it was . . . different than I'd expected. She wasn't angry at all, she wasn't bitter or resentful or anything. She wasn't asking for money. She wasn't trying to strike up anything romantic. She told me about her situation, about her husband's abuse, about the legal issues. She wanted my help, and she wanted me to find a way to tell you, for it to all be aboveboard."

"So you decided to go for it?"

"No," Max said. "I said I needed time to think. She told me that she could get a paternity test and I could meet her back there next week. I told her I'd think about it, but yeah, I ended up meeting her again. She got the samples from Sutton and gave the kit to me, and I took it home and got my samples. I had to keep everything on me, but I was so afraid you'd find the packaging, so I shoved the box under the mattress in the guest room, which I'm guessing you saw if you found the phone."

I nodded.

Max let his hands drop to his sides. "I sent it all in, paying extra to expedite it. When she filled it out, she put in her friend's address to receive the results. This woman, Erica, was the only person Rae felt she could trust. We met up again the next week, which was just last Wednesday—same time, same place—and Rae showed me the results. There's no doubt about it. He's mine." Max swallowed. "I knew I had to tell you, but I wanted to wait until the right time. And I was planning on it, as soon as Liana and my parents had gone."

I nodded him along, but then froze, thinking of the bartender's words, the way she'd been so sure. "Wait," I said. "You're skipping something. Someone saw you last Wednesday. The bartender told me. Some woman who was angry to find you two together. The bartender assumed it was your wife, but we know that's not possible. So who did she mean, Max? *Who?*"

"Oh," Max said. "I'm sorry. When you mentioned some other woman, I didn't put it together that *that's* who you were talking about." He reddened, and he looked down at his hands. When he looked back up, his voice was strained.

"That was Liana."

46

8:14 p.m.

LIANA.

For a second, their whole relationship flashed before my eyes. How Molly always thought it was so strange for a straight guy and girl to be so close. How Liana was gorgeous and talented and smart and funny, and could it really be possible that nothing had ever happened between them? How they were so close—too close—and no good ever came of that.

For a second, I was back in the kitchen, on Friday night, watching Liana and Max talking quietly, earnestly, while they were supposed to be doing the dishes. I was in the living room, seeing Liana's lack of surprise when I told her Max changed his password.

What if something had happened between them, a betrayal even worse, even more personal, than anything that happened with Grace?

What if Liana had only been helping me out of some sort of misplaced guilt?

"You and . . ." I started. "You and Liana?"

Max's eyebrows crinkled up. "What? Oh god, no."

"Because I thought she was my friend," I said miserably. "Was I stupid to think so? Was it all a big lie?"

Max leapt from the bed and came to me, kneeling down, taking my hands in his. "No," he said. "No, I promise you."

I shook his hands away, and he backed up, returned to the edge of the bed. "Liana saw Rae and me at the bar. She assumed I was having an affair. She started yelling about how I was ruining everything, how I was being so stupid. I guess when the bartender saw it, she assumed that Liana and I were together. Trust me, Liana wasn't mad because she was jealous. Liana was mad because she thought I was hurting *you*."

I shook my head, trying to make sense of it. "So why didn't you tell Liana the truth? You could have told her the whole story right then."

"When Liana saw us, she stormed out, and the next time I got her alone was on Friday, when we were doing the dishes. I told her I wasn't having an affair and I was going to explain everything to you right away. I didn't—I couldn't—tell her all of it. I thought if anyone should find out next, it should be you. Liana basically told me that if I didn't come clean to you about whatever was going on, she was going to tell you herself."

Liana's words flashed to mind. *Max leaves when things get hard.*

"So Liana thought you lost your nerve and bailed on us. She thought you disappeared, because you'd done it before."

"Probably," he said. "That's probably exactly where her mind would have gone."

"I don't understand," I said. I got up from my chair, went

to the bed, sat next to him again. "Why did you use to disappear like that, and why didn't you ever tell me about it?"

Max's cheeks reddened. "I'm so . . . so embarrassed about it. I'm not proud of that part of my life at all. I've been over it plenty with therapists over the years. There were times where things were so overwhelming, when I felt like I was disappointing myself and my parents and well—everyone—that it felt like it would be easier on everyone if I weren't around for a few days. It was like hitting a power-off switch or something. I didn't tell you about it because I was ashamed, and I also knew that I was done with it, and I promise you, I am. This was different."

"Liana still should have said something," I said. "I've been driving myself crazy, thinking there were multiple people—thinking you were screwing every single woman in Kingston. God."

"Janie," Max said, taking my hand in his. "I know that's what it looked like, but you have to believe me. I never cheated on you. With Rae. With Liana. With anyone. I love you. I know I made so many mistakes, I know I should have opened up to you, but I promise you, I never did anything like that."

"Maybe you didn't cheat," I said, still processing. "But you had secrets. You all did. Liana never even told me about seeing you on Wednesday. She was always defending you to me. For all she knew, you *were* having an affair, and she never told me. She covered up for you even if she didn't fully understand what she was covering up for."

"I know," Max said. "I'm sorry. But I'm sure Liana just didn't know what to do. I'm sure she hoped there was a way I could tell you everything myself. Don't blame her, please. It's not her fault that all of this happened. And I promise you she cares about you so much. She never would have gotten so angry at me that night if she didn't. Please forgive her."

I felt an ache, deep in my chest. I wanted to forgive Liana, I wanted to forgive Max, I wanted, even, to forgive myself. But we'd all kept things from one another. None of us had been truthful.

Max looked down, then back up at me. "I promise you, I was only trying to do the right thing for Rae and for Sutton. I know I fucked up at just about every step of the process, but that was always my motivation."

I wanted to believe him—I really did—but there was still so much to understand.

"Why didn't you at least tell me on Friday? You could have, as soon as everyone was gone. You knew that Liana already knew . . . something. Why did you go back out to Rae when you could have come to me?"

Max bit his lip. "I wanted to—that was the plan. And when I came home from dropping them off and you seemed so upset, I thought you may have even found out. I thought maybe when you saw Rae looking at us at that concert you put it together."

"Why was she there, Max? Did you arrange that?"

"No," he said. "It was a coincidence, truly. A small town. Only so much stuff to do with kids. But yeah, it was awful that she was there, and that she was looking, and that you noticed. I knew I had to tell you, even if Liana hadn't seen us on Wednesday. And I wanted to, but then you said what you did about Freya, and I could see that you weren't yourself at all."

Shame filled me up again, turning my cheeks hot.

"I know you didn't mean it. It's not that, Janie. But I also knew that telling you then would break you. I thought if you could get some sleep, if I could wait until you were in a better headspace . . ."

Tears spilled over my lids as guilt shook through me. "So this is all my fault, then? Because I was a mess, right. A terrible mother, who confessed those horrible thoughts to you?"

"No," Max said, reaching for my hand again, squeezing it. "You aren't a terrible mother at all. God, you'd do anything for her, I know that. And you must know that, deep down. But you weren't—" He glanced to me. "You aren't in the best place. And I didn't feel I could tell you then, while you were already so raw. I decided to give it a couple of days. And I really thought I would have another chance."

I looked up at Max, the pieces fitting together in my mind. "But then she called you," I said. "Grace. *Rae.*"

Max nodded solemnly. "She was absolutely frantic. I guess she sent a bunch of WhatsApp messages to the other phone, but I didn't see them, because you were already asleep, and she called my actual phone number, which freaked me out. I thought maybe she was calling because she'd seen us all at the park that morning and it had upset her somehow, but it wasn't that at all. She was in a panic, and she begged me to come meet her. She wanted me to come straight to her house, but it felt like crossing a line, so I insisted on the bar, and she agreed."

"Then what?" I asked. "How did it get to this? To you running? To you and . . . and Sutton."

"It happened so fast . . ." His voice trailed off, and his eyes locked on mine. "On Friday night, it all got totally out of control."

47

8:28 p.m.

I WHIPPED MY HAND AWAY, DUNCAN'S WORDS ABOUT GRACE'S death ringing in my mind.

You don't fall that hard without being pushed.

"You . . . you didn't hurt her, did you," I stammered. "By . . . by accident?"

Max's head shot up. "No, Janie. God, no. I would never hurt anyone. Tell me you know that."

"I thought I did," I said. "But it's hard to know anything now."

Max pressed his hands to his thighs, his eyes trained on mine. "As soon as I got to the bar, Rae was frantic. She'd spoken to Daniel only a couple of hours before, and he'd caught her out in a lie. She'd made up this story about a boozy book club with her friend, Erica, for the nights we met up, and that's why she had to go to the bar on Wednesdays, but she fumbled when he asked what book she was reading—she told him the wrong title. He called her out on it and asked her if she was meeting me, and I guess the whole thing blew up. He was threatening her, saying he was going to make sure she never saw Sutton again. He was sending messages to her, the works, calling her all sorts of names. She was terrified. He had a business thing in the city that she knew he couldn't miss, and she told him Sutton was at a sleepover, that they could talk everything out as soon as he got home." Max sighed. "The thing is, Sutton didn't have a sleepover—it was a lie she made up on the spot—and she told me she needed me to drive her and Sutton to Erica's house. She told me to get the car and come back, park in front of her house, across the street. She said she'd get Sutton and all the evidence of the abuse and we'd drive to Erica's house. I asked her why Erica couldn't drive her, and Rae said Erica wasn't answering her phone, and she had to get out of there before Daniel got back that night."

"And you just did it?" I asked. "Why didn't you both call the cops?"

"One of Daniel's brothers is in the Kingston Police Department. Rae didn't trust them. And I don't blame her. You read these stories all the time. Women dead. Whole families murdered. The cops, their friends and their families, they never took them seriously. I couldn't live with myself if something happened to Rae and Sutton, if Daniel did something, if it was all my fault."

Max's shoulders shook.

"What?" I asked. "What happened?"

"When I got back with the car, Rae was standing on the sidewalk with Sutton in her arms. He was wrapped around her like a koala, obviously exhausted. She opened the back door and laid him across the seat, tossed a small backpack in. She opened the front door, but instead of getting in, she pushed a scrap of paper at me. She said she was sorry, but she'd gotten more texts from Daniel, directly threatening

Sutton, and she didn't think Erica's place was far enough away from Daniel to keep Sutton safe. She asked me to take him to the address written down on the paper. It was an aunt of hers, the only other family Sutton had."

"I don't understand," I said. "Why didn't she want to go with you if Daniel was that dangerous?"

"I asked her that," Max said. "Rae said she had evidence of the abuse, that it was in the back of Sutton's closet, mixed into all his things. She said she needed to return to the house to get it, and then she was going straight to Erica's. It was too far to walk with Sutton, but on her own she'd be okay. She started to close the car door, but then she started freaking out again— she said she'd left her phone in the bar—and she couldn't do any of this without it. I told her I'd wait, but she told me to shut the fuck up and drive, that Sutton's safety depended on it. She begged me." Max's voice cracked. "She obviously didn't realize Daniel was back from the city already—and I don't think she believed he'd actually kill her. Rae thought she could get all her evidence together, hole up at Erica's, and petition the court for a restraining order, at least until she could remove Daniel as the father. She believed Daniel wasn't above hurting—even killing—Sutton to punish her."

"But you must have realized this was crazy?" I asked. "You must have known that there had to be a better way?"

"I know," he said desperately. "But she just ran, straight into the bar. I waited for her—I did—I thought I could reason with her once she came back out. But then ten minutes went by, twenty minutes, and she still didn't come. I left the car idling, and I went back into the bar, but I couldn't find her. And so I go back to the car, and the kid's in the back seat, and I have this address in my hand, and what was I supposed to do? Go to the cops? Explain why I have a kid I have no legal right to laying in my car? When Rae told me the cops were on Daniel's side anyway? Sutton started crying, and I didn't know what to do, so I plugged the address into my phone, and it was nine hours away, and I knew I couldn't do that in one night. I'd been drinking, I was losing it, nothing felt safe. So I headed north, and when I was a half hour away, I stopped at a motel. I tried to get Sutton to sleep, and once I did, I crashed."

I shook my head, anger surging in my belly. "Why didn't you call me? I was worried sick."

"I know," Max said. "Believe me, I wanted to, but I didn't know where to begin, what to say. 'Hi, Janie, sorry to wake you, but I can't feed Freya tonight because I'm taking my biological son to an address on a scrap of paper so he's safe'?"

"You could have said *something*," I said. "You could have said there was an emergency but that you were okay. I thought something had happened to you. I walked to the bottom of the basement, terrified you'd slipped and split your skull in two. I woke up to Freya screaming," I said, my voice cracking. "I woke to her covered in her own shit, and you weren't there, and I didn't know what to do, and I was all alone, and I—"

"I'm so sorry," he said, reaching an arm around me. "I'm so incredibly sorry."

A sob escaped my throat. "And when I called your family, when I called Liana, they didn't even sound that surprised," I said. "You treated me like everyone else. Disposable. Disappear when things get hard. That's what you do, right?"

Max dropped his hand and shook his head, tears in his eyes, too. "No," he said. "It just happened so fast. We woke up early the next morning, and I had Sutton, and I didn't know what to do. And I still thought, I don't know, that I could get him to where he needed to go, and I could go back to you, and I could explain, and I knew you'd hate me, I knew you'd be furious, but at least I could explain it in person. I was acting on impulse, trying to put out every fire that popped up. Sutton was hungry, and I realized she hadn't even given us a car seat, and I thought—what if something happens in the car and he gets hurt and it's all my fault? So I went to Walmart that morning, and I got a booster seat, and I bought snacks and waters and food for us. I was going to go straight to Maine, straight there and come back, but in the midst of all the calls from you, I started getting these calls from a number I didn't recognize. I looked it up, and it was the Kingston Police Department. I just knew. God, I knew that something had gone terribly wrong and that I could be in trouble, too. That, hell, this could be a kidnapping. But if I turned around, Sutton would go to Daniel, and what would happen then? So I looked up the directions, and I copied them onto the paper, and I tossed my phone to the side of the road. I was too scared by then. Too scared of what I'd already gotten myself into. I thought if I could only get Sutton to Maine, I could think about the rest later. But then, of course, I saw the news. I saw Rae was dead, and I knew how bad it looked. I had to call you. I used some cash to get one of those prepaid phone cards, and it took me forever, but I asked around at shops until I found one that would let me use their phone. I still didn't know what to say but I wanted you to hear my voice. I wanted to know if Freya was okay."

"I heard Sutton," I said. "When you called. I heard his voice, and it terrified me."

How much longer?

"I'm sorry, Janie. I'm so sorry that every time I tried to

make it better, I only made it worse," Max said, pressing on. "I took back roads the rest of the way. I stopped at a parking lot—my dad always told me to keep a set of tools in the trunk, even for a rental, and I guess his advice paid off—I used a screwdriver to switch my plates with someone else's. But I got him there. I got him there this morning. I did what she asked me to. Rae's dying wish."

"Then you just came . . ." I looked around. "Here?"

"I went by our place first," he said. "I had the llama pacifier, and I knew how much you needed it. I didn't see any cops on the block, so I drove by and rolled down the window and tossed it onto the porch. It took everything I had not to stop the car and rush in and see you, but I knew it was too risky. So I headed here instead. I called you as soon as I found another phone to use at a gas station out of the way." Max turned around, his eyes trained on mine. "I swear to god, I never hurt her. I never wanted to hurt anyone."

He leaned forward, his face so close to mine.

"Do you believe me?" he asked. "Please say you believe me."

"I want to," I said, all the emotions of the past few days leaking from my eyes now, water through a sieve. "I really, really want to."

48

8:47 p.m.

MY BRAIN RACED, TRYING TO PIECE IT ALL TOGETHER, BECAUSE I wanted to believe him, I really did. But there were still too many questions. Sticky thorns, hooking in. Scratching.

"What is it?" Max asked, squeezing my arms with his hands, like he used to do when he wanted to reassure me. "I can see you thinking. Whatever it is, tell me."

I pushed up from the bed and walked to the chair opposite Max. My boobs had begun to throb. Right then, I should have been feeding Freya. I should have been sitting in the rocking chair, her tiny baby body swaddled tightly, I should have been getting ready to put her in her cot, praying she'd drift off for at least a few hours. For the first time since Freya was born, I missed her, feeling the space where her body should have been, the emptiness in the crook of my arm, the ache of my body longing to fulfill her hunger, her needs. For the first time, I wanted to be feeding her. I wanted to be home taking care of her. I stared at Max.

"What about the handkerchief?"

His face scrunched up, confused, and his eyes looked entirely lost.

Maybe that was what did it for me, over anything else. My partner was not a good actor. There was no doubt that he could evade the truth by omission, as he had done with me, but I truly believed if I'd ever found something, questioned him outright, he wouldn't have been able to fool me. He wore his emotions, all of them, right there on his sleeve. That was how it had always been, how it had been on Friday night, too, when I'd confessed to him my darkest of thoughts.

That was how it was now. The most genuine surprise and confusion were painted all over Max's face.

"The handkerchief," I said again.

Still, nothing.

"*Your* handkerchief," I clarified, testing him one more time. "One of the ones I got you."

"What handkerchief?" he asked, his eyes scrunching up at the corners. "What are you talking about?"

I licked my lips, preparing. "One of the teal ones that had your name printed on the bottom. The cops found it near the scene."

"Are you sure?" he asked. "That doesn't make any sense."

"Yes, I'm sure."

"That's . . . impossible," Max said.

"Why?"

He reached into his pocket, pulled a hankie out. "Because I have it on me."

I stared at it, the edges of teal, the bold lettering. *M-A-X.* The blank canvas around it, the absence of blood.

"I saw it, Max. I saw a photo and everything. And when I

checked your top drawer at the rental, I found four left. It was a set of six. That means one was missing. And that one is in police evidence right now, covered in blood."

Max's shoulders slumped, and his face found his hands again. "Oh god," he said. "I knew I was a murder suspect, I knew I would have so much to explain for taking Sutton, but I didn't think—I didn't think they'd find something that actually tied it back to me. I thought it would all be circumstantial. I still thought, god, I thought somehow this would be okay."

"There has to be some explanation. Did you give one of those to Grace?"

Max's eyes widened. "Oh shit," he said. "Fuck."

"What is it?" I asked.

"She was so upset. On Friday. She was crying, and . . . and my jacket was sitting on the table between us, and . . . I told her I usually kept an extra handkerchief in the pocket. She reached in, and . . . I didn't even see which one it was. I thought she put it back, but obviously she didn't. It was probably there, wherever she left her phone. Fuck."

"Daniel must have found it," I said, the truth, the answers, finally clicking together. "Or she had it on her when she . . . when she died. It was the perfect way to frame you."

"Jesus," Max said. "Jesus Christ."

"That's not all," I said. "Duncan, the investigator, she says there are payments, too. From a trust of yours, to Grace and Daniel."

Max shook his head vehemently. "I have no idea what you're talking about. Did you see proof of that, too?"

"No," I said. "Duncan only told me. She thought Grace was threatening to come to me with the whole story, and you were paying her hush money. That you didn't want me to know you were an absent dad to Sutton."

"That's impossible," Max said. "I swear to you, Janie, I never even knew I had a kid. There was nothing to pay off, because I didn't know."

"Is there any way Grace told her husband otherwise? Because everyone seems to think you *did* know."

"I promise," he said. "I didn't. But——" He shrugged. "I did ghost her, and that was shitty, and she told me she found out she was pregnant a couple of weeks after. I guess I could see how she might . . . adjust the timeline a bit. Tell people I wasn't ready to be a dad and left her." He sighed. "Even if I didn't know, I don't blame her for saying whatever she felt she needed to say to save face."

"So who made these payments, then?" I asked.

"There were no payments," Max said. "There is no trust, apart from the one we emptied to put into the apartment. If they didn't show you proof, I have to think that the police made it up to turn you against me."

I sighed, exhausted by the mental gymnastics, by evidence, by circumstance, by all the information I was still trying to process. All of it so new, so foreign. I glanced around at this room. The haphazardly put-together walls. The exposed pipes. "What is this place, Max? Why *did* you come here?"

"It's my aunt Tammy's," he said sheepishly. "She was at the baby shower."

"The hippie lady?" Max's aunt Tammy had been the only one of Brenda's guests at the Westchester baby shower who hadn't had that buttoned-up, moneyed, WASPy look to her. She'd floated in in a long black dress, drunk three mimosas, and left early.

"I don't understand. She knows you're here?"

"No," he said. "Maybe. I don't know. She hasn't said anything. Obviously."

"I still don't get it."

Max winced. "It wasn't always so . . . calm . . . between my parents. Now things are okay, but my mom would be so difficult and controlling, and it would set my dad off. So when I turned eighteen and graduated from high school but was still living at home, Tammy told me to use this place anytime I wanted. It had mostly been used by her husband, my uncle, who died when I was in high school, and she couldn't bear to sell it—too many memories. She said I could always come here, anytime I needed to get away, to get some space. Use it to make music, connect with nature, whatever, but I knew it was really so I could get some time from my parents."

I blinked, taking in this new info. I did know about Max's parents, about how there had been years when things weren't so good, when they almost split up. I'd always thought Carl would have been so much better suited to someone warmer, more laid-back, but now, he seemed happy enough. I never knew Brenda was so difficult that Max's aunt was literally sweeping him off to a secret getaway. "You never told me any of this."

Max shrugged. "I should have. It's just the times I did use it were those times I disappeared, and I felt so ashamed about that part of my life. I thought you'd judge me if you knew that's how I used to act."

"I wouldn't have," I said. "I would have listened. I would have loved you anyway."

"I know that now," he said. "I'm sorry."

"Have you come here?" I asked tentatively. "Since you met me?"

"No," Max said. "Never. Not until now, and that's only because I was desperate and didn't know where to go." Max's eyes caught mine. "Don't you see, I never *needed* to come here since meeting you. When shit would hit the fan, I'd go to you, not run away."

"Except for when this shit hit the fan," I said. "Except for now."

"Yeah," he said, abashed. "Except for now."

I stared at my partner, at the father of my child. I loved him, and I knew he loved me, too. I knew he never would have meant to hurt me or Freya. He'd made all the mistakes in the world, but his love for me, for Freya, was as true as ever. He'd risked his freedom—everything—to give us something small, yet so meaningful. The llama in place of your mama. It was so very Max. Such a sweet gesture and yet altogether foolish. The action of a man fueled by emotion, by caring and compassion and love, the sort of man who would take a child across state lines because someone begged him to.

Part of me still hated him for scaring me, for omitting the truth, for meeting Grace and going to the bar without ever telling me. I hated him for his secret phone and his secret hideaway and a past I knew less about than I'd thought. I hated Max for all the things that he'd kept from me.

But how could I, really? I had secrets of my own. "Max," I said. "I made mistakes, too. I wasn't always . . . I wasn't always entirely honest, either."

Max looked at me, and his eyes were open so wide, taking in my words, and if he'd asked, I would have told him, I really would have, but he didn't. He only squeezed my hand, letting the moment pass. "It's okay, Janie. Whatever it was, it's not as bad as this. Whatever it was, I forgive you."

Did he know? Somehow, in some way, did he already know?

Maybe he did, and maybe he really had forgiven me. Maybe we were two fucked-up people who *wanted* to be good to each other, who *wanted* to do the right thing, even if we failed.

For once in my life, I didn't care what anyone else thought about me. The worst had already happened now, and there was no way to worry about it anymore. I had worn my shame so close to my heart, all these years, just as my parents had taught me to, but now, it was all out, my relationship laid bare, naked for the world to gawk at. My partner, hated, all across the internet. And in real life, too. He'd been tried and found guilty in the court of public opinion already, there was no denying it. And there were no appeals there, either. The damage was done. Yet, it somehow didn't matter now. Max was mine, and I loved him.

"I believe you," I said.

Max risked a smile. "You do?"

I nodded. "I do."

He leaned forward, embracing me, and it felt good, so good, even though I knew the feeling couldn't last.

When we finally pulled away, I stared at him. "But what do we do now? What is your plan, Max? Because you can't stay here forever. The police are looking for you."

"I know," he said. "I've been over it a hundred times, and I think the only thing that can possibly save me—that can possibly save Sutton from going right back to Daniel—is to find proof of what Rae told me. The proof she was going to collect."

"Are you *sure* it was Daniel?" I asked. "Are you sure he killed her?"

"Janie," Max said. "You have to understand. She was terrified of him, of what he could do to Sutton. She was so scared she practically threw her only child into the back of a relative stranger's car without a car seat. She wasn't a bad mother. She wasn't careless. She was desperate. She knew she had to get Sutton away, however she could."

I tried to reconcile the image of the sad, heartbroken man I'd met twice with the picture Max had in his own head, the one Rae had painted for him. It was hard to make sense of, but at the same time, was it, really?

That's what they always say, after something like this happens . . . he didn't seem the type.

That's what the bartender said, and it was true, wasn't it? I could no sooner figure out whether Daniel was a killer from two meetings than I could make sense of why my partner was wanted as one. Things like this, they weren't comprehensible.

Was Daniel's grief an act? What if his sweet, sensitive husband routine, his swoop-in-to-parent-the-bastard-child routine, was just that: a routine? Something to trot out when with friends or family, something to show the community that he was a good guy after all. What if, behind closed doors, there wasn't any hint of that man?

"So how are you going to get it, then?" I asked.

"I have to get Daniel out of his house," Max said. "Rae told me she had stuff in Sutton's closet. I know I can find it if I can only get Daniel to leave."

I blinked twice. "That's it?"

Max nodded.

"Okay," I said. "I think I can do that for you."

"What do you mean?"

"I'll ask him to meet me," I said.

"What?" Max said, rearing back. "No, you can't. He's dangerous, Janie."

"You don't understand," I said. "I've already met him. Twice."

Max's jaw hung open.

"I needed answers, Max. I was turning over every stone I could."

"No," Max said. "No, no, no. I can't believe I brought you into this. I can't believe I put you at risk."

"I chose to go see him, Max. I chose my own way."

"Still," he said. "Still, it's all my fault."

"Listen," I said. "Do you really believe Daniel could hurt Sutton?"

"Yes," he said. "Yes, I do."

"And do you really believe that there is some sort of proof in that house?"

"Yes," he said. "But I don't want you meeting him. I don't want to get it like that."

"Officer Duncan told me that Daniel is taking the first flight to Maine tomorrow. Sutton will be right back with him unless we do something that changes that tonight."

"Christ," Max said. "Christ."

"I know it's a risk," I said. "I know we're playing with fire, but what else can we do? Duncan will never believe you without something. And that boy could be in serious danger. He's your biological son. He's Freya's half brother."

"There has to be some other way," Max said.

I knew there wasn't. The clock was ticking. Sutton's—
and ours.

Before Max could stop me, before he could argue, reason,
try to put my safety over this existential risk to our family, to
this poor sweet child, I pulled out my phone, found the contact, shot off a quick message.

*I found something you'll want to see and I need to talk. Can you
meet me in an hour at the same spot?*

49

10:11 p.m.

THERE WAS NO SIGN OF DANIEL WHEN I ENTERED THE BAR, just a few minutes before our agreed-upon meeting time. The same bartender was there from before, and he smiled when I walked up.

"Hendrick's, correct?"

I forced a grin, tried to stay calm. The place was as dark and dim as it had been before, but a feeling of menace had settled in since my last meeting with Daniel. Hazy, with a hint of horror lurking around the corner, like a noir film approaching one of its final climactic scenes.

"You remembered," I said, leaning into the banter. Something about it felt safe and comforting.

"Same thing again?" he asked.

I hesitated. I didn't want a drink, really, but I needed to buy time, and ordering seemed to do that. "Sure thing." I would take a couple of sips, to calm my nerves, to loosen myself up for what was about to be a hell of an acting job in front of Daniel. I was suited to the art, unlike Max. I was the one who'd entertained clients, I was the one who'd reflected back to them exactly what they desired, in any given moment.

"And you're meeting someone again, right?" the bartender asked as he reached for a martini shaker. "Because the guy still hasn't been caught."

"Yes," I said. "I'm meeting someone."

I'm meeting the person who did it, I thought. But Daniel couldn't very well attack me right here in the bar, could he? Right here in front of this jovial bartender? Only he had managed to kill Grace, just outside Three Crows. The thought sent a chill up my spine.

It was okay, I told myself as the bartender went to work on my drink. It was a necessary risk. To save Max. To protect Sutton.

I checked my phone, opening the baby camera.

There Freya was, fast asleep, the rise and fall of her chest rhythmic beneath the night vision of the HD camera.

I slipped my phone back into my pocket and watched as the bartender shook the martini, taking extra care.

Max hadn't wanted me to do this, but he knew there was no alternative. I'd sent the text and told him I was going, with or without him. And so, I'd driven us back in Liana's car, and I'd stopped, car idling, a block from Daniel and Grace's home, a block from where she'd been killed, and Max had gotten out, taking with him a backpack he'd found in Liana's trunk, a leopard-print thing that looked almost painfully out of place on him. The plan was for him to wait until he saw Daniel leaving to find a way in, use the time I bought him to get the proof that Grace had been gathering, anything that would back up his story, that would prevent Daniel from going to get Sutton the next day.

"Sorry I'm late."

I jumped at the voice behind me, then turned to see Daniel leaning against the bar, his stubble still unshaven, his shirt undone at the collar. A scent of booze wafting right off him.

"Scotch and soda," he said to the bartender.

"He makes a mean martini," I said. He makes a long martini, I thought, and every second was precious now.

Daniel shook his head. "Scotch for me." His eyes caught mine. "You okay?"

"Yes," I said. "Thank you for coming. I'm sorry it was so last minute."

"It's okay," he said. He raised an eyebrow. "What did you find?"

I hesitated, not wanting to rush. "Let's wait till we're at the table."

He nodded, and as the bartender finished my drink and poured Daniel's, I imagined Max jimmying a window, squeezing his body through. He could do it; I knew he could. The house was old, and old houses came with easier points of entry. Window locks that didn't quite latch. Rickety doors waiting to be jammed open. In any case, we'd found a bottle of wine in Liana's back seat, and in a pinch, he could use it to bust open a window, get in that way.

I turned, heading toward a table in the corner, and took a seat, steeling my breath, crossing and uncrossing my legs, Daniel opposite me, already sipping his drink. I had to play this right. If Daniel left, if he went back to his house, there was no way to warn Max. He didn't have a phone.

"How are you doing?" I asked, trying my best to stretch this out.

"Better, now that Sutton has been found," he said. "Now

that I know he's safe. I'm flying out to Maine to get him to-morrow. But I can't help but think about how Grace won't be there. How she should be there."

"I can't even imagine," I said. "But you must be so re-lieved about Sutton."

Daniel's eyes narrowed, and for a moment, the feeling was almost written across them, naked and plain: *I don't give two shits about that kid.*

Or was I imagining it? Was I seeing what I wanted to see so I could fully believe Max?

"Yes, I'm relieved," Daniel said, the look in his eyes disap-pearing as quickly as it had come. He took another sip, and his voice softened. "He's my son, after all. No matter what his genes say, I'm his father. Not Max."

"Of course you are," I said, making my voice warm, calm, reassuring. I took a small sip of my drink.

"So?" Daniel asked, taking a gulp of his. "What is it? What did you find? Like I said, I have a flight tomorrow. I'm only here because you made it sound urgent."

I bit my lip. I'd run through it all in the silent moments of the car ride, my hand in Max's, squeezing, reassuring him as much as myself, and I'd landed on the truth. It seemed, some-how, the simplest.

"I found a phone," I said. "Of Max's. One I didn't know about."

Daniel raised an eyebrow. "And?"

"And there were texts on it. WhatsApp messages. Between Max and . . . and your wife. Did you ever see anything like that? On her phone?"

Daniel shook his head. "No," he said. "I know she had WhatsApp, used it to talk to the other moms in Sutton's class.

But no one knows where her phone is now. The police said it wasn't found on her, and it's not in our house. Can I see the phone you found? Does it confirm these meetings?"

"It does," I said. "But it's still back at my place."

"Did you tell the police?" Daniel asked.

"No," I said. "But I will. I know it's time to cooperate with them. I can't keep holding out, hoping Max will somehow turn out innocent in all this. I just . . . I called you first. I didn't know what to do."

Daniel stabbed the straw around in his drink, then took another sip, leaving only a little bit left. "You should tell them. You have to. But I don't know what you need from me. Why you need me here. Like I said, I have a flight tomorrow."

"I'm sorry," I said. "I just, I had to speak to someone. I couldn't sit with it, on my own. My brain was running, and I—"

"I know you've been dealing with a lot, and I've tried to be understanding, but, god, what else do you want from me?" he asked. "I'm sorry that you've learned that Max is a horrible human being, but *I'm* the one who lost someone. Me. I'm not the one who's supposed to be consoling you, telling you it's going to be okay. Because it's not, and maybe you're only just figuring that out, but it's been very clear to me since the cops called me on Saturday morning, telling me my wife was dead." He finished his drink in one last gulp. "I have to go."

My heart raced. Max. He was inside Daniel's home. I'd ruined this. I should have made up something. Anything to keep him here with me.

"Wait," I said, reaching my hand out, lightly grabbing his

arm. "Have another drink. Come on. No one understands it but us. It's different, but you know it's true. Max isn't dead, but he might as well be. He's long gone, he's abandoned me and our new baby. He's done—" I shook my head, pulling it all out, every ounce of pain I could. "Unspeakable things, and I'm left—alone—to pick up the pieces. Just like you."

Daniel stared, and his eyes softened, if only for a moment.

"What I want from you is someone to talk to," I said. "That's all. And I know you want that, too."

"My flight," he said.

I squeezed his arm, let my hand rest upon it, heat coursing, skin on skin. "*Please.* You're the only one who understands."

"Okay," he said. "One more drink, then."

I tried to hold back the sigh of relief as Daniel walked up to the bar, ordered another.

I bought you ten minutes at least, Max. Find something, anything. Find something and get the hell out.

Daniel returned, set the drink down, took a sip. "I'm sorry," he said. "I know you're right. It's just been so hard."

I sipped my drink as well. "I know."

Go, Max. Go, go, go.

"You're a beautiful woman, you know," Daniel said, as if only now taking me in. He took another sip.

I did as well, knowing I had to play this right. Knowing that Daniel loved a woman in despair. "Thank you," I said. "I don't feel it. I feel sleep-deprived and lost and like I don't know what to do with my life."

"What *are* you going to do?" he asked. "Now that you know the truth?"

I met his eyes, then looked down at my hands. "I'm going

to take this to the police, help them in any way I can. I'm going to get my baby and go be with people who care about me. My parents are coming on Thursday. I'm going to try to . . . to move on however I can."

"So you believe it, finally?" Daniel asked. "The things I said."

I nodded without looking up. "There's nothing else that makes sense now."

Daniel leaned forward, reached across the table for my hand. I hesitated only a minute before I let him take it. My heart was racing, and my palms were sweating, and I prayed he didn't feel it.

"Does it scare you? To know that you built a life with a murderer? Does Max scare you now?"

I looked up, winced. "When you put it like that—I mean, yes, I guess. Yes, he does."

Daniel whipped his hand away suddenly, leaving mine hanging there, in the middle of the table. I pulled it back.

His brow furrowed as he took another sip. "The thing is, you don't seem scared of Max." He slammed his drink down on the table. "In fact, you almost seem scared of *me*."

My heart beat even faster, and I looked at him, tried to hold it together. "Why would I be scared of you?"

Daniel let the question hang in the air for a moment, but there it was anyway: a glimmer in his eyes, like someone finally being seen.

"Why were you so eager to have me stay for another drink?"

"I told you, we're the only ones who—"

"Understand each other, I know." Daniel smirked, but it

was an awful smirk, mean, a hint of aggression brewing beneath.

The hairs on the back of my neck stood tall, and my face began to go hot.

"You must be angry," Daniel went on. "What he did to you. And with this new proof. This new confirmation. You must be furious."

I swallowed, my throat feeling suddenly dry. I took a sip of gin, tried to calm my nerves. "I am," I said. "You know I am."

He cocked his head to the side. "Then how come you don't look it?" He leaned forward. "You think I don't know manipulation," he said, his voice quiet now, so only I could hear. "You think I don't know when someone's lying, playing me? You think she didn't try about a million times? Pretty girls, they think they've got you under their thumb if they so much as look your way. But I'm not like those other guys. Chads drooling over a pair of nice eyes and C-cups. I have a brain." He pounded the table between us, and I jumped, my heart racing. "You wanted me out of my house, didn't you? You wanted me out of my house for some reason, that's why you brought me here. It is, isn't it? I can see right through you."

"Daniel, wait—"

"I'm not stupid," he said. "I won't be a fool."

I grabbed his arm then, desperate to buy time, some way, any way.

"Stop it," I said. "I don't know what you're talking about. *Really*. Please stay."

Daniel shook me off, pushing himself up and bolting out of the booth.

I turned, my head swiveling to follow him as he burst out of the bar, practically running now.

Oh god oh god oh god.

I jumped out of the booth, grabbed my bag, and followed him out of the bar.

Daniel was already halfway down the block, breaking into a run.

50

10:41 p.m.

I HADN'T RUN SINCE BEFORE I'D GOTTEN PREGNANT. IT USED to be something I tried to do a few times a week at least, but first-trimester morning sickness had knocked me out, and after that, I'd either been too big—or too exhausted and uncomfortable—to do anything more than a brisk walk.

My feet pounded hard against the pavement, and my breaths came quick and shallow, my insides roiling and my breasts as heavy as rocks, painful and tender as I rushed down the sidewalk, toward Daniel's.

I couldn't warn Max—he had no phone.

We had known this, and yet I had hoped to buy him more time.

All I could do was get there, hope and pray that Daniel wouldn't do something rash.

That he wouldn't . . .

Daniel turned, rounding the corner, disappearing from view, and I pushed myself harder, rounded the corner as well, the streetlights dim, illuminating only the cracks in the sidewalk, the tree roots breaking through, threatening to trip me, send me straight onto my face.

I spotted Daniel again, his profile lit up by a streetlamp. He was running up the walk now, onto the porch, fumbling with keys, opening the front door.

Finding all the energy I had left, I ran even faster, my boobs aching, screaming with pain, my heels rubbing raw against the edges of my boots.

I rushed through the open gate, up the walk, and onto the porch. The door was unlocked, and I pushed in before thinking, past the coatrack I'd seen that first day, strung up with items from people who weren't there anymore—Grace, dead; Sutton, safe for now, but endangered by the man who'd been playing father for his whole life.

All that mattered was that Max was safe. I could get through it all if only Max was safe.

Then, as if materializing from my mind, there Max was, running down the staircase, Liana's backpack in his hands, Daniel behind him.

Daniel pushed Max at the last step, and I watched, horrified and unable to stop it, as Max fell forward onto the floor, the backpack flying.

There was a moment of quiet when I stared at my partner, splayed onto the ground, and stared at the backpack, full of what I could only hope was proof, and I didn't know which Daniel would lunge for, but Max's voice quickly cut through the silence. "She deserved so much better than you," he spat, grabbing Daniel's attention.

"No, Max," I called, rushing toward him. "Don't make it worse!"

Already, Daniel was on him, picking him up, slamming

his body against the wall. I scrambled for Liana's backpack, tossing it back toward the door as Daniel railed, "What the fuck were you doing in my house?" He shook Max, slamming harder. "In my fucking kid's room?"

"Janie," Max said, his eyes on the backpack near the door. "Janie, just leave—"

The front door was still open, and a cool gust of air rushed past us. I could grab the backpack now, pray it had the evidence we needed. I could go.

Daniel punched Max swiftly in the gut. Max keeled over, bending in half, grabbing his stomach.

"Stop it," I screamed, but already Daniel's fist was connecting with Max's face, making an awful cracking sound, followed by a squish. I reached for Daniel's shoulder, my fingers grasping at the back of his jacket. He pushed me away forcefully, and I stumbled back, the pain from my C-section scar blazing. A hot white line of fire.

Me out of the way, Daniel threw another punch, his hand connecting with the other side of Max's face. Another crack. Another squish.

Max splayed onto the ground, and Daniel stood over him, kicked him in the ribs.

"You think you could take her away from me like that?" he asked, taunting. "You think you're so special? Who's special now?"

Max pushed himself up, his eyes on mine again. "Janie," he said weakly. "Janie. You don't need to be here. Janie, go."

Another blow. Another kick.

I knew what Max wanted. For me to turn and run, protect whatever it was that was in that backpack, whatever it was he'd found. Get back to Freya. Get the hell out of here.

But I couldn't leave him like this.

I loved him. I loved him so much.

"No," I screamed, trying to get Daniel's attention. "Stop it, please. Jesus, you'll kill him!" Scar singing, breasts still aching, I ran forward, leapt onto Daniel's back, trying to take him down, pull him away, but he shook me off again. I stumbled backward and stepped on something—an errant toy car, left by the staircase whenever Sutton had been here last—then stumbled more, fell straight back, my tailbone vibrating, sending shock waves of pain through my body.

"You think you're such a hero," Daniel said, turning back to Max, kicking him once again, his words coming fast now, practically spilling from his mouth. "But you're the one who left her high and dry. You're the one who abandoned your own fucking child. I'm the one who saved her. I'm the one who loved her. I'm the one who did everything for you. And it still wasn't enough. She still went running to you. If it wasn't for you, it never would have come to this," Daniel said, his voice cracking with genuine emotion. "She'd be happy still. She'd be *alive*. She'd be mine. I *loved* her, I *adored* her. I was there for her when you—fucking—weren't—" Daniel said, punctuating each word with a kick. "But you don't care, do you, because you never cared for anyone, did you? You never cared for Grace, you certainly didn't care for *her*." Daniel nodded to me, then delivered another swift kick. "You never cared about anyone but yourself, you sick fuck. I'll fucking kill you for what you did."

Daniel pulled back, rearing for another kick, one that could destroy everything, because I believed him; in that moment, I believed that he would kill Max if he could.

That he would try, at least.

"Wait!"

Daniel's head whipped around, and mine did, too.

Liana was there, standing on the porch. "Stop it," she screamed. "Stop it. The police are on the way. Just stop."

Then I heard it—through the chaos of everything—Liana's screams, Max's labored breathing, Daniel's steps, walking past me—I heard the worst thing I could possibly hear.

A wail, an animal's shrieking.

I heard my baby. I heard her scream.

51

10:51 p.m.

FREYA.

She was here. With Liana.

She was tucked in the stroller, next to Liana on the porch.

Oh god oh god oh god.

"Who the fuck are you?" Daniel asked Liana, walking forward, toward the front door.

Toward Freya. Toward my baby.

I gasped for breath, tailbone throbbing from where I'd fallen, boobs leaking through my bra, making spots on my chest, and as I pushed myself up, fear seeping through every inch of skin, every cell of my body, something happened, something I hadn't expected.

Time slowed down, and as Freya's cries continued and Daniel took another step toward the door, the images, all the terrible fears, flashed through my mind.

The stroller tipping over. Freya spilling out. Her tender, fragile body, falling. Crushed.

Oh god oh god oh god.

And as I rushed toward Daniel, it was like a door opened inside me, and love for Freya came gushing through, like a dam coming down, a river flowing, so fast it felt like it would never, ever stop. My insides exploded with a love so fierce, I felt it might destroy me. My heart seemed to burst from my chest, beating perilously outside my body. Tears came to my eyes, then coursed down my cheeks.

I loved her, I really did, and I had *always* loved her. From the moment I met her. From the moment I knew she was in my belly.

I loved her, but the fear that had been bubbling, growing inside me, had taken over, the fear that I couldn't do it, that I couldn't care for her as I should, had caused me to numb it all, had made me too fucked up to feel it as I thought I should. I loved Freya desperately, and I wanted so very badly to give her a good family, a good life.

I loved her so much, and if something happened to her, I felt I would die. Perish on the spot. Somehow cease to exist.

I loved her, and I needed her. To breathe. To go on. To live.

She needed me, too.

Daniel was there, hovering in front of the doorway, walking toward Liana. Liana was screaming about the police being on their way. Max was whimpering behind me. The leopard-print backpack was still on the ground, only a few feet from Daniel.

None of that mattered. All that mattered was Freya.

I slammed my body into Daniel's, knocking him down so he fell into the doorway, and then I leapt over him and rushed past Liana, to the stroller.

"Why would you bring her?" I shouted as I ripped Freya

from the stroller, and she wailed, sucking air into her lungs, screaming again so loud it sliced through everything, splitting the world in two.

My body began to shake as I pulled her to my chest.

"Why the fuck would you bring her here?"

"I was worried—I wanted to see—" Liana stammered.

I rushed down the porch steps just as the car turned the corner and pulled in front of us, lights flashing, officers rushing out. I moved out of their way and looked back to see Daniel pushing himself up, to see Max on the ground, blood pouring from his nose. To see Liana, eyeing me, asking me to forgive her for bringing Freya into this mess.

"Hands in the air!"

A gun held out, pointed at Daniel and Max.

It happened so fast. One officer was on Daniel, restraining him, placing him in cuffs. Another was on Max, doing the same. And then Liana rushed into the thick of it, calling out words I couldn't hear.

I knew one thing and one thing only.

I had to get Freya away from this.

From these men. From this anger. From cops and guns and noise and flashing lights.

I stepped backward, horrified.

"Ma'am," one of the officers said, turning back to me. "Ma'am, we'll need you to give a—"

Already, I was flying down the walk and through the gate, holding Freya to my chest.

Protecting the only one I could protect now.

Being what I was always meant to be.

Freya's mother.

52

11:11 p.m.

I WAS ACHING ALL OVER BY THE TIME I GOT US BACK HOME, Freya loud as could be and writhing in my arms, angry from being woken, from being ripped from her stroller, from the cool wind that wasn't meant for her new-baby cheeks.

I dug in my bag for my keys but couldn't find them, and as Freya's crying grew, I flipped over my bag, shaking the contents to the ground. It all spilled onto the faded slats of the front porch, cast in a strange yellow from the porch lights, made hazy from the tears still swimming in my eyes: a veritable museum of my life this past year. Newborn-sized diapers. Nipple cream. Ginger chews for the morning sickness. A pen with a skinny, spongy boob figurine on top that we'd gotten from our new parenting class at the hospital. Napkins crunched and molded with dried spit-up. The receipt from Three Crows. And beneath the napkins and papers, a gleam of silver. My keys.

I snatched them, quick as a cat, and wiped the tears away with the back of my hand, found the right key, and jabbed it into the door as Freya cried even harder, as if sensing the adrenaline still pulsing in my blood.

Inside, I sank into the sofa and did what I knew how to do, what I had been doing, hour in and hour out, for the last six weeks. I pulled her close to me and offered her warmth and nourishment and comfort. She latched on immediately, and the screaming finally stopped, and the tears seemed to let down in time with my milk now. Flowing freely, from one duct and another.

I rocked back and forth, keeping her comfortable, satiated and happy, and as we sat there, just the two of us, I looked at my child, here in my arms, safe and sound. My shoulders shook, and sobs threatened to rock me, but I forced myself to stay still, to not disturb her peace.

Freya was safe, and she was mine.

Freya was safe, and I loved her so deeply, so dearly.

Freya was safe, and as hard as this was, it was worth it.

My family was worth fighting for.

"I'm here," I whispered to my baby, now angelic and peaceful. "I'm here, and I love you, and your daddy loves you, and we'll always love you, no matter what."

I sighed, releasing a long breath, as Freya continued to nurse. I closed my eyes and took in the sound of her sucking, the smell of her baby skin and the sweetness of the milk, knowing it would be okay—somehow.

When I looked up, the front door was opening. Liana stepped through.

She rolled the stroller in and positioned it near the wall, then walked toward the two of us, slowly, as if shamed.

"They arrested Max," she said, her voice shaking. "And

Daniel, too. They arrested them, and they took my statement, and—"

"You shouldn't have brought her," I said, pulling Freya closer to me. "You shouldn't have come."

"I'm sorry," she said, walking closer, sitting across from us. "I'm so sorry. I didn't—I didn't know what to do. I knew you were with him, and—"

"How did you even know that?"

"I saw it on my tracker, that you were across the street from that bar, Three Crows."

"Your tracker?"

"I have one of those GPS things on my keys, because I was always losing them and kept being late to gigs and stuff. You go on the website, and it shows you where they are. I saw that you went west, and I thought you were going to wherever Max was, but then I saw that you came back, that you were on the same street as that bar, and I knew that's where the guy lived. You told me."

I shook my head. "Jesus, Liana. I brought a *tracking* device to see Max?"

"I'm sorry," she said. "I knew it was a risk, but it—it made me feel better to know where you were."

I held Freya tighter. "But why did you bring her? She could have gotten hurt. Daniel could have . . . he was so angry, and what if he, what if . . ."

I couldn't bear to finish the thought. Freya pulled off, looked at me sweetly, as if there was nothing in the world to be afraid of. Fresh tears filled my eyes then, and I adjusted, switching her to the other side.

"I know," Liana said. "But I couldn't leave her, could I?

She's a baby. You can't *ever* leave a baby. And she didn't stir when I woke her, so I thought I'd just go by and check to see if you were okay, and then I saw you, running into that house, and I called out to you, but you didn't hear me, so I followed you, and I heard yelling and fighting, and I called 911, and I wasn't going to get any closer, but then I heard him say, 'I'll kill you,' and I was so scared, I couldn't just stand there, and—and—"

Liana's head fell into her hands, and she began to cry. "I didn't think anyone would hurt Freya, I swear. But I didn't know what to do."

Liana's shoulders shook, and I felt my anger warm and soften, melting into something more subtle—into exhaustion, fear, and grief. Into the knowledge that I couldn't protect my child, my partner, even myself, from the world. I could only try. And loving that deeply while knowing you were powerless to prevent hurt and tragedy and loss, it made you raw. As if you were walking around with your heart fully exposed. And there was nothing you could do to change it.

"It's okay," I said. "Really, it's okay. I know you were trying to do the right thing, and if the police hadn't come when they did, god, I don't know what would have happened, but it was still terrifying. To be in the middle of that and to be scared for Max, for myself, and then to hear her cry, to know that she was there—it was too much."

Liana stood, crossed the space between us, sat next to me on the sofa, reached a hand out to Freya's down-covered head.

"She's safe now," Liana said. "Because you protected her like no one else could. Because you're her mother," she went on. "The best a girl could ask for. Seriously. It was superhuman, the way you just knocked him down to get to her. I've never seen anything like it."

I laughed, in spite of myself. "I didn't even think. I just did."

Liana rubbed at Freya's head. "I know."

I turned to her then, this woman who'd been with me through everything, through my most difficult days in the world, and her gaze held mine. "Why didn't you tell me that you knew?"

Liana's eyebrows narrowed. "That I knew?"

"You don't have to play dumb," I said. "That you knew Max had met up with Grace. That you saw them on Wednesday."

"Oh," she said, and her face reddened.

"Were you covering for him?" I asked. "Because he's more important to you than I am?"

"No, Janie. Not at all. I love you. I hope you know that. You're as much a friend to me as Max is. I wouldn't be here if that wasn't true. And you have to understand, when I saw him with her, in that bar that night, I thought she maybe looked a little familiar, but I didn't put it together. I thought she was just some random woman, but I did think it was some kind of an affair. And I told Max that if he didn't tell you, I would. And that's what I said to him in the kitchen on Friday, when you walked in on us. And when you called me the next morning, I thought—oh shit, I confronted Max, and he freaked out, and he bailed, like he used to do."

Liana sighed. "I know I should have told you everything right then, but I wanted to give him a chance to collect himself and come home and tell you himself. And then the whole murder thing happened, and I swear I still didn't know that any of it was connected to this person from his past. And then I was so worried that if I threw that at you in the midst of everything else, you'd believe he was capable of something like this. And I believed, the whole way through, there was no way Max would kill someone. That's why I went down to the police station on Sunday morning. I told Duncan about Max disappearing, but I also told her I suspected he'd been cheating and that I confronted him, and I believed that's why he'd run off. I'm not sure how much Duncan knew then, but she never showed me a photo of Rae or anything. I had no idea until *you* showed me that photo on Facebook. That's when it all clicked, that the woman I'd seen Max with was Rae from forever ago. And knowing that she was the woman who'd been killed, god, knowing that I'd gone down to Duncan and basically hand-delivered more evidence that might lead them straight to Max, I didn't know how to tell you without you losing trust in me altogether. I'm so, so sorry. I know I fucked up, but I promise, everything I did was because I loved you *both*. And Freya. I was trying to do the right thing for your family. Because I consider your family like *my* family, Janie. I really do."

I stared at Liana. She wasn't perfect, she hadn't made all the right choices, she hadn't been honest every step of the way, and neither had I. And yet, she had been there for me, in ways that no one else had. And I remembered how broken I'd felt, knowing my parents couldn't ever take care of me in the way that I wanted, and for the first time in my life, it felt like maybe that was okay. Like there were people who would take care of me when the shit hit the fan. Be it Liana or Molly or even the college crew, if I would let them. Hell, even Carl and Brenda had been there, offering to hire me a night nurse and sweep me away to Westchester, connecting me with the lawyer. Maybe it was okay that support came from other sources.

Maybe that didn't have to determine the kind of mother I would be to Freya.

"Do you believe me?" Liana asked. "How much I care about you?"

I nodded. "I do. I know you do. And just so you know, it wasn't an affair."

"It wasn't?"

I shook my head. "It's a long story, but Max was only trying to help her. And I believe him."

Liana smiled. "I'm so glad. What can I do for you, Janie? Just tell me, what can I do now to help you, to help Max? To help Freya?"

"There's nothing to do," I said, fully aware of the mess we were still in. "I was trying to get Daniel out of the house so Max could find proof of his guilt. Max must have put whatever he found in the backpack from your trunk, but he dropped it, and I was going to grab it, but then I saw Freya, and all I cared about was protecting her. It was all for nothing."

Liana stood, rushing back to the stroller. When she returned, she had the backpack in her hands. "You mean this?"

My heart swelled. "You grabbed it?"

Liana nodded. "I mean, it's my backpack," she said. "I figured if you guys had taken it, it must be important. No one saw me in the chaos of all the arrests."

"It is important," I said. "Oh god, I think it is, at least. Hand it to me."

Freya still latched on, I took it from Liana, then snaked open the zipper with one hand.

There it was, a folder. Papers, photos. A thumb drive.

"Max found it," I said. "Max found what he was looking for."

"That's good?" Liana asked.

"Yes," I said. "Yes, Liana, that's very good."

53

11:25 p.m.

CARL ANSWERED ON THE SECOND RING, AS IF HE WAS HOLD-ing the phone in his hand, waiting for everything to blow up.

"Janie," he said. "It's late. Is everything okay?"

"No," I said, adjusting Freya on my breast. "Max is back, but he's been arrested, and they arrested Daniel, too, Grace's husband. He's the one who did this. He's the one who hurt her."

"Of course he is," Carl said. "Did something . . . happen . . . between them?"

"Daniel attacked Max," I said, failing to mention that Max was in his home when he did so.

"Oh god," Carl said. "Is Max okay?"

"Yes," I said, and as I did, Freya popped off, her eyes closed now, her lips coming to a line. She was asleep, as if exhausted by the events of the day.

"What happened, Janie?" Carl asked.

"Too much to tell you over the phone. Rick Courtland is coming up tomorrow. You and Brenda should, too. There's still loads of evidence stacked against Max, and I don't think even Daniel's assault will throw the police off Max entirely. We need to get ahead of this, as much as we can."

Carl took a deep breath, and for a moment the line was silent.

A knock on the door. Then another knock. An urgent pounding.

"I have to go, Carl. I can explain everything in person."

"Okay," he said. "First thing in the morning, then. We'll take care of this. We'll fix this."

"Thank you," I said.

"Love you, Janie," he said.

Already, I was ending the call, the door pounding again. I moved carefully, propping Freya on the snuggly pillow we kept on the couch.

I took a few steps forward, just in time to see Liana open the door for Duncan.

"Ms. Walker," Duncan said, her eyes flitting from me to Liana. "I've been told you ran off."

I looked down at my feet, then back up at her again. "I was afraid for my baby. I had to get out of there."

Duncan tilted her head slightly. "And she's okay?"

"Yes," I said, glancing back toward the couch, as if to reassure myself again. "Yes, she is."

Duncan nodded. "Mr. Akins is being held for aggravated assault. Mr. Bosch is in custody as well. But we need your statement. And more than that, we need your cooperation—your full cooperation," she said. "We have your partner now, there's no running anymore. We have evidence. We're building a case. This is over. No more evasions. No more lies. That's the only possible way I can protect you, that I can make sure your daughter doesn't lose you, too. You understand?"

"I understand," I said, but for the first time I'd ever spoken to her, I felt confidence pumping through my blood, a Mama Bear urge to protect my family. "But like I told you before, I need my lawyer with me. He'll be here tomorrow. We can do it then."

Duncan raised an eyebrow. "It will look a lot better for you if we talk now."

I shook my head firmly. "Tomorrow. It can wait."

She sighed, as if realizing the battle was already lost. "All right then, I'll see you tomorrow."

"Wait," I said. I turned, walked back to the living room, grabbed Liana's backpack, took out the folder, and pushed it toward Duncan. "Before you go, please take this."

Her eyebrows narrowed as she opened the folder, glancing over the contents. "How did you get this, Ms. Walker?"

I pressed my lips together, not answering. "Sutton isn't safe with Daniel. Grace's dying wish was to get him out of town so Daniel couldn't hurt him. You don't have to believe me, just look at what's in there. Please." I took a deep breath. "And please keep Sutton from Daniel however you can. I'm begging you."

Duncan looked up at me, her eyes cautious but kind. Understanding. Somehow.

"Please," I said again. "Mother to mother."

UPSTAIRS, DUNCAN GONE, Freya nestled sleepily into the crook of my arm, I leaned over the bassinet, carefully set her down. She didn't stir, and I counted her breaths, watched the subtle rise and fall of her chest, the way it tugged at the snug cotton of her swaddle, the way each breath shushed out of her tiny nostrils, the way her eyelids stayed shut so tightly, lashes like black crescent moons.

I love you, I thought.

I love you, my baby girl.

I love you, and I don't regret a single thing, not a single thing that brought you into my life.

I love you, and I will be there for you, every second, every minute, every hour, every day and every week and every month and every year.

I will be there for you no matter what happens, no matter how difficult it is, no matter how scared I am.

I will be your mother.

I may not be perfect, I may not even be all that good, but I will be what I can.

That will have to be enough for both of us.

THURSDAY, MARCH 21

54

1:15 p.m.

WE HAD TURNED INTO THOSE PEOPLE IN THE TRUE-CRIME documentaries, set up around the dining table, a triage of sorts, making the most of the time before Freya woke again. Me; Max; Carl and Brenda; Max's fancy lawyer, Rick; Rick's hungry young associate, a woman who wore four-inch heels and took meticulous notes in swirling script; and, finally, my own parents. Mom and Dad, getting off their cruise ship earlier than they'd anticipated, taking a red-eye to New York and driving straight from JFK, arriving bleary-eyed and tanned by the Mediterranean sun. Out of place and out of sorts, but *here*. And that was something.

Liana was upstairs in the guest room, catching up on sleep so she could watch Freya later. Molly had left Ani's and was back in Brooklyn, but I'd updated her on what had happened, and she was ready to help in any way she could as soon as we were back in the city. Bree and the college gang had arranged a week's worth of takeout dinners so none of us would have to cook.

Beneath the table, my mom squeezed my hand as her eyes

flitted from Rick to Carl and back again. "Can you explain that part again?" she asked. "About the handkerchief?"

"Yes," my dad piped in. "Shouldn't DNA be back by now?"

Rick cleared his throat. "Any moment, really. It's never as fast as they show you on TV."

My dad reddened, and my mom took his hand.

Brenda and Carl remained quiet, as they had been for the most part. Our parents had never all been in the same room like this—after all, Max and I had never gotten married—and it was strange and horrifying that it was this of all possible eventualities that had made the meeting possible.

Max leaned forward, nudging me under the table with his knee. "You sure you don't want to nap?" he asked. "You must be exhausted."

"Yes," my mom said. "Go, get some rest. I can give Freya a bottle if she needs it."

I shook my head, turning back to Max, my eyes taking in the bruises on his face, the yellowing on his cheekbone, the purple beneath his eyes, the way he winced when he took too deep of a breath. "I want to be here for this."

Rick had spent the last hour detailing every piece of evidence that we knew there was against Daniel, which we would use to cast doubt on the charges against Max. The papers Max had found included bank accounts, photographs, and a thumb drive of voice recordings—all of which chronicled a pattern of emotional and financial abuse, as well as an injury Daniel had inflicted upon Sutton. There was a will there, too, one that gave custody of Sutton to his great-aunt in Maine, should anything happen to Grace, and though it was legally questionable—Daniel's name was on the birth certificate, and his rights couldn't so easily be given away—it was enough to grant

Sutton a temporary guardianship with his great-aunt, at least until the investigation into child abuse had been completed. Sutton was safe for now. Thanks to Max.

Rick had moved on to the evidence against Max, the handkerchief, chiefly, which he kept referring to as "the smoking gun."

Rick tapped his pen against the papers. "If the DNA is a match, and if Daniel's DNA doesn't turn up on that handkerchief, like we're hoping, charges will certainly be pressed against Max. I believe that is all they're waiting for."

Once the DNA came in, this would be an entirely different conversation, an entirely different game.

Max squeezed my hand again. "I'm so sorry for all of this."

"It's okay," I said quietly, pulling his hand into my lap. "I'm glad you're here."

When I'd gone with Rick down to the police station on Tuesday morning and given Duncan only the details Rick had deemed necessary—that I'd asked to meet Daniel at that bar and followed him from there to his house, where I'd found him in an altercation with Max—I hadn't thought Max and I would have this moment. I didn't think I'd be seeing him anywhere else than some cold, anemic visitation room, a guard watching us the whole time.

Max's injuries turned out to be substantial but superficial, and when he was cleared from the hospital, he was released into police custody. Though the murder charge hadn't come yet, his run from the police and his taking Sutton without any communication had drummed up a whole host of others.

Rick and his team had jumped into action. He was one of the preeminent defense lawyers in the city—if not the whole country—and he'd miraculously managed to get bail set yesterday, even though Max was the very definition of a flight risk, having run before, to the tune of one million dollars, money that Carl and Brenda had somehow been able to procure within twenty-four hours.

His parents had picked him up this morning, my parents had rolled in around noon, and we'd hardly had a moment together before all was being set up on the dining table, before plans were being made.

"There's got to be more on Daniel," Carl pressed. "Has anyone checked his phone?" he asked, as he had asked several times already. "Because he must have threatened her. There must be something."

Rick shrugged. "Like I told you, Carl, all of that will come out in discovery. For now, we simply don't know."

The monitor crackled, and Freya's cry cut the tension with a knife. "I'll get her," I said, standing up.

"Good," Rick said. "Let's take five anyway. We have plenty to still go over, and we need to be as clearheaded as possible."

"Do you need me to come with you, Janie?" my mom asked. She was laying it on thick, had been since she'd arrived, but I appreciated it. It was nice to be the one taken care of, not the other way around.

"Thanks, Mom," I said. "I'm okay."

I looked to Max, catching his eyes.

"I promise. I am."

55

1:45 p.m.

WE WERE ABOUT TO RECONVENE WHEN THE KNOCK CAME AT the door.

My limbs tensed up and I looked to Freya in her swing, then to Max at the table. His parents, his lawyers around him. My parents, barely keeping their eyes open, lost puppies who didn't know quite what to do. It was so abnormal, and yet it felt like this might be the last bit of seminormalcy for so long. Once Max was charged with murder, everything would change.

"I'll get it," I said, and stood, pushing back from the dining table, my pulse pounding. I didn't want it to be Duncan, but at the same time, I almost did. I couldn't handle much more of the waiting, the feeling that a guillotine was hanging over our heads.

"Hello," Duncan said as soon as I opened the door. She walked past me, striding toward the group.

"Oh, no, no, no," Rick said, standing and puffing up his chest like a bird. "No, you are *not* speaking to my client like this."

Duncan ignored Rick and looked back at me. "There have been some updates," she said.

"Updates?" I asked.

"What updates?" my mom echoed.

"This is really not appropriate," Rick went on. "Max, you don't have to say a word."

"It's okay," Max said. "I want to hear, too."

I walked closer, catching Duncan's eyes, and there was kindness there, though there was firmness, too.

"What happened?" I asked her. "What are these updates?"

Duncan cleared her throat, and Rick tossed up his hands, frustrated. "We've gotten more clarity about the payments from the trust. Do you know anything about these, Mr. Bosch?" She looked at Max.

"Don't answer," Rick said. "For Christ sake, Max, don't answer that."

Max ignored him, shaking his head. "Janie knows as well as I do that we emptied the trust a year ago. We converted it into equity in our apartment so we could get the monthly mortgage payment down. You must be mixed up somehow. It's impossible."

Duncan cocked her head to the side. "There is a trust in your name. And there are payments, I can assure you. But what we've learned, just recently, after finally getting clearance on the financials, is that you don't have access to the account . . ." She paused. "Only the person who opened it does."

Silence stretched through the room, and in the midst of the looks of confusion—of disbelief—one person stood out. Carl, sitting there, tight-lipped and stoic, staring at his hands.

"Mr. Bosch," Duncan prompted.

"I told you I don't know anything about it," Max said.

"No," Duncan went on. "Not you. Mr. Carl Bosch. Do you want to illuminate us?"

"Carl?" Brenda turned to him, her eyes wide. "Carl, what is she talking about?"

"You don't have to say anything," Rick said loudly. "Any of you."

"Carl?" Brenda asked again. "Carl, what's going on?"

"Dad," Max said. "Dad, whatever it is, just say it."

Rick and his associate started to object, but Carl cleared his throat, eyeing Max. "I didn't think it was wise for you to empty your trust, especially since you had no protections. You two weren't even married. The apartment isn't even in your name."

"I told you," Max said. "It was my money to spend. It's not your business how I spend it. Not since I was twenty-five."

Brenda huffed, as if she agreed with Carl on this one, but then stared at her husband. "What does that have to do with anything?" she asked. "It's all in the past."

My parents exchanged a look, and I caught their eyes, too. Trust funds, such a foreign thing to most people. Certainly a foreign thing to us. Meanwhile, Freya swung happily, unaware.

"Mr. Bosch," Duncan said again. "I'm sure they'd all rather hear it from you than me."

"Carl," Rick said. "You don't have to—"

"There were tax benefits," Carl said. "So I opened another trust for Max. It wasn't a big deal."

"And you never told me?" Brenda asked.

"Or me?" Max said.

"I was going to tell you." Carl glanced briefly at Duncan. "I was going to tell you all. Today." He sighed and eyed Max a bit desperately. "I just didn't have a chance to explain. It's all been so chaotic."

"What is it, Dad?" Max asked. "There's still something you're not telling us."

"Carl, please," Brenda prompted.

I stared at the father-in-law I thought I'd known so very well. The one who, in some ways, had taken care of me more than my own dad ever had.

Carl sighed. "The payments—the ones she's talking about—" His eyes flitted to Duncan, then back to Max. "Those came from me."

56

1:55 p.m.

WE STARED AT CARL. DUMBFOUNDED. HORRIFIED.

"Don't look at me like that," Carl said desperately. "He approached me. Daniel Akins, the husband. He . . . he blackmailed me. Don't you see? I didn't have a choice. *He's* the madman. *He's* the horrible person. He's obviously the one who killed her. And yet here we are, all tied up in it."

"What do you mean, he approached you?" Max asked. "When?"

"Spring last year," Carl said with a sigh. "March, I think. He said Max was the biological father of his son, and that he and his wife wanted restitution. That . . . they wanted support. Or else they were going to tell Janie. They were going to blow up Max's whole life."

"And you agreed to this?" Brenda demanded. "Without even coming to me?"

Carl shook his head. "I didn't believe him. I thought it was some nut out for our money. But then . . . then he kept pushing, he sent me a photo of Max and that girl together, and . . . and he sent me a photo of the kid, and it looked like Max, and . . . by then it was right after Janie got pregnant, and she wasn't even sure if she wanted to keep it—"

My own mother gasped, and I shook my head as the shame I'd been battling so long came roaring back. "Jesus, Carl," I said. "That's not your business to divulge."

"Come on, Dad," Max echoed. "I told you that in confidence."

"I know," Carl said, his own voice breaking. "I'm sorry. I just knew, I knew if all this came out that Janie would definitely not keep the baby. She wouldn't want to have a baby with you if she knew you'd left this other kid, and I knew that was a part of your old life, like how you used to disappear when things got tough—I knew it was over, and I wanted to protect you. I wanted to protect my grandchild."

"Fuck," Max said, and again my mother gasped. My father looked at his hands, as if wishing he'd never come, wishing he were still back in the Mediterranean, forgetting the problems of the world, as he was always wont to do. "Fuck," Max said again. "You actually thought I *knew*? You thought I left my own kid?"

Carl looked up, his eyebrows raising. "You didn't?"

"Of course he didn't," Brenda said, heat and anger rising to her bony cheeks. "Don't you know our son at all?"

"That's not who I am, Dad," Max said. "Jesus."

"I—" Carl shook his head. "I . . . I only wanted what was best for you. For you and Janie. For . . . for Freya. Mr. Akins— he and that *woman*—they promised they wouldn't bother you if I gave them enough money. That they'd never, ever contact any of you so long as I did." He turned to Brenda. "I didn't want to stress you out, either, so I made the payments from the trust, since you didn't even know about it. I'm sorry," Carl said. "I really am. I was trying to make it right. I promise."

Silence among us, all of us trying to reconcile what he'd just said.

Finally, Max turned to Duncan. "And now this is all going to be used against me, I suppose? Payments I didn't even fucking know about?"

"None of this is going to be used against anyone," Rick interjected. "Because as everyone can very clearly see, my client was completely unaware of this trust, of these payments, of any of it. Clearly, this is no more than a misunderstanding, an overstep by a father who was worried about his son and his future grandchild." He eyed Duncan. "No jury on earth is going to blame Max for that."

Duncan cleared her throat. "I didn't only come here to talk about these payments. There's been another update, too. We've got the DNA back."

No no no.

All this bullshit about Carl, it was only a distraction. The smoking gun was finally here.

Oh god oh god oh god.

Duncan looked at Max. "The DNA did come back on that handkerchief. It's Mrs. Akins's blood, but as for the other DNA present—the hair we found—it was only a partial match."

Max shook his head. "Partial?"

"It wasn't yours," Duncan said. "But interestingly, many of the markers were similar to yours. Enough to establish some sort of connection."

"No," I said, shaking my head. "DNA has to be exact. There's no partial . . ."

Duncan turned to Carl. "Is there anything else you'd like to share with us, Mr. Bosch?"

A gasp, splitting the tension in two. From Brenda.

"No," she said, turning to her husband. "No, you didn't."

Carl's mouth remained shut.

"Dad," Max said, and his voice was so hurt, so wounded, so much like a little boy's. "Dad, what's going on?"

Brenda began to cry, her shoulders hunched, tears drawing lines in her flawless, almost-airbrushed foundation. The woman I'd always thought so uptight, so cold, so unfeeling was pouring out emotion like a sponge just squeezed.

My own parents sat there, jaws gaping with horror.

Rick stood, objecting to any questions like an attorney in court.

My heart cinched up, the place within that Carl had occupied shrinking. He was my father-in-law, the man who'd treated me like a daughter from the moment I first met him. The glue of Max's family, and in ways, ours. The shining example to me of all the things my parents weren't. There in a crisis. With the resources, the disposition to back it all up. More than all of that, the grandfather of my daughter. Someone linked to me through Freya's very own blood. I looked at my daughter, imagined telling all of this to her one day. The thought was horrifying. The thought was heartbreaking.

"You couldn't, Carl, could you?" I asked desperately as Rick tossed up his hands, lost. "Why would you? Why would you hurt her? Why? Carl, look at me," I said. "Please."

He wouldn't look me in the eyes. I had a strange and terrible feeling that he never would again.

"Carl," Brenda was saying. "Carl—"

"Dad?" Max echoed. "Dad?"

That finally broke him. Carl's body shook, racking with sobs. Tears streamed down his cheeks, and his face reddened as he looked at Max, his only child. His son.

"You don't understand," Carl bellowed. "They promised me. They promised me they would never contact Max, they would never tell Janie. And then I see her there on Friday, sitting with you, Max. And . . . and I know she's threatening to blow up your life, to tell Janie. I know she's going to ruin everything. Then you both left, and she left her phone right there, and your handkerchief, too, and . . . and she came back, and . . . and I only wanted to talk. I wanted to talk before I gave her back her phone. I wanted to ask her what she was thinking, why she'd broken her promise. After . . . after all that money I gave her. But as soon as she saw that I had her phone, she attacked me. She . . . she lost it. I pushed her off me. It was to defend myself, I swear." Carl's shoulders shook even harder. "It was to defend myself," he said again, his eyes finding his hands before connecting with Max's again. "It was to defend you."

Brenda cried out, more sobs escaping.

Max shook his head, unbelieving.

And Freya, as if sensing all that had been broken, let out a horrible, awful scream. Like she knew how her own history would never be the same. That the mother of her half brother had been killed by her own grandfather.

I jumped up, running to her, lifting her from the swing,

pulling her tight. I lifted up my top, latched her on, soothed her, like only a mother can.

"Mr. Bosch," Duncan said, her hand landing on a pair of cuffs. Her eyes were trained straight on Carl.

"Mr. Bosch, I'm placing you under arrest for the murder of Grace Akins."

FOUR MONTHS LATER

57

5:32 a.m.

MY EYES SHOT OPEN. THE ROOM WAS DARK, ONLY THE TINIEST bit of light peeking through the edges of the curtains. Freya was gone.

But she was supposed to be gone. She was in her own room now, something I'd been so excited for once, but now felt strange, like a missing limb.

I turned, took in Max, snoring softly beside me, sleeping as deeply as Freya still was. Sleeping like a baby.

Not me. It had been happening all week. Freya was beginning to sleep through the night, but my boobs still woke me around five a.m., ready for a feeding.

And once my brain was awake, that was when everything else started.

I grabbed my phone from the nightstand, checked the video monitor, counted Freya's breaths, then did what I had been doing these past few mornings.

I opened Google, typed in Max's name. I'd turned off the alerts, but still I couldn't help searching Google News for any new hits.

Sure enough, there were plenty. A new witness had come forward a couple of days earlier, and the news was quickly picking it up, the music sites shortly behind. Headlines flashed at me.

NEW WITNESS COMES FORWARD IN VELVET HOPE MURDEROUS FAMILY DRAMA

FRESH DEVELOPMENTS IN THE CASE OF FORMER VELVET HOPE ROCK STAR'S FATHER

ROCK THAT SHOCKS: 10 MUSICIANS WHO GOT CAUGHT UP IN MORE THAN SEX, DRUGS, AND ROCK AND ROLL

I skimmed each story, looking for any new details, but none of them told us more than what we already knew, straight from Carl's mouth that horrible afternoon. That his drinking, his simmering anger, had gotten out of control. That a push had turned deadly.

Grace's phone had fallen when Carl pushed her. He'd picked it up, used Max's handkerchief to wipe his own fingerprints and Grace's blood off it, but had seen threatening text messages pop up from Daniel as he did. Carl had slipped it into his own pocket in case it could somehow help him later. He thought he'd put the handkerchief back, too, but in his drunken, adrenaline-fueled panic, it had dropped at some point as he fled down the alley, where it was eventually found by the police.

Max had opened up to me, only a few weeks earlier, about his dad's rare but terrifying bouts of rage. Most of the time, he was warm and genial. Most of the time, he was working so hard to make everyone in his family happy, to deal with Brenda's exacting standards, but sometimes, it got to be too much. Sometimes, he just snapped.

Brenda said she didn't know a thing about any of it, just that Carl had gone out again that evening, after Max had taken them back to their rental, to have another drink, and had come home sometime after she went to bed. She'd assumed it was nothing more nefarious than an old-man alcoholic. For what it was worth, I believed her. Over the intervening months, she'd made it beyond clear that she would always choose Max over Carl. That no matter how cold or controlling or difficult she could be, in the end she'd come through for Max.

Because she was a mother. That was what mothers did.

In exchange for Brenda's sworn testimony and Max's as well, the kidnapping charges against Max had been dropped.

Sutton was living in Maine, and apparently doing okay, as much as a kid could be who'd lost his mother and was separated from the only father he'd ever known. His great-aunt had been granted temporary custody, and a child abuse investigation was still underway for Daniel.

After months of discussion, we'd made the decision to go out to Maine today. To meet Sutton. For Max to find a role with his biological son, whatever that meant for us.

It scared me, it did, the idea of merging our life with Sutton's, but at the same time, I knew he was, in some ways, our responsibility now. The boy had lost his mother to such a horrible misunderstanding—neither Max nor I believed that Grace even knew Daniel had been blackmailing Carl, given how rigorously Daniel controlled their finances. Being present in this boy's life, helping him, however we could, could never make up for what he'd lost, but it was the right thing to do.

Besides, I knew Max wanted it. After all, Sutton was his child. He was Freya's own half brother.

I tapped out of Google and into my texts. I had loads of unread ones. I was so bad at clearing them out, especially since Bree and the college girls were always checking in on me. I found Molly's latest at the top, sent around midnight.

HR says the offer should come through any day now!

Spurred on by Molly, I'd been in talks the past few weeks about returning to the agency. Not as a VP, as I'd always wanted, but in a role that seemed almost better—director of client services. Flexible hours, giving me more time with Freya, but with all the client interaction I'd always loved— and across many accounts, not dedicated to the one Bryan handled. Benefits, which we were in dire need of. And a regular paycheck, too. It was still something I was wrapping my mind around. Returning felt impossible, most days. But starting over did, too, when so many other things in our world had been shaken.

There was a text about toddler insomnia from Bree at 10:38 p.m. and then just under that—

My heart clenched up at the name.

Ani. She'd reached out several times since everything hit the news, but I'd never responded. Until I'd texted her last night, just before I went to bed, desperate for answers to a question I simply couldn't put out of my mind, especially now that I was considering returning to the agency.

I hadn't expected to hear back so soon.

Fingers shaking, I tapped to open the thread.

My eyes scanned the words frantically, first my own text

and then her response, looking for an answer, then read it over slowly again, the realization—the horror—dawning.

> Ani! I know it's been forever and I know I haven't responded to all your texts checking in. I'm sorry! But you may have heard from Molly. I'm thinking about coming back to the agency, and I have this very random question about forever ago. Do you remember that night we all went out to karaoke in K-town with Bryan, right before we re-signed the account? Bryan and I were singing "Islands in the Stream," and I think you were one of the last people there? I was just wondering if you remembered how the night ended? Like did you stay till the end with Bryan and me? Or did you head out beforehand? It's a little embarrassing, but I can't remember exactly how we left it, and I'm trying to get a handle on my drinking and was hoping you could let me know how I was as I don't quite remember. I hope I didn't do anything too humiliating especially since I might be about to return!

I'd been careful in how I phrased it because I couldn't very well tell her everything, and the drinking part wasn't a lie in any case. Only it wasn't the drinking that bothered me; it was what happened after. I hadn't expected her to remember, much less have an answer, and yet, there it was.

> Janie, my love! Great to hear from you. I am sooooo sorry about everything that happened with Max and with his father. I've been reading the news, and I still can't believe it. How horrifying! I hope you are all hanging in and Freya is doing well, all things considered. And yes, Molly told me you were potentially returning to the agency and I'm thrilled! As for that night, haha, I actually do remember. And please, do not be embarrassed. We

have all been there! Anyway, yes, how could I forget your incredible rendition of Dolly and Kenny, and yes, to be totally honest, you were pretty far gone. Slurring your words, stumbling around, babbling on about how much you loved Max, the works. I left right after that song, and I told Bryan to make sure you got in a cab. Bryan is super chill, so I'm sure he didn't care that you were drunk. He just wanted to get you home like I did. Anyway, do not fret, please! We have all been drunk with clients in this business. I can't wait for you to come back so we can work together again!

I took a deep breath—I hadn't exhaled the entire time I'd been reading—then reread Ani's words yet again, key phrases standing out—

You were pretty far gone

Slurring your words, stumbling around

Babbling on about how much you loved Max

I told Bryan to make sure you got in a cab

He just wanted to get you home like I did

A knot formed in my chest as I read her text again and again.

I closed my eyes, felt tears forming behind them, then opened them again, wiped the tears away.

I'd never voiced it aloud. Not to Molly. Not to myself. And certainly not to Bryan.

I'd never voiced it, and yet somehow, deep down, I'd known it. The truth.

I hadn't wanted this. I hadn't chosen this.

I hadn't even consented at all.

58

5:42 a.m.

IT'S NOT LIKE IT WAS AN ATTACK.

No one was waiting for me in the bushes of the park. No one jumped behind me on an empty subway platform. No one even drugged me.

No one held my arms down.

No one covered my mouth while I tried to scream.

I didn't even say no.

I doubt I said much of anything at all.

My stomach tightened, acid curdling, as I forced myself to go back there, to that night.

I didn't remember much past singing "Islands in the Stream"—Bryan on Dolly, me on Kenny. That was where things got super hazy. All I knew for sure was that another round of drinks was suddenly on the table before us, and Bryan and I were clinking to the future of the account and the fact that he was going to absolutely *demand* that I be promoted to VP at the agency once they signed back on, about how good this partnership was going to be.

That was the last thing I can clearly remember. Bryan, yelling, at the top of his lungs, "You're a fucking VP!"

There was only one more flash of a memory after that—blurry and nothing more than an image, but there all the same—the yellow goldenrod of a New York City taxicab, ready to take me home . . .

Only it didn't take me home. And it was supposed to take me home. Now I knew that beyond a doubt. Ani had said as much.

The next thing that was there, in the Swiss cheese of my brain that night, was opening my eyes to see a white ceiling, a gold, sculptural chandelier.

I knew it, then. I knew everything was terribly wrong. I sat up quickly, my head pounding, throbbing, like someone was pulling my skull back from the wrinkled gray tissue of my brain. The sheets were impossibly silky, must have been a thousand thread count, but they were rumpled, a mess.

The bed was empty beside me, but the dented pillow betrayed someone else's presence.

The Paul Smith blazer and Acne Studios jeans that Bryan always wore were tossed over the desk in the corner, and my skirt and silk shirt were crumpled on the floor. I was in my bra, and pulling back the covers, I saw my underwear on, too.

The shower was running, steam coming from the closed bathroom door, and I struggled out of bed, took too long to find my purse but did, checked for my ID and my corporate Amex card, and discovered a receipt from the karaoke place for seven hundred dollars that I had absolutely no memory of signing, and my phone, which was filled with texts from Max.

Love you

Have fun

Get that account, girl, I know you can do it

Struggling to balance, I managed to get my skirt and blouse on and slipped into my heels. I hesitated outside the bathroom door, wondering if I should say anything, but I was too mortified to so much as open my mouth. I slipped out the front and pulled the door shut behind me, and it locked automatically—there was nothing more to do.

As I rode the elevator thirty floors down to the lobby of the W Times Square, in my hungover (still drunk?) haze, I almost thought that maybe nothing really had happened. Perhaps it was a kiss, and we'd passed out, and that was all. My underwear had been on, after all. There was that.

In the lobby's bathroom, gleaming with shimmering, metallic surfaces, all reflecting my awful state—hair a mess, mascara clumping beneath my lids—like some kind of sick, twisted funhouse mirror, I walked into the first open stall, pulled up my skirt, tugged my underwear down, and sat on the pristine white toilet seat.

That was when I knew what had happened. The burning of my urine, washing over every tiny little abrasion on the opening of my vagina.

The worst had happened, then.

We had had sex.

It was already after nine, and there was no way I could get home to Brooklyn, shower, and get back to the office in time for my first meeting, at ten o'clock. So I walked the ten blocks to the office; took the freight elevator up, not the main one; snuck to my desk; and found the bag of makeup and the change of clothes I always kept in my bottom drawer, just in case I spilled on my blouse before an important client meeting. In the bathroom, I cleaned myself up as best as I could, took two Advil, and was at least somewhat presentable by the time people began arriving at nine forty-five.

Max was on the road, traveling with the band, and I texted him that I was sorry for going to sleep without writing him back. I ambled through my meetings, and I went into the bathroom once at eleven to throw up, but I chewed mint gum and I took more Advil, and somehow I made it to the afternoon.

At three, Eli's wisp of an assistant—his girl Friday, as Molly called him—said that Eli wanted to speak to me. I walked to his office, my heart beating mercilessly, sweat pricking the back of my neck, bracing for the worst. I walked in, and Eli cleared his throat, asked me to shut the door behind me.

That was when Eli told me that Bryan's account was signing on for another two years.

Now, remembering it in the only way I could—a flash here, a flash there—now, staring at Ani's chilling words, I knew it. It was undeniable.

I remembered nothing, but Bryan remembered everything.

He'd been the one who was supposed to take me home. He'd been the one to usher me into that cab. He'd been the one to lead me up to his hotel room.

He'd been the one . . .

It had never been me.

It wasn't simply a bad decision, a drunken mistake. It wasn't a momentary lapse in fidelity.

It was something else entirely.

As if listening to my inner thoughts, Max stirred beside me, then opened his eyes.

"Why are you up?" he asked. "Can't sleep?"

I set down my phone and turned to him. "No," I said. "No, I can't."

"Nervous about meeting Sutton?" Max asked, blinking sleepily.

"Kind of," I said.

"Caught up in the news?"

"That, too." I hesitated, wondering if I really was about to do it. Drop the bomb I'd been holding so precariously for so long.

I'd been so close to telling Max what had happened, that night I went to meet him in that little shack in the woods, but he'd seemed so desperate to get past it.

It's okay, Janie. Whatever it was, I forgive you.

I swallowed. Max had to know. He had to know what had really happened. That there was plenty to forgive—not telling him sooner, not realizing it myself sooner, what had happened that night—but at the same time, that it wasn't something to forgive, because it had never been a betrayal.

"There's something else, too," I said. "Something I've actually wanted to tell you for a long time. I just didn't know how."

A flicker of nervousness passed across his face. He and I knew very well that bad things could happen. His father was a guilty man, splashed across the headlines. His family was torn apart. The whole idea that bad things were something that usually happened to somebody else had been burst right open, before our baby was even two months old.

"It's okay," I said. "It's not anything scary. And it's not irredeemable. I mean, I hope it's not."

Max sat up. "Just tell me, Janie. Whatever it is, just tell

me." He pressed his lips together. "And I love you, I really do. No matter what."

"I know," I said, tears already coming to my eyes. "I'm just so, so sorry."

I laid it out then, baring my secrets, my shame. There in the bed between us. There at not even six a.m. To the man who had seen so much. Who didn't know that in some ways, we could bottom out even further. Who didn't realize that I had secrets, too.

When I was done, Max stared at me, tears in his eyes. Emotions flickered across his face like film-projector slides. Anger. Hurt. Betrayal. Injustice. Rage.

After a moment, I asked, "Are you . . . are you okay?"

"No," he said. "I need a minute."

I nodded, and I slipped out of the bed. I went into the bathroom, splashed water on my face, stared at myself in the mirror.

He knows. He finally knows.

I closed my eyes, then opened them again. Stared into my deepest self.

He knows, and it's okay. It's better this way.

When I returned to the bedroom, Max's eyes were kind. "It's not your fault," he said. "You must know that. And *I* know that, no matter how angry, how furious, it makes me. No matter how much I want to—" He stopped. Talking about killing someone, casually, as common parlance, it didn't work for us anymore. Not after Carl. "It's not your fault, what happened to you. It was assault," he said. "Rape."

Tears filled my eyes, running down my cheeks. "I think I always did know that, somewhere deep down, but it's been hard to accept. I thought I betrayed you, and I hated myself for it."

Max squeezed my hand. "Do you . . . do you want to press charges . . . or to at least let work know?"

I imagined the chaos of that, another media circus, the he-said, she-said that would entail. I couldn't go through it. Not after everything else I'd been through.

"No," I said. "No, I don't." I paused. "You have to be okay with that."

I could see the veins in his neck, the way his muscles tightened, but Max sighed. "Okay," he said. "Okay, I guess that's your choice."

"And I'm sorry," I said. "I really am. I'm sorry for not telling you sooner."

"I wish you had," Max said. "I wish you would have turned to me, but we can't go back in time, can we?"

"No," I said. "We can't."

Silence passed between us. Brokenness. Raw hurt. Fragility.

"I know I should have told you," I said. "But . . . you should have told me. What you did, Max, the way you kept everything going on with Grace from me . . . I know you didn't mean to hurt me, but it *did* hurt. It terrified me. And sometimes I wonder if I'm ever going to be able to fully forgive you for that. Sometimes I wonder if it's not going to stick with us. The way you've hurt me. And the way I hurt you. And now I wonder if you can forgive me for keeping this from you. If maybe the two of us are broken, and that means our relationship is, too."

Max reached over, took his hand in mine. "Maybe we are broken. You and me. But we love each other, and maybe what matters isn't that we fucked up but that we're doing everything we can to fix it. Maybe that's what we show Freya, that things can break, but things can also heal. And we can learn from this. We can turn to each other when things get difficult, instead of trying to handle it all on our own."

Tears cascaded down my cheeks. "You think so?"

He nodded. "I know so."

"Okay," I said. "Okay."

Max pulled my hands to his lips and kissed them tenderly, then held them together in his lap. "Everything you just told me, is it . . . is it why, you think, why things were so hard for you—mentally, I mean—when Freya was born? Because you were so worried about all this?"

I looked down at the creases of our sheets, the crumpled duvet, the stain on our bedsheets from Freya's spit-up that I'd never quite gotten out.

When I looked up, I had my answer. "I don't think so," I said. "Not entirely, at least. Sometimes I think being a mother is just hard. Giving yourself to this creature, this creature you love so much and you're so afraid you won't be able to protect—it's its own kind of trauma, isn't it?"

Max laughed. "It sure is."

He looked at me then, and I could see the question in his eyes before it found his lips. "So do you think there's a chance that she's not mine? Biologically?"

"You're her dad," I said. "She looks just like you. She acts just like you. She loves you more than anything in the entire world." I laughed. "She loves you maybe even more than me." I smiled softly. "I know in my heart she's yours."

Max hesitated a moment, and then his eyes locked on mine.

"You're right," he said. "I do, too."

59

9:01 a.m.

IT WAS ONLY LATER, AS WE WERE PACKING OUR BAGS FOR Maine, Freya rolling around in her playpen, scooting about as she'd learned to, that I did what I had to do.

I went into the bedroom, closed the door behind me, reached beneath my side of the mattress, and retrieved the envelope I'd been too afraid to open before.

I'd sent in the test a few weeks after we returned to Brooklyn, and I'd received the report more than a month ago, but I hadn't done anything with it but stuff it beneath the bed.

The envelope was sealed tight. The one from Family Solutions Testing.

I slipped my finger beneath the edge, prying it open, then paused.

Through the shut door, I could hear Freya's laughter, the sound of Max blowing raspberries on her stomach.

My heart swelled. We loved her so deeply, so truly. We were her parents. And we were doing the best we could. That had to be enough.

Fingers working quickly, I ripped the envelope into shreds

and tossed it all into the trash, before I could be so much as tempted to look at the actual results.

Then I whipped open the door, plastered on my best smile.

"Mommy loves you," I said to Freya.

I looked at Max, and I knew he was her father.

I knew he was her father in all the ways that could ever matter.

Then I looked at my baby, my love, my Freya.

"And Mommy loves your daddy, too."

ACKNOWLEDGMENTS

No book is written in a vacuum, but this one, more than any of my others, was particularly inspired by the people and circumstances surrounding it. After a complicated pregnancy and a traumatic emergency birth, my daughter burst onto the scene just a few months ahead of a global pandemic. In those early weeks and months, I found myself struggling to adapt to sleepless nights and the trials of new motherhood, and was at a loss trying to feel all the feelings I knew I was "supposed" to have. Add in an unexpected lockdown, and I didn't feel quite myself until around six months into parenthood. Then, in the summer of 2020, baby napping and sun blazing through my home-office window, I sat down to write, and in only a few short days, the first seventy-five pages of what would become *You Should Have Told Me* poured out. I'd opened up to so many other mothers in the early days of new motherhood, and what I'd found was that so many women felt exactly as I did, but were afraid to share these complicated emotions—even to those closest to them. Writing down these feelings, dark and intense and difficult as they might be, felt so crucial to me, and became the basis of the book that would be the closest to my heart yet. Above all, this book could not have been written without the women and parents who supported me early on, who trusted me to listen to their own struggles, and who told me it was all going to get better when I feared it never would. From the bottom of my heart, thank you.

Of course, writing is only half the battle, and this story wouldn't be out in the world without the brilliance of my incredible publishing team. To Elisabeth Weed, thank you, as always, for being such a dedicated advocate of my career and for "gabbing" with me anytime I need a pep talk, strategy session, or even a friendly chit-chat. A huge thanks to the entire TBG team, and especially to D.J. Kim, who makes sure I never miss a deadline or payment!

To Danielle Dieterich, thank you for taking an interest in this book from the moment I first pitched it over Brooklyn cocktails! You are an incredible editor and champion of my work, and I am so thankful to have you in my corner. To Sally Kim and the whole Putnam team, thank you so much for the work you do in creating amazing books and ushering them into the world. Elora Weil and Nicole Biton, you are the best publicists an author could ask for, and I am so thankful for every single one of my clips. Emily Mlynek, thank you so much for tirelessly marketing my books and getting them into readers' hands.

I am blessed to have an equally amazing team across the pond, and this book would not be what it is without the brilliant guidance of both Joel Richardson and Grace Long, whose notes always get me thinking and challenge me to improve my writing with each new draft. Thanks as well to the entire Michael Joseph family for finding creative ways to get my books in front of each and every wonderful UK reader.

To Jenny Meyer, Heidi Gall, and your whole team, I am so appreciative of the care you've taken in pitching my books around the globe. Jenny, I trust your opinion so very much and look forward to hearing your thoughts on every project I work on.

To Michelle Weiner and everyone at CAA, how do you continue to work magic with my film rights? I am so thankful for the work you do and am excited for many more pinch-me moments in the future.

This book simply could not exist if not for the meticulous and inspired notes of my longtime beta readers, Andrea Bartz and Danielle Rollins, as well as my newest beta reader, Kamala Nair. Thank you so much for being incredible writers yourselves and for sharing a little bit of that genius with me.

My book about motherhood would not have been possible without the advice and support of my own legion of fellow moms, especially Christine Burnside, Kate Lord, and Beth Ziefle. You all are family to me, and I am thankful for you every single day.

To my dad, thank you for always believing in me and for encouraging me to follow my dreams and write from a young age. To my sister, Kimberly, having you as a dedicated reader who always finds a way to shout-out my books to people near and far is an amazing gift.

But above all, to my mom, I never knew how hard it was until I had a child of my own. Thank you for every late night you spent with me, for every time you hugged me and told me how much you loved me, for every time you took care of me when I was sick, and for being there to answer the phone no matter when I call you, always. You taught me how to be a mom, and everything I learned about unconditional love is from you.

To Thomas, thank you for making it so easy for me to balance motherhood and my writing career, and for creating an environment where I never have to choose between one or the other. To my wonderful dog, Farley, you are my favorite office mate, and thank you for being by my side through every book.

Finally, to Eleanor, thank you for making me a mom and opening up new worlds inside me that I can write about!

You Should Have Told Me

LEAH KONEN

———

A Conversation with Leah Konen

———

Reading Group Questions

———

A CONVERSATION WITH LEAH KONEN

Where did the inspiration for *You Should Have Told Me* come from? When did you first begin to think about this story?

Every book is personal, but *You Should Have Told Me* is one that's particularly close to my heart. The early scenes poured out of me when my daughter was around six months old. I was still feeling the effects of a complicated pregnancy and a traumatic emergency birth, not to mention a global pandemic, and when my daughter started napping long enough for me to get some writing time in on a new book, the pages came almost easily. The story was—and still is—a way for me to process some of those emotions.

Was the novel impacted by your own experience as a new mother? What makes this novel feel so personal to you?

Absolutely. Feelings during early motherhood can be extremely complicated and cause a lot of shame. But the more I opened up to other mothers about what I was going through, the more I saw that nearly all of these feelings were incredibly common! It was so important to me to be able to chronicle some of this through Janie's story. I hope that anyone reading who has had a similar experience can know they're not alone and that it does get better.

Do you have a favorite character in *You Should Have Told Me*? If so, who, and why do you think you connect to them?

I really admire Liana. She doesn't always make the right decisions, but she's always acting from a place of love, compassion, and kindness. I think it's wonderful that her friendship with Janie grows independently of her longer friendship with Max, and the way she steps in for Janie and really fights for both her and Max is incredible, even if she has a few missteps along the way. I also thought it was a wonderful chance to portray a woman who was child-free by choice but who loved kids and was quite good with them—it's interesting to let different characters take on those roles, regardless of whether they have children themselves.

Your three most recent adult novels have all been set in upstate New York. What do you find intriguing about this location?

I've lived in small towns, the suburbs, and major cities, but nowhere to me has been such a unique combination of all three quite like the particular corner of the Catskills where I live and write. The towns are small and have a village-like feel, but with New York City so close, and with so many transplants coming up from there, there's a natural tension of two worlds that I think is a perfect location for a thriller. Plus, who doesn't love to set murder mysteries near mountains and woods?

Do you have any favorite scenes from the novel that you would be willing to share?

There's a moment when Janie first ventures out to the bar where Grace was killed, when she has a chance to look back on the last few weeks with Freya and have some separation from her daughter for the first time. I remember in early motherhood my own first small trips to a coffee shop or a bar for a drink, knowing I had only an hour or two on my own and how precious it was. There's a natural thrill in those moments, and I loved getting to explore that through Janie's eyes. It's also a scene where she digs into the idea that mothers have more expected from them, societally and sometimes also biologically, than fathers do. One of my favorite passages is when Janie is able to have the headspace to really come to that realization:

> Mothers didn't leave, did they? It was too horrible, too antisocial, to even comprehend. Mothers didn't disappear. Mothers didn't get caught up in things like this, things that took them away.
>
> I remember watching that movie, the one with Meryl Streep and Dustin Hoffman, several years before, long before there was any talk of a child of my own, before I'd met Max, even. Kramer vs. Kramer. Meryl Streep gets fed up with motherhood and just . . . goes. It was so easy to hate her in that movie, so easy to paint her as a monster. What she'd done was so evil, wasn't it? So wrong?
>
> I remember in high school, reading A Doll's House, internally cheering for Ibsen's brand of feminism, however imperfect, and then being horrified when Nora simply leaves her children behind.
>
> A mother exits. A door shuts. Fin.

Alternatively, were there any scenes that were particularly challenging to write?
Anything to do with Grace's death was very difficult for me to write and even think about it. It broke my heart to write those scenes and knowing that this loving mother had died, especially when Sutton needed her so much. One of my closest writing friends kept having to reassure me that she was just a character and not a real person!

What was your experience of writing *You Should Have Told Me* like? How was it similar or different to writing your past novels?
In the beginning, I definitely had a looser writing style than I typically do. I think I was so inspired to capture the postpartum experience that the writing felt pretty instinctual and free. That said, I definitely did more plotting as I got deeper into the story, especially the mystery, as I do with all of my books.

Did you always know how the book would end, or did it change throughout the writing process?
Just once I'd love to write a mystery without a million changes draft to draft, but it really just isn't my process. For me, the ending is always in my head as I write, but it changes many times as I go through the process.

Janie's past trauma comes to play an important role in the novel, and it's heart-wrenching to read about. Why did you feel it was important to explore this topic?
Unfortunately, a lot of women and people have stories just like Janie's, and I really wanted to chronicle a sexual assault

that lived in that gray area, even for Janie herself. Her coming to terms with the fact that it was, indeed, a rape is so important to her journey, and one that sadly many people can relate to.

What authors do you enjoy reading? Do any of them impact your own work?
I'm a huge fan of British thriller novelists, and right now Ruth Ware and Lucy Foley are two of my absolute favorites. I think everything I read impacts me in some way, whether it's mystery, sci-fi, horror, classics, or literary. I truly believe that the best way to become a better writer is to read and read widely. I don't think there's any better way to study the craft.

What is next for you?
I'm working on another thriller set in upstate New York. It's a murder mystery packed with mom friends, mind games, class conflict, and con artists, and I can't wait to share it with my readers.

READING GROUP QUESTIONS

1. *You Should Have Told Me* examines the challenges of motherhood in the context of a thriller. Does the genre of the book change the way you think about Janie's emotional journey?

2. Compare and contrast the different portrayals of motherhood in the novel, particularly looking at Grace, Janie, and Brenda. What makes a "good" mother? Conversely, compare the different fathers in the book—what similarities and differences do you find between Carl and Max?

3. How are the expectations of mothers and fathers different in our society? How do those expectations influence the events of *You Should Have Told Me*?

4. Do you think that Max is a good partner? Were his decisions justified, and was Janie right to help him? Why or why not? Going further, how does their relationship change through the novel?

5. How does Janie's experience of past trauma and her associated guilt transform throughout the course of the novel?

How do you think she will continue to heal after the end of the book?

6. Do you think that the setting of the novel impacts the events in the book? Does Janie and Max's relative isolation from friends and family change their decisions and actions?

7. Several men in *You Should Have Told Me* appear to be "good" but are revealed to have been violent toward women. How are their secrets uncovered, and what are the consequences? Take a specific look at Bryan, Carl, and Daniel.

8. How does Janie's own childhood influence her parenting style?

9. Compare and contrast Janie's female friendships, particularly with Molly and Liana. What makes them good friends, and where are their blind spots?

10. At the beginning of the book, who did you suspect had killed Grace? Did your suspicions change throughout the novel? Were you ultimately surprised by the ending?

LEAH KONEN

'Intense, unpredictable and
completely addictive'
T.M. Logan

WHICH BOOK WILL YOU READ NEXT?

He just wanted a decent book to read ...

Not too much to ask, is it? It was in 1935 when Allen Lane, Managing Director of Bodley Head Publishers, stood on a platform at Exeter railway station looking for something good to read on his journey back to London. His choice was limited to popular magazines and poor-quality paperbacks – the same choice faced every day by the vast majority of readers, few of whom could afford hardbacks. Lane's disappointment and subsequent anger at the range of books generally available led him to found a company – and change the world.

'We believed in the existence in this country of a vast reading public for intelligent books at a low price, and staked everything on it'
Sir Allen Lane, 1902–1970, founder of Penguin Books

The quality paperback had arrived – and not just in bookshops. Lane was adamant that his Penguins should appear in chain stores and tobacconists, and should cost no more than a packet of cigarettes.

Reading habits (and cigarette prices) have changed since 1935, but Penguin still believes in publishing the best books for everybody to enjoy. We still believe that good design costs no more than bad design, and we still believe that quality books published passionately and responsibly make the world a better place.

So wherever you see the little bird – whether it's on a piece of prize-winning literary fiction or a celebrity autobiography, political tour de force or historical masterpiece, a serial-killer thriller, reference book, world classic or a piece of pure escapism – you can bet that it represents the very best that the genre has to offer.

Whatever you like to read – trust Penguin.